To Jane,
Best Wishes and
Happy Reading!

[signature]

DEADLY APPARITION

Acknowledgements

I must acknowledge my editor, my inspiration and my companion in life's journey, Mary Beth Smith. Thank you for all your help and encouragement, dear.

I would also like to give credit to Amy Siders, Jen Dunsmore and Robert Reid at 52Novels for doing the chapter graphics and layouts.

Thanks to commercial artist Shaunna Heth for the cover art.

Thanks for insights from Ex-Navy torpedoman, Jeff Smith, my brother.

Thanks to actor Jack Nolan who with his expert knowledge of accents and dialects did a great narration for the audiobook. He also helped me with Spanish phrases and inaccuracies in the text.

And thanks to my daughter, Mona Guerrero, for doing a fine job of managing the G. Ernest Smith Facebook site.

DEADLY APPARITION

G. Ernest Smith

Prologue
Aboard the Florencia
English Channel
20 Miles off the Flemish coast
August 4, 1588

"God smiles on us, Francisco!" exclaimed Gaspar De Sosa. "He gives us a beautiful morning for victory and a good wind."

"Yes, and he keeps Drake and his English dogs locked up in their pen. There is nothing to stop us now, sir."

"It is a magnificent sight, is it not?" De Sosa swept his arm at the view. Ships as far as the eye could see with taut sunlit sails pitching up and down as they plowed through sequined green waves. He breathed in the cool salt air. "We are God's fleet carrying on God's mission, Francisco." He pointed at the great galleon 200 yards to the north. It rolled more slowly because of its great size. "Look at the San Leandro, Francisco. Look at the size of it. The power! How could one doubt it came from God? It must have dropped directly from heaven, for how else could you explain its perfect lines. The perfect way the deck sweeps in such a pure artful manner. It's a force of nature, is it not?" De Sosa laughed a hearty laugh that made his great belly tremble and his black beard quiver.

Francisco laughed too. His thin shoulders shook, and he showed his gap toothed smile, and nervously pulled at his shirt. "I think after we make our landing, we should make every Englishman line up and kiss his Holiness's ring. What say you, De Sosa?"

"A good idea, Francisco, but the Pope is a busy man. He doesn't have time for English scum."

"Maybe they could kiss Admiral Sidonia's ass then. Same thing!"

Both men roared with laughter. De Sosa scanned the horizon ahead and saw nothing but the empty sea and cottony white clouds. There was no sound except the snap of banners in the wind, the rattle of block and tackle and the creak of hull planking as the ship plunged through the waves. Both men gripped the rail tightly to keep their feet as the deck heaved under them.

"Sail!" called the lookout from above. "One point on the bow." He pointed.

Every deck hand turned to where the lookout was pointing.

"That's not a sail," said Francisco.

"What is it?" asked De Sosa.

It was like a tentacle from a Portuguese man of war. One fibrous tentacle extending upward from the sea. It pointed to the sky…up and up. Then it curved down.

"It looks like it's coming toward us," said De Sosa with concern. He extended his spy glass and looked at it.

"I know what it is!" cried Francisco, his brown eyes alive with excitement. "It is a message from God. I have read it many times in the Bible. Heavenly messengers always come from the sky or the sea. It is an angel come to give us a joyful message. God is pleased with us, De Sosa!"

De Sosa's eyes were troubled. He wasn't so sure this was a good thing. It was streaking across the water toward them very fast now. Faster than a racing falcon. He had never seen anything so fast! It was coming straight at them…no…it was coming toward the San Leandro. The men on the San Leandro saw it too. They were at the rails, pointing. There was a sound building like the roar of a lion. It was almost on them. It was…

BOOM!

There was a bright flash and the gunnel beneath De Sosa's arm exploded into fragments and a great invisible hand slapped at him, knocking him end over end. He tumbled from one side of the deck to the other. He grabbed at Francisco and tried to stop him from going over the rail but he failed. He saw the frozen open-mouthed look of horror on Francisco's face as he went over. The Florencia rolled hard over away from the blast. He waited long seconds for the ship to right itself, and when it finally did, he staggered to his feet. There was a sharp pain in his side and when he looked there, he saw a large shard of wood sticking out from between his ribs. Fighting against the pain, he struggled to the rail. The San Leandro was gone! There was nothing but jagged smoking pieces of wood and broken charred planks floating in the water. He also saw bodies floating in the wreckage and heard the cries and entreaties to God of dying men. What could have done such a thing?

De Sosa looked up and saw most of Florencia's sails had been shredded and the mizzen mast had been snapped like a twig. There were only two top gallants still intact. He quickly looked around at the surrounding ships. The Antonio De Palma's sails were fluttering free, having been ripped free of their moorings. Most of the sails of the San Juan De Portugal were shredded like Florencia's. La Trinidad also had shredded sails.

"Capitan!" shouted a crewman. "The larboard hull planking has collapsed, sir! Water is rushing in! We can't stop it!"

"Get boats in the water!" ordered De Sosa. Then he noticed all the nearby ships were listing and putting boats in the water. Others had put up distress flags and were turning around. A distress flag meant the ship had suffered heavy damage and was out of the action.

What could have done this? Is this the hand of God?

"Sir," said a crewman. "You've been injured!"

He looked down at the piece of wood sticking out of his side. "I know." He looked to where the flying demon had come. That's when he saw another one. Another long tentacle reaching toward the sky. It arched, then plunged down and built speed as it came directly at them…no…this time it was going to pass on the other side about 100 yards away. As it roared by, he was able to see it for a split second. It was like a white stove pipe spewing white smoke with triangular attachments on it.

BOOM!

This time the flash was farther away, but it still knocked De Sosa and the crewman next to him off his feet and rolled the Florencia. De Sosa pulled himself up on a rail, crossed himself and said, "We've angered God in some way! He has sent a great demon to smite us!"

Chapter 1
Norfolk, Virginia
Operational Test and Evaluation Force Headquarters

If one had to guess what Don Castillo did for a living, one might guess he was an insurance salesman or maybe a stockbroker. He was 37, of average height, slightly frumpy and carried a bit of a paunch. He was obviously not a manual laborer with his soft hands. He had thinning wavy hair the color of dark oak and a round pleasant-looking affable face with brown eyes that seemed to disappear into slits every time he smiled. He seemed always to be on the edge of chuckling at something. One would never guess he was submarine commander in the United States Navy, unless of course one saw him in uniform.

Commander Don Castillo sat in his dress whites in the windowless first floor conference room, waiting. The room was dominated by a large white screen against one wall and a polished mahogany table around which were wooden chairs with padded leather seats. There were four khaki clad stone-faced admirals sitting opposite him at the table doing an impression of Mount Rushmore. Gold stars glittered from their collars. Behind them were aides and support staff. He wasn't sure what this was about, but it had to be big to draw this much brass. He was looking at three two-stars and a four-star! Admiral Zeke Montgomery, Director of Naval Nuclear Propulsion himself! Maybe I'm being court marshaled, thought Castillo briefly. No, I've never screwed up *that* bad. He glanced around the room at pictures of Navy ships and groups of important looking Navy men in silver metal frames. Whatever they were about to discuss, it was big and it was sensitive. He had to go through two security checks and three scans to get into this room. He was afraid the evil looking guy at the badging station was going to ask him to drop trousers and bend over, but he didn't. Thank God!

They smiled at each other uneasily. They were waiting on Castillo's boss, Admiral Nate Baynes, head of Submarine Group 2. Castillo couldn't help but feel he was being sized up. He was an outsider here. There were also some civilians. They all had that clean cut look of people who had been vetted and scrutinized by many agencies and eventually approved to do sensitive work for the American military. He knew Dr. Susan Lambert, of Quantum Vital Research Corporation. He had worked with her before on the test phase of the TAL-TAC system, an ingenious system of transducers that when directed at an enemy torpedo could destroy its guidance system. He smiled at her and she returned his smile. He didn't know Lambert's companion, Crystal McConnell according to her badge, also of QVR or the other QVR guy, whose name he couldn't read. Chet something? He could feel the weight of their stares as they took his measure.

Admiral Quentin O'Keefe, Naval Special Operations, nervously cleared his throat and said, "How's your family, Don?"

"They're doing good, sir," replied Castillo. "Kelly's science project won first place this year at her middle school and Robin will start middle school next year."

"Sounds like Kelly's a chip off the old block."

"Yes sir. But she'd die if she heard you say that."

O'Keefe chuckled. He had a bony face that seemed to be all angles. He looked at a nearby painting of a sailing ship. It was an old square-rigger from at least two centuries ago. "How's Liz?"

A dark shadow fell across Castillo's face. "She's in good spirits. Weak, but the doctors say she's in remission."

"That's good! She's in our thoughts and prayers."

"Thank you, sir." The looks of scrutiny changed to looks of sympathy.

The door opened and Admiral Baynes rushed in wearing crisp service khakis trailed by his aide, Lieutenant Cal Moore, and another older bespectacled snowy-haired gentleman in a dark suit.

"Good!" exclaimed Baynes. "We're all here!" The admiral's aide handed tan folders all around.

"As you well know," began Admiral Baynes, settling into his chair at the head of the conference table, "Naval electronic detection and counter measures have always been a seesaw of technology. When the Russians developed a better Q processor, we developed a quieter propulsion system. When their advanced generation detection set began detecting our flow noise, we developed anachoic polymer hull coatings. Whenever they become quieter, we improve our sonar arrays. It's a game of one-upsmanship. Who's to say who has the advantage at any one time? And now the Chinese are getting into it with their own boats, and they've gotten some help from the Russians." Baynes tented his hands over his chest and said, "But what I'm going to tell you about is going to change all that." He paused dramatically.

Castillo only stared at Baynes, waiting for the delivery…the punch line, but he said nothing. Baynes had a broad face and dark skin around his eyes. It made him look like a raccoon, Castillo thought. This had to be a sign of poor health. It probably indicated a lack of sleep, but Baynes had always looked that way. Maybe it was just a natural discoloration caused by genetics or something.

"QVR has come up with something that is so remarkable, it borders on magic." Baynes was animated now. Well, as animated as he ever got. "We'd like to use the Kansas as our proof of concept ship."

"Why Kansas, sir," asked Castillo.

"Well, I could say because of your engineering background, Don. Or I could say because of your excellent work on the TALTAC system or the C303 anti-torpedo system. You and your crew are very professional and do damn good work! And you work well with the QVR folks."

Castillo sighed. "Yes, sir, but the crew was hoping to get a break from this kind of thing for awhile."

Baynes frowned. "And do what? Go out on long boring patrols? Wait 'til you see what this thing does, Don. And tell your boys they're going to get a few weeks of liberty in Glasgow. They're going to have the time of their lives!"

"Glasgow?"

Now the bespectacled man to Baynes left spoke. "The Glasgow division of QVR developed the Hyper-density Spherical Conversion Emitter, sir. We thought it would be easier to take your ship there to be outfitted, rather than bring a crew and all the equipment here." The man had a strong British accent.

"Oh, sorry," said Baynes. "This is Dr. Nigel Hill of QVR. He's the director of the project. If you will open your folders, you will see a test schedule and the important dates. There's also a brief overview of project Apparition and what it does. I want you all to read these and ask any questions, but these folders do not leave this room. Understood?"

"Project Apparition?" asked Castillo.

"That's easier to say than density emitter…whatever," groused Baynes. "It's going to be our working title for now."

"What exactly does this Apparition do, sir?" asked Castillo.

"It's easier to show you than it is to tell you about it. That's why Nigel and I have set up a little demonstration for you."

• • •

They exited the conference room and followed Baynes and Dr. Hill down a long hallway, across a courtyard and soon found themselves in a white tiled test facility reminiscent of a municipal swimming pool natatorium complete with pool and an observation balcony. It even had that ubiquitous chlorine smell that swimming pools always have. Castillo and Dr. Hill went up a stairway onto a metal platform looking down on the test tank. Floating in the center of the blue water was a small boat no more than 3 feet long. Castillo thought it resembled a world war II battleship more than a submarine. He heard footsteps, turned and saw a cadre of civilians come up onto the platform behind them. Among them were Susan Lambert and Crystal McConnell.

"When does the show start?" he asked Hill.

"Soon," responded Hill. "We've set up a miniature emitter array on the model ship to reproduce the sphere phenomena."

"What kind of phenomena?" asked Castillo in puzzlement.

Hill removed his glasses, extracted a small cleaning cloth from his pocket and began to clean them as he considered his answer. Susan Lambert and Crystal McConnell came up to within earshot. "This breakthrough is a result of an accident, as are so many great discoveries. I assume you are all familiar with the Hadron Supercollider in Switzerland?"

"Yes," replied Castillo. Lambert and McConnell both nodded.

"There was an accident there in 2008. A magnetic quench during a high energy beam rotation and approximately 6 tons of liquid helium was explosively released. It made a real mess!"

"I remember reading about it," said Lambert.

Dr. Hill replaced his glasses and sniffed. "Yes, but you didn't read about the niobium-titanium hypercompression phenomenon, did you?"

"That's used for making high powered magnets, isn't it?" said Castillo.

"Yes. We had a block of the stuff in one of the detection chambers, just to have something to focus on. At the moment of the liquid helium release, it disappeared!"

"Disappeared?" exclaimed Castillo. "How?"

"Well, that's what we thought at first anyway. We had high speed cameras rolling and when we backed up the video, we could see that the block was there in one frame and gone in the next. It was most perplexing. Then one of the scientists observed a crystalline grain of something very dense in the chamber. The metal block was still there, but it had been hypercompacted."

"What? How's that possible?" asked Crystal McConnell. She was a thin woman with fine features and large fawn-like brown eyes. Castillo guessed her age to be about 34.

"Our bodies, the air, this rail," said Hill slapping the metal rail in front of them. "Everything is made of atoms, but these atoms are held in a structure at a certain distance from each other by forces we don't fully understand. If you could remove the space between all the atoms in our bodies, you could reduce us down to the size of a BB. But it would be a very heavy BB because it would not lose any mass. In my case, my BB would weigh about 12 and a half stone, or 180 pounds as you Yanks like to say."

"I think we're ready," shouted Baynes from below. He and Admiral O'Keefe and several other men, some in lab coats, were standing next to the test tank. There was a man in a black wet suit standing in the tank about ten feet from the model boat.

"I'm switching on the emitter now," said a technician at a nearby work station with a flat display screen.

Castillo felt the hairs on the back of his arms and neck stand up. It was like having an electrostatic charge applied to his body. That same feeling you get when there's a lightning storm nearby. At once a shimmering 5 foot silver colored circle appeared on the surface of the water around the boat and the water level dropped. Violent ripples spread through the water and sloshed against the sides of the tank. The silvery circle was thin like the shell of an egg.

"What you're seeing," said Baynes, "is a barrier that surrounds the model on all sides and beneath in a perfect hemispherical pattern." He nodded to the man in the pool. "Our first test is a high-powered spear gun, capable of penetrating quarter inch steel plate."

The man in the wet suit took a heavy spear gun from the side of the tank, lowered it into the water and said, "Everyone ready?"

"Go," said Baynes.

The man pulled the trigger and a spear shot forth through the water and bounced off the silver barrier and fell harmlessly to the bottom of the tank.

Castillo blinked, unsure of what he had just seen. "Could you do that again?" The man in the wet suit reloaded the spear gun and repeated the demonstration.

This time Castillo knew what to expect, but still had a hard time believing his eyes.

"Holy Mackerel!" exclaimed Susan Lambert.

"Bear in mind," said Baynes, "that if the ship and its emitters are completely underwater, like a submarine would be, the protective barrier is a sphere completely surrounding the boat offering protection from above as well."

"What's this barrier made of?" asked Castillo.

"Water," replied Hill.

Castillo frowned, saying nothing.

"The water at a specified distance has gone through a molecular compression. Scientists are calling it hyperdensification. The atoms in this layer of water are bound so tightly they resist any force trying to separate them."

"Any force?" asked Lambert incredulously.

"Well, we haven't found any force yet that will penetrate it, but we haven't tried everything."

"Why doesn't a sphere enclose this model?" asked Lambert.

"Because our hyperdensification process only works with water and the air just doesn't contain enough water molecules for the molecular compression to work. It takes an enormous amount of water for this to work… and an enormous amount of energy too."

"Okay," said Baynes. "Are we ready for the next test?" He nodded to a technician. "We've placed a small explosive charge in the bottom of the tank right beneath our model to simulate a torpedo explosion."

A blond young man in a white lab coat said, "Fire in the hole in three…two…one…"

BLUP!

Water erupted violently straight up into the air from everywhere in the tank, spraying the bystanders. Everywhere except inside the silver barrier. The model ship was barely disturbed.

"The pressure wave from the blast is dissipated across the barrier and hardly any of it carries through to the ship." Baynes had a triumphant smile on his face.

Castillo's mind reeled at the implications of what he was seeing. This was a protective shield that could be deployed during a battle and completely protect a submarine and her crew. Whoever possessed this technology would have a great tactical advantage. He understood the need for secrecy too. "This is amazing!"

"There is a downside to this thing too," said Admiral O'Keefe. "Tell him, Nate."

"Well," began Baynes. "The worst effect is the guillotine effect when it's first deployed. If you're trailing an array, it gets chopped off. If you have wire guided ADCAP's in the water, you'll lose your guidance. Your sonar will be useless as well as acoustic communications. Nothing penetrates this barrier. And it consumes quite a bit of power, so we're recommending deploying it in short bursts as needed."

"You must have a large scale version of this somewhere," said Castillo.

"As a matter of fact we have several," replied Hill. "At a remote test site on the Irish coast away from prying eyes. We've even conducted tests with animals and a few brave humans, and so far, so good."

"No after effects at all?" asked Lambert.

"Doctors have given everybody a clean bill of health. No harmful after effects. Most people report a tingling sensation over the skin, but that's about all."

"I think we're ready for the next phase of testing," said Baynes. "What do you think, Don?"

Castillo didn't like playing the guinea pig, but he knew for the sake of his career and the lives of many sailors in life and death situations at sea the correct answer. "Let's go for it, sir!"

"Yes!" Baynes smiled broadly and punched the air with his right fist.

• • •

The Kansas was a Virginia class attack boat built out of sequence. Originally it was intended to be a full sized test platform for evaluating new weapon systems and electronic counter measures. It was not much more than a hull and a crude power plant and propulsion system that could get it out of a slip and back in. It served well in its test capacity until defense cutbacks and the sequester happened and money started getting tight everywhere. Many new proposed submarines were cut from the Navy budget. Navy officials decided to press their test platform into service. It would not be as costly to outfit the test platform with full systems as it would be to build a brand new submarine from scratch. So, the test platform was completely fitted with new systems and a new reactor and it was christened the USS Kansas, after the 34th state and home of the Jayhawks, SSN 849.

The Kansas was assigned a crew and a commander, Commander Don Castillo. It was assigned to the Submarine Squadron 6 and patrolled the Eastern seaboard, but after a year was asked to perform tests on a new system. There was some grumbling. Some of the men would rather be performing normal duties with the *real* Navy instead of performing test operations. Conducting tests involved long hours of boredom while scientists and engineers made observations and recordings and checked settings and rechecked them. This was *not* high adventure!

When the crew of the Kansas were told they were going to be testing another counter measures system, they were not happy. Castillo was not allowed to talk about the top secret project with anyone except his executive and engineering officers. But when Castillo told the crew about spending extended liberty in Glasgow, they seemed more accepting of their new assignment.

When the SSN Kansas arrived in Scotland it was late summer. There was a hint of autumn in the air suggesting at what was to come but the temperatures in the highlands were mild, the purple blossoms of heather were still prominent and the hills were still very green.

The submarine base was at HMNB Clyde which is actually part of Faslane Naval Base twenty miles to the west of Glasgow. The Royal British Navy made the Kansas crew feel at home, showing them to their temporary quarters and welcoming them, although they were not told why the Kansas was here. Indeed, most of the Kansas's crew didn't know why they were here either. The first thing they wanted to do was visit Glasgow.

Glasgow is a city of contrasts. The third largest city in the UK, it is a modern bustling city with shopping malls and mass transit but also with ancient reminders of a rich history. It boasts a cathedral that dates back to the 12th century with soaring stone gothic arches and grinning gargoyles, a throwback to the Renaissance. It also has a modern university performing cutting edge research in the fields of physics, chemistry and medicine. It has the Burrell Collection which is an astounding mix of Egyptian, Greek, Roman and Chinese artifacts as well as old European masters. The oldest parts of the city puts one in mind of medieval Europe with its narrow old cobblestone streets, old gray stone buildings and slate roof pubs and stacked moss-covered stone walls. Stone is evidently a plentiful building material here for some of the bridges and even some fences are made of stone. There are always festivals and renaissance fairs going on in the streets or in parks where actors perform Shakespeare or play medieval street entertainers, jugglers and troubadours for tourists.

A popular tour with the crew was the Glengoyne whiskey distillery where they were guided through the cask rooms, the still house, the storage house and got free samples of the world's finest Scotch.

• • •

When Kansas first arrived at the Clyde Royal Naval Base the first thing that happened was her identity was erased. Her identifying number and markings were painted out. The high American and British command did not want her identified, although the shipyard workers knew quite well that this was the attack submarine Kansas from America. Then she was moved to a dry dock and a large structure was erected over her. It looked a lot like a gigantic boathouse made of canvas, hiding Kansas from prying, spying eyes and satellites.

Many vans and trucks traveled the long pier, and boxes and instruments were dollied aboard. Technicians swarmed over Kansas like fire ants over a bratwurst and welding arcs sputtered like flash bulbs inside the structure as work progressed, and the scent of ozone wafted on the air. After many days, the work was complete and Kansas was scheduled for deployment.

A meeting was called to order at the Clyde Royal Navy Headquarters building. Present were Commander Don Castillo, Nigel Hill, Admiral Nate Baynes, Admiral Quenton O'Keefe, Dr. Susan Lambert, Crystal

McConnell and Kansas's executive officer, Lieutenant Commander Mason Taylor. There were also a great many high-ranking British Naval officers whose names Castillo had forgotten.

"What you're holding is a list of people," said Admiral O'Keefe, "we deem necessary to this test. I trust that you can accommodate them all."

"But…there are seventeen names here, sir," said Castillo.

"Is that a problem?" asked O'Keefe.

"Yessir, a big one. Kansas is pretty cramped, as are all submarines. Where will I put all these people?"

"You'll think of something," chuckled O'Keefe.

"There's no way, sir," said Castillo. "Unless I leave some crew ashore."

"Okay," said O'Keefe.

Castillo blinked. He couldn't believe what O'Keefe was suggesting. "You're asking me to leave some crew ashore, sir, and take on these people? How many of these people are sub qualified? Can any of them help out during an emergency?"

"Oh, C'mon, Don!" snapped O'Keefe. "It's just during a few test runs. It's not forever."

"I don't like it, Admiral. There are too many unknowns during test runs. Too many things can go wrong as you well know." He said this deliberately to remind the admiral of the tragic second AMTOK test in 2007 that caused a fire and claimed the lives of 6 people aboard the SSN New Hampshire.

Admiral O'Keefe's nostrils flared. "I don't need reminding, Commander!" He shifted in his chair. "I know quite well this is dangerous work. Do *you* need reminding of exactly what's at stake here?"

Castillo said nothing. He knew this was an important advancement in naval warfare. He immediately began considering what crew he could do without. He would need Damage Control in case they had an emergency. Engineering also. He had eight SEAL team births available. They had not come to Scotland. Did he need the weapons crew on this run?

"We eventually plan to outfit all NATO ships with this countermeasure," said Admiral Baynes, "but for right now, this is a joint American/British venture. It's important, Don, for our relations with our allies."

Castillo still didn't like leaving part of his crew behind and taking on all these civilians, but he said, "I understand, sir."

• • •

On the day before deployment, Kansas's executive officer, Lieutenant Commander Mason Taylor, showed the civilians aboard and to their assigned births. They weren't all civilians, however, there were two British Naval officers, Captain Miles Simms and Commander Lauren Gastmeyer.

Dr. Susan Lambert surprised Castillo in the passageway outside his stateroom. "Isn't Glasgow fabulous, commander? I've had a ball here!" Her blue eyes were doing the highland fling.

"Really," responded Castillo. "What did you do?"

"Crystal and I toured the museum at the Glasgow School of Art and the Burrell. Then a bunch of us took a tour of the highlands by bicycle. The first two days it rained, and we went from tavern to tavern, trying to stay dry and sampled the ale, then the rain cleared up and it was glorious! There were these beautiful clear lakes that reflected the surrounding peaks and blue sky and the heather was in full bloom and it was so green! It was like you were looking at a picture postcard in every direction. It was just so beautiful! God! What a place, huh? What did you do, commander?"

"I spent most of my time back in Virginia Beach, I'm afraid."

"Oh." It dawned on Lambert that Castillo might want to spend his off time with his sick wife back home. "How's your wife?"

"She's good. I got the feeling she would rather have been here touring Scotland. I had to promise to bring her back one of those thick woolen tartan blankets they're famous for here."

Susan laughed. "Well, you'd better do it then."

Castillo liked Dr. Susan Lambert. She had a good sense of humor and a pleasant square face which displayed lively expressions. Her short sandy hair hugged her head and stopped at her thick neck. Her muscular build gave her the look of an athlete, and, in fact, she was. A triathlete to be exact. She could run, cycle and swim faster than any woman in the state of Virginia. She had proven it twice! And although her doctorate was in computer science, she was the best systems analyst, Castillo had ever seen. He had worked with her twice and she seemed to have been gifted with an ability to sense when a test was not ready. Either equipment had not been prepared, or people had not been trained properly or a procedure had been overlooked. She had a sixth sense about test preparations. Castillo couldn't help but notice she spent a lot of time with Crystal McConnell. He wondered briefly whether they were a couple. Oh well, it was none of his concern.

"You're the chief test conductor for QVR for this run. Correct?"

"Yes, sir," she responded.

"As captain, I'm going to appoint you as test liaison. Okay?"

Lambert compressed her mouth thoughtfully then said, "Sure. What do I do?"

"Just serve as a go-between for me. Relay messages and advisories to the rest of the test people."

"Sure, commander. I can do that."

"Good!" Castillo smiled. "And call me Don. I'm an informal type. Remember? You can start by telling everyone there will be a meeting in the crew's mess at 1700. We'll be discussing tomorrow's schedule."

"Will do, Don." And Lambert rushed off.

Castillo was impressed by the professionalism of the civilian test crew. They were all concentrated on their mission and talked about little else. Whenever Castillo asked a question they always answered with that humorless sincerity scientists often have. Even when he was joking.

In the aft equipment room Castillo spied an Apparition test set with a large display screen on it and said, "Hey, can you get the Panthers game on that thing?"

The technician said, "No, sir," seriously. "It's an M91 controller, sir. It communicates with the accumulator when the reactor plate charges."

"Oh." The smile faded from Castillo's face and he moved on.

At 1700 they all crowded into the Kansas's mess. Castillo chose this space because it was the largest room on the boat, about the size of a small living room, having five tables attached to the bulkhead and benches. It was obvious that some of the scientists and technicians were not able-bodied seamen. One man was so obese, his body could not fit in the space between table and bench. After trying to squeeze in several times without success, he decided to stand just inside the doorway. Castillo frowned at him. This man was very out of place in the cramped confines of a Virginia class attack submarine. Whenever he stood in the narrow passageway, he blocked it completely. No one could get by him. He must be very important to this test for the QVR people to send him here.

Castillo stood in the front of the room and addressed them. "I'd like to welcome you all aboard the Kansas. I hope no one here has claustrophobia because as many of you have already discovered space is at a premium here." There were 31 people crammed into the tables and benches. They were sitting shoulder to shoulder on padded benches around metal tables and those who arrived late were standing against the aft bulkhead. "I'd like to start by going around the room and have everyone introduce themselves and tell us who you work for and a little about yourself." This took about 35 minutes. Of the 15 civilians, 11 worked for QVR Corporation and most of them sounded British. The other 4 civilians were from U.S. Navy Test Operations. The two British Naval officers were from British Naval R and D and were here to observe.

Then the Kansas senior staff introduced themselves. They were the heads of the various departments vital to the operation of the boat: engineering, navigation, weapons and fire control, sonar and comm, safety and damage control. There was also the senior enlisted man and Chief of the Boat, COB for short, Chief Greg Brown and the boat's Executive Officer, Lieutenant Commander Mason Taylor.

"We usually travel with a SEAL team when we deploy, but we didn't bring them with us to Scotland because we didn't think they'd be needed. To get the additional berths for the test crew, we left a few of our people ashore, weapons and supply people. Some of you got state rooms, but most of you will be bunking in general enlisted birthing. It's very important that you don't make any unnecessary noise when we are ultra quiet, which we will be for part of our mission. If there's an emergency, please, listen to the crewmen. Do what they tell you and stay out of the way of damage control parties." Castillo looked around the room smiling at all the serious faces and said, "We're doing some ground-breaking work on this mission and I'm glad to be a part of it. To make you all honorary crew members, I have a gift for each of you. A crewman opened a cardboard box and Castillo took out a ball cap and held it up. "This is the official Kansas crew cap. You are each going to get one." There was a smattering of applause. It was a handsome black ball cap with gold submarine insignia dolphins embroidered on it. Above the dolphins was USS KANSAS and below was SSN-849 also in gold. "Well, that's all I have. I'm going to turn the meeting over to Dr. Lambert now who will be discussing the first day's tests."

Dr. Susan Lambert in a brisk businesslike manner went over the first day's tests and the division of responsibilities and who would be performing the briefings at each session. After a brief question and answer period they adjourned and settled into their assigned quarters. They were a group electrified with purpose and charged with the importance of their mission. No one could sleep.

Chapter 2

On the morning of departure tugs swung Kansas away from the pier and out into the Gare Loch current. A harbor pilot was aboard to help navigate the loch and the upper Firth of Clyde which is a large many-fingered bay opening to the Atlantic. Castillo was glad to have him aboard. There were treacherous rocky shoals in the loch and firth that had done in many a sailor over the years, and it was good to have an expert who knew these waters. The pilot would depart after about 25 miles where the firth widened.

The surrounding hills were draped in an earthy olive and shrouded in a white early morning wispy mist. At the water's edge there were small cream colored houses and taverns and occasionally a truck or car scurried rodent-like between them along a coastal road.

Castillo, the harbor pilot, and the watch stood in the Kansas's weather bridge high in the conning tower, or sail as the submariners liked to call it. It was late October in western Scotland and the air had a bite to it. Castillo's cheeks colored against the chill breeze. He wore his gray Navy foul weather jacket and his black Kansas ball cap. He also had a headset so he could communicate with Kansas's control room below. A cabin cruiser slowly passed them on the right, two people waved and Castillo waved back. The bright tangerine sun was just above the horizon and threw sparkling diamonds across the rippling water in the V-shaped wake of the small boat.

"The lahrd has smiled on ye this dee, Cap'n," said the old harbor pilot in his thick Scottish brogue. His leathery face cracked a smile.

"Yes, he has!" replied Castillo. He pulled the collar of his coat tighter against the wind and turned to look behind them. They were doing about eleven knots and at that speed Kansas's big screw was not churning the water very hard, but still creating a frothy white wake as wide as Glasgow's main boulevard. Castillo took a deep breath and relished the salt air. This was the best part of putting to sea. The smell of the brine, the brisk refreshing wash of the wind on your face. This was all lost as soon as the sub submerged. Once you're in the sealed metal tube breathing artificial air, you might as well be on the moon.

He heard a gull scream and looked up to see three of them circling. "The gulls look different here. They're bigger and have black wingtips and feet."

"Those be gannets," said the pilot. "They leke to nest in the rocks 'round about. They pester us to death and sheet on evrythin'" The old pilot sniffed disdainfully and added, "flyin' rats."

Castillo chuckled. The petty officer standing watch behind them at the watch's station said, "Sounds like a sea gull to me, sir."

The pilot started giving directions over his headset to the control room, adjusting Kansas's course. Castillo heard a voice in his ear, "Sir, this is Comm. We have secure voice coming in from the Connecticut."

"Pipe it up here, Comm."

"Yessir." There was a delay, then. "Go ahead, sir."

"What can I do for you?" said Castillo.

"Potato! Is that you?"

He immediately recognized the voice of one of his drinking buddies from Submarine Command School. "Hi, Scorch," he laughed. It was Commander Al Peterson, skipper of the Connecticut, a Seawolf class submarine. He could picture Peterson's sunny smile. "Where are you guys?"

"We're at the firth outflow, waiting on you. That boat under you is called a *fast* attack, you know?"

"Yes, I know. What's your point?"

"Y'all seem to be draggin' your feet. It'd be nice if you'd join us some time *today*!"

"What's your rush, Scorch? You have a plane to catch or something?"

"You know me. I'm a man of action!"

"Yes. That's how you got the name Scorch, isn't it?"

"Hey! That can was supposed to have *water* in it, not *kerosene*!"

They both broke into a fit of laughter. "Good times!"

"Yeh," said Peterson. "I'm just glad the officer's club didn't burn down."

Their laughter trailed off into an awkward silence.

"Does Connecticut have point for us on this?"

"No. We have your back door. The Brits have point. The Ambush."

"Ah…an Astute boat. Supposed to be good."

"Yes. I met her skipper a few months ago. Geoff Baldridge. A really sharp guy."

"Anything to report?" asked Castillo.

"There are a few onlookers here. We've identified a Russian Akula, a Kilo, a French Triomphant and possibly a Chinese Yuan."

"A Yuan! Are you sure?"

"Yes."

"Man…Those are quiet. You could sooner hear a butterfly whisper."

Petersen said nothing.

"Do you know the nationality of the Kilo?"

"No. Since Russia had their two-for-one sale on the things, we don't know who it might be. Iran? Vietnam? India? Who knows."

Castillo considered this. The Kilo was a very capable diesel attack boat built by Russia, and when the Soviet Union collapsed, Russia had a garage sale and parted with about 40 of them. They sold them to anyone with the money. 200 million each in American dollars.

"I don't know what you guys are testing," said Peterson, "but word has leaked out that it's something *big*.

There seems to be a lot of interest out here. That's why I was trying to hurry you."

"Understand. We'll be there shortly, Al. Thanks for the heads up. Have you notified SUBGROU 2 or TEST OPS of the situation?"

"Yes, both of them."

"Good. See you soon."

"Okay, Don. Connecticut out."

The line went dead. Castillo sighed. He was expecting this. Whenever something big is happening in the submarine world, there are always plenty of interested parties. All the major players, Russia, China, even allies like the French want to know who has the next big breakthrough. This complicated things, but he and Admiral Baynes had anticipated it and had come up with a plan.

He watched a circling gannet fold its wings and dive into the loch. Its body looked like a sleek spear as it entered the glassy water. After a few seconds it came it with a silvery fish in its beak. Castillo heard footsteps on the ladder behind him. He turned and saw his executive officer Mason Taylor's fine featured brown face smiling up at him. He was also wearing his official Kansas black ball cap and his gray foul weather jacket. He looked kind of lumpy, thought Castillo. Like he was smuggling something inside his coat. Taylor stepped up onto the sail deck, unzipped his jacket and extracted a cardboard box.

"Fresh coffee from the galley," said Taylor. He removed four white ceramic cups of coffee with plastic lids and handed them all around.

The old harbor pilot cackled, accepted a cup and made the sign of the cross in front of Taylor. "Bless ye, me son!"

"Thanks, Mase!" said Castillo. He spilled coffee on his coat sleeve when he removed the lid from his cup. "Oops! The coffee's on me!" Taylor and the pilot chuckled. Castillo's cup piped a long banner of steam into the chill breeze.

"Thank you, sir," said the watch.

"I was in the radio shack and heard your conversation with Connecticut just now," said Taylor.

"We seem to be attracting some unwanted attention, but it wasn't totally unexpected," said Castillo. "Admiral Baynes has come up with a plan I think will work."

Taylor nodded. They stood for a time in quiet reverence watching the sun rise and listening to the scream of sea birds and the hiss of water sluicing over Kansas's bow and off her round sides. Another boat passed them traveling in the opposite direction. It was a large sloop, but it wasn't under sail. The wind was calm, so it was slowly motoring up the loch, its image perfectly reflected in the mirror-like surface of the water. Two people waved from the boat's cockpit. Castillo and Taylor both smiled and waved back.

"So…," said Taylor. "Potato, huh?"

Castillo winced. "You heard that?"

"I did," said Taylor, then added thoughtfully, "It's okay. You don't have to tell me if you don't want to. If it's simply too embarrassing…"

Castillo caught the twinkle in Taylor's dark eyes. "When I was in Submarine Command School in California, some of the guys in my class were motorcycle crazies. That's okay with me. So am I. But they all favored these fast rockets, sportbikes. I preferred my Harley Road King. It's a '95, candy apple red with a custom tooled leather saddle. It's beautiful and runs like a dream! They kept after me, but I was stubborn about my Harley. I like how comfortable it is and the sound of the exhaust when I'm on the road. It sounds like the hooves of a galloping horse, you know?"

Taylor began to sing and strum an imaginary guitar. "*I'm a cowboy. On a ste-e-el horse I ride…*"

"Exactly!"

"So where's the potato come into this?"

"Oh. A columnist for one of the trade magazines said that a well-tuned Harley at idle says, 'potato… potato…potato'."

"Really?"

"Yeh. I always thought it said, 'bodega…bodega… bodega', but anyway, a few of my mischievous class mates passed the word that I liked potatoes. I was in *love* with them, they said. I started to find potatoes everywhere. In my shaving kit, in my bike. One day my locker was filled with potatoes."

Taylor shook his head in mock dismay. "They can be relentless."

"For sure. You'd know, wouldn't you…*Elvis*!"

"Aw man! I was drunk when I did that." Taylor removed his hat and scratched his bald head. "I should've known when I chose to make a fool out of myself someone in the crowd would have a camera."

"Yes, I saw your performance on YouTube. It was actually pretty good. I liked your *Hunk a Hunk a Burnin' Love* best."

"I think my classmates were just amazed to see a black man doin' Elvis in a karaoke bar."

They spent the rest of the ride down the loch in silence, sipping their coffee. Eventually the old harbor pilot removed his headset, turned to Castillo, saluted and said, "I'm turnin' 'er over to ye, cap'n! Ye kn teek 'er from 'ere."

Castillo returned the salute and pronounced, "You stand relieved, sir." Smiling, he shook the old man's hand, then watched him disappear down the access hatch. He exited the sail through a door below and stepped onto his waiting small boat which had been moored to Kansas. A crewman cast off his lines and the small vessel separated from Kansas and a short time later made a U turn and went back up the loch.

"Time to go to work," said Castillo.

"Yeh, I'd better get back to the control room," said Taylor stepping onto the access ladder and descending down the access trunk.

Castillo turned his back to Taylor's receding steps. Castillo reflected on how lucky he was to get Taylor as his executive officer. It was the responsibility of the skipper to make decisions and establish policies that best facilitate successful completion of a mission. He's also entrusted with a billion dollar Navy ship and the protection and well-being of her crew. The executive officer is responsible for implementing the skipper's policies. He makes sure all Navy rules and regulations are followed. He's the bad guy when he needs to be. Castillo liked Taylor's command style. He is very sharp and is good at following up on details. And the men seem to love him. At least he hasn't heard anything negative on the rumor mill.

He wondered how Liz was doing. It was about 2 in the morning in Virginia Beach right now. Was she up? Possibly. He decided to chance it. Cell phones were strictly forbidden aboard Navy submarines, but Castillo had a bulky satellite command phone. He was supposed to use it only for emergencies, but he could bend the rules from time to time. He pulled out, dialed and waited long minutes it seemed while the call was passed through the switching centers and finally connected. She picked up on the third ring.

"Hi, Honey."

"Hi." She sounded sleepy. "Are you awake?" He realized how stupid that question was as soon as it was out.

"Well…evidently."

He could hear the smile in her voice. And he could picture her sweet face. She was pretty but gaunt, thinned by the ravages of cancer and chemotherapy. Her chestnut hair was just now beginning to grow back. "How do you feel?"

"Pretty good. Is Kansas outbound?"

"Yes, we are. I just wanted to hear your voice." Awkward silence, then. "I hope you're getting enough rest."

"Yes! God, you and sis are too much. What I really need is a nice relaxing day away. I've been trying to talk sis into driving us to Nags Head this week-end."

"It should be nice weather there, right now." A thought crossed Castillo's mind. "I'll tell you what. When I get back to Clyde, if you're up to it, I want to fly you and the girls out here."

"To *Scotland*? That would be so great! But the girls are in school."

"They're both earning top marks. They can miss a week."

"Are you *sure*, honey?" She was bursting with exuberance.

"I'm sure. I want you all with me. I haven't really had a chance to see Scotland myself. We'll all explore it together."

"That would be so *great*!"

"Make sure it's alright with Dr. Shah." Her oncologist.

"I will!"

"I'd better sign off and get busy commanding. I'll call you again in about seven days."

"Okay. Do good on your test!"

How many times had he heard that same phrase from his mother when he was a kid. "I will. Love you!"

"Love you too!"

Castillo disconnected and put his phone away, a smile lingering on his face. What would he do without Liz, Kelly and Robin? They were the sunshine in his day. The north star in his night sky. Just knowing that they were somewhere waiting for him, made all his struggles worth it.

He cleared his throat and then spoke into his headset. "XO, Captain."

"XO here."

"Do we have a position on Connecticut?"

"Yes, she's about fifteen miles ahead, stationary, inside the mouth of the firth."

"Surfaced?"

"No she's down about 100 feet."

"Okay, good. Let me know when we're within three miles."

"Will do. There are a couple civilians here who would like permission to join you."

"Send them up." Everyone wanted to be on the sail. There was a spectacular view from up here, but it had limited room. But right now there was only the watch and him so he didn't mind a little company. He wondered who was coming up. He heard footsteps on the ladder and turned to see Susan Lambert's head pop up, followed by Crystal McConnell.

"Hi!" said Lambert. "This is Crystal's first time aboard a submarine, so I'm showing her around."

"I see," said Castillo. Crystal smiled shyly. She was almost as tall as Castillo, had a delicate fine-featured face with a small mouth. Her complexion was flawless cream and her hair was rich cocoa. It streamed away from her face like a banner in the wind.

"She asks a lot of questions I can't answer," said Lambert. "But I'm sure you can."

"I'll try," said Castillo.

Crystal looked at Castillo self consciously and said, "Why is Kansas a *boat* and not a ship?"

"Oh! Well, the first submarines in the Navy were less than 125 feet long. By definition that makes them boats. But as they got bigger, the Navy continued to call them boats. Kansas is 377 feet long and almost 8000 metric tons. That's way bigger than a boat, but we still call her a boat. It's become a tradition now."

"I see," said McConnell. "Why is a ship always a *her* and not a him?"

Castillo laughed. "You got me there! I suppose because most crews are men and ships are kind of mysterious temperamental creatures."

McConnell and Lambert both smiled. "But you do have a woman on your crew. Your navigation officer."

"Lieutenant Maria Guerrero. Yes. There are a few women on active submarine service now and we have one of them. She's very good at what she does."

Something caught Castillo's eye. It was a boy bundled in a bulky brown coat running down the nearby beach with a dog. Behind him was what looked like a primitive vine-covered tavern or inn made of stacked gray stone and a slate roof. It looked like it could have emerged from the ancient outcropping of rock behind it. It blended perfectly with its surroundings. How long had it been there? A century? Two? On a grassy hill above the rocks was a tall steel tower with microwave horns at the top. A cell tower. Just another example of the old juxtaposed with the new. They all watched the boy and his dog run and laugh in the straw-colored sunlight, perfectly mirrored in the water. He seemed to notice the submarine and stopped running. He shaded his eyes with one hand and waved at them, and Castillo, Lambert and McConnell smiled and waved back.

"So Crystal, what do you do?" asked Castillo.

"I authored the test plan for this mission. I had lots of help, of course, from QVR as well as Navy people."

With that accent she was obviously English, thought Castillo. She seemed very different than Susan. Crystal was taller and thinner. Susan's face was very expressive. Her eyebrows were always dancing when she told a story, but Crystal's seemed to be expressionless, in fact, she barely moved her lips when she talked. She would make a great ventriloquist, thought Castillo. "So what do you do during a test?"

"I initial each test step as it is performed and record when we deviate from the test, I have to record how we deviated and why. I sign off, then the senior test conductor has to sign off on it and then the Navy has to sign off on it." Then she added. "That would be *you*, sir."

"Please, call me Don." He wanted to ask her if she had ever tried ventriloquism, but he thought it would probably come across as impertinent, bordering on disrespectful. "Do you expect us to deviate?"

"Oh sure. This is very complex equipment. We're bound to run into something."

He turned to Lambert and said, "Do you see any problems for tomorrow's test, Susan?"

"No," replied Lambert. "But I don't like the communication arrangements. When Apparition is activated, we have no communications link to the outside world at all. We're essentially cut off."

"True," agreed Castillo. "Not the best situation to be in."

"When things go wrong with something like this," said Lambert, "they tend to go wrong fast. We could be in big trouble before any observer knows about it."

Castillo didn't like this possibility. "But some of the tests are designed to test different communication devices and procedures. Correct?"

"Yes."

"Well, let's hope that at least one of them works." He playfully punched Lambert on the shoulder and said, "Stay positive!"

She chuckled and saluted. "Yes, sir!"

• • •

The nerve center for the Apparition test was at a QVR facility near Glasgow. The project had taken over a large open room on the third floor of one of the R & D buildings in the QVR industrial compound near the Glasgow airport. Before they could use the room as a Navy test monitoring facility however, they'd had to beef up security and install some specialized communications equipment. They'd been rushed to get all the modifications done on time. Even now, one day from the first official Apparition test, the room looked like chaos. Workmen and technicians were still hooking up cable and testing screens with colorful test patterns. People rushed around the room, shouting requests for information or file access. There were civilians, U.S.

Navy personnel in blue uniforms and Royal British Navy personnel in similar blue uniforms.

At the back of the room on a raised platform were four U.S. Navy admirals sitting in comfortable chairs along with three Royal British Navy admirals. Apparition was a very important cutting edge technology and everyone understood the ramifications if it succeeded. It would change naval warfare forever, and everyone wanted a piece of it. After a successful test everyone would be rushing to claim credit for this groundbreaking technology whether they had been a part of it or not. Such was the politics of the military.

The admirals were all watching the large overhead screen showing a view of the Firth of Clyde. It appeared to be a satellite shot of the firth, dotted with ships. Kansas was clearly marked, as was Connecticut and all the observer ships, authorized and unauthorized.

Admiral Baynes was addressing the other admirals on the platform. "Peterson thinks that tango 3 is a Chinese Yuan, tango 1 is a Kilo of unknown nationality, tango 2 is the Vigilant, a French Triomphant class boat, tango 4 is a Russian Akula and tango 5 is another Kilo of unknown nationality."

"Quite a crowd!" said one of the British admirals. He pulled at his large nose and said, "Word has leaked about this thing."

"And more are arriving by the minute," grumbled Baynes. With his jowls and darkly ringed eyes he resembled a disgruntled raccoon. "We also have a flotilla of surface ships. The usual Russian and Chinese trawlers and one Spanish destroyer."

"Do you have a plan for losing the looky-loos?" asked O'Keefe.

"Yes. Kansas, Connecticut and Ambush are going to execute a 'stop-n-drop'."

"Do you think it will work?" asked O'Keefe.

"If it's done right." But Baynes's gray expression was anything but confident.

Chapter 3

"Cap'n, this is the XO in the control room. We're three miles from rendezvous with Connecticut."

"Very well. Prepare to dive," said Castillo into his headset.

Immediately they heard the command blare from the 1MC loudspeakers.

Now, prepare to dive! Prepare to dive!

Then they heard the dive warning alarm.

WHOOOP! WHOOOP!

Castillo turned to Lambert, McConnell and the watch and ordered, "Clear the bridge!"

The watch said, "Aye, sir! Clear the bridge!" He immediately began unplugging his headset and securing the plexiglass spray shields.

"After you, ladies," said Castillo gesturing to the ladder. McConnell went down first, followed by Lambert and then Castillo. The petty officer of the watch came down last and spun the dogging wheel on the hatch to secure it tightly.

They went to the control room where Castillo took his command chair in the center of the room. Lambert said, "Well, we'll leave you now. You're going to be busy."

"No, stay," said Castillo. "You won't be in the way. I enjoy explaining things. It's the instructor in me."

Several of the men smiled at Castillo. Mason Taylor said, "I think he just enjoys female company."

"Oh, pipe down," said Castillo. "Pilot, take us down to 100 feet."

"100 feet aye, sir," repeated a man setting in the front of the control room.

"He used to be called the helmsman, but with the Virginia class boats they began calling him *pilot* and the bow planesman is now called the *copilot*," explained Castillo.

"I see," said McConnell nodding. The deck under them began to tilt downward slightly.

"And with all the automation and with the Navy constantly pushing to save money and increase efficiency, we have done away with many positions. For example, Virginia class boats no longer have a diving officer or a maneuvering officer. The con officer talks directly to the pilot and the throttleman in maneuvering now. No redundant relaying of commands up and down the line."

"Well, that makes sense," said McConnell.

The control room was very dark, but every man's face was lit by the ghostly luminescence of the flat screen before him. Some men stood, but most were sitting at keyboards and counters talking into headsets.

The screens displayed a dizzying number of graphs, plots and alphanumeric readouts. Behind the quiet whispers and murmurings of operators there was an undercurrent of electronic whining and the soft purring of blowers. The room smelled of electronics and sweat. Every square inch of the ceiling was covered with pipes, conduits and junction boxes. Susan Lambert looked around and recognized some of the people here. She had met some of them before on previous test missions. She waved at Maria Guerrero who was leaning over the large horizontal navigation plotting station in the back of the room. Guerrero smiled and waved back. Guerrero looked like she had two small display screens mounted on her nose. It was only the reflection of her display monitor in her rectangular glasses.

"Virginia boats have a very open layout in the control room because we don't have a periscope, which used to dominate the control room."

"No pcriscope?" asked McConnell, surprised.

"You have a photonics mast. Right?" said Lambert.

"Thats right," smiled Castillo.

"See? I remembered something from my last mission on Kansas."

"Very good!" said Castillo.

"What's a photon mast?" asked McConnell.

"A *photonics* mast," corrected Castillo. "It's a mast we send up with high definition cameras and sensors. It can tell us way more than a periscope ever could."

"We're level at 100 feet, sir," reported the pilot.

"Very well," responded Castillo. He pointed at the large view screen on the bulkhead in front of the control room and said, "There is the navigation display. It shows where Kansas is and her surroundings." Kansas was a small icon in the center of the display with nearby land masses outlined in bright green. It resembled a standard GPS moving map display. "The small red blip ahead of us there is the Connecticut. And the one next to her is the Ambush, a British boat." Castillo removed his ball cap and wiped at his brow with his left hand and said, "And our first job is to disappear!"

"Disappear!" said McConnell doubtfully.

"Not really, Crystal. But to the watchers we'll seem to disappear."

"How?"

"We'll go very quiet."

Crystal said nothing.

"We're going to go quieter than a falling snowflake."

"Really?" said Crystal doubtfully.

"This whole deck structure is on shock absorbers. It doesn't contact the hull anywhere. Very little sound we make gets transmitted through the hull. And we have very quiet pump jet propulsion and…"

"Sir, Connecticut is on the Gertie."

The Gertie was an acoustic voice device which could be used ship-to-ship at close range. Castillo held up a finger of pause and picked up what looked like a telephone receiver and said, "Put 'em through." Castillo heard a click then a hiss. "Hello, this is Kansas."

"Hey, you ready to do this?" It was Peterson.

"We're ready. Do you have the play?"

"We've got the play. Geoff Baldridge from Ambush is on the line with us too."

"Hello, Commander Castillo," said a Brittish voice. "Baldridge here. We've got the play. Are you the quarterback?"

Castillo was surprised that a Brit would know what a quarterback was. "Yes, I'll be calling the play. I want Ambush to take the lead and Connecticut to follow. We are going to form up on Connecticut in close formation all the way to the drop point. I want direct communication between the pilots so there won't be any mistakes. I want to make about twelve knots."

"Only *twelve* knots?" asked Baldridge.

"Yes, Kansas has some hull attachments, and I'm not sure how that's going to affect our flow noise at high speed. I know our unauthorized observers are going to be recording us with every device they have, trying to get a clue about what we're doing. I don't want to give them too much to analyze."

"Ah! got it!" responded Baldridge.

"Okay," said Peterson. "Let's do this!"

"Let's go," said Castillo and disconnected. He turned to Mason Taylor and said, "Rig for ultraquiet."

Taylor picked up a microphone and immediately his voice was heard in the overhead speakers:

Now, rig the ship for ultraquiet. Rig for ultraquiet. All hands not on active watch retire to quarters. All hands not on active watch retire to quarters.

Susan Lambert and Crystal McDonnell looked askance at Castillo. Castillo smiled and said, "Here's the part where we become like a falling snow flake. All unnecessary fans, blowers and machinery will be turned off, and all nonessential personnel will go to their quarters and read or sleep."

"Should we…" whispered Lambert.

"Stay right here," said Castillo. "You're okay. But if you make any noise, you'll be shot." Crystal McConnell's brown eyes enlarged. It's the closest Castillo had yet seen to an actual facial expression on her.

Lambert said, "He's kidding."

"Are you?" asked McConnell.

Castillo nodded. "The Navy and QVR would probably frown on such a thing."

The three ship formation left the firth and emerged into the Irish Sea. Admiral Baynes had instructed the task force ships what to do. A frigate and two destroyers began cruising in circles near the unauthorized observers at flank speed.

There are basically two types of sonar used by the Navy. The first type is the *passive* type. Passive sonar listens for noises made by ships or oceanic installations. Passive sonar is very sensitive to the sounds a ship makes as it passes through the water. There are noises made by the water flowing over her hull. These are called *flow* noises. There are noises made by her propeller. The faster a propeller turns, the more it cavitates and creates a noisy turbulence behind the ship. There are also mechanical sounds like pump noises, valve noises, vent noises and even sometimes human noises: the clattering of mess hall pans and hatches slamming shut.

Admiral Baynes rendered the enemy *passive* sonar useless when he ordered the Navy ships to cruise at high speed near the unauthorized observer ships. Their sonar operators would not be able to hear anything but the racket raised by the task force ships. That solved one problem.

The second type of sonar is called *active* sonar. It works by sending out a powerful sound pulse or *ping* and reading the echo returned by another ship's hull. This was an accurate way of seeing what was in the water, but most sub skippers didn't like to use it because it also gave away the position of the ship sending out the pulse. If a skipper was trying to hide, this would give him away.

Castillo wondered which of the boats shadowing them would ping. Some one would have to. It would probably be one of the surface ships. They are not as concerned about staying hidden. He didn't have to wait long.

PING!

He heard it through the hull and saw it register on the sonar displays. It looked to be one of the trawlers, but he wasn't worried. When the enemy observers analyzed the return, they would see *two* submarines in formation, not three. Connecticut and Kansas were traveling in parallel less than fifty feet apart. They looked like one submarine on a sonar display.

This tight formation was made possible by the new wide aperture sonar array Kansas was using. They also had the laser system on the photonics mast allowing them to get very accurate distancing information. The Ambush's pilot was steering a course for an undersea trough formation. A mile behind her was the Connecticut with the smaller Kansas in her shadow. Kansas's pilot only had to think about one thing: maintaining a fifty foot separation from Connecticut. Beads of sweat formed on the pilot's forehead as he concentrated on his displays. Behind him a technician called out distances. "48…49…49…49…50…50…50…" Because all vents and blowers had been secured during the ultraquiet run, the air was beginning to get warm and stuffy. The odor of sweat was becoming more pronounced.

They continued like this for what seemed an eternity. The pilot grew fatigued and handed off to the copilot who had a control stick identical to the pilot's.

Finally Castillo picked up his receiver and said, "Okay, Engine room, get ready. We're approaching point bravo."

"Ready, sir," replied a voice.

As soon as the Connecticut and Kansas were both shielded from sonar by a trough formation, Castillo gave the command and Kansas stopped, dropped and hovered just feet off the sea floor. This was made possible by Kansas's auxiliary maneuvering devices at the bow and stern. This allowed them to keep their station in shallow water, which was what Virginia class submarines were designed to do. They were intended to take SEAL teams into shallow water and wait for them to return if necessary. A new weapon in the war on terrorism.

Ambush and Connecticut continued on course without so much as a twitch.

Kansas waited silently. "Do you think they fell for it?" asked Taylor.

"I think they did," said Castillo. "We'll know shortly. Engine room, make turns for three knots. Sonar, deploy the TB-29. Let's listen."

"Aye, sir. Making turns for three knots."

"Aye, sir. Deploying TB-29."

The TB-29 was a state-of-the-art thin towed sonar array which was extremely sensitive. It would quickly tell them if there was anyone within a hundred miles.

After the chaotic ruckus had stopped, the Kansas slowly emerged from her hiding place and began listening for other ships with her towed array, but all she could pick up were the ships heading away, trailing the Ambush and Connecticut.

"Good!" said Castillo. "Let's get some ventilation going in here. It's stuffy." Immediately a quiet whir started and cool fresh air began to flood in from overhead vents. "Navigator, plot us a course for the Apparition test area."

"Aye, sir. Plotting a course to test area," replied Lieutenant Maria Guerrero.

"I'm hungry," said Castillo and then with a whimsical tone in his voice, "Where would you ladies like to go for lunch."

They exchanged puzzled glances.

Castillo picked up his receiver, turned a dial and said into it, "Jonesy, why don't you announce lunch for our guests."

After a delay a voice came from the overhead speakers:

"*Good morning, ladies and gentlemen, for lunch today the Jayhawk bistro will be featuring New York style pepperoni pizza made with a special homemade marinara and a sourdough crust. This will be served with a tangy Greek salad made with feta cheese, fresh tomatoes and green peppers, onions, black olives and your choice of dressing. Or you may prefer our homemade minestrone and lasagna topped with cheese tortelinni, meat sauce and mozzarella cheese. Also available will be our fabulous garlic knots topped with olive oil, fresh garlic and Parmesan cheese. Lunch will begin at 1100 hours. Thank you.*"

Susan Lambert's eyebrows shot up. "Sounds great!"

"Yes!" agreed McConnell.

"We have pretty good food here," said Castillo.

"But," said Taylor, "I think Jonesy is showing off a little for the civilians."

"Could be," admitted Castillo.

• • •

Admiral Baynes clapped his hands as he saw the small ships on the big screen moving off to the north. "They fell for it!"

The admirals laughed and smiled all around, nodding to each other. Baynes picked up a handset mounted on his chair and spoke into it. "Call Apparition 2 and tell them Kansas is clear and on her way.

She'll rendezvous with them sometime today in the test area."

Apparition 2 was actually the British research vessel Balthazar on loan to the British Royal Navy from the National Oceanographic Society based out of Edinburgh. She had been anchored in a remote Scottish cove for two weeks preparing for the Apparition test. She was a 600 foot white trawler with the NOS crest on her sides, a blue codfish with a crossed trident and quill pen behind it. She looked like any other research vessel with a large stack, several large booms and two satellite dishes. Beneath her hull however, were some very highly specialized sensors and cameras.

The Balthazar crew had established a cover story of doing survey work on plankton in the area. They had even gone so far as to hire local villagers to get plankton samples for them.

The young sonar operator aboard the Balthazar was bored as he stood his watch. He was reading an article on his iPad and only paying attention to the displays peripherally. That's why he jumped when a voice came from the console speaker. The voice said, "Apparition 2, this is Kansas checking in."

He turned his selector to the Gertie and said, "Jesus, you guys are spooky quiet! I didn't hear a damn thing!"

"We're not called the *noisy* service, you know."

Kansas had silently approached the Balthazar and stopped and gone to station-keeping at a depth of 100 feet and a distance of 600 feet.

"I know." He contacted the captain of the Baltha-zar, and he and Castillo talked briefly about when they would start tests tomorrow.

That evening the Kansas crew dined on beef welling-ton, steamed broccoli, glazed carrots, corn chowder, Caesar salad and the chef's signature garlic cheese bread. For dessert there was apple cobbler.

The following morning after a hearty breakfast of bacon, eggs and for those watching their weight, bagels and low fat cream cheese, the Kansas crew got ready for the first Apparition test.

The air seemed to be charged with the angst of an-ticipation. Castillo sat in his command chair in the control room. He ordered all ship's alarms be tested first to make sure all ship's hazardous warning systems were working properly. Fire, chemical, nuclear, colli-sion. All were working perfectly. The weapons stations to his left had all been taken over by the Apparition test crew, the workstations there having been repro-grammed to perform test monitor functions. Susan Lambert was sitting at the first weapons station with a notebook in her lap, speaking into her headset. She was on the line with the Apparition control center in Glasgow and the Apparition 2 ship and her techni-cians on board. Next to her was Crystal McConnell also with a notebook and a headset. She seemed to be listening to Lambert with a laser-like focus. There were two more testers next to her. In the back of the control room were the two British officers, observing. To Cas-tillo's right was the sonar operators and Mason Taylor, who looked preoccupied. This is pretty much out of my hands now, thought Castillo. He had taken Kansas down to 150 feet, activated station-keeping and then kicked back. The Navy is just along for the ride at this point. He tried to hear what Susan was saying.

"So…" said Lambert, "do you have the amendment to steps 5 point 2 and 6 point 3? Good. And we have a replacement for step 7…substeps 4 through 8. Okay… okay…but we can't do that today. Tomorrow, yes. We ran into an initialization problem."

It was boring! Castillo looked at the large screen in front of the room. It had an image of Kansas on it. It was feed from a live underwater camera on the Balthazar. Castillo reached down to his small control screen built into his chair arm. He switched the feed to another camera. Kansas was ringed with cameras. Some were mounted on the Balthazar and some were on buoys. They showed Kansas from every angle, even from above and below. Castillo finally switched to Kansas's own cameras on her photonics mast. He could see the hull of the Balthazar and on other cameras the bottoms of the sensor buoys as they bobbed in the water.

Finally Lambert said, "Okay, let's do this! Everybody report in."

Castillo could see messages streaming across the screens before Lambert and McConnell. Blue green phosphorescence flickered across their features. McConnell typed quickly and in spurts on her keyboard.

Lambert said, "Ready for stage 1. Initiate!"

More messages scrolled on Lambert's screen. It looked like alphabet soup to Castillo.

SZ167-1 charging…SZ167-2 charging…TT78388-code 2398…SZ167-1 37%…SZ167-2 32%… TT37-9-code 2322…SZ167-1 55%…SZ167-2 51%… TT877751…SZ167-1 83%…SZ167-2 79%… TT5599-code 7878…SZ167-1 100%…SZ167-2 100%

"Stage 1 complete," said Lambert. "Ready for stage 2. Initiate!"

More alphabet soup messages, observed Castillo.

KMM129 phase 1 regression in progress… SS7171…34SS-2 detector initializing…SS7172… HUF2 amplifier initializing…ST4838-C…3…2..1… KMM129 regression complete…

"Stage 2 complete," intoned Lambert. "Okay, we're almost there, folks. Power up the emitter arrays."

EMIT22-3 beginning induction…GH1004… GH1005…GH1011…Error 1447 - Modal anomaly…terminating…

"Shit," sighed Lambert. Castillo could tell by the consternation on her face this was not good. "What happened, Norm?" She pulled at the skin under her chin. "Can you reset?" McConnell picked up a pen and began writing. Then her fingers flew over her keyboard throwing words onto the screen, pen dangling from her mouth. Lambert listened intently, then she sat back and said, "Okay, everybody. We have an emitter problem. Just stand by and let Norm take a look at it. We may not be terminated yet."

Lambert turned and looked at Castillo, shrugged. Castillo returned the shrug. Nothing to do but wait. "You're used to this, aren't you?" said Castillo.

"There's always something," said Lambert. "I've never had a test go flawlessly. And I expected trouble on Apparition but that's because of the complexity of this thing. We have subsystems and processors and networks and circuits and there's so much connectivity and so much critical dependency, if there's so much as a hiccup anywhere, it's going to affect us. This is brand new cutting edge technology here. Once all the kinks are worked out of it, it'll be a stable reliable system, but right now…"

Castillo shifted and found Taylor staring at Lambert with a curious expression. Something was on his mind, and knowing him like he did, Castillo was sure he would get an earful sooner or later. He turned to face Lambert again, but she was talking on her headset.

"Okay…okay…want to try it again? Alright everybody. We're going to try it again. Start where we left off. Power up emitters, now."

Castillo saw McConnell cross her fingers on both hands. Messages once again scrolled across Lambert's screen:

EMIT22-3 beginning induction…GH1004… GH1005…GH1011…initializing accumulator…startup successful…EMIT22-2 beginning induction…GH1055…GH1024…GH1012… initializing accumulator…startup successful… EMIT22-1 beginning induction …GH1031… GH1044…GH1013 …initializing accumulator… startup successful

"Woo hoo!" said Lambert. "I think we're ready!" She wiped both hands on her slacks and exhaled loudly and glanced at Castillo, smiling. "Okay, Don. You've got the switch."

Castillo nodded, picked up his receiver, and when he talked, his voice was heard throughout the ship.

"*Attention, all hands! Apparition will be activated in 3…2…1…mark!*"

At the word *mark*, Lambert hit a key on her keyboard and at first nothing happened, then a sensation of pins and needles washed over everybody. Some squirmed at the discomfort. Then abruptly the deck fell away like a large airliner encountering wind shear. McConnell screamed and several men swore as coffee cups, notebooks and pens hit the deck. From the sound of the thuds, Castillo knew that several bodies had hit the deck too: people caught by surprise by the sudden deck plunge. It took a few seconds for Castillo to recover and get his breath back. Everywhere he turned he saw panicked faces.

Mason Taylor was one of those who had fallen. "Christ! What happened?" he said regaining his feet.

"I don't know," said Lambert.

"I imagine," said Castillo, "that was the result of several feet of sea water under the boat going through molecular hypercompression. It probably creates a void under us for just a few milliseconds." He picked up his receiver and addressed the crew again from the overheads:

"*My apologies, folks. That caught us off guard. Please, report to the infirmary if you have any injuries and assess all areas for any damage and report it to damage control.*"

The forward view from the photonics cameras suddenly caught Castillo's eye. A pale shimmering blue iridescent veil was in front of the ship. It was incredible! He cycled the view through every camera and it was the same. A pale iridescent sphere was surrounding the boat. It had to be about 400 feet in diameter. He wanted badly to see what how it looked from Balthazar, but there was no communication while the sphere was up. Nothing penetrated it. Castillo felt very queasy and the pins and needles over his skin had turned to flame and seemed to be getting worse.

"My skin feels like it's on fire," said Taylor scowling.

"Mine too," said Lambert. "Alright, we've proven that it works. Lets turn it off now."

"Wait," said Castillo. He picked up his receiver again and made another announcement:

"*Okay, folks. We're going to deactivate the Apparition system now and we're likely to get a reverse effect from the one we got the first time. My suggestion is to brace your backs against a bulkhead or lay flat on the deck to avoid injury.*"

He looked at Lambert, and when she gave him the thumbs up, he said into his receiver:

"*Apparition deactivation in 3…2…1…mark.*"

At the word *mark* Lambert hit a key on her keyboard and after a short delay the deck suddenly heaved upward about 3 feet. McConnell screamed again and there was more cursing and muttering. Castillo felt as if his spine had been compressed from the jolt but he was otherwise okay. He shifted to look at Taylor, but he was gone! Then he saw him laying on his back on the deck beside him, smiling.

"I was ready this time," he chuckled.

"You were!"

They reestablished communications with the Apparition control center and Balthazar. Castillo was able to see a replay of what Balthazar saw with her underwater cameras. It was dreamlike image of a pale blue shimmering sphere. One second they were looking at a portside profile of Kansas and the next the Apparition sphere. The sphere activation created quite a bit of turbulence in the water. Surface cameras showed agitated waves racing across the cove, lapping onto the far shore and rocking Balthazar gently. When the sphere was deactivated, more turbulence.

They still had more testing to do. The test team activated Apparition again, this time with a different staging protocol, just to test different emitters to see which ones were more efficient. The crew was ready for the plunging and heaving of the deck this time. The third test was an effort to see how long the sphere could be sustained using Kansas's power. They were able to keep the sphere activated for six minutes, sixteen seconds before the heat exchanger began overheating. It was a very uncomfortable test because the flaming skin phenomenon turned to first degree burn and many experienced feelings of nausea.

After the third Apparition test it was 1134 hours, so they broke for lunch, but with all the upheaval of the morning, not many ate. There was a run on peptic aids from the infirmary.

When it was time to begin testing again, Castillo took his command chair and said, "I feel like I've been on a roller coaster all morning."

"So do I," said Taylor, collapsing into a watch chair. "How many more of these do we have to do today?"

"Three more," replied Lambert. "What page are we on, Crystal?"

"Uh…23, I think," replied McConnell, flipping pages in the notebook on her lap.

Castillo thought she looked pale. On the next test they were testing a gradual charging of reactor plates after the accelerators were started in an effort to control the force of the compression. It failed utterly! The Apparition sphere never activated and white smoke issued from the stage 1 accelerator, sending a foul acrid stench throughout the boat. It took two hours to cleanse the air, assure that there was no fire and to recertify that the accelerator was healthy.

When they were ready to test again, Castillo took his place in the control room again. He caught the dark glare from Taylor.

"Okay," said Lambert. "In this test we are going to try and adjust the diameter of the sphere after it's activated. We're on page 34 of the test plan."

Everyone braced for the activation, knowing what to expect now. McConnell no longer screamed when the deck dropped away. It was more of a yip.

"Gain adjustment beginning now," said Lambert.

Castillo watched the view from the photonics mast cameras. There didn't seem to be any change. He wondered what it should look like. Would they be able to see any difference? Would they…something was happening, but it was happening to him. His insides were rumbling…or something. He could feel waves of nausea washing over him. It got stronger with each wave. He suddenly stood up and a cramp hit him deep in his intestines and doubled him over…like a giant hand had gripped his insides. He turned to Taylor and his face was registering distress as well. He was holding his stomach and grimmacing. Suddenly, Castillo was sure he was going to evacuate his bowels. He quickly sat down before it could happen.

"Shit!" screamed one of the sonar operators.

"Cut it off!" screamed Castillo to Lambert.

Lambert nodded, hit a key on her keyboard, the deck heaved upwards and the discomfort gradually subsided. Castillo had fought against emptying his bowels and he could tell from the aroma in the room, someone had lost that fight. He picked up his receiver and addressed the crew:

Attention crew, a*nyone who needs to leave your station to…freshen up may do so.*

The control room almost emptied, and men began to stack up outside the head like airliners on approach to Atlanta.

Castillo turned to Lambert and said, "Susan, could I see you in my stateroom immediately!"

Chapter 4

"Explain again in simple words what happened?" said Castillo, struggling to understand what had happened during the last test. He had a slight headache and his body was aching as if he'd been bull riding all day. Crowded into his stateroom was Mason Taylor, Susan Lambert, Crystal McConnell and Norm Bloomberg. Norm was the obese man Castillo had noticed earlier blocking the passageway. Castillo was sizing him up. The man was Apparition's head engineer and obviously important to the project. In fact he seemed to be the only one with any explanation of what had happened. He was of average height, but he had to weigh close to 400 pounds, thought Castillo. His blue denim shirt was half untucked, his huge belly lapped over his belt and his jeans stretched tight over his tree trunk legs. He had thick lenses in his black-rimmed glasses, long thinning black hair that covered the back of his neck like a hat flap and wore a black goatee on his chin. Well, on his first chin anyway. He stood before Castillo uneasily swaying rhythmically like a caged hippo.

"In NASA's early research," said Bloomberg, "they determined that there was a resonant ultrasonic frequency for every muscle in the human body. Each muscle can be contracted with an ultrasonic transponder tuned to its resonant frequency. Unfortunately, we accidentally hit the frequency today for the male bowel."

"Ultrasonic?" questioned Castillo. "Are you using ultrasonics?"

"No, sir," replied Bloomberg. "We have nothing designed to produce an ultrasonic signature, but the plunge attenuator in the accelerator caused a reflected wave when we varied the signal voltage to it. This in turn hit a resonant frequency in one of the particle chambers which translated into a mechanical oscillation. It transmitted through the hull of the ship and well, you know the rest."

"Well, when you put it like that, it makes perfect sense," said Castillo, dripping with sarcasm. He removed his cap, laid it on his desk and made a washing motion over his face with both hands.

"I'm sorry, sir," said Bloomberg, looking at the floor. "It won't happen again. We've got it fixed now, sir."

Castillo sniffed. What could he say? He couldn't be angry at them. It was an accident. He could still smell the aroma of feces in the air. The air scrubbers were probably working overtime to clear the scent. "Okay, what's next?"

"I'm terminating testing for today," said Lambert. "We've got a debriefing at 1700. We'll be hooked in with Glasgow and Balthazar. They'll be wanting to discuss the day's events."

"Oh good!" said Castillo. He still had some sarcasm to get out of his system. He could already picture the sullen faces. Lambert cast him an apologetic look but it was lost on him. "Okay, I'll see you all there." The QVR people all left. Mason Taylor stayed behind.

"How long are you going to let these people go on with this farce, Don?" queried Taylor. He sat down in a chair and crossing his long legs.

"What do you mean?" asked Castillo.

"I mean these people do not seem to have control of this thing. Apparition needs to go back to the drawing board for a while."

Castillo sighed. "Have you seen what it does?"

"Yes, Baynes granted me access to the test vids. It was very impressive."

"Impressive!? It was mind-blowing, Mase! As a kid, I used to watch science fiction. I thought it was so cool when the captain said, 'Raise Shields'. It made them invulnerable to attack! I never in my wildest dreams thought that we would some day have the same thing. If this works, it'll save thousands of lives at sea! Don't you think it's incredible?"

Taylor held Castillo's gaze and said nothing for a time. Then he crossed his arms and said, "I shit my pants two weeks ago when I saw what they were experimenting with."

"What? Why?"

"Do you know what that Hadron Collider does?"

"Sure, it…uh…" Castillo scratched at the side of his face.

"It is exploring the forces that formed the universe, Don. It is delving into the unknown, the dark elemental forces of nature that created our world. I'm not convinced that we should even be going there. Maybe God kept this information from us for a reason. If we had access to these forces, could we control them? Would we do more harm then good? Some experts think these experiments could cause a black hole that would engulf and destroy our planet."

Castillo had never seen Taylor this worked up. "Well, I don't know about any of that, but I think this thing's important. Think of the lives it will…"

"If we were in a shooting war, Don," interrupted Taylor. "But we're not. And there's no knowing when we will be again."

"But this is a huge breakthrough in electronic countermeasures, Mase! I think you're overreacting."

"Have you read about this Higgs boson, Don? It's called the God particle. It existed before all matter in the universe. This is an area where the laws of physics meet God. This is the kind of technology they're developing at that collider, and they're barely in control of it. They're trying to answer questions they have no business asking. And sometimes it gets away from them with disastrous results and now we have it on Kansas! Have you seen those tubes they attached to our hull? Have you seen those strange spheres and boxes in the aft equipment room? Whenever I ask what something does no one can explain it to me. Are you listening to me, Don? These test people don't even know how it works! If something goes wrong, what might we unleash on the world? We're one misstep away from a catastrophic nuclear accident here or maybe something worse!"

Taylor's eyes were wild. Castillo was shocked and at a loss for words.

"And if today's events didn't convince you these guys don't know what they're doing, then I don't know what will. This is the stuff of nightmares, Don."

Castillo could tell by Taylor's compressed lips and furrowed brow, he was agitated. "Your concerns are very disturbing, Mase. I would appreciate it if, for now, you kept these views to yourself and didn't share them with the rest of the crew." Taylor uncrossed his arms and plunged both hands into his pockets. Castillo read his body language. "You already have."

"Unger approached me weeks ago with his concerns, then Tanaka. I think the whole crew is spooked about this thing. I was nominated to talk to you about it." Taylor pulled out a handkerchief and wiped the beads of sweat from his broad brown forehead. "But don't worry. I'll do my job. If you insist on continuing, then I'll tell them all not to worry. The skipper knows what he's doing."

Castillo nodded uncomfortably. This was a revelation to him. He had no idea the crew felt this way. He knew this would be dangerous work. Testing untried systems is always dangerous, but the big question was *is his ship and crew in any real danger?* He didn't think so, but after talking with Taylor, he wasn't sure. *The dark elemental forces that created the universe?* That sounds like something they shouldn't be experimenting with. He would have to give this some thought.

• • •

"I'd like to begin tomorrow's testing at test eight in the test plan," said Admiral O'Keefe. "That starts on page 112."

Everyone started rattling pages trying to get to the right page. Castillo knew which test O'Keefe was talking about. He was looking at the large screen on the rear bulkhead of the ward room. It was Mt. Rushmore again plus two. There were four stone-faced U. S. Navy admirals plus two British admirals. On another screen was the crew of the Balthazar which consisted of a British captain and three QVR people, among them Dr. Nigel Hill.

"That's the test of a communication procedure, isn't it, sir?" said Castillo. "Using a partial Apparition enclosure."

"That's the one," replied O'Keefe. The flat planes of his narrow face caught the light and made him look alien. "I think it's important that we find a way to stay in communication with you during these early tests." The admirals all murmured agreement.

"After today's events that might be a good idea," agreed Castillo. He shifted in his chair and cleared his throat. "After the last test, some of my crew expressed a concern that this technology may not be ready for test phase. Is it possible that we're rushing this thing, sir?"

"I don't think there's anything to worry about," said O'Keefe. "Dr. Hill do you have any thoughts on this?"

On the side screen, Nigel Hill spoke in his familiar baritone, "I think it's safe, commander. Of course, that's not to say we may not have a few minor mishaps here or there. We *always* do, it seems, especially with a new technology. I guess I don't have to tell you that. But we wouldn't have approached the Navy with this thing if it were not ready. My company, QVR, prides itself on its accomplishments and its safety record. These systems are designed to protect people. We've never caused an injury or a fatality with one of our systems."

"That streak came to an end today," intoned Castillo. "When the deck dropped out from under us the first time, we weren't ready for it. One crewman suffered a broken leg and we had five concussions."

This statement was met with silence from Hill. He blinked rapidly, trying to absorb it. Admiral Baynes was the first one to speak. "I'm sorry about that, Don," he said weakly. "Are your injured men okay?"

"They'll live. Doc set the broken leg and gave the man some pain killers. That will hold him until we can transfer him to a hospital. He's off duty until then. The concussions too."

They went over the order of events for tomorrow and the debriefing concluded. They all dispersed. Castillo had a report to write as did Lambert and McConnell.

That evening the Kansas mess served chicken Piccata with rice medley and Tuscan stuffed mushrooms, but hardly anyone ate. Their stomachs were still upset from the jostling they had been through during the day. The Kansas's food staff was disappointed.

Castillo tried to sleep but he kept having the same nightmare. He was an ancient explorer, like Christopher Columbus, sailing to a new unexplored land, but he kept sailing off the edge of the world. He would awaken just as his ship fell into the abyss.

• • •

The next morning there was a good crowd for breakfast and the chief food specialist, Clint Jones, or Chef Jonesy as he was called on board, was greatly heartened by it.

The plan was to bring Kansas to a depth where the top of the Apparition sphere would not be able to form completely. Above the ship, the hyperdensification process would not have enough water molecules to use, so there would be an open hole in the sphere through which they could extend an antenna and communicate. It sounded like it would work.

They decided not to risk any of Kansas's antennae. Instead they tethered a communications buoy directly over head and linked in to a comm mast on Kansas. When the test crew determined they were at the proper depth, they announced all was ready. This time Castillo was looking at Dr. Nigel Hill on the forward control room screen. He could also switch to a photonics camera with enough up angle to see the bottom of the comm buoy sitting over them. It looked like the buoy was doing quite a bit of pitching. Kansas was also doing some rolling from wave action.

"How's the weather look up there?" queried Castillo.

"It's deteriorating," said Hill.

"What do you think, Hill? Is it good enough to test?"

"I think so. We have some rain four miles to the south of us right now and winds out of the southeast at 28 knots and in our little cove here only about 6 foot seas."

"Any lightning with it?"

"Yes, but it's pretty far off. About 22 miles."

"That doesn't sound too bad."

"It's up to you and Dr. Lambert."

Castillo looked to Lambert for a sign. She gave him a thumbs up. "Okay, let's do it!" Castillo didn't want any delays at this point. He just wanted to get all this testing over with. The sooner its done, the sooner they could all go home.

Susan Lambert and her team began going through the Apparition initialization…stage 1 activation… stage 2 activation…emitter arrays power up and activation. Finally they were ready. Castillo made the announcement to the crew and almost everyone laid flat down on the deck. This was the best way to handle the jolt of dropping 3 feet. The deck fell and the Apparition sphere formed. Castillo could still see Dr. Nigel Hill with total clarity, and on his photonics camera he could see the buoy above them. The sphere stopped short of forming completely around Kansas, leaving a hole about fifty feet wide at its top.

Castillo beamed at Lambert, then turned to Taylor on his right. "It worked!"

"Sure," griped Taylor, "but how're we going to use this when we're down 600 feet?"

"Well, I don't know. But…one step at a time. If we can…"

Suddenly there was a sharp report and a flash, and ship's alarms began screaming. All the display screens went black.

"What the hell was that?" shouted a concerned Lambert.

"I'm guessing a lightning strike," shouted Castillo. "Is everybody okay?" He began statusing his departments through his headset. "Engineering, Nav, Weapons…report."

Lambert did the same. "Talk to me, Norm. I'm blind here. What are you seeing?"

"How about Command and Control?" asked Castillo. He turned to Taylor, "Mase, I'm not getting an answer out of weapons. Could you check?"

"I'm on it," said Taylor, springing out of his seat and sprinting away.

"What do you mean?" shouted Lambert over the cacophony of ship's alarms. "What's going critical?" There was tension in her voice and Castillo caught it.

"See if you can reset the ship's alarms," barked Castillo to a crewman in the back of the room.

"Yessir," replied the crewman. He ran to a workstation and began typing furiously.

"Well, shut it down, Norm," cried Lambert. "For God's sake! Pull the breaker! Do whatever you have to!"

Castillo stared at her. She was bordering on hysteria now. "What's going on?" he demanded.

"We've got an accelerator that's in full runaway! Accumulators are going critical! Norm's trying to stop it, but so far…" She stopped and listened. "Shit! No! No! No!"

"That sounds bad," shouted Castillo, standing up. "What does it mean? In plain language!"

"In plain language. The containment tubes for the emitters are about to breach. When that happens…I don't know… I have a feeling we're about be blown to kingdom come." Crystal McConnell's mouth was twisted in anguish and she began to wail, tears filling her eyes. It was the hopeless wail of the banshee. Her mask was gone now. Lambert's eyes began to fill too as she choked out, "I'm… so… sorry."

Castillo was in denial. This couldn't be the end. The end of him, his ship, his crew. No way! He wanted to say something comforting, but he couldn't. His mouth was suddenly dry. He opened it, but when nothing came out, he closed it. The alarms abruptly shut off, and it became eerily quiet and without the illumination from the display screens it was very dark, but there was an undercurrent of something else. It was a fine fluctuating vibration he could feel through the soles of his feet. The vibration seemed to be building and the temperature in the room was dropping. A glow bloomed on the bulkheads and room surfaces like you would see on a sunlit meadow of mustard flowers. When he looked around the room, he saw worried faces looking to him for answers. He had none. How long did they have? Minutes? Seconds? He could feel a hissing inside his skull like a radio tuned to nothing.

"Taylor was right," he said to nobody. *We have no business experimenting with the dark elemental forces that created the universe.* My God! What have we done?

He heard McConnell weeping softly and a sob from someone to his right. He had never felt so helpless. The dreadful hissing in his head was intensifying. He wanted to scream and cry hysterically, but he was still a Navy commander and decided to act it right to the end. It would do no good to break down in front of his men in their last moments.

The only thing he could think of to say was, "It's been a pleasure, gentlemen." He put a grim expression on his face, came to attention and snapped a salute.

• • •

"What do you mean it's gone?" screamed Admiral Baynes. He was staring at the ashen visage of Nigel Hill on the control center monitor.

"The ship, Kansas, and all her crew have simply vanished, sir. We're sending you all the footage we have, but I don't think it will help you much. We have two search crews out right now looking, but they've not found anything so far."

"Vanished?" bellowed Baynes. "Nothing just vanishes! Kansas has got to be somewhere. It didn't just drop off the face of the earth, did it?"

"It happened shortly after a lightning strike, admiral. A bolt scored a direct hit on the communications buoy tethered to Kansas and traveled down to the ship. We lost all communication at that point. As you can see from the video, there was an aura of some kind and then a collapse. When we run it back we can see the collapse of the Apparition sphere."

Everyone in the control center watched the big screen where they saw a video from one of Balthazar's surface cameras. It showed a yellow buoy with a whip antenna on it riding on an angry gray sea amid frothy waves. An unearthly underwater golden glow formed under it, wisps of steam rising in streamers from the water's surface and then the buoy and the adjacent waves collapsed inward as if there were a vacuum under it. An angry whirlpool of foaming water boiled and the buoy resurfaced.

"That's the damnedest thing I've ever seen," said Admiral O'Keefe. "Could Kansas have gone down?"

On screen Nigel Hill said, "We've sent a drone down to look, but nothing so far."

Baynes could not wrap his mind around it. Kansas and all its crew gone. It was unthinkable! Had they simply been vaporized? A lump formed in his throat and his eyes were suddenly wet as he thought about those brave men and women. This was a catastrophe that would hit the Navy hard. He suddenly felt very old. He glared accusingly at Nigel Hill on the screen and shouted, "This thing was not ready for test, Hill! You assured me it was! We pushed it too fast. And I wanted it too badly. Now, men are probably *dead* because of that!"

The color drained from Nigel Hill's face but he said nothing.

"If that ship isn't found, your career is over, Hill. I'm going to make sure of that," said Baynes angrily, then he quietly added. "I think all our careers are over."

No one spoke for long seconds, the depression in the room heavy. Finally Baynes said, "I'd better make some calls," He rose and left the elevated VIP platform in the control center.

• • •

Admiral Baynes made his calls and notified the authorities at Naval Atlantic Command headquarters who in turn notified the Chief of Naval Operations who in turn notified the White House.

The Navy quickly put together an emergency search and rescue force which included the attack submarine Connecticut. The British also responded with a ten ship task force which included the attack boat Ambush and the research ship Balthazar. They did an intensive thorough sweep of the cove where Kansas was last seen and fanned out from there to the storm-tossed sea. They also used air-dropped deep transit search drones. The Navy spared no expense. They were very thorough, but as the day wore on and light faded to darkness, spirits waned and the mood grew very heavy. They knew the truth. Kansas was gone without a trace.

Chapter 5

He had a migraine. Not just a migraine. It felt like the top of his head was going to blow off. He was certain someone had implanted an expanding bladder of some kind in his brain. When it reached a certain point, it was going to burst. He wanted to open his eyes, but he was afraid it would just invite more pain. With effort he forced his eyes open, but saw only blackness. Maybe his eyes didn't work. No. Wait. He could see a small red glow in the corner of his vision. There was a strange smell, a mixture of ozone and scorched microchips, and he could hear something. What was that? Moaning? And a cough? Why was he laying in the darkness on his back?

Then he remembered! Castillo sat bolt upright. They were about to be blown to kingdom come. But they hadn't been. Had they? Relief washed over him. He heard the moaning again and he went toward it. It was Susan Lambert laying on her back, her face gently dusted by the red emergency lights.

"Susan," he said taking hold of her face. He saw Crystal too laying beside her, but she wasn't stirring. Susan's eyelids fluttered open.

"Wha…happened," she rasped.

"I don't know."

"My head hurts," she groaned. "I think…wait…" Her eyes popped. "We made it?"

"Well…I…"

"Oh, God! Don, we made it!" She reached up and embraced his neck with both arms, hugging him tightly. "We made it, we made it, we made it!" Then she held him at arms length and said, "Didn't we?"

"I don't know. We have red emergency lanterns on which means we're under emergency power."

Castillo stood up and began to walk around the control room. Some men were regaining consciousness and groaning. From the back of the room he heard someone throwing up. The odor of vomit hit him and he thought he might join them. He touched each man as he passed them. They all seemed to be okay, just unconscious. He began statusing the systems: communications, sonar, navigation, weapons, engineering, command and control. All the panels were black.

"What h-happened?"

Castillo turned and saw the groggy young face of Lieutenant Eric Tanaka, Kansas's engineering officer.

"I don't know, Eric, but I need a reactor status immediately."

"Yes, sir." Tanaka staggered off.

"And switch us over to full battery power."

"Will do, sir."

"Kansas has batteries?" asked Susan.

"And a diesel too," replied Castillo. "In the event our reactor shuts down." He helped a crewman to his feet. "Is everyone okay?" He was met with stunned stares from crewmen bathed in the red emergency lights.

"My head is throbbing!" said a crewman.

"Mine too," sobbed Crystal McConnell.

"Crystal!" exclaimed Lambert. "How do you feel, dear?" She went to McConnell and looked into her eyes with concern.

"Like shit!" she said weakly.

"It's an aftereffect from this…thing…I don't even know what to call it," said Castillo.

"I'm going to check on Norm and the rest of the test crew," said Lambert. She stood up and exited through the rear of the control room, feeling her way in the dark.

Castillo heard a chirp. He walked to his chair and picked up the receiver. "Castillo."

"Skipper, the reactor has safed itself."

"Can you restart it?"

"I'm getting my engineering crew on it right now, sir. Fred's running diagnostics. I'll know soon. Batteries look good. I'm switching over everything to full battery."

"Good! Keep me informed." Castillo hung up and went to the command and control panels in the front of the room and began powering up the displays. "Power up the systems, everybody. We have full battery power." All displays around the room began to flicker to life. Soon the room was awash in the bluegreen phosphorescence of the big screens.

Castillo noticed according to ship's status screens they were at 334 feet and slowly descending. Station-keeping was obviously off. "Pilot, bring us to periscope depth. Let's take a look around. Comm, raise Balthazar."

"Roger, sir. Coming to periscope depth," replied the pilot.

"Yessir. Hailing Balthazar." replied the comm operator.

Castillo closed his eyes tightly, trying to make the pain go away. He had to concentrate. He picked up his receiver and turned the selector. "Hello, Doc. I think we could all use some Advil up here."

"Be right there, sir," replied the chief corpsman.

Mason Taylor staggered in. "God, what happened? I feel hung over and I don't even remember the party."

"How's everybody in weapons?"

"There are only two of them, but they're okay. That lightning strike took out some of our weapon systems though."

"What did we lose?

"All horizontal tubes and five vertical."

"Shit! Well, I don't think we'll need them today."

"That's good."

Castillo caught the look from Taylor. "What?"

"Nothing."

"Go ahead. Say it."

"I'm not one of those I-told-you-so types."

Castillo said nothing.

"Why? Would you feel better if I did?"

"Well, you did tell me so, and I ignored you. But, I'm pulling the plug on this operation now. Better late than never as they say. Let's go home!"

"Now you're talkin', skipper!" There were murmurs of agreement all around the control room.

"We're getting no answer from Balthazar, sir," said the communications man.

"We're at scope depth, sir," said the pilot, turning on the photonics cameras.

Castillo stared at the camera screens and frowned. "Is there something wrong with our cameras? It looks black."

"Cameras appear to be operating normally, sir."

"What time is it?" asked Taylor.

"According to ship's clock," said Castillo, looking at the time display in his command screen, "9:36 in the A.M."

"That's what I have too," said a crewman.

"The test started at exactly 8:57. So we were out for 39 minutes." Castillo considered this. "Considering the ship's drift and sink rate, that sounds about right. Pilot, switch to night vision."

The screen blinked off then came back on with a green cast. They could clearly see the green ghostly outlines of the coastal hills ringing the cove. Castillo sat down in his command chair and took control of the big screen. He cycled through all the mast cameras, looked in all directions and scanned the surrounding hills and waves.

"Where's Balthazar?" asked Taylor.

"Good question," said Castillo. "And why is it night?" He drummed his fingers on his chair arm for a few seconds, then shook his head and said, "I need some answers. Comm, send up the thirty four masts. I want to make some calls."

"Yessir! Deploying comm masts, sir."

"Navigation, plot us a course back to Clyde. Let's get out of here."

"Aye, sir. Plotting course back to Clyde," replied Lieutenant Guerrero.

Castillo wanted to get back to Glasgow and put this whole fiasco behind him. Of course there would be many debriefings and meetings during which the high brass would engage in finger pointing and second guessing what should have been done and where they fell short. He didn't care. All he cared about was getting back and reuniting with Liz and the girls for a carefree few days in Scotland. He couldn't wait to hug and kiss his girls. He could picture Robin's sunny little face and Kelly's brace-filled smile. He only hoped Liz was up to the trip.

As Kansas progressed toward the Clyde naval base, Castillo and Comm officer, Lieutenant Bud Unger, were becoming increasingly concerned. They weren't able to get a response from the Clyde naval base, nor could they get a response from the Apparition Control Center. They decided to try SUBGROUP 2, COM-SUBRON 6, TESTOPS. Nothing!

"This is strange, sir," said Unger. "We're not picking up anything. I mean nada! We've tried EHF, marine VHF, High Speed downlink. We can't even get a GPS fix. What the hell?"

"Are you sure our equipment is working?" asked Castillo.

"The diagnostics all say yes. But…I just don't know."

Castillo considered this, then turned abruptly to the sonar operator at his left elbow. "Anything on sonar?"

"No, sir. Nothing," replied the young petty officer.

"Is it working?"

"Yes, sir. I've got biologicals. Whalesong and crustaceans."

"Put it on speaker."

The overhead speakers came alive with croaking and chirps and something that sounded like a mournful cello searching for the proper key. "Okay," said Castillo. He made a slashing gesture across his throat and the speakers cut off. "Where the hell is everybody?"

"What about your special phone?" asked Lambert.

"We'd have to surface to use phone," replied Castillo.

"Can't we surface?" asked McConnell.

"I don't like to," sighed Castillo.

"Because of stealth," said Lambert. "Right?"

"That's the main reason, but it goes beyond that." Castillo took a deep breath before launching into his explanation. "A submarine when it surfaces, startles people. And a submarine on the surface looks evil."

"Evil! Really?" asked Lambert.

"Yes. Ancient seaman feared the weather, the sea, the rocks, but more than anything they feared what they couldn't see. Things that lurked beneath them, in the deep. They made up stories about sea monsters and the supernatural to explain disappearances and strange sightings. They were a superstitious lot. We've come a long way since then, but still when someone sees a submarine surface a few hundred yards away, some ancestral memory springs unbidden into the mind. Fear grips a man when a denizen of the deep floats threateningly close and sinister."

"Still?"

"Oh yes."

"Hey," said Mason Taylor. "Do you remember that time we surfaced off Cape Henry too early?"

Castillo chuckled. "I remember. A transceiver had overheated and we wanted to clear the ship of smoke, so we surfaced early."

"Right next to a cruise ship! The cruise skipper went into a panic. He called the Coast Guard, the Navy, the Portsmouth harbor master…"

"He even called the Merchant Marine demanding action," said Castillo, scratching his chin. "And the week before when an aircraft carrier passed them, the very same skipper ordered his crew to render honors." He shifted in his chair. "We have to face facts. A submarine just looks evil. It represents the dark nightmarish monsters that lurk in our subconscious. We're not always aware of them, but they're always just beneath the surface able to abruptly spring forth and scare the hell out of us."

"Now that you mention it," said Lambert. "I've always thought submarines were kinda creepy looking." Castillo elevated his left eyebrow. "That was before I started working on them," she hastily added, smiling and wrinkling her nose.

"Okay," laughed Castillo. "Let's start working another problem. What time is it? There should be a way of telling time by simply reading the stars, but I'm not an astronomer and I don't know anyone who is. Do you?"

"Yes, I do," said Lambert. "Our chief engineer, Norm."

"I met him, didn't I?" asked Castillo.

"Yes, should I ask him to come up?"

"Please." When Norm waddled into the control room, he was noticeably limping. "Are you alright?"

"I had a bum right knee when I started working on Kansas, sir, and all the jostling hasn't helped it any. In fact, I can barely walk." He grimaced.

"Did you get some pain killers from doc?"

"Yes, but they don't help much, sir. I'm afraid I need surgery."

Castillo shifted in his chair and cleared his throat indicating a change of subject. "I understand you're an astronomer."

"I dabble in it, sir. Amateur only, but I have an excellent telescope. A professional quality 9 inch reflector, gimbal-mounted, clock-driven, fully programmable and…"

"Good," interrupted Castillo. "Do you think you could guess what hour it is if we could get you a good view of the sky?"

"Uh…maybe…I could try."

He didn't sound very positive, thought Castillo, but he decided to try him anyway. He angled all HD cameras on the photonics mast up toward the night sky. "Take a guess, Mr. Bloomberg."

"Polaris is…" He staggered closer to the big screen and scrutinized it. "There…no…there…no…wait…" He looked from the big screen to the smaller screens on the left and right. "Something looks wrong." He frowned and turned to Castillo. "I need an unobstructed view of the whole sky. Is there anyway we could go up, sir?" He pointed to the ceiling.

"Oh, why not," sighed Castillo. "Pilot, take us up."

"Aye, sir. Blowing tanks." The deck began tilting upward and shortly the pilot announced, "Surfaced, sir."

"Do you think you can climb a ladder, Mr. Bloomberg?"

"I'll try, sir."

It was a huge effort for Bloomberg to haul his obese torso through the necessary hatches to get through the lockout chamber and to the ladder which leads to Kansas's aft deck. Castillo went up first, emerging onto the open deck behind the boat's sail and feeling the cool night air wash over his face. Bloomberg climbed the ladder in an torturous manner letting his left leg do all the work, heaving him up, step by agonizing step. He grunted, perspired profusely and stuck out the tip of his tongue with the effort. Kansas was never designed for a man Bloomberg's size. Castillo tried to help him as best he could, but he could only give him a hand on the last two steps of the ladder. Bloomberg sucked in his gut to squeeze through the last hatch, but still lost a button off his shirt as he scraped through the opening. Lambert, McConnell and Taylor followed.

Bloomberg took a deep breath, blinked and began swinging around with his eyes on the night sky. "Well… what the…something's not quite right."

"What's wrong, Norm?" asked Lambert.

"The stars are wrong!" There was alarm in his voice.

"What, Norm? Talk to us!" insisted Lambert.

"The constellations have…shifted."

"Shifted?" said Castillo.

"Look right there," said Bloomberg, pointing. "Ursa Major. The tail of that constellation is what we know familiarly as the Big Dipper. Do you see it?"

Castillo concentrated on where Bloomberg was pointing. "Yes."

"The two stars at the end, Dubhe and Merac, are the pointer stars to Polaris, popularly called the North Star. There." He pointed again. "All you have to do to find Polaris is take seven times the distance between the two guidepost stars, Dubhe and Merac. Every amateur astronomer knows this. Do you see anything wrong?"

Castillo studied it for a few seconds before saying. "Did you say seven times the distance?"

"Yes, sir."

"But Polaris is closer than that."

"Yes, it is. It looks to be about six times the distance if that. The constellations all appear to be closer to each other, which is…impossible! Our universe is always expanding. Constellations move further apart with each year."

"How fast are we talking?" asked Taylor, stepping closer to Bloomberg.

"It's not fast enough to notice, usually. It's only about 1.4 degrees per century."

"What kind of shift are we looking at here?" asked Taylor.

"I don't have anyway to measure it, but I would guess at least six degrees. It's enough that you can see it with the naked eye."

"But that's…that's…" Castillo couldn't finish his thought. A small trickle of dread worked its way down his spine and he shivered slightly.

"A four hundred year shift," said Taylor, finishing Castillo's thought.

"A four hundred year shift backwards?" questioned Lambert.

No one spoke for a few seconds, trying to grasp the possibility of it.

"As for the hour," said Bloomberg. "It's about 7:30 in the morning. Look, it's already getting lighter in the east."

They all swung toward the east and saw the pink glow backlighting the rocky landscape.

"Let's go back down," said Taylor.

"Wait," said Castillo. He pulled out his satelite phone and powered it up. After a few seconds he said, "No satellites. Odd."

Bloomberg pulled out a phone and turned it on. "Nothing," he said, his face lit by the small screen.

"How did you sneak a cell phone past security?" asked Castillo.

"I didn't mean to," said Bloomberg apologetically. "I forgot it was in my bag."

Castillo extended his hand and Bloomberg gave the phone to him. "You'll get it back when you leave the ship."

"Okay," nodded Bloomberg, looking chastised.

After they went below and secured the hatch, Kansas submerged and got back on course for the Clyde Royal Naval Base.

Castillo took Taylor aside in the passageway and said, "What do you think, Mase?"

"I don't know, Don. Bloomberg gave us a lot to think about." They stepped aside to allow a crewman to pass by. "Do you think he's full of shit?"

"I don't know. Is there any way you can check on that Polaris thing?"

Taylor frowned, smoothed the imaginary hair on his bald head with his left hand then said, "The boat has a pretty extensive ebook library. I can probably find something on it there."

"Thanks, Mase. It's not that I don't believe Mr. Bloomberg. It's just that I would like a second opinion, if you know what I mean."

"I know exactly what you mean," nodded Taylor and hurried off.

Castillo sat in his command chair silently. Why was there such a wide spread communications outage? It had to be an equipment problem. But he'd never seen a failure that affected every receiver on the ship. It's very odd! He looked around the control room at all the profiles painted by the bluegreen glow of the displays. The Kansas crewmen looked thoughtful. Lambert and McConnell looked troubled. They all suspected something was wrong. The mood seemed to be heavy, so Castillo decided to lighten it.

"Well, I guess it's time for breakfast but my stomach is telling me I just had breakfast. It's confused!"

There were a few chuckles.

"We haven't had second breakfast," said Lambert, arching her eyebrows.

"Oh," laughed Castillo. "That's right. Hobbits do it all the time, don't they?"

"Let's become Hobbits," said Lambert. "I've heard middle earth is nice this time of year."

"I'm game," replied Castillo.

"Sir!" said one of the young sonar operators. "I've got something on the array."

"What is it?"

"I…don't…know."

Castillo could read the confusion on his face. "Put it on speaker."

He flipped a switch and they heard a faint sound. "Let me amplify it," said the operator.

It got louder but was still muffled:

rumble rumble rumble thunk rumble rumble rumble thunk rumble rumble

then nothing. After a few seconds it started again:

rumble rumble rumble thunk rumble rumble rumble thunk

Castillo couldn't identify what it was either. It almost sounded like something heavy rolling down a wooden board. What? A large rock? "Where's it coming from?"

The young petty officer studied his screen then switched to another view. "It's about 18 miles out, sir. Bearing 188."

"That's not too far out of our way. Let's have a look. Pilot, come to new course 188."

"Aye, sir. New course 188."

Castillo picked up his receiver, turned a dial and said, "Maneuvering, make turns for 20 knots."

"Aye, sir. Making turns for 20 knots."

They didn't hear the sound again, but within 30 minutes they had closed the distance to the contact to 7 miles. That's within visual verification distance. Castillo ordered their speed reduced to 6 knots and periscope depth. He deployed the photonics mast and swept the horizon ahead of them.

"Wow!" he said. "Look at that!"

"It's an old sailing ship," said Lambert.

Mason Taylor came in and stared open-mouthed at the forward view screen. Castillo touched his controls and magnified the view until the ship filled the screen.

"That's a replica of a Spanish Galleon," observed Lieutenant Tanaka. "16th century. I wonder who it belongs to."

"It's not flying any flags, but it's perfect in every other detail." Taylor walked up close to the screen, craning his neck. "A proud old man-of-war. 1000 tons at least. 48 guns!"

"Whoever built her did a good job!" said Castillo.

"They did!" agreed Taylor.

The three-masted ship was the color of dark oak with red gunnels and masts in black. It had an elaborate black bowsprit with a walkway extending beneath and two rows of 12 gun portals. The early morning sun glinted off the raised black and gold decorative window shutters beneath the high afterdeck, or stern castle, where the captain's quarters usually were, and just above them was a row of colorful coats of arms in bright reds and blues and greens and a detailed carved gold colored rail attached to the aft weather deck. There was a balcony-like observation platform extending off the aft gun deck with men walking on them. It appeared to be getting under way. Sails were unfurling on all three masts with men in the rigging. Large white square sails slowly swelled like great balloons, emblazoned with the pronged blood red empirical Spanish cross of old. At the top of each mast was a long white fluttering pennant also with the red Spanish cross.

"Man, it's perfect in every detail," marveled Lieutenant Tanaka, his onyx eyes twinkling.

"Do you study those things, Eric?" asked Castillo.

"Sure," replied Tanaka. "I was a guide on the Constitution for one summer and I crewed on the Coast Guard's tall ship, Eagle, in college."

"Coast Guard? How did you swing that?"

"My dad pulled some strings."

Castillo recalled that Tanaka's father was Sacirro Tanaka, CEO of Advocate Shipping and running for a California senate seat. "Any idea who this one belongs to?"

"None. I've never seen this one before."

Castillo said nothing for a long time. He folded his hands in his lap and lowered his head. He looked like he was praying, but the crew knew he was trying to come to a decision. He nodded his head slightly and his lips silently formed words as if he were having an internal dialogue. Finally he looked up and said, "Screw it. Let's go up and get a better look. Pilot, take us up."

"Aye, sir. Blowing tanks."

"Really?" said Tanaka, beaming like a little boy about to look at model trains.

"Yes, besides I'd like to ask some questions of the skipper. Maybe these guys have a working radio we can use."

Chapter 6
Aboard the San Luis Hidalgo
Western Irish Coast
July 28, 1588 A.D.

Capitan Martin de Cordova would be glad to be rid of this place. He had regretted this mission from the outset and had tried to protest to Admiral Medina Sidonia, but it had been a waste of his time. The duke had been set on getting his spies into England. Well, he had succeeded. He had delivered the men into the hands of the duke's Catholic allies in Ireland, and now they must leave. They were deep into enemy waters, cut off from any reinforcements and caught in the daylight hours without protection. This was a suicide mission. But God had watched over them so far, and his men had eaten well here and gotten their fill of Irish whiskey.

He took hold of the broad brim of his black felt hat of office with the gold imperial lion insignia, removed it and mopped his broad bearded face with a handkerchief. The early morning air was cool for July, but he was sweating anyway. He replaced his hat on his head then replaced the handkerchief in his red uniform coat. He watched a crewman come out onto the main deck with a bucket. The man stuck a finger up to test the breeze. Always a good idea when you're about to throw something overboard. The man emptied the bucket overboard on the leeward side and immediately the seabirds began screaming and squawking as they dived into the slick of food scraps and started a feeding frenzy. Cordova walked to the opposite side of the deck and peered down. Good! His men were back aboard and the small boat was pulling away.

"Jesucristo, give me wind!" he prayed softly with his gray eyes to the sky. There were only a few flat high clouds overhead. He came inside, climbed two ladders that creaked with his weight and emerged on the upper weather deck of the stern castle behind the stern mast. He heard a fluttering and tilted his face upwards. His prayer had been answered. The breeze was freshening and the high pennants were beginning to pop. The wind appeared to be out of the south southwest! Where was Estevez?

"Estevez!" he screamed.

"Yes, capitan!" came an answer.

Where was that skeleton? He could hear him, but couldn't see him. He was below somewhere. No matter. "We have the tide and we have wind! We go! Retrieve anchor!"

"Yes, capitan!" Estevez's whip thin visage soon appeared on the main deck below and began screaming and clapping his hands, "Anchor crew to stations! Anchor crew to stations! Hands aloft! Hands aloft! Look alive!"

Men began to scramble. Some ran forward, others began climbing the ratlines. Cordova looked up and saw a lookout in the crow's nest scanning the horizon. He screamed, "Anything?"

"No, capitan!" he replied.

It didn't hurt to check these things. He didn't want to be caught here by the English. Cordova faced the breeze, closed his eyes and breathed the fresh salt air. The breeze was getting stronger. If the wind held, they could rejoin the main fleet in two days. He would much rather be with his family in Madrid, but duty calls.

rumble rumble rumble thunk rumble rumble rumble thunk rumble rumble

Cordova smiled. It was the sound of the anchor windlass drawing up the anchor. It took eight men to turn the large spoked wheel that slowly drew up the large links in the anchor chain. The *thunk* was the sound of the bottle pin dropping to arrest forward progress. It took tension off the wheel and allowed the men to renew their grip on the wheel.

rumble rumble rumble thunk rumble rumble rumble thunk

The masts creaked and halyards moaned as the sails filled and thundered. They started putting a strain on masts and rigging. Men swarmed like monkeys down out of the rigging and tied off halyards and sheets. Cordova watched the bow plunge forward out into the frothy olive Irish Sea. He screamed through a command port to the helmsman two decks below, "Just keep us on this course until Mr. Estevez tells you otherwise."

"Yes, capitan!"

"I must prepare a message for Sidonia. Mr. Marten, bring a pigeon."

"Yes, capitan," replied a serious young man standing behind Cordova.

• • •

Cordova was in his stateroom composing his message to Admiral Medina Sidonia when he heard the commotion, feet running and raised voices. A cabin boy put his head through the door and said, "A leviathan, capitan!"

"A *leviathan*?" Cordova scratched his chin under his salt and pepper beard. "What do I care about a leviathan?"

"It is not a normal leviathan. Mr. Estevez says it is most unusual." The boy withdrew his head and closed the door.

"Unusual?" Cordova tried to continue his message, but found he could not. He had to see this *unusual* leviathan. He put down his quill and shrugged on his red uniform coat and donned his black captain's hat. When he emerged onto the weather deck of the stern castle, he found Estevez on the larboard rail with a spyglass trained on something in the water.

"What do you make of that, capitan?" He handed the spyglass to Cordova.

Cordova put it to his eye and saw nothing at first, just empty sea, then he swept over it and quickly returned to it. It appeared to be a great leviathan with something attached to its back. A sizable box of some kind, and there was another box attached to its tail. But as it turned toward them, he realized they were not boxes at all, but large square fins.

"That's not natural," said Cordova. "It has great square fins and it's black as satan's heart!"

"It came up from the depths like a sea dragon straight out of hell!" shouted a young seaman.

"It's coming straight for us!" screamed the helmsman.

• • •

Castillo and Tanaka climbed the ladder inside the Kansas's sail and emerged at the top. Tanaka smoothed his jet black hair and tugged on his black Kansas ball cap. Then he put the binoculars to his eyes.

"Magnificent!" he exclaimed.

Castillo donned a headset, then put on his black ball cap and his aviators. He said, "Okay, pilot, ease us up next to the galleon. We want to be within hailing range."

"Aye, sir. I'll get us close."

"What do you think, Eric? Who are these guys?"

"I would guess they're re-enactors, sir. I've read about them. There are clubs and societies that get together and re-enact famous battles. In the U.S. It's mostly the Civil War. These guys are re-enacting a sea battle probably."

"Really?"

"They're dressed very authentically. I don't see a T-shirt in the bunch. The guys in red coats and black broad-brimmed hats are Spanish officers, and the guys in the white shirts are seamen. These guys are a class act."

Castillo put binoculars to his eyes and studied the galleon. "They seem to be running around quite a bit, aren't they? Are they conducting a drill of some kind?"

"Don't know, sir."

• • •

"To quarters! To quarters! Gun crews to stations! Gun crews to stations!" screamed Estevez. There was concern in every face that passed him.

Cordova didn't know what to make of it. Whatever this evil thing was, it was on a collision course with them. He wanted to alter course, but they couldn't point much higher against the wind to maneuver away. They could however make a ninety degree turn to downwind. Then they would pass behind the monster. It was worth a try. "Helmsman, ninety degrees to larboard! Now!"

"Yes, capitan. Ninety degrees to larboard."

"Estevez, resheet mains!"

"Yes, capitan," responded Estevez from the main deck. He and several others began playing out sheet lines on the larboard side, taking them in on the starboard and trimming jib and spanker lines. As the ship slowly turned, boards and masts creaked and groaned with the stresses of wind against sail and the rolling sea against hull, but the big ship gradually increased speed and began surging through the troughs and waves once again with a rocking motion.

Castillo put the spyglass to his eye and scrutinized the sea creature. This thing was large. At least twice the size of Hidalgo. After a few seconds it turned and was back on an intercept course with his ship. This monstrous thing is stalking us, he thought. The skin on the back of his neck crawled and his hands began to sweat. What is it? All about him he could see the faces of his terrified crew.

"It's turning too!" screamed a voice, hysterically. "It's coming for us."

"It won't take us without a fight!" shouted another.

• • •

Kansas was within 300 yards of the galleon and closing. Tanaka and Castillo watched the deck activity on the galleon through binoculars.

"Hey," said Tanaka. "They're opening their gun ports."

"Really?" said Castillo.

"And now they're rolling their guns out. I can see the muzzles."

"Maybe they're going to give us a gun salute."

Tanaka squinted and refocused his binoculars. "I don't like the looks of this. I can see the expressions on some of their faces. They look kind of freaked out. And the guns…"

"What about them?"

"The gun crews are taking direct aim at us."

Castillo's eyes went wide as he realized what was about to happen. "Shit!" He barked into his headset, "Emergency dive! Emergency dive!"

"Aye, sir," said the pilot. "Emergency dive!"

BOOM!   BOOMBOOMBOOM!   BOOM!
BOOM! BOOM!

The big guns opened up on them and scored several direct hits to the sail. The sail lurched violently and Castillo tumbled out. He clung briefly to plexiglass spray shield with his right hand, then he lost his grip and fell. He glanced off the rounded deck of Kansas before hitting the water. Pressurized air roared from three ballast vents in Kansas's bow throwing geysers of water 200 feet in the air and three more geysers roared from her stern as Kansas flooded her ballast tanks and prepared to dive.

"No," shouted Castillo. "Wait!" But no one heard him. He had lost his headset.

Tanaka slid down the sail's access ladder in one smooth slide using his hands and feet on each side of the vertical supports. When his feet touched down on the deck, he felt Kansas tilt as the ship began its downward descent. He looked up through the open hatch expecting to see Castillo descending, but there was no one! The sea began to pour in, so Tanaka secured the hatch then ran to the control room.

"No! No! We have to go back up! The skipper is still on the sail!" he screamed, anxiety in his oriental features.

Mason Taylor shouted, "Emergency blow! Emergency blow!" He flopped down in the captain's command chair and began cycling through the cameras on the mast intently watching the forward screen.

"Aye, sir. Emergency blow!" The dive systems screen before the pilot showed iconic images of valves turning red and closing and other valves opening and turning green. Eventually the slope in the deck leveled and then began to angle up.

"There he is," said Mason. They could see Castillo in the water swimming after them. "Shit!" As they watched, the galleon changed course and began bearing down on him. "They're going to reach him before we can. Who are these guys, Eric?"

"I don't know, but they're definitely hostile."

• • •

"Stand by to slacken sails," screamed Cordova. He was sure they had wounded the beast. After they'd fired on it, it blew and sounded. Six blowholes! Three in its nose and three in its tail. A strange leviathan indeed. And something had fallen from its square dorsal fin. He'd seen it hit the water. He wanted to see what it was.

He was coming up on it now and… It looked like a man!

"Slacken sails," Cordova ordered. His men played out sheets until the sails flapped loosely on the yardarms. "Estevez, see if you can hook it with a cargo hook."

"Yes, capitan!" Estevez began swinging a metal hook from the end of a long line. On the third try, he was able to hook the thing and pull it aboard. It collapsed in a heap on the deck and the crew gasped. It was a man!

Castillo stared up angrily at the men surrounding him. "Hey, you ruined my coat!" He stuck a finger through the hole the cargo hook had made in the collar of his weather coat. They parted and a large aggressive bearded man in a red coat and black hat came up and started screaming at him. He was speaking Spanish. That's okay. Castillo spoke Spanish fluently. His grandparents had come from Puerto Rico and he'd learned Spanish at an early age. The man was demanding to know who he was.

His Spanish was a little rusty, but he told the man he was Commander Don Castillo, United States Navy.

This seemed to enrage him. He began spouting a lot of words. This is when Castillo realized that this was not the Spanish he was used to. This man had a heavy accent and the verb forms were slightly different, but he was able to understand what was being said. If these guys were re-enactors, they were carrying it to an extreme. He had to get some answers.

"Where are you from?" he demanded in his best Spanish.

"Quiet!" screamed the big man and backhanded him. He frowned and ran a hand over Castillo's cheek. As Castillo looked around he noticed that all the faces were bearded. And he couldn't help but notice this man had a rather strong fetid odor.

"Take him below," said the man.

Two sneering men stepped forward and seized Castillo's arms. These men had a personal hygiene problem as well. They had an even worse aroma than their captain. They had long greasy hair and lined faces. The one on his right had a long scar down his left cheek and was missing three fingers from his left hand.

• • •

The crew watched helplessly as their captain was un-ceremoniously hoisted onto the deck of the galleon. Taylor zoomed the picture in tightly on the galleon's deck. They could see only the top of Castillo's head. They also saw the big man strike him.

Susan Lambert had to stifle a sob. "We have to help him!" she cried.

"Damn right," spat Tanaka. "Bastards!"

"Why the hell would an old windjammer like that fire on an American warship?" questioned Taylor.

"They're waging some imagined war against the U.S.," said Tanaka. "Terrorists do it all the time."

"Terrorists with a windjammer," muttered Taylor. He had to say it out loud just to see how insane it sounded. He shook his head and slumped in the command chair. "My first impulse is to put a fish into that thing. But that won't help Don, will it?" He took a deep breath and looked around the room. "I'm open to suggestions."

As they watched the screen, the sails of the galleon filled and it began to get under way again.

"Pilot, shadow that thing. Stay within a mile of her."

"Aye, sir. I'll stay with her."

"How much damage do we have?" Taylor asked Tanaka.

"I don't know, sir. I'll go up and take a look."

"I'll go with you."

Tanaka and Taylor emerged through the deck hatch behind the sail and began to inspect the ship's hull.

There were three 8 inch dish-shaped indentations in the sail, four flaps of anachoic panels were hanging off the hull and one of the Apparition hull tubes had been smashed.

"I don't think we suffered any serious damage, sir," said Tanaka. "The pressure hull seems okay. It's made of six inch HY-100 grade steel. We have superficial damage to the sail where the steel is thinner."

"Yeh. But we need to cut away these panels. We can't reattach them, and they're just going create drag in the water. Tell that torpedoman to come up with the torch and get to work."

"You mean Haberman, sir?"

"Yes. I think that's his name."

"He's one of those we left behind to make room for the test crew."

"Great!" Taylor blew out breath loudly, like a boiler venting. "Maybe you could get some people up here with hack saws."

"Yes, sir. I'll think of something."

Taylor stared off to the south at the distant galleon. "I wonder what's going on over there."

• • •

Castillo was tied to a wooden chair in a dark windowless room with heavy foul air that was ripe with the rotten odor of decay, and there were dark stains on the floor. Blood? There were two flickering iron lanterns hanging on opposite walls and chains and shackles attached to the stained wall facing him. There was also a table against the wall next to him with a cross, knives and a grill with red hot coals in it. There was just a hint of some kind of incense in the air. The overall effect was stomach-churning.

"The sea beast is following us, capitan," said Estevez.

"I know," said Cordova. "Keep the guns loaded and ready. If it moves on us, notify me immediately."

"Yes, capitan."

Estevez exited, leaving only Castillo, Cordova and the two other serious-looking men standing in the corner.

Cordova was looking at the contents of Castillo's pockets. He could not identify anything here. He held up a long black thing and said, "What is this?"

"A pen," replied Castillo.

"A what?" asked Cordova.

"You don't know what a pen is?" asked Castillo, incredulously. "Let me go! You have no reason to hold me!"

"I don't think so. Demons are full of tricks."

"I'm not a demon! I'm a man just like you. Enough's enough! I'm American. You have no cause to hold me. I don't know where you come from, but…"

"Silence," bellowed Cordova. "You are aboard his majesty Phillip's ship San Luis Hidalgo, and I am captain Martin de Cordova, second Duke of Almaguer."

Oh my God, thought Castillo. These re-enactors play it right to the hilt. They go for very tight realism. He didn't see a cell phone or even a wrist watch on anyone.

"I saw you fall from the demonic leviathan. Do you control it or does it control you?"

Castillo said nothing. He only glared indignantly.

"Do you work for Satan?"

"Satan?" Castillo blinked in disbelief. "What's wrong with you people?"

"I saw you!" roared Cordova. "Do you deny that you came from the sea beast?"

"No…y-yes…" sputtered Castillo. "Wait…"

"Prepare him for questioning, Francisco."

The man missing fingers on his left hand stepped forward and cut Castillo's shirt away, so that he was bare chested. Then he brought forward the grill of red hot coals and a branding iron. He began to heat the iron in the bed of coals, blowing gently on it, making the coals glow.

"What are you going to do?" asked Castillo, eyeing the coals nervously.

"You are going to confess that you work for Satan," said Cordova. "Or are you in league with Drake?"

"Who's Drake?" asked Castillo, trying to keep the tension out of his voice.

"Drake is the Godless queen's hound. She slips him from his leash and orders him to attack us from time to time."

He picked up the branding iron and held the glowing end close to Castillo's bare chest. "Are you one of the Godless queen's mongrels? Eh?"

Castillo said nothing. This man was psychopathic. No telling what he was capable of. In fact this ship was probably full of them. He had to get away from here.

Cordova laid down the iron and picked up Castillo's command phone. "What's this?"

Castillo said nothing.

Cordova pushed a button and the screen lit up. He sucked air and dropped the phone to the floor and stomped on it with his boot as if he were trying to crush an insect.

"Satan!" He pointed a finger at Castillo. He took the cross from the table, held it toward Castillo and began reciting a rite of exorcism.

• • •

"I'd give anything for a SEAL team right now," said a frustrated Taylor.

"We don't have a SEAL team or the swimmer sub, sir," said Tanaka, "but we have two inflatables and all the SEAL weapons and equipment aboard."

"Weapons? What kind of weapons?"

"Assault rifles mostly," answered Tanaka. "MP-5's, and there are a couple grenade launchers, and a sniper gun, and a 50 caliber, and…"

"A 50 caliber? That's a big gun! What the hell do they have one of those for?"

"I've no idea, sir."

Taylor closed his eyes tightly, massaged them with his finger tips. "Is there anyone on board who can handle a sniper gun?"

"There is a supply guy who is a competition shooter, sir," said Lieutenant Maria Guerrero from her navigation station. "Green, I think his name was."

"Green?" said Tanaka reflectively, shaking his head.

"Don't tell me," said Taylor.

"We left him behind. I'm pretty sure," said Tanaka.

Lambert cleared her throat. Taylor turned toward her and elevated his eyebrows. Lambert turned to McConnell and whispered something. McConnell whispered back.

"Do you have something to contribute, Miss Lambert?" asked Taylor.

"Well, Crystal and I have worked together at QVR for awhile, but not until we met at a gym in Glasgow did I discover that we're both athletes. She represented England in the Olympics. Her sport was the biathlon."

"That's nice, but…" Taylor stopped short. "Wait. Isn't biathlon that thing where they ski and shoot?"

Crystal McConnell nodded and smiled shyly.

"Did you win a medal?" asked Taylor.

"No," said McConnell, "but it wasn't because of my shooting. I had a perfect score, but I'd sprained my ankle."

"Do you think you can handle a sniper rifle?"

"I don't know. I'd have to see it."

Taylor turned to Tanaka. "Let's get that gun up here and let Miss McConnell take a look at it."

"Yes, sir." Tanaka raced off.

They waited silently until Tanaka returned with a long black hard case. He opened it and McConnell came forward and knelt down next to it. She picked up the rifle and got its heft. "It looks like an SR-25," she said quietly. "Light, about 12 pounds, probably fires a NATO round, a 7.62, a big magazine, 20 rounds." She laid the rifle down, picked up the scope, flipped up the end caps and put it to her eye. "Nice!" She expertly slid the scope into its receiver on the back of the gun and locked it down. She stood up, put the stock to her shoulder, took a shooter's stance. "Ejects brass to the right, about a two and half pound trigger pull." Finally holding it by the barrel, she set the rifle's stock down on the deck and said, "Yes, I can handle it. It's a very fine gun."

"Good!" Taylor smiled broadly showing white even teeth and clapped his hands. "Now, I'm going to jump right to the bonus round and ask you the 64 dollar question." He leaned forward and pinned McConnell with his eyes. "Do you think you could shoot a man?"

McConnell began to shake her head in the negative, but Taylor put his right palm up to her and said, "Before you answer. I want you to know that 90 per cent of all people who are asked that question say, 'no', but when put in the proper context, they find they can. If they are defending themselves or saving the life of a loved one…a son, a daughter, a mother or father, the answer changes for 75 percent of them. When you have to choose between shooting a low life or allowing your loved to be murdered, the decision is much easier." He paused to allow McConnell to absorb this. She only blinked. He wasn't sure he was getting through to her. She was hard to read. "I'm going to ask you again.

Do you think you can shoot a man to save Don Castillo or a member of this crew? Take your time with your answer."

McConnell compressed her lips and stared at Taylor. She knew this was important. She turned and looked into Susan Lambert's anguished face and something passed between them. She turned back and took in Taylor's intent stare. His eyes were the same shade of brown as the comfortable old padded leather wingback chair she had back in her flat in Glasgow. She loved the comfortable way it embraced her and made her feel secure. "Okay," she said to Taylor. "I can do it, but may I practice first?"

"Yes!" exclaimed Taylor, slapping his thigh. "We'll find a way for you to get some shooting in up on deck, but we have to move fast. We need to get Don back before something happens to him. He would do the same for any one of us."

Agreement all around.

Chapter 7

Castillo liked to think of himself as a tough hombre, cut of the same cloth as strong football heroes and determined title characters in the John Wayne movies. But he was not. As soon as the pain started, he caved. After two applications of the red hot poker, he admitted he was Satan. He would have admitted he'd fathered a rattlesnake to get them to stop. The burnt skin on his chest was still smoldering and the searing pain was so crippling, he couldn't breathe. He could only gulp small mouthfuls of air. He no longer tried to conceal his sobbing. Tears from his eyes were dripping down his chest now and when his salty tears got into his wounds it renewed the pain. His vision was bleary, his sinuses were filled, and his heart was hammering. He was afraid he was going into shock.

Cordova was looking quite smug. He had gotten his confession. But it had come too easily. He was not ready to stop yet. "So now, *Don* Castillo, I want to know about the bastard queen, Elizabeth."

Castillo wished to be gone from this place, but more than that he wanted to strike at this man. He hoped that Kansas was nearby. He hoped Mason Taylor would put a fish into this floating band of lunatics and blow them to smithereens. He didn't want rescue. He didn't want his crew to see him like this. He had peed himself. He only wanted to die and take these miscreants with him. "Come on, Mason. Do it! Put a fish into this barge and kill them all!" he said to himself in English.

"So," sneered Cordova. "You know the language of the godless queen and her mongrels. What is she planning, *Don* Castillo?"

He said his name mockingly as if the Don was a title of nobility as it used to be in old Spain. "I…don't… know," croaked Castillo through swollen lips.

Cordova stepped forward and back-handed him sharply.

• • •

Taylor came up on deck to hurry along the crewmen who were cutting away the damaged acoustic panels. He was in a rush to get Castillo back. He didn't know what these pirates might be doing to him. The wind picked up and the sea got rougher causing the boat to rock. Submarines wallowed on the surface because of their round hulls. They were only stable when they were underwater.

Crystal McConnell came up on deck with the sniper gun slung over her right shoulder and Taylor hardly recognized her. She had a totally different demeanor.

She was wearing a brown leather jacket, black calfskin gloves with the fingers cut out of them, her chestnut hair was fastened in a ponytail which protruded through the opening in her black Kansas ball cap, and she had on a pair of wrap-around reflectors. He could read determination in the set of her mouth. She walked with purpose. All business. She called to Taylor's mind a line from an old song:

> *She's a Killer Queen*
> *Gunpowder, gelatine*
> *Dynamite with a laserbeam*
> *Guaranteed to blow your mind*

She had brought an assortment of jars and bottles as targets. She turned and said, "Could you throw some targets for me?"

"Sure," answered Taylor. She slammed home a magazine, cocked the firing mechanism and laid down on the deck. She adjusted the set of the bipod twice, then nodded to Taylor. He picked up a mayonnaise jar and threw it as far as he could.

POW! POW! POW!

She shattered it on the third try.

"This is hard!" she said. "I've never tried to shoot from the pitching deck of a ship before."

"I never said it would be easy," said Taylor. He threw more jars and bottles for her. She expended twenty rounds and on her last six targets, she'd hit them on her first try. "I think you're ready," said Taylor.

"I think I need more practice," she answered.

"We don't have time for more practice," said Taylor. "We need to get Don."

She studied Taylor's face. "He's your close friend, isn't he?"

"You could say that. We've known each other for about three years, but I think we've gotten to know each other pretty well in that time. We've been very involved in the day-to-day operations of the Kansas and her crew, and we've had many drinks in celebration and in sorrow."

She studied his handsome face. Taylor gave her a protected feeling. They were about to go into danger yet she felt oddly comforted knowing Mason Taylor was in command of the operation. He seemed so confidant, so sure. She smiled at him and he smiled back.

Taylor called a meeting in Kansas's wardroom and went over the plan. Taylor had asked for volunteers for the assault team and had gotten 57 volunteers, but the SEAL inflatable assault craft could only hold 8 so he selected people he thought most capable. Susan Lambert insisted on leading the assault. He at first refused but finally gave in because of her relentless insistence. She did not know weapons, but she was probably the most fit of the crew. He put an MP-5 assault rifle in her hands and showed her where the safety was.

A problem with Taylor's rescue plan was getting the 50 caliber to the top of the boat's sail. The big gun weighed nearly 100 pounds and each ammo box also weighed in at 100 pounds. The Browning 50 caliber was designed to stop armored vehicles and aircraft. The brutish weapon could punch holes in one and a half inch steel plate. Taylor still questioned why the SEAL team needed such a diabolical thing, but at this point, he was only thankful. The big gun was going to be very useful in the upcoming operation.

When all was in readiness, they took their positions. Taylor knew the Browning 50 caliber because of his time on a Navy destroyer. This was before his submarine days. He had fired the big gun only twice, but he remembered the specifics of its operation. The crew had securely set the gun into position in Kansas's sail anchoring it on the edge of the bridge well and Crystal McConnell manned the sniper gun in the watch well in the sail right next to it. She and Taylor knelt side-by-side in the top of the sail ready to provide fire support to the boarding party. Although McConnell was not military, she had made a connection with Taylor. They were comrades in arms about to go into battle. He had her back and she had his. This is the type of operation that bonds warriors forever. It's in the heat of battle that they discover who they really are and what they are truly capable of.

"Let's do this," said McConnell, sighting through her scope.

"Right," said Taylor. He donned a headset and said, "Is everybody ready?"

"Assault team ready," said Lambert.

"Control room ready," said Lieutenant Maria Guerrero, who was in the command chair and monitoring camera views.

"Okay," said Taylor. "Maria, start closing the distance. Move us up to within a hundred feet of the stern of the galleon."

"Aye, sir," replied Lieutenant Guerrero. "Closing on the galleon."

Tanaka was crowded in beside Taylor. His job was to feed ammo belts to the Browning when it started firing. It consumed an enormous amount of ammunition when it fired. Tanaka was huffing loudly with the effort of laying out the heavy belts.

"Could this be construed as an international incident, sir?" asked Tanaka.

Taylor couldn't believe what Tanaka was implying. "I'd say when they fired on an American ship and kidnapped the skipper, *they* created an international incident. And I don't care what country is involved in this, in firing on us, *they* initiated hostile action. Besides, I'm more concerned about getting Don back than operational protocol. His life may be in danger."

"Okay, okay," said Tanaka apologetically. "I was just asking."

"The first thing we have to do is slow down the galleon," said Taylor. "And give our people a good shot at getting on it."

"I would suggest taking down the center mast," said Tanaka. "This ship is most likely made of oak, but the masts are softer wood, pine. Also, see the row of windows in the stern castle? The second row?"

"Yes," replied Taylor.

"The windows at each end are not windows at all. They are gun ports. There are two stern-facing guns there. Expect them to use those against us when we get in range."

When Kansas had closed the distance to 500 yards, the doors to the two stern gun ports opened and the gun muzzles extended.

"Show time!" said Taylor. He aimed the Browning at the left gun port first and braced against the expected recoil.

BOOM! BOOM! BOOM! BOOM! BOOM! BOOM! BOOM! BOOM! BOOM! BOOM!

When the deafening roar had died, all that could be heard was the clink of empty brass shells hitting the deck below. The left gun port on the galleon was destroyed. It was a gaping jagged hole ten times bigger that it should be. The gun sat sideways in the port aimed at the port bulkhead. There were two bodies, one against the rear wall and one draped across the gun.

Taylor turned his attention to the right gun port. Right before he fired, he saw through the windows the gun crew abandon their stations.

BOOM! BOOM! BOOM! BOOM! BOOM! BOOM! BOOM! BOOM! BOOM! BOOM!

The right gun port appeared to be wrecked now too with a wide irregular hole. There was also a hole in the wall behind it as well. Suddenly there was a voice in his ear.

"Sir, we're seeing a man, possible sniper, on the stern rail."

"Thanks, Maria." He turned to McConnell. "Sniper on the rear rail. See him?"

McConnell put her right cheek against the stock of her weapon and sighted through her scope. "Got him." She took in a breath and held it, moved her chin in a circular motion until it felt right. The sail was swaying back and forth with the roll of the boat in a very distracting manner. She closed her eyes, let out the breath, then opened them. It seemed forever to Taylor, but he didn't want to interfere with her process. He sat very still feeling the sway of the sail with each wave.

POW!

"Nice!" said Lieutenant Guerrero from the control room. "Got him in the arm. He dropped his rifle."

"Were you trying to hit his arm?" asked Taylor.

"What do you think?" replied McConnell sweetly.

"Hey," screamed Tanaka. "She's turning to port! They're trying to get guns on us."

"Maria," said Taylor. "Stay on her tail. Don't let her get a broadside into us."

"Yes, sir. She won't shake us." Kansas turned right slightly and picked up speed, staying on the tail of the tightly turning galleon.

"I'm going to try to take out the center mast," said Taylor. He turned the Browning toward the mast, sighted down the barrel, braced and fired.

BOOM! BOOM! BOOM! BOOM! BOOM! BOOM! BOOM! BOOM! BOOM! BOOM!

The mast looked unharmed. "Let me see the binoculars." Tanaka handed them over and Taylor put them to his eyes. He could see large splinters projecting out from the base of the mast. "I hit it! I'm going to try again." He handed the binoculars back to Tanaka and picked up the gun again.

"Another sniper, sir," said Guerrero. "First yardarm, stern mast."

"Another sniper, Crystal. Stern mast, first yardarm."

McConnell's eyes went to the rigging on the stern mast. "I see him." She went through her process again. Breathing, closing her eyes, opening. She was a picture of concentration.

POW!

It was a miss. The man sitting on the yardarm fired and a bullet pinged harmlessly off the sail a few feet below them.

"We don't have to worry about him anymore," said Tanaka. "Those old flintlocks were single shooters. It will take him a while to reload." He looked through the binoculars and said, "Oh shit! He has another gun!"

"Let me try again," said McConnell. She began going through her process again.

Then the galleon reversed direction and began to turn to starboard. Kansas reversed direction too and stayed on the galleon's stern. The two ships were locked in a deadly dance.

POW!

This time McConnell scored a hit. The man plummeted from the rigging and hit the deck below.

As soon as the stern castle swung by and Taylor had a clear shot at the center mast, he fired at it again.

BOOM! BOOM! BOOM! BOOM! BOOM! BOOM! BOOM! BOOM! BOOM! BOOM!

But the mast held fast like a mighty pine tree rooted in the deck. "I know I got at least six rounds into that thing." Taylor took the binoculars and inspected the mast again. He thought he saw a few more jagged splinters protruding from it. "Alright, I'll try again." He shifted his position and sighted the gun. Just then a gust of wind came up, and the mast made a sharp crack. It was the same sound a big tree makes when it's about to fall. Taylor yelled, "Timber!" There was another crack, then a crunch and finally the mast slowly toppled forward taking out ratlines, halyards and rigging from the first mast. The man in the crow's nest hit the deck, the sails on the galleon began to flutter impotently, and the galleon almost slowed to a standstill.

Taylor hung his upper body out over the edge of the sail and looked back at Kansas's aft deck. He could see the inflatable assault craft sitting on the deck. It was full of people. "Okay, Lambert, get ready," said Taylor into his headset.

"We're ready," she responded and waved.

"Maria, trim ship and flood the aft deck. Assault team is ready to launch."

"Yes sir. Flooding aft deck."

Stern vents hissed loudly and Kansas dipped just enough to allow water to wash across the aft deck and float the small boat. In a short time the inflatable sped past Taylor, McConnell and Tanaka, bouncing from wave to wave, throwing spumes of spray from its propane-powered outboard. It looked like a team of SEALs going into action, complete with assault rifles, black helmets and body armor.

"Susan, see that thing that looks like a balcony coming off the stern?" said Taylor.

"Yes."

"I think that's your best bet. It's only about ten feet off the water."

"I agree. We'll go there first."

Lambert, COB Brown and Lieutenant Anderson all had SEAL blue tooth communicators tuned to Kansas's control room. Lambert and Brown were also transmitting a live video feed to the control room through their helmet cameras.

The assault team arrived at the balcony projection and threw a grappling hook over the rail. The rope trailing from it had stirrups attached to it. Lambert tugged on it and the hook held fast. Just then a voice in Taylor's ear said, "Someone came out a door onto the balcony. They have a gun!"

"Crystal! The guy on the balcony. Can you get him?"

"I see him," she said sighting through her rifle scope. The figure looked down at the assault team and leveled his gun at them.

"Hurry, Crystal!"

"Shit!" She ripped off a shot.

POW!

The rail next to the man's hand splintered. He was startled and looked toward Kansas in shock. She fired again.

POW!

This time the window frame next to the man's head exploded. He quickly ducked back through the door.

"Damn it!" cursed McConnell.

"That's okay. You did it, girl! He's not a threat anymore, and the team has been alerted."

Lambert made climbing to the balcony look easy. She must be a good triathlete, thought Taylor. Chief Brown, who was much bigger, struggled, but he made it. When there were only two men left to go, Taylor got another call.

"Armed men on the rail…three…no four…"

Taylor saw them. They were leveling rifles at his people on the balcony. He decided there was no time for the finesse of sniping. Brute force was needed here. He aimed the heavy gun at the rail where the men were gathered.

BOOM! BOOM! BOOM! BOOM! BOOM! BOOM! BOOM! BOOM! BOOM! BOOM!

When he stopped there were no men at the rail. There was no rail either, just uneven broken posts like bloody teeth projecting from the deck. And there were bits of meat and a man's severed arm impaled on them. The Browning had reduced the men to slabs of muscle, bone and gristle.

Someone on the command circuit whispered, "My God!" Violent death was a brutally shocking thing when it was in living color.

Taylor felt he needed to say something. "I didn't want to do that, but they didn't give me much choice."

"We know," replied Guerrero softly.

Now there was nothing for Taylor, McConnell and Tanaka to do but wait. Taylor could hear the voices of

Lambert, Brown and Anderson, but he had no way to see the helmet cams.

Below in the control room, the crew was very tense. There were 59 people crammed into the small room. They watched Lambert's helmet cam as she entered the ship. They had all expected resistance there, but the man who had tried to take a shot at them earlier had fled.

"Jesus, it stinks in here," said Lambert.

"You can say that again," said Chief Brown. "It smells like a cesspool in a slaughterhouse! How do they stand it?"

"Lights everybody," said Lambert. They all switched on the halogen lights on their weapons and pointed them into the gloom extending down the passageway. When they turned the corner, they illuminated the grubby blinking faces of three crewmen with muskets and cutlasses. They were wearing muslin shirts and pants smudged with soot and tar. Their eyes went wide in surprise at the black clad intruders.

"Drop your weapons and get against the wall," barked Chief Brown. The crewmen just stared in disbelief at what they were seeing. "Drop your weapons and against the wall! Now!" roared Brown and thrust his rifle at one for emphasis. The men threw down their weapons, got down on their knees, began speaking softly and crossed themselves. "Good enough," said Brown as he stepped forward and kicked their weapons away from them and made them lay flat on their faces.

"Anybody have any guesses where they're holding Castillo?" asked Anderson.

"The quickest way to find him," said Lambert, "is to ask somebody."

"Do you think they'll tell you?"

"I'm not going to ask nicely," said Lambert darkly.

"The officers are wearing red," said Taylor into his headset. "One of them should know."

"Yes, sir," replied Chief Brown. "We'll find one." They proceeded down another passageway, made a turn and came face to face with an armed band of men. There were five men kneeling with rifles leveled and five standing behind them also with rifles leveled. They were backlit by the outside glare just beyond. A show of force. Lambert dove for the deck as the first one fired.

POW!

The bullet missed her, and Brown and Anderson both went prone and returned fire.

POP!POP!POP!POP!POP!POP!POP!POP!POP!P OP!POP!POP!POP!POP!

POW! POW! POW!

POP!POP!POP!POP!POP!POP!POP!POP!POP!P OP!POP!POP!POP!POP!

When the shooting stopped, the galleon crewmen all lay groaning and wounded. They had only gotten off four shots.

"Did anyone get hit?" shouted Lambert.

"I don't think so," said Brown looking around at everyone.

Lambert jumped up and ran to a big man in a red coat laying on the deck. She roughly grabbed him and screamed, "Where's our captain?"

The man was wounded in his left leg and arm. He disdainfully snapped something at her.

"What's that? Spanish?" asked Lambert.

"Yes," replied Maria Guerrero in her ear. "He said something derogatory about your womanhood."

"Let *me* ask him," said Chief Brown, smiling evilly. "I know a little Spanish." He walked up, knelt down so he was nose to nose and gripped the man's injured arm and began to squeeze. The man grimaced, showing yellow teeth with black gaps in them. "Donde esta capitan?" growled Brown.

The man looked hatefully at Brown's black face then spat on him. Brown stood up, wiped the spittle from his face then stomped down on the man's injured left leg. The man roared in anguish and rolled away from Brown. Brown stepped forward and delivered a vicious blow to his stomach with the butt of his gun. The man gasped and turned the color of a dead mackerel.

Lambert turned her back on them. She didn't have the stomach for this part. She heard blows landing and the man screaming, then silence.

When she turned back around, the man was pointing down the passageway with his good arm. He muttered something in Spanish.

Maria Guerrero translated. "Down the ladder and the room on the left."

"You just have to ask the right way," said Brown with satisfaction. He yanked the man forcefully to his feet and growled, "After you, pal!"

Brown forced the man to hobble down the hall and then descend the ladder with the Kansas team trailing.

The ladder creaked and complained with every step of the heavy men.

When they reached the floor below, they saw two crewmen brandishing cutlasses, but the astonished crewmen quickly assessed the situation, laid down their weapons and knelt in surrender. Anderson stepped forward and forced them face down on the deck.

Chief Brown went to the door of the room and took the iron door grip and pulled, then pushed, but it was bolted from the inside. He could see the bolt across the crack between door and frame.

"We're going to have to break this thing down." Chief Brown, who had the build of a fullback, backed up and put his shoulder into the door, but the door held. Someone inside screamed something in Spanish.

Maria Guerrero translated over the comm net, "Someone just screamed, 'If you come in, he dies'."

Brown and Lambert exchanged concerned looks.

"What do we do?" asked Lambert.

"We don't have much choice," replied Brown. "We've *got* to go in. Maria, how do I say, 'if he dies, you die'?"

Guerrero gave them a phrase to say and Brown bellowed it. He heard nothing in return. He turned to his team and said, "Okay, get ready to flood the room."

Anderson said, "Come on, chief. Let's hit this door together."

They backed up against the wall on the other side of the passageway, took two strides and slammed the door hard. It burst open to reveal two men, one stripped to the waist, bloodied and tied to a chair and another bare chested man with a scar on his face standing over him with a cutlass. He raised the knife to strike, and Brown fired a burst.

POP!POP!POP!POP!

The man did a spastic dance, his mouth wide in a silent scream, then collapsed. Lambert ran to the bloodied man in the chair. "It's Castillo!" He had wounds on his chest and there was a large pool of blood beneath him. His chin was on his chest and he was unresponsive.

"It looks like they used him for target practice," said Brown.

Lambert picked up his head and looked at his waxy swollen face. "He looks terrible…but he's alive."

Their corpsman stepped forward and said, "Lay him down here so I can dress his wounds. I can't do much for him here, but I can get him ready to move." He expertly applied antibacterial ointment to Castillo's wounds and dressed them. Then Brown and Anderson stood him up, and began walking him out, a man under each arm.

"You guys," said Anderson, pointing to two team members. "Go make sure the path's clear ahead." They exited with rifles at the ready.

• • •

Norm Bloomberg sat in the tension-filled perspiration-laced atmosphere of Kansas's control room watching the view from Lambert's helmet cam on the big screen. He was wheezing. He needed his asthma inhaler, but he didn't want to leave the room to go get it. He didn't like what he was seeing. Something was wrong. Something about the men, the old ship. He slowly and painfully hauled his bulk up out of his seat at the rear of the room and slowly limped to the command chair.

"Lieutenant Guerrero," he said. "I have a request. It may be important."

Guerrero turned her bespectacled face to him. She was tall, almost as tall as Taylor, and with a lantern jaw and light brown shoulder length hair. "Right now?"

"Yes. Have Lambert ask one of the galleon crew the date."

"We're a little busy right now, Mr. Bloomberg."

"I know, but this may be important. I need to know what date these men believe it to be."

Guerrero studied him and deliberated. Finally, she sniffed and said, "Miss Lambert, Mr. Bloomberg has a request."

Guerrero relayed the request to Lambert, who was none too pleased with having to approach a skeletal foul-smelling galleon crewman and repeat the Spanish phrase to him: ¿qual es la fecha? and when he responded with day and month, Guerrero further prompted: ¿el año? When he answered, Guerrero was stunned.

"He says it's July 28, 1588!"

Chapter 8

L ambert and Brown carefully supported Castillo and walked him up a ladder and down another ladder. They walked him past several galleon crewmen, but the men offered no resistance. They only stood and stared with gaunt hollow faces. Some of them crossed themselves as the black clad strangers moved warily by them with their strange rifles and lights.

• • •

"There are men on the stern," warned McConnell as she sighted through her scope.

"Keep an eye on them but don't shoot," said Taylor. "I don't think they're a threat. They seem to be more curious than anything else."

Fourteen galleon crewmen were standing along the stern and hanging out windows watching the assault team rigging a sling for Castillo. They lowered Castillo into the inflatable and transported him to Kansas. Once the inflatable was securely beached on the aft deck, they carefully lowered him through the access hatch in the deck.

"What do you think we should do with these guys?" asked Taylor.

"Put a fish into that barge! Send her to the bottom," said someone over the command circuit. Sounded like Chief Brown.

There was some agreement. "Damn right!" "Let's do it!"

"No," said Taylor. "They don't represent a threat any more." He removed his shades and blew a piece of lint out of them. He turned to McConnell and asked, "What do you think, Miss McConnell?"

"I think they should answer for what they did. They fired on us and they hurt Don Castillo."

"True. They've violated international maritime law and should answer to the authorities. I'd like to throw a line on that thing and tow it back to base, but I doubt they would hold still for it. There would probably be more bloodshed." Taylor stood up and arched his back, stretching his tall frame. "Maria, get a lot of pictures of that thing and save the video of the attack on us. I have a feeling authorities will want to review it after we file our complaint."

"Aye, sir. Archiving today's video, and we'll also get some HD stills of it."

"I'd like to call in medical help for Don Castillo and the injured men over there, but we still can't get anyone on radio." Taylor thought it over before finally saying, "They don't seem to have much fight left in them, so I'm going to send an armed medical team back over there with a couple corpsman to patch up their wounded. It's the least we can do. They're drifting toward the Scottish shore, aren't they, Eric?"

"Yes, sir," said Tanaka. "If the wind holds, they should be there in about fourteen hours."

"Good," said Taylor. "They can get their injured off and call for help when they get there."

When they had recovered their medical team, Kansas backed away from the galleon and crew members lowered the big Browning down into the ship along with the ammo cases. The inflatable was deflated once again and stowed below decks, and when the ship was buttoned up tight, it submerged.

• • •

The man the crew called Doc was first class corpsman George Aultman. He was the head of their medical staff. He performed first aid and dispensed pills mostly. He could stitch up wounds and set broken legs, but that was about it. Anything else had to be done at a Naval hospital. The crew was lucky to have him, however, because he wanted to be a surgeon and had finished his pre-med at Virginia Commonwealth. When he examined Castillo, he knew at once that Castillo needed blood. He knew the commander had AB positive blood so it shouldn't be hard finding a match and there were plenty of willing donors. He set him up in Kansas's small two bed dispensary.

When Taylor looked in on Castillo, he was hooked up to a crewman being transfused.

"How do you feel?" asked Taylor.

"How do I look?" rasped Castillo.

Castillo had a puffy plum colored face and his left eye was swollen shut. He had bandages across his chest and one on his left hand. "Like you lost an argument with a piece of agricultural equipment."

Castillo chuckled slightly, then winced at the pain it caused him. "What did you do to the galleon?"

"We let them go. The authorities should be able to find them easily enough. A ship like that can't hide."

"Oh." Castillo looked disappointed.

Taylor decided he needed some cheering up. "But not before we kicked their asses!"

"Really?"

"Hell yeh! Well, we decided we had to get you back, so we dug out all the SEAL's weapons and put together a team. Did you know they have a 50 caliber?"

Castillo brightened. "Really?"

• • •

Doc Aultman's copper eyebrows knitted as he talked to a concerned Susan Lambert and Crystal McConnell.

"None of his injuries are life threatening. His face has substantial bruising. He has knife wounds and severe burns on his chest and two knife wounds to his left hand. Also the two smallest fingers on his left hand were amputated. These wounds are all designed to inflict pain, not kill, but he still might've died from the blood loss and shock."

"Oh my God!" said an appalled Lambert. "Why would someone do this?"

"Don't know." Aultman stroked his copper mustache. "He's stable now. We've had more than enough blood donors come forward. That was my biggest concern. His loss of blood. We'll transfer him to the infirmary at Clyde, but I think he'll make a full recovery."

• • •

"How many dead?" asked a troubled Castillo.

"About ten, I estimate," said Taylor. "And another six wounded. I sent them some medical assistance. Corpsman Bailey and Corpsman-in-training Rouse patched them up as best they could and administered some pain killers. They thought they would last long enough to make it to a hospital. I didn't expect a *thank you*. They seemed very…distant."

"I don't think I was worth all those lives," said Castillo quietly.

Taylor said nothing. Castillo was different. He had gone through a lot in the few hours he was in the custody of those mad men.

Doc Aultman swept in and disconnected the crewman laying in the adjoining bed. "You're done, Teddy!" The sailor sat up and rolled down his right sleeve. "I think you're out of the woods now, skipper."

"Thanks," said Castillo, reaching out and shaking the smiling sailor's hand.

"Glad to do it, sir!" The man replaced his ball cap and exited.

"I owe you all so much." Castillo's one good eye was abruptly very wet and he had to wipe away a tear.

"You'd do the same for any one of us," said Susan Lambert from the doorway. Her eyes were wet too and her lips were trembling. Crystal McConnell was standing directly behind her, tall enough to see easily over Lambert's shoulder.

"Hey!" said Castillo, waving with his good hand. "I'm in your debt. You're quite the pair."

"We just did a small part. It was a team effort."

"That's not what *I* heard. From now on I'm going to call you *Rambo* and Crystal, *Annie Oakley*!"

They both chuckled softly, but cast sad glances at the wreck lying in the sick bed. "How are you doing?" asked Lambert.

"I hurt, but the doc has me on some pretty strong pain killers to take the edge off it. If I say something stupid, blame it on the drugs." He stopped, grimmaced and shifted his body in the bed, trying to find a more comfortable position. "I'm not fit to command that's for sure, but I'm not worried. Mr. Taylor's more than up to the task."

"I hope so," chuckled Taylor. "But if I say something stupid, what can *I* blame it on?"

"Too many dead brain cells from all your partying," smiled Castillo.

"He's gonna be okay," said Taylor.

• • •

Castillo rested in the ship's small infirmary and caught up on his reading. He had a NERD ereader that allowed him to connect to the ship's ebook library, which was extensive. NERD stood for Navy Ereader

Device and the ebook library was still an experimental program. But with all the drugs in his system, Castillo found it hard to concentrate. He drifted off and dreamed of his girls, running down the beach and laughing in Virginia.

He didn't know how long he had been asleep when he awoke. He knew immediately Kansas was surfaced by the gentle rocking. One of the corpsmen brought him a bowl of corn chowder and he discovered he was hungrier than he thought. The chowder was excellent! There was a knock on the door frame. He looked up to see Taylor looming there.

"How are you feeling?" he asked.

"Better, I think."

"I've run into a problem. We're inside the firth now and surfaced, but we still can't raise anyone. I'm reluctant to navigate the firth without a harbor pilot." There was angst in Taylor's eyes.

"How much daylight do we have left?"

"Maybe an hour."

"What do the Brits have to say?"

"Brits?"

"The two British officers we have aboard?"

A light came on in Taylor's face. "I forgot about them. What were their names?"

"One was named…uh…" Damn these drugs, thought Castillo. "Gas…something…Gastmeyer, I think. Yes, a commander."

"Good enough!" Taylor picked up the receiver next to Castillo's bed, dialed to the ship's general announce system and spoke:

Would Commander Gastmeyer please report to the infirmary. Commander Gastmeyer please report to the infirmary.

He hung up and they waited.

Soon a young woman appeared in the doorway. "You wish to see me, sir?" Taylor and Castillo both stared at her. She had a pretty freckled face and mid length straight brown hair with bangs that fit her head like a bronze helmet. She appeared to be about 25, which both men knew was impossible. She was a full commander.

"Yes," said Taylor. "Are you or your companion familiar with the firth? And would you recommend navigating it in the dark?"

She blinked at him, then said, "I take it you weren't able to reach harbor control and contact a pilot."

"That's correct."

"I would not recommend trying to navigate the firth at night. You might ask my companion, Captain Simms."

"Could you go get him for us?" asked Castillo. "Thank you."

She disappeared and returned a short time later trailing a British captain. Castillo had seen him before in the control room. He always looked like he was about to deliver bad news. He had kind of a permanent sour look on his face with bushy gray eyebrows and a mouth that turned down at the corners.

"Can I be of help?" he asked.

"Maybe," replied Taylor. "We were thinking of proceeding in the dark up the firth and to Clyde without a harbor pilot. Do you think you could serve in that capacity?"

"Um…" He considered it. "Sure! I know these waters, and I used to sail here as a boy. It's not impossible."

"Good!" said Taylor.

Castillo studied them both. What is it with the British? They drive on the wrong side of the road, name tags on their uniforms are backed in white instead of black. And what's with the shoulder epaulets? They put them on everything. Even their informal service shirts.

• • •

They stood in a cold pouring rain and fading light squinting through binoculars at the horizon. Lieutenant Commander Mason Taylor, U.S. Navy, Commander Lauren Gastmeyer, Her Majesty's Royal British Navy, and Captain Miles Simms, also of Her Majesty's Royal British Navy. They wore black rain slickers and hats as they stood in the bridge well at the top of Kansas's sail. They were traveling up the Firth of Clyde at 6 knots and Simms was perplexed. Taylor could see it in his eyes and his tense face.

"I don't understand," said Simms.

"What's wrong?" asked Taylor.

"Where are the channel markers? They should be right here. One red and one green."

"Are we in the right place?" asked Taylor.

"I'm pretty sure we are." Simms turned left and put the glasses to his eyes. "Yes, that's Little Cumbrae, isn't it, Gastmeyer?"

"Yes," said Gastmeyer. She had to raise her voice to be heard over the strumming of the heavy rain against Kansas's metal surfaces. She swiped water away from her eyes before bringing the glasses up again. "But I don't see the Clydeport Hunterson terminal. It should be right here."

"What's that?" asked Taylor.

"A rather large shipping terminal where coal carriers load," replied Gastmeyer. "It's hard to miss!"

"Something's wrong," said Simms. "We should be able to see the city of Millport dead ahead."

"Alright," said Taylor, sighing. "Without a harbor pilot and navigational aids, I think the best thing to do would be to keep station right here and try it in the morning. What do you think, Captain Simms?"

"I concur." Taylor could tell by their faces Simms and Gastmeyer were very troubled by what they were seeing.

The following morning the skies were clear and an apricot sun was breaking over the eastern hills lining the firth. After breakfast, the three climbed up to the sail on Kansas. Taylor had to chase some of the crewmen below: it was a little crowded. But he could use all the help he could get, so crowded into the sail's bridge well was himself, Simms, Gastmeyer, Tanaka and Chief Brown. In the watch's well was Lambert and McConnell. Down below in the control room were about fifty people watching the camera screens.

Taylor heard Lieutenant Guerrero's voice in his ear. "According to our charts and radar, we're at the mouth of Clyde Chanel at the Little Cumbrae Elbow. We're ready down here, sir."

"Still no word from harbor control?"

"No, sir. Nothing."

"Alright, Maria," said Taylor. "Lets make turns for 6 knots. I want to go slow with this."

"Aye, sir," replied Guerrero. "6 knots."

Taylor turned over control of Kansas to Captain Simms who expertly made course corrections to maneuver the ship into the Clyde Channel and then head north toward Gare Loch. Simms and Gastmeyer grew increasingly alarmed at the changes they were seeing. There were no roads, no towns, only a few buildings. They passed a few small sailing vessels, the crews of which stared at them in open-mouthed awe as if they were seeing a sea monster straight out of a nightmare.

"Hey," said Lambert. "A few days ago, there was a cell tower there! Remember, Crystal? There was a boy playing with his dog beneath it."

"Are you sure it was here?" asked McConnell. "These hills all look alike."

"I'm sure. Remember the stone house that was there before that outcropping of rock?"

Crystal McConnell frowned and said, "I think you're right." She looked up channel and added, "How do you explain it?"

"I can't."

Simms called out landmarks as they passed them: Holy Loch, Cloch Point, Gallow Hill, Rosneath Point. But it was with increasing dread that they approached the Clyde Naval Base. They were afraid of what they would find…or *not* find. They proceeded up Gare Loch until they arrived at the proper place and stopped.

The Clyde Naval Base was not there!

No one spoke. They only stared in disbelief. The atmosphere in the control room was the same. Disbelief! Guerrero double checked her charts and the radar repeater. They were at the correct location, there was no doubt. Guerrero's logical mind wanted an explanation, but what could explain the disappearance of a burgeoning British Naval Base? She stared at the camera screens showing the rolling green hills. It was devoid of any activity. There were only grass-covered hills, and outcroppings of gray rock dappled with white bird droppings and at the water's edge, craggy trees.

"Okay, Maria," said Taylor. "Let's shut down and go to station-keeping here."

"Aye, sir. Engaging station-keeping." The submarine stopped its forward motion and held position in the middle of the loch.

• • •

Castillo shook his head in disbelief. "Nothing?"

"Nothing," affirmed Taylor. He sat down heavily in a chair at Castillo's bedside. "I can't explain it, Don. Are we all mad?"

Castillo stared at a spot on the wall and said nothing. He was in deep thought.

"No sign of Clyde…or any other sign of civilization." Taylor slouched as if a weight had descended on his shoulders.

"Did you have time to verify the star shift Mr. Bloomberg pointed out to us?"

"Yes," replied Taylor. "I found several good astronomy books in the ebook library and I think Norm Bloomberg knows what he's talking about. The star drift, the Polaris pointer stars, all of it. Something's happened, Don. It's in the heavens."

A chill went through Castillo. "Could you go get Bloomberg? I'd like to talk to him."

"I think Doc Aultman has ordered him to stay off his feet. He has a blown right knee."

"Oh! I forgot. Okay, we'll go see him then." Castillo pulled out his IV, and swung his legs over the edge of the bed.

"Should you be up?" asked Taylor.

"My legs work fine. Besides I'm tired of laying here."

Castillo stood and steadied himself, gripping the door frame until his dizziness passed. Castillo and Taylor went to Norm Bloomberg's stateroom. They found him laying in bed on his back reading. His trousers had only one pant leg. The right one had been cut away to expose his right knee. It was very inflamed and swollen. When he saw Castillo and Taylor, he put down his ereader and propped himself up on an elbow. "Well, hello, gentlemen! I would invite you both to sit, but I only have one chair. Sorry. Not much room in here. How are you feeling, sir?"

"Better, thank you," answered Castillo. "How's the knee?"

"It's killing me. I was supposed to have surgery in Glasgow, but I think that possibility has slipped away if reports I'm hearing are correct."

"You've heard?"

"Yes, Susan told me. I was afraid of this." He pushed his glasses up his nose with a single finger.

"If you understand what's going on," said Castillo, "I would appreciate an explanation."

"Certainly," said Bloomberg, tenting his hands. "Indulge me first. You had direct contact with the galleon crew. Do you think they were acting?"

"Acting?"

"Yes, you know, were they re-enactors?" Bloomberg squinted, seeming to focus completely on Castillo, awaiting his answer.

Castillo took a breath and said, "Well, if they were, they were damned convincing."

"I've watched the video recordings several times, and I can only come to one conclusion." His mouth worked to form the exact words. "The crewmen looked like scarecrows. They were pale, malnourished and some of them had open sores. The same kind of thing you would see in sailors of 400 years ago, before refrigeration and modern medicine. On Kansas we dine grandly, but 400 years ago it was salt beef and hard tack. Maggots and rats infested the food stores. They often got dysentery from their water stores because they went bad. That's one reason they drank grog. Many sailors in those days were in terrible shape. They would look exactly like those men you saw on the galleon. Now, did you see the weapons they were using?"

"Yes," answered Castillo, "knives, cutlasses, flintlocks."

"Not flintlocks! Matchlocks!" corrected Bloomberg. "The flintlock was not introduced until the 17th century. The matchlock used a slow burning match to ignite the flashpan, and it was very unreliable. The match would go out and the weapon would misfire half the time. But they were still capable of killing. Now, I ask you. If these men were re-enactors, why were they using live ammunition?"

"Well…" began Castillo, laying his good hand on his right cheek.

"And if these men were terrorists, why were they armed with matchlocks? One of the most unreliable firearms in history. Not very smart."

Castillo looked at Taylor, who shrugged. "So… what's your conclusion?"

Bloomberg took their measure, his gaze going from one man to the other. "I have concluded the galleon crew were not deluded in any way. We are!"

Castillo frowned but said nothing.

"They knew exactly who they were and what their mission was. We, on the other hand, believe we are still in the modern world…the year 2014!"

Castillo exchanged glances with Taylor again. Taylor opened his mouth to say something, then closed it again.

"When the Apparition system went critical, it caused either a portal in the terrestrial timescape or a dimensional rift. There are two schools of thought on the subject. I was just reading up on it." He held up an ereader with a cover page to a book on quantum mechanics displayed.

"So…" began Castillo slowly, feeling for the proper words. "What you're suggesting is…" He stopped, stuck.

"Either we have slipped the bonds of time and made a huge leap backwards, as the stars suggest, or we are in another dimension, very similar to our own home dimension, but we have entered it at a time that is not our own."

Castillo blinked. "Well, there must be a way to undo this and get us back."

"I don't know of one. This happened as the result of a catastrophic accident."

Taylor erupted and slammed the bulkhead angrily with his palm. "I knew it! I knew we were fucking around with something dangerous! Didn't I try to tell you, Don?"

Castillo put his good hand on Taylor's shoulder and said, "Easy, Mase. Finger-pointing isn't going to help us now. We need cool heads." He took a deep breath and turned to Bloomberg. "Norm, I'd like you to make a presentation to the rest of the crew. We have some very fine minds on board. If we all think on this, maybe we can come up with a solution. Use Power Point or whatever you need and do it on the mess deck where we have the most room. Can you have something by this evening?"

"Uh…sure…I don't know what I'll say exactly."

"Say what you just told us, then we'll throw it open to questions and answers."

"I have a feeling there'll be many more questions than answers."

Chapter 9

Norm Bloomberg had erected a large 4 foot screen slaved to a laptop on the mess deck On it he displayed a colorful graph of a timeline. It showed centuries and important events that occurred in history. The messdeck was crowded with more than 60 crewmen and civilians. They were transfixed by Bloomberg's presentation, listening with hushed attention. Castillo made arrangements to record the presentation so the watchstanders could view it too at their leisure.

"We were here!" He balanced on his crutches and pointed to the section representing the 21st century. "Now we are here!" He pointed to the 16th century.

There were confused faces all around. "How do you know exactly where we are?" asked a crewman.

"I don't really know. All I know for sure is we have shifted in time. The alignment of the stars supports this and the crewmen of that Spanish galleon believe it is the year 1588. And the Spanish were using the Gregorian calendar, the same as we do now."

"What exactly is a parallel universe?" asked another crewman.

"It is something supported by the theory that at the inception of the universe, the big bang, many universes were created. Universes we cannot see and are completely unaware of because of dimensional boundaries. A parallel universe is an alternate reality. A world similar to ours but with differences. Perhaps, there were no ice ages, or no moon, or something much smaller like no WalMart."

"Well," asked Susan Lambert, "how do we know whether we are in a parallel universe or simply displaced in time in our own?"

"We don't. At least I don't. I'm not really an expert. I just read a lot." Bloomberg shifted his great weight on his crutches.

"But," said a crewman. "If we're in our own dimension, won't we affect our own timeline, the future of our civilization, Dr. Bloomberg?"

"Please! Not doctor! I work for a living!" This elicited a few laughs and glances toward Lambert. "Yes, any action we take will have an effect in the future." Bloomberg hit a key on the laptop and the picture on screen changed to two people in cartoon form, greeting each other. "If you shook hands with a man in this time, and delayed him long enough that he didn't catch the eye of a young lady who is about to enter a shop." He changed the picture again to a cartoon of a young woman entering a shop. "A young lady he is supposed to marry and father two children with." He changed the picture again and it showed an ancestral tree with many branches. "Lets say that each generation produces two children, on average. That means that over 500 years these two people have populated the earth with over 65,000 people! By shaking this man's hand, we have wiped out 65,000 people! This is extreme, but it's a good example of the multiplicative effect of a small action over time. And what if one of these people was an important leader or an educator who touched many lives. The ripple effect just gets worse and worse."

No one said a word. They just stared at Bloomberg, stunned. The breath had been sucked out of them.

"Now, let's talk about the moral imperative." Bloomberg changed the picture again. It was a picture of the starship Enterprise from the old Star Trek TV series. "How many people here remember Star Trek?"

Almost every hand went up.

"Good! Do you remember the *prime directive*? What was that all about anyway?" He didn't wait for an answer. "It was based on the moral principle that an advanced civilization should not interact with a primitive society. Because to do so could do great harm to that society. The slightest interaction could influence the development of that society artificially. It could cause them to become a society of paranoid schizophrenics and stunt their artistic and philosophical growth. They could never achieve their full potential simply because they were made aware of an advanced civilization before they were ready to accept it." Bloomberg stopped to let this sink in.

Chief Brown snorted. "This is all a rather moot argument, isn't it? We've already *interacted* with these people to the extreme."

"Yes," said Bloomberg heavily. "We have. There's no way to undo that, but perhaps we could limit any further interaction and thereby contain the damage."

The air seemed unbreathable. Everyone in the room was struggling with this concept of time shifting and parallel universes. They looked askance at each other. Several people coughed nervously.

Finally Susan Lambert said, "Norm, is there no way we can undo this and get back to where we belong?"

A shadow fell across Norm Bloomberg. He shook his head, scratched at his goatee and said, "I can't think of a way." There was sadness in his voice.

"Can't we duplicate the Apparition accident?" asked a crewman.

"It would be impossible to duplicate the exact conditions. And if we did," said Bloomberg, "I wouldn't trust it not to throw us another 400 years back. This is clearly something we have no control over. Besides, when the galleon attacked us, it severely damaged one of the Apparition emitter tubes so I think the Apparition system has been lost to us."

The seriousness of their situation gradually began to dawn on the crew. Kansas was isolated and cut off from civilization with no way to get back. All their families and friends, everyone they had ever met or loved… gone… irretrievably lost.

• • •

Normally when Kansas was in port, the crew switched to their *in port* routine. They manned the ship's systems with minimal crew, three shifts of watch standers. Lieutenant Commander Taylor assigned watches. This meant those not actually on watch could take liberty, but this time, they were uncertain where to take their liberty. There was nothing for them here.

The crewmen continued to perform their assigned functions but it was different. It was unusually quiet and the atmosphere seemed heavy with little chatter and very little laughing.

Crewmen were depressed at the sobering prospect of being stranded in time, and one of the hardest hit was Castillo. He sat shut away in his stateroom looking at the framed pictures on his small metal desk. There was a picture of his smiling mother and father in their Sunday best and a 5X7 of his family: he was in his dress blue uniform and Liz was beaming at his side in her fuschia jacket and skirt and white blouse and in front of them was Robin and Kelly in matching golden taffeta dresses. The picture was taken a couple years ago. They were so happy then. That was before Liz got sick. He had just taken command of Kansas. They were on top of the world. There was another smaller framed picture of Robin standing in the front yard holding her big yellow cat Stinky. He adored her chubby-cheeked smile. Everyone said she looked like him. And there was a picture of Kelly, tall and skinny in a bathing suit standing on the pool deck. It had been taken right after she'd gotten her braces. She was sunlit and exuberant.

Castillo's heart was aching with the thought he might never see them again. He choked back a sob and dabbed at his eyes with a tissue. His girls were the reason for his existence and kept him going through difficult days. They enabled him to function on an even keel when it seemed the world had gone mad. Because no matter how bad his day was going, boring meetings, systems failures, failed tests, he knew at the end of it, his reward was waiting for him: his beloved Liz, Robin and Kelley. He loved them more than life itself. How could he go on without them?

There was a knock, followed by Mason Taylor's familiar face poking through the door. He came in, stretched, yawned noisily and collapsed into a chair. "What a situation, huh? The people who have liberty are afraid to go anywhere because of what Bloomberg said about interfacing and affecting the future. And also they're afraid what happened to you could happen to them." He sized up Castillo and didn't like what he saw. "Are you okay?"

Castillo was uncharacteristically quiet. Taylor looked from Castillo to the photos on his desk.

"There *has* to be a way back," said Castillo without conviction.

"I don't know about that, Don. I've got my hands full right now just trying to run the ship. The NWP 1-14M covers just about everything that can happen to a naval vessel and what a commander should do, but there's not one word in there about a dimensional shift. We're making it up as we go now."

"There *has* to be a way back," repeated Castillo.

Neither one said anything for a time preferring to sit in the oppressive silence.

"When's the last time you saw your father?" asked Castillo.

"I was back home in May. We went fishing."

"That's good." Castillo took a tissue and blew his nose.

Taylor stared at a spot in the floor and turned reflective. "If we never get out of this…fix we're in, I'll never see him again and that's depressing. He was my pal and my best advisor. And Lani and I were getting serious, I think."

"Really?"

"Yes. We had chemistry. We hadn't really talked about taking the next step, but I think it was obviously a *ring*."

"You two were good together."

"What bothers me the most is the Navy's going to notify dad of his son's death…lost at sea."

"Oh shit! I forgot about that." Now he was picturing Liz's shocked face at seeing a Navy staff car pull up to the house and two white-gloved officers coming to the door. She'd know immediately why they're there. He pictured her pretty mouth distorted in anguish.

"Shit!" said Taylor. "I want them to deliver my dad a message saying his son is alive and well, but in a different dimension. He'd be sad at not seeing me again, but he'd be relieved I'm okay."

Castillo looked a mess, thought Taylor. Kind of like a balloon that had lost all its air. How long had he been wearing that robe?

"Anyway, not to change the subject, but Jonesy has expressed concern to me that we only have enough food to last another ten days. Then we'll be out. We have to replenish our food stores and I'm not sure how we're going to do it. Have any ideas, Don?"

No response from Castillo.

"Don?"

"What?" responded Castillo quietly. He was in another world.

Taylor just shook his head and said, "Never mind." He stood and decided to go discuss the problem with someone else.

• • •

Lieutenant Eric Tanaka was the Command Duty Officer. He sat in the command chair watching the camera screens. The shoreline outside was shrouded in a curtain of white mist. He could barely make out Kansas's stern fin. Then something emerged from the fog. He picked up the receiver, turned a dial and said, "Mr. Taylor, could you come to the control room, please?"

Taylor was there in seconds. "What ya got?"

"Take a look, sir."

They both watched as a small gray wooden skiff bumped against the hull of Kansas. Two young men stared at the submarine in wonder. They looked to be teenagers and one wore a black wool sweater and cap and one wore a heavy gray coat. The one in the sweater reached out with an oar and touched the submarine's hull. After some discussion they decided to row around the submarine and examine it from every angle. They were like two boys with a found elephant. Taylor could imagine the discussion: *What should we do with it? Let's take it home. But me mum won't let us keep it, there's no room, maybe we could keep it in your backyard.*

"I knew this was going to happen sooner or later," said Taylor. "I was hoping for later."

"Want me to blast the ship's horn?" asked Tanaka. "That'll scare the hell out of them."

Taylor chuckled. "Tempting, but no. Are we buttoned up tight? They can't get in, can they?"

"No, sir. Hatches are locked down."

"Keep an eye on them." Taylor went back to his stateroom.

As acting commander of Kansas, Taylor was facing a serious problem. He commanded a crew with no mission and no purpose. They awaited orders that would never come. He decided to start having daily meetings with senior staff to try and gage the morale of the crew. He tried to keep them focused on the day to day running of Kansas. He got them busy on solving the food shortage problem. The reports he received on the crew's temperament were not good.

After three days Taylor began to notice small things that were very telling. Crewmen were not even trying to hit the trash receptacles any more. Wrappers and tissues were littering the floor. Taylor found half a tube of toothpaste smashed on the floor of the forward head.

It seemed cleanliness and personal hygiene was a low priority.

In one of the daily staff meetings Taylor heard about two fistfights on the messdeck. One erupted out of a *discussion* on which state had the best fried chicken and one about whether Commander Taylor's mother or father was white. Taylor couldn't believe men coming to blows over such things. "And for the record," said Taylor, "my grandma Taylor was of the pale persuasion."

By the end of their fourth day at Gare Loch he could feel the despair settling over the ship. The despondent crew was talking, sharing information and speculating, and it was all negative. Taylor could see the fear in each haunted face. They were looking to him for an answer to their desperate situation. They needed to know there was a way back, and they were not stuck forever in this strange place and time, cut off from the real world. Taylor wanted to tell them not to worry, he had a plan. But he couldn't say that, and his silence worried them even more.

Everyone suspected the truth, but they were all afraid to give voice to it. They were never going back home. In every direction Taylor saw sullen faces and thousand yard stares. He decided to get some advice. He went to Castillo, but was dismayed by what he saw.

Castillo looked like a haggard phantom of his former self. His swollen left eye was looking better, but there was a deadness to his eyes now. He was still wearing the same robe he had been wearing days ago and he was still sitting in the same chair. And from the ripeness of the air, Taylor knew he hadn't bathed. *Had he slept? Had he eaten?* Castillo turned his bearded face to Taylor and looked through him. Taylor realized he was not going to get any help from him. Castillo was in a bad place. He decided to go elsewhere.

Everywhere Taylor went crewmen avoided eye contact. Some men appeared on the edge of breaking down. This was *bad*, he thought.

He found Susan Lambert in the control room staring at the big screen. "Look!" she said. "They're going to tow us away."

On screen were three small rowboats full of men stroking hard under an overcast gun metal sky. They had thrown ropes over Kansas's stern fin and were trying to tow it.

"We're not going anywhere," said Taylor. "Our maneuvering thrusters can keep us on station against a strong current. They'll get tired and quit."

"Are you sure?"

"Yes." Taylor regarded Lambert. She looked good. He didn't see any of the inner turmoil the rest of the crew seemed to be going through. "I'm more concerned about what's going on *inside* the ship."

"I know what you mean. There's a funeral-like atmosphere."

"Aren't you concerned about our predicament?"

"Sure, but I don't think it will serve any purpose to brood on it. Our mission now is one of survival."

"Exactly! The crew needs to hear from their captain, but he seems to be pretty bad too."

"Really? I haven't seen him in a few days."

"Do you think you could talk to him? He doesn't seem to hear me at all."

Lambert nodded affirmative. "I can try."

• • •

Castillo looked at the loaded pistol sitting on his desk. Some called it the coward's way out, but he was okay with that. He knew what he was. He'd had to face the truth when he was being tortured by the Spaniard. He'd been measured and had come up short. He was not the man he'd always thought he was, a towering figure of strength. When put to the test, he'd folded like a poor poker hand. A hard thing to admit. And now he'd lost everything that had mattered to him. He'd even lost his symbolic bond to his precious wife: his wedding band. It had been on his finger since he had exchanged vows with Liz. He hadn't removed it even to shower. Now it was gone, savagely cut away along with the finger that wore it. His life was basically over. There was nothing left for him in this life. He couldn't go on.

There was a knock at the door. "Don? It's Susan. Can I come in?"

Go away, thought Castillo.

The door handle rattled. "Why's the door locked? Don? Open the door."

Leave me alone, thought Castillo.

He heard her footfalls as she left and went down the passageway. She returned after a short time, and he could hear a key click into the lock. She must have gotten a key from Taylor. He quickly pulled out his desk drawer and slid the pistol into it.

The door opened and he heard her gasp. She came to him, knelt down and said, "Don, what's happening to you?"

He only glared balefully at her.

She pulled up the guest chair and sat. "Talk to me, Don. Your crew is worried about you."

He started to talk and discovered his lips were glued together because of dryness. He wet them with his tongue, opened his mouth and croaked. His voice wasn't working either. He coughed softly, cleared his throat and said, "My crew is better off with Taylor."

"Don, your crew is falling apart. It's quite a bit for Taylor to handle. He needs help. The crew respects you."

Castillo could not hold her intense eyes. It was like looking into a pair of blue spotlights. He looked at the photographs on his desk and said, "I could have gone to work in my father-in-laws firm, you know. Civil engineering. I'd be sitting pretty right now. I could've owned it some day, but no. I was bull-headed. I wanted to be a submarine commander." He snorted derisively. "And now I've led you all to this."

"This self pity thing you're doing, doesn't do any of us any good now, Don." She took hold of his face and turned it so she was eye to eye with him. "We've all made our decisions. Some good, some bad. But we've learned from our mistakes and moved on because it doesn't help to relive them over and over." Her eyes went to his family pictures. "You have a beautiful family, Don! You can mourn them if you want, but they're not dead. They're alive somewhere! They're going to feel remorse at never seeing you again, but they will eventually recover and move on. Your little girls will grow up and have families of their own and Liz may find another man like yourself who'll be a good husband to her and a father to the girls. You have to picture them happy and living their lives. Because somewhere they are! And if they knew you were alive somewhere, they'd want you to do the same."

"But I need them."

"Yes, and they need you too. But they have lots of loving support don't they? Your wife has a sister and her parents. It's not the same as having a husband and father, but they'll move on with their lives and you'll have to do that too. You want to know who else needs you? We do!"

Castillo looked blearily at her, then down at his bandaged left hand. "You don't know what kind of man I am, Susan, or you wouldn't say that."

Lambert followed his gaze and guessed the problem. "Don, I'm a pretty good judge of character, and I think I know what kind of man you are. You're kind, intelligent, insightful, caring, generous…firm and forceful when you need to be. A leader! You came face to face with a man that was pure evil, and lesser men would never have recovered from that, but you will." Lambert's eyes began to fill and her voice suddenly got tight with emotion. "Don, do you remember when Apparition went critical and we all thought we were about to die? Everything looked very black and I was petrified to my core. We had seconds to live and were facing certain death, but I looked for deliverance, grasping desperately for anything, and I saw *you*, Don. You were standing there in the middle of the control room, calm and confident, like a shining beacon of hope, and somehow I knew we were going to come through it, and we did."

"*I* had nothing to do with…"

"Don, I'm convinced that you *did* have something to do with it. Whether it was divine intervention or fate, somehow we were *meant* to be here at this moment."

Castillo cast her a doubtful look. She could read his expression like a traffic sign.

"Okay," she said, "believe what you want. But your life isn't over. How old are you? Thirty seven? You have a new family now with 113 children, yes, even the civilians. And they regard you as the father figure. They're depending on *you*."

He looked at her and for the first time saw her in a new light. She was very smart and perceptive, and he had never before noticed how attractive she was. She had these marvelous high cheekbones and enormous expressive blue eyes and sculpted eyebrows. "You shouldn't stand so close to Crystal all the time."

She gave him a look of puzzlement.

• • •

The men trying to tow Kansas had given up. Lieutenant Tanaka watched the big screen as two men stripped down and got into the water.

"They're looking under us to see if Kansas is hung up on something," said Taylor.

Lambert walked up. "What's going on?"

"They can't figure out how Kansas is riveted to this one spot."

"I can't either," said Lambert, shrugging. "But I talked to Don this morning."

"Do any good?"

"I don't know. He's a wreck!"

"I know. I've never seen him like this." Taylor and Lambert stepped aside to allow a watchstander through. "But it's understandable. A lot of people are struggling with this. Some are in denial and think this is just a temporary thing, and we'll figure it out any day now and go back to where we belong."

"What are we going to do, Mason?" She searched Taylor's face. He had a strong chin and seemed so earnest, but a lot of Navy officers were that way. She watched him struggle for an answer.

"I don't know, Susan. I'm going day to day right now." Taylor took a step back and nearly tripped over a multimeter someone had left on the floor. "Who left this here?" He kicked at the meter, frowning. "People are getting pretty lax. It's against Navy regulations to have something like this in a passageway unattended." He glared at two nearby crewmen and one muttered something.

"What was that, Mr. Harris? Did you say something?"

The young watchstander glared insolently at Taylor. After a few seconds he broke his silence. "I said, 'What Navy?', sir. The U.S. Navy doesn't exist anymore. Not for us anyway. Why are we even bothering with watches. Look!" He pointed to the big screen as more people arrived outside on the aft deck of Kansas.

Kansas had become a bunker and they were under siege, and a siege mentality was setting in. They were all probably thinking the same thing, thought Taylor. How long could they hold out here? They were almost out of food.

Taylor heard a familiar voice coming from behind him. "The Navy may not exist for us, Mr. Harris, but your shipmates still do." It was Castillo. He was dressed in fresh khaki and the swelling had gone down in his face. "Please, pick up the meter before someone trips over it. We must be more vigilant than ever. The only ones looking out for us now is…us. We must treat each other as shipmates and something more. Family! We will obey all Navy rules and regulations unless it does not make sense to do so. Then we'll discuss it as a crew and decide if there is a better way to do something." Harris, smiled sheepishly, stood and retrieved the meter at Taylor's feet. Castillo observed the men working on Kansas's deck hatch with pry bars. "I think we're attracting too much attention here. It's time to leave, Mr. Taylor. Set the maneuvering watch."

"Yes, sir," chuckled Taylor. "What's the matter? Couldn't find a razor?" He reached out and touched Castillo's stubbly face.

"I want all crew members to stop shaving immediately. We're going to have to fit in with the locals here. How many do you see that are clean shaven?" He pointed at the bearded men outside working on Kansas's hatch.

"Good idea," said Taylor. He picked up a receiver and dialed to the address system and said, "Attention all hands! Attention all hands! Set maneuvering watch! Set the maneuvering watch!"

Lambert went up to Castillo and smiled. "You look better. How's your eye?"

"It still hurts, but it works."

• • •

When Kansas began to move under the men, their first reaction was one of amazement. A few men jumped into the water, but nine men stayed on deck and cast perplexing looks at each other. The ship silently did a pirouette, slowly turning 180 degrees until its bow was pointing south. Then it began forward motion. The men riding Kansas saw a frothing angry white trail stirring behind the ship. It was such a frightening sight, seven men jumped off, but two stayed. As Kansas picked up speed, the small barnwood skiffs tied to Kansas's tailfin began to bobble and collide on the boiling water. Two of the skiffs broke apart and the third filled with water and the line holding it snapped. The two remaining men on Kansas's aft deck hunkered down and pulled their coats tighter against the stiff breeze coming down the deck.

After a time something truly amazing happened. A voice spoke to them from above. "Hey!"

They looked up to see two men at the top of the tower behind them. Where had they come from? They were talking to them, but at first they didn't understand them. Were they speaking English?

"Name…Casteeyo…yours?"

I think he wants to know our names, thought one. "I bae Will," he said. "An' 'e bae Kevin."

The man on the tower said something else he didn't understand. He was speaking English, but he had a funny accent. Something about *inside*. Inside what? Then another amazing thing happened. A round door opened about ten feet away and a man stuck his head up and beckoned to them.

"Thahr bae a man in 'er, Kev," said Will with astonishment. "wot think yae?"

"Daemon cast, Will. A trick!"

"Look not a daemon tae me."

"See many, do yae?"

Will jumped up and went up to the round hole and looked in. There was a man there with his hand extended. Will edged closer cautiously and looked down into the hole and saw a ladder made of metal and a floor down below. And he could see the face of a pretty lass smiling up at him.

"Dinna do 't, Will!" screamed Kevin hysterically. "Bae a trick!"

Will took the offered hand and stepped onto the ladder and descended.

Kevin fretted and scowled, but finally got up and went to the hole too.

• • •

"You're on a ship," said Lambert a little too loudly as if they were deaf. They only stared back at her dumbly. One of them rapped knuckles on a bulkhead as if testing it. The other stared in slack-jawed awe at an overhead light.

"I recognize these guys," said Tanaka. "They were the first to find us and explore."

"Maybe that's why they were the last to leave." Then to the nearest one, she asked, "Why didn't you jump?"

"We kinna swim," he replied.

Lambert decided that these boys didn't have much. The one in the black woolen sweater had holes in the knees of his pants and in the elbows of his sweater. His right boot was held together with several wrappings of twine. His name was Will. The other one, Kevin, had a gray coat of heavy canvas-like material with patches sewn over the holes. They had stubbled, dirty faces and smelled like a barnyard. Maybe everyone was malodorous in this century. The boys…if they were boys…they seemed young, 17 maybe…were different in their demeanor. Will smiled a broad smile at her with a space where there should be an incisor, whereas Kevin looked grimly about him, distrustful of everything. She would bet that they're brothers. They had the same fine flaxen hair and ruddy complexions.

"Are you hungry?" She asked them. "Would you like to eat?"

They seemed to understand that fine. Kevin brightened slightly. She led them down the passageway and down a ladder to the messdeck, only losing them once when they passed a large computer screen. They stared in reverence at the bright display with symbols, numbers and letters streaming across it.

"Hell's 'ammer!" said Will. "What bae?"

"That's a status screen," said Lambert. "It helps us run the ship." She could tell by his look that he had no idea what that meant.

"Yahr speech bae strange. Wot country yae?" asked Kevin suspiciously.

Here we go, thought Lambert. "We are from a powerful ally of Scotland. The United States of America." She beckoned to McConnell. "We have several Scots on board. See this lady? Her name is Crystal McConnell."

Kevin's face lit up. "Of Tess McConnell's clan in Doogan?"

"Sorry, no," Crystal replied sweetly. "Different clan."

When they reached the messdeck, they were too early for dinner, but chef warmed them two helpings of barley beef stew he had in the refrigerator. They ate it hungrily with saltines. The chef decided they deserved seconds. They repeated the disappearing act!

Chapter 10

Simms and Castillo were on Kansas's sail in the bridge well, navigating down Gare Loch under an overcast sky. Castillo's hot swollen face felt better in the chill breeze. His left eye was almost fully open now although it was still watering. His disfigured hand was giving him the most pain. He felt sharp stabbing pain in the fingers no longer there.

"Let's hole up in Holy Loch," said Simms. "It's fairly isolated."

"That sounds good," said Castillo.

"So…are we completely out of food?"

"Well, not really. Chef says he has plenty of flour and sugar, but we're just about out of any kind of fresh vegetables, chicken, beef, that type of thing."

"Well," said Simms. "We might try hunting for meat. There are deer in the Argyll Forest." He pointed toward shore.

"Hunting? Sure. We could try that. I'm hoping our two local lads can help us with locating the best markets where we can procure produce."

"With what? We don't have anything to barter with."

"True," shrugged Castillo.

"These two young men probably think they've been *impressed*."

Castillo looked questioningly at Simms. "Impressed?"

"A few hundred years ago, the British Admiralty was allowed to *impress* able-bodied men to serve on his majesty's ships. It's the only way they could man them all. They *shanghaied* men from surrounding villages."

"Really? They were allowed to do that legally?"

"Oh yes. It was their version of the military draft."

"I'll have a talk with these two young men and assure them, they're not being kidnapped."

"Do you intend to release them?"

"Of course. After we get as much information as we can from them."

"They'll tell everyone about their adventure on Kansas."

"Probably. But it can't be helped. I don't think they'll be believed, but if they are, we're not a big secret anymore."

"Do you have a plan, commander?" Simms studied Castillo's face.

"I have a rough start to a plan, but I need to discuss it with the crew. I think we'll have a meeting tonight."

• • •

Castillo was getting ready for his all hands briefing when there was a knock. It was Susan Lambert.

"I have someone I'd like you to meet." She escorted Will and Kevin in and introduced them.

When Castillo shook their hands he couldn't help but notice their calluses. These were boys who worked.

"How old are you boys?" he asked.

"I'm 15 'n' two 'n' Kev's 16 'n' fahr, yahr lahrdship."

Lambert chuckled.

"Don't lord, me," said Castillo. "Just Don. I'm not sure what you just said, but I think someone is going to miss you boys. We should get you home."

The one called Will looked pained. "Ahr da was teeken by the press gang last yahr. And ahr ma's gone, Sahr Don. The gang ceeme back fahr us, but wae wahrn't thahr. They'll git us shore next visit."

"So…what you're saying is you have no family and this impressment squad is out to abduct you?" summarized Castillo.

Will looked perplexed. "Is 'at wo' I said?"

Kevin finally spoke up. "Wae've a sister, Maggie, but she lives wi' the duke."

"Could we stay on Kanzits?" pleaded Will. "Wahr good men, sahr. And 'is *is* a ship."

"But wo' kind o' ship has nae sails 'n' nae wood?" asked Kevin.

"'N' howzit go?" asked Will. "'N' 'o toed it?"

"Whoa!" said Castillo. "Too many questions." He looked at Lambert and said, "Could you take responsibility for these guys temporarily?"

Lambert rolled her eyes. "Okay."

"All righty then. Miss Lambert here will be your mother while your aboard. You can stay with us for awhile and contribute by being our liaison with the local community, and you'll do everything Miss Lambert or I tell you to do. Agreed?"

Castillo caught Lambert's look. She raised her eyebrows and mouthed the word 'mother?' Castillo smiled at her. She stuck out her tongue at him.

"I've no scone wo' yae said," said Will. "'cept aboot mindin' yae 'n' Miss Lambert. I agree! How 'boot yae, Kev?"

"Agree," said Kevin.

Castillo shook both their hands, smiling. Lambert glared at him.

• • •

That evening the entire crew of Kansas assembled. All 113 men and women. They filled the messdeck and the adjoining wardroom and the galley and both passageways. People were crammed into every adjoining space, even the food pantries. There were five men sitting on the steam tables and four were on the floor crammed under tables. The passageways were full in both directions. Every man on the ship was within earshot, but Castillo decided to use the overhead address system anyway. This was an important meeting.

He squeezed his way through the crowd to the front of the messdeck. There was applause when he entered. He held his arms up in acknowledgement and smiled so broadly his chubby cheeks eclipsed his eyes. They were mere slits.

He wore a small headset with an outrigger microphone. He touched a switch on his belt and said, "Test, test, test." His voice spoke loudly from over the speakers in the ceiling.

"I don't know," he began, "how to thank you guys for getting me back from the bad guys. I'm forever grateful, and I could never have asked for a better crew. And I'm going to do my best for you."

"But," said someone, "we didn't get you *all* back, skipper."

"You got *most* of me back," said Castillo, holding up his bandaged hand. "I never used these fingers much anyway." There was laughter. "We have two guests aboard." He indicated Will and Kevin sitting nearby. "Stand up, boys." They got to their feet and Will waved. "This is Will and Kevin Kincaid from the village of Glasbergen. Did I get that right, guys?" Will nodded, smiling. "They're going to help us with procuring food and other supplies from the local community."

Castillo shifted gears and his expression became serious. "*Those were the best years of our lives!* How often have we heard that expression? And just exactly when were the best years of our lives? Well, we don't know, of course, until our lives are almost over, and then we can look back and say, 'The best years of my life were those I spent in college. Or those raising my children. Or those I spent in Europe.'" He took a deep breath before he continued. "We are facing a situation no other Navy ship has ever faced before to my knowledge. We're cut off from the world we once knew and I'm afraid there's no way back. And although we'll never see our loved ones again, we can take solace in the fact that they're alive and living their lives somewhere, happy hopefully." A tear formed in his eye and began to roll down his cheek. "Our mission is now one of survival. There's a strong temptation to look back and say, 'those were the best years of our lives.'"

Castillo looked around the room at all the hopeful faces and caught Lambert's eye. "But as a friend reminded me recently, we're not at the end yet! It's too early to quit. Our loved ones would want us to go on. We are *family* now. The Kansas family. And like family's everywhere, we are going to give thanks and celebrate and mourn together. It won't be easy surviving in this new world. The struggles we face will try us and cause us to despair but they will also bond us and make us stronger. We will work through our problems and look to the future. But…beyond being a family, we are also a culture. We're the most advanced culture with the most incredible technology on the planet. We're the only ones in this world who've ever heard of Starbucks, the Internet or the Beatles. We should try to preserve our culture as long as possible, although that is going to become increasingly more difficult."

Castillo extracted a tissue from his khakis and wiped at his eyes. "Our world is powered by a nuclear reactor. It has enough fuel for 30 more years. That seems like a lot, but 30 years will go by before you know it. We need to start making plans now. We need to establish a base of operations somewhere and we have the means to go anywhere in the world. I'll be taking suggestions and then we'll take a vote." Castillo pulled a piece of notebook paper out of his breast pocket and glanced at it. "Oh yes. I encourage you all to *read*. We have a lot of ereaders and an ebook library with almost a million books in it. The Navy in their attempt to determine reading tastes, threw in the towel and gave us just about everything. Storage is not an issue with ebooks. We have books on farming, hunting, horticulture, carpentry. We have medical texts, engineering texts, music books. Pick a subject that interests you, preferably something that will help us set up a thriving new colony and start reading everything you can on it, and take good notes. When the power goes out in 30 years, we will lose this knowledge base."

Castillo looked at his notes again. Then he turned to the Kincaid boys. "Will, Kevin what do people here eat normally?"

"Uh…" Will scratched his arm and twisted his face in thought. "Krip, 'aggis, cabbage, poots, beetroot, beef."

"Condus and tack," added Kevin and Will nodded in acknowledgement.

Castillo shook his head in bewilderment and there were a few chuckles. "I guess I asked for that. What we're interested in is vegetables. You mentioned cabbage and beetroot. We want to get some of that and whatever greens you eat. For meat we're going to try hunting."

"'ahr bae 'art and 'are near 'ere," volunteered Will. "Mae 'n' Kev could show yae. But wae dinna 'ave ahr 'untin' bows."

"That's okay we have something better than hunting bows. We would appreciate your assistance however in locating game Chief Brown is heading that group and he'll also need help with the transporting and butchering of the game. I'm hoping we'll have enough to feed the boat and some left over to trade in the market for vegetables. We're figuring this out as we go."

Castillo looked down at his notes again. "Uh… Lieutenant Tanaka is forming a garbage detail. He may recruit some of you to help with that. And…what else…oh yes…if any of you go ashore and we have a situation that requires a hasty departure, we will sound the ship's horn. When you hear the horn, you'll have 15 minutes to get back. So if you go ashore, stay within earshot of the boat."

Castillo folded his notepaper and stuck it back in the pocket of his khakis. "Are there any questions?"

Lieutenant Guerrero asked, "Are we no longer concerned about our footprint in the event timeline?"

Castillo's forehead furrowed and his lips formed a tight thin line. "Yes and no. I think we need to be concerned about the Star Trek prime directive and all that, but the only way to reduce our impact on these people to zero or to negate our impact in history is to make this ship and her crew disappear off the planet. I don't know how to do that. And I don't think you good people deserve that. You deserve the opportunity to live out peaceful fulfilling lives…as citizens in a new society. We'll have to carefully plan each encounter with the locals. As I already said, we're figuring this out as we go." Castillo looked around the room. "Any more questions?"

After a few seconds, a young man said, "If we're to become a village, we're pretty lopsided gender-wise. Not enough women."

There were some murmurs. "A good point! A very good point!" answered Castillo. "We'll have to fix that, but short of abducting a boatload of women, I'm not sure how just yet." He heard Lambert giggle. "But I'm open to suggestions." He looked around. "Any more questions?"

"How fair, sahr?" asked Will Kincaid, a frown on his features.

"Sorry. How fair?"

"How fair from the…fuchore 'ave yae come?" He said the word *future* as if it were a foreign concept.

"Oh! Well, let's see." Castillo put a finger to his lips, then, "Let me put it into perspective for you. If you had children and they grew to adulthood. And they had children and grew to adulthood. You would have about 13 generations added to your family before you reached our time. That's about 426 years."

"426 yahrs! Hell's 'ammer!" Will looked to Kevin, astonishment on both their faces.

• • •

The following morning there seemed to be a change in the atmosphere aboard Kansas. Crew members walked with a purpose and greeted each other with genuine warmth. They all seemed to understand that they were in this thing together...for the long haul. This was not a short term commitment, and it was not going to be easy, but they had a challenge facing them and they would not shy from it. Their captain was back and they had a new confidence. The same kind of confidence a championship team has when they know they have all the talent in the league.

Maria Guerrero decided they needed to act more like a family so she organized the very first Kansas family activity. They had a picnic on the beach. Kansas's two 15 foot inflatables acted as ferries shuttling crewmen to shore. Once on shore they spread sheets and drop cloths and made tuna salad sandwiches with the last of their canned tuna. They drank iced tea and when one crewman produced a soccer ball, they erected a makeshift volleyball net between two trees and chose up sides. By the time Castillo arrived the sun had come out and many men stripped off their shirts and enjoyed the feeling of the sun on their backs and chests. Castillo heard something from his crew he had not heard in a long time. Laughter.

He walked down the beach which was not composed of sand, but fine smooth brown and gray pebbles. Small gray and yellow birds chirped greeting and watched him from adjacent trees. He saw Susan Lambert and Lauren Gastmeyer walking barefoot down the sunlit beach, ducking an occasional overhanging branch. Every few feet they would stop, stoop and examine something.

"Hello, ladies!" called Castillo, coming up from behind.

"Hi, Don," said Lambert shading her eyes.

"Beautiful day, isn't it?" remarked Gastmeyer.

"It is. What are you finding?"

"We were looking for shells," replied Lambert. "We found a few. See?" She held out a hand with a few nut-colored periwinkles.

"Good ones," said Castillo.

"And we found these things. Not sure what they are." Lambert held out some flat white bony-looking objects about the size of a cell phone.

"I don't know," said Castillo picking up one and turning it over.

"Norm would probably know. He knows everything," said Lambert. "He wasn't able to come."

"How's his leg?" asked Castillo.

"Bad. I don't know if he can even walk anymore." The wind blew her sandy hair into her eyes, and she finger-combed it back into place.

"It's kind of ironic," said Castillo, "that the smartest guy on board is also our least capable physically."

"Yes." Lauren Gastmeyer walked on ahead, Lambert fell back and walked side by side with Castillo. "Have you noticed the change in the crew?" said Lambert. "It's just like someone flipped a switch."

"They just needed to see there's a tomorrow for them," said Castillo. "I showed them a future. The same as you did for me." He turned to Lambert and a lump formed in his throat. "I've never properly thanked you, Susan." He looked down at her small bare toes, then back up. "I was in a…lonely place. The future for me looked…pretty grim, and I didn't want to go on. I was weak, but you found me in the darkness and gave me strength. You led me out of my emotional wilderness. Thank you, Susan! That's twice you've rescued me. You're a true friend."

Lambert chuckled softly, her bright eyes watery and sad. "The strength was all yours, Don. I just gave you a gentle shove."

There was a moment shared between them that did not require words. They walked down the beach watching shore birds running in the shallow water, occasionally dipping their beaks. Then they were both distracted by the laughter of a woman coming from just beyond the bend. It put Castillo in mind of a whinnying horse. One of those small cute miniature horses with beautiful mane and tail. When they came to the bend, they saw a smiling Crystal McConnell laying on a blanket with someone. She punched at him playfully.

"I don't believe I've ever heard Crystal laugh before," said Castillo.

"She doesn't laugh very often," offered Lambert.

Castillo shaded his eyes trying to see who was with her. A figure waved at them. It was Mason Taylor. Castillo and Lambert waved back.

"There's something there," said Lambert. "She started asking about him a few days ago. You know. 'Is Commander Taylor married? Is he seeing anyone? How old is he?'"

Castillo thought about this. "But I thought you and Crystal were…" He stopped, realizing that he had already gone too far with the thought, and there was no taking it back.

"Crystal and I were what?" asked Lambert.

"Nothing! I was just…" Castillo felt tongue-tied.

Abruptly it dawned on Lambert what he was trying to say. "You thought Crystal and I were lovers?" Her eye brows flew up, her eyes bulged and she began to laugh. It was a hearty laugh and it seemed to get the attention of everyone within ear shot.

Castillo colored and said, "You two are always together, so I just thought."

She stopped walking and placed fists on her hips. Her body language spoke volumes. "I was thinking the same thing about you and Commander Taylor," she said. "You two are always together too. Anything going on between you two?"

Castillo scratched at the bandage on his left hand, then mumbled, "I'm a pig."

She stabbed him in the chest with her finger. "And don't you forget it." Castillo winced and grabbed her finger. "Oh! I'm sorry." Lambert's face tightened. "I forgot about your wounds. Did I hurt you?"

"No. Just my self image. I've always thought of myself as being objective and professional. Ouch!"

• • •

Chief Brown recommended going at night on their hunting expedition. They would have an advantage with their infrared vision and rifle scopes. Brown hand-picked two men and the three of them along with the Kincaid brothers and Crystal McConnell went ashore. McConnell handled the sniper rifle and Brown carried a SEAL MP-5 assault rifle. The Kincaids proved their worth as guides by locating several groups of deer. When the night was over, they had taken five deer. The Kincaids proved their worth again as experts at cleaning and butchering the animals. They ferried the meat back to Kansas and loaded it into Kansas's cold storage. Chef Jonesy was very pleased with the quality of the venison. He decided to keep half of it. They would trade the other half.

The Kincaids were farm boys and had been working on a dairy farm outside of Glasbergen. As such, they knew where the best markets were and helped the Kansas crew get their venison to market. They borrowed a horse and cart and took two hundred pounds of venison in to the town market. Castillo wanted to send an armed escort with them, but he thought it would attract too much attention, so he equipped them with remote comm units. They returned with several hundred pounds of vegetables. There was a root vegetable called crall which looked like a turnip and there were garden greens called eggweed and a large wheel of cheddar cheese and a wooden drum of flour and a keg of ale. Their trip proved so successful, they decided to repeat it the following day. This time they returned with squash, tea, milk, eggs and a keg of whiskey.

Castillo had mixed feelings about the alcohol being brought aboard. He knew it was inevitable in a society to have social drinking, but he would like his crew to stay sharp in case they needed to do some critical maneuvering or other functions. He decided it would be okay for those not actually on watch to sample the ale and whiskey, but only on the messdeck. No alcohol in the berthing or work spaces. Everyone agreed.

They mounted two more hunting parties and brought back deer, rabbit and some large crane-like birds. They were getting better at stalking and bringing down game. Castillo was beginning to feel his crew could do anything. Maybe we should try fishing, he thought. He'd seen fishing boats out on the firth. He ordered Lieutenant Anderson to come up with a plan.

He encountered a crewmen carrying a tray down the hallway one afternoon. On it he had a large bowl of stew, buttered biscuits and a glass of ale.

"Holy Mackerel! Who is it getting room service?" asked Castillo.

"This is for Mr. Bloomberg, sir."

"Oh, I see." Castillo hadn't seen Norm Bloomberg in a while. "Give it to me. I'll take it to him." He took the tray down the passageway to Bloomberg's stateroom. Bloomberg was reclining in his rack and reading as always. Castillo rapped on the door frame. "Hi, Norm. How's the knee."

"Don't ask," replied Bloomberg grimacing. "I can still manage to make it to the head, but that's about it. I don't know what will happen when I can't even do that anymore."

Castillo sat the tray next to Bloomberg's rack, and regarded him. A smaller man would be able to get around by hopping on one foot, but a man Bloomberg's size probably couldn't.

Bloomberg promptly sampled the stew. "This chef of yours, Jonesy, is amazing. You could give him possum and he would turn it into cordon bleu!"

"He's a culinary artist."

"How's your hand, sir?"

"Oh, as good as can be expected I guess." Castillo had his bandages off. He held up his left hand and displayed the two stubs where his pinkie and ring fingers should be. They had been cut off between the hand and first knuckle of each finger. The phantom pains were still strong and at times he could feel ants crawling on the missing fingers. "Why would a person do something like that?"

"Part of the national mentality, I suppose," replied Bloomberg.

"Say again?"

"You have to remember the Spanish Inquisition is in full swing right now."

"The Spanish Inquisition?"

"Yes, remember that from the history books? It was established by Queen Isabella and Pope Sixtus, the fourth. Originally it was intended to find Jews and other non-Christians, but expanded to include all non-Catholics. Spain tortured and killed thousands during this period. They were a very paranoid culture. They didn't trust anything or anyone who wasn't Catholic. They were determined to root out all enemies of Spain."

"By torturing suspects?" Castillo looked skeptical.

"They believed it worked. The thinking was that if a person was guilty, he would confess, but if he was a good God-fearing person, well then God would help him withstand the torture. And of course, if a person confessed, they were justified in sentencing him to death."

My God, thought Castillo, Spain must be a whole nation of psychopaths.

"So when this Spaniard picked you up, the first thing he wanted to do was find out if you were an enemy of Spain, so he put you to the tried and true test."

"He never even asked me. He just accused me of being in league with the Devil and forced me to admit it."

"Well…same thing. Anyone who's an enemy of Spain is in the employ of Satan since God loves and protects Spain."

"I wonder how many people withstood this type of torture."

"Not many, I'm thinking. They were able to get a confession out of nearly everyone who went before the Grand Inquisitor." Bloomberg took a spoonful of stew and a sip of ale. "This ale is excellent! Your Scottish lads did well, sir."

"They're good boys!"

"King Phillip, the second, of Spain wanted to spread his holy war all over Europe and he almost succeeded. There was only one thing that stopped him. He sent his mighty Armada against England with instructions to crush them, but they got their asses kicked by the English fleet commanded by Lord Howard and Sir Francis Drake."

"The Spaniard kept asking me if I was working with Drake and the Godless queen."

"The Godless queen. Yes, that would be the protestant queen of England, Queen Elizabeth. Actually the Armada thing's happening right now. August 1588!"

"Really? Right now? Wow, we could actually go see it. One of the greatest naval battles in history."

Susan Lambert trotted in and gasped, "Don, Will Kincaid just called in. He and Kevin are on their way in, but they're being pursued. He thinks it's either the English press gang or reavers. He's not sure."

"Okay, we better go give them an escort."

"Oh, Don," wailed Lambert. "They're going to be captured."

"Not on my watch. Come on." They bolted out of the room, down the passageway and to the control room. Castillo turned to Lieutenant Guerrero and said, "Sound the horn. Recall all crew."

"Aye, sir," replied Guerrero. "Recalling crew."

"Tanaka, hand pick five men, issue MP-5's and meet me on deck. The Kincaids are coming in hot. They're going to need help."

"Yessir!" Tanaka sprang from his chair and started barking orders. "Harrison, Douglas, Ford, McReady, Phillips. Follow me!"

Chapter 11

When they had assembled on the aft deck, Tanaka and his hand-picked squad launched in an inflatable for the far shore. Several crewmen were standing on the beach having heard the blast of the ship's horn.

Lambert, Castillo and Taylor all stood and watched them go. They all wore headsets so they could keep track of the action. They heard Will's voice: "I dinna think wae're gonna meek it, Miss Susan!"

"Hang on, Will," cried Susan. "We have an armed escort coming to meet you." Her tight mouth expressed her upset.

"Try not to kill anybody, Tanaka," said Castillo.

"I'll try, sir," came Tanaka's voice in Castillo's ear.

• • •

Kevin Kincaid was trying to squeeze more speed out of the little horse drawing their cart, but he was already at full gallop. They were beginning to lose some of their load as they bumped violently down the rutted road.

Two boxes of beets had fallen off the back of the cart and spread litter on the path behind them. It didn't seem to slow their pursuers though.

He turned and saw the four horsemen coming… no…there were five now. The one in the lead was riding a large black and swinging a heavy wooden cudgel, and his eyes were dark and his lips were set in a grim line. He would be on them before they ever reached the loch. Kevin knew help was coming from Kanzits. He could hear Will talking to them over the air talker Miss Susan had given them. The wind pried at his coat and he felt the first drops of rain on his face from the heavy-looking clouds. Just what we need, thought Kevin. Rain!

The pursuers were coming very fast now. Kevin was pretty sure they were outlaws, not government men. They looked too rough to be English. Will stood up and flung a large beet at the one in the lead, but he easily ducked it. He was almost on them now. He could hear the large black horse snorting and its hoofs thundering. Will picked up another beet and threw it and almost lost his balance. Their little horse was tired and slowing. He was not a runner.

The man on the black pulled up next to Kevin and took a swing at him with his cudgel. Kevin ducked it. Then there was another rider on a thundering, blowing chestnut on the other side of the cart next to Will. The rider rode up next to their little horse reached over and grabbed his halter. He pulled on the halter and slowed the cart to a gradual stop. Soon they were surrounded by tough-looking men on horseback.

"Wahr yer off to in such a 'urry, lads?" said the leader dismounting. He began poking and prodding at the produce in the cart with his cudgel. "'o yer werk fer, boy?" When he didn't get an answer from Kevin, he reached up and drug him from the cart. Kevin lost his balance and went sprawling in the dirt.

Will jumped down and ran to his brother. "Leave us bae. Wae weren't derin' yae any hahrm," he said defiantly. A man behind Will hit him behind the head with a club and sent him to his knees. Will shook his head trying to clear his vision and his foggy brain.

POP!

A geyser of dirt kicked up next to the leader's foot. Shocked, he looked to his left and saw six men at the turn in the road running toward them. They were carrying something rod-like. Too small to be rifles. Then one raised his rod-like weapon.

POP!

Another patch of ground sprayed a geyser of dirt. They *were* rifles! But the rain began to come down harder and the bandit knew no gun could fire when it was wet. He threw down his cudgel, yanked Will to his feet, took out a large knife and held it to Will's throat. "Stee back!" he screamed. "Or Ay'll slit 'is throat!" The armed men slowed to a walk, but continued advancing with weapons leveled. "Stee back, Ay say!"

The leader of the armed men began talking. "Let the boys go and you'll live. Harm them and you die. Do you understand?"

He talks with a strange accent and has the look of an oriental, thought the lead bandit. No matter, it was now raining so hard, a firearm wouldn't work. "Lee down yer weepons! Now!"

"I'll say it again. Let the boys go and you live. Harm them and you'll die! Do you understand?"

The stalemate lasted long seconds, neither side moving or blinking, rain dribbling down off noses and chins. The armed leader began talking in a very low voice. Evidently he was murmuring to the man standing to his right. Two could play that game. The lead bandit nodded to the man on the chestnut who then began inching his hand down toward his belt. The armed leader continued to murmur to his man. Abruptly the man on horseback drew a knife, drew back his arm and…

POP!

He clutched his chest and fell off his horse. The leader of the armed men quickly swung his firearm back at Will's captor. The men on horseback expressed alarm and two of them wheeled their mounts around and raced off, leaving only Will's captor, one man on horseback and the wounded man writhing in the mud. *Special guns that fire when wet!* The armed leader began murmuring again at the man next to him. His murmuring was beginning to infuriate Will's captor. "Got anythahn' to see to yer lad 'ere afore he dies, eh?"

"I'm warning you," said the gunman.

Will's captor tilted Will's head back and slowly began to draw the knife across. A stream of blood started flowing down.

POP!

Will's captor gasped and dropped the knife. The bullet had passed through his right elbow.

"Will, Kevin, get back in the cart and go," said Tanaka. "We'll hold these guys here."

Kevin got shakily to his feet but Will was still suffering from the blow to his head and he had blood streaming down his front from the cut on his neck. "Douglas, go with them. Make sure they make it to the boat." One of the men slung his weapon and helped Kevin and then Will up onto the cart. He climbed up and took the reins, and they trotted off down the path.

The squad held guns on the bandits until the cart had disappeared around the bend, then they slowly backed away from them until they judged they were out of danger. They turned their backs and began to jog away down the path. When they had almost reached the bend in the road, they heard hoofbeats.

Looking back, the leader said, "Uh oh. We've got company!"

• • •

"I showed them a movie last night on my laptop," said Lambert. "*High Noon* with Gary Cooper. I thought they should learn a little about our culture. It was a good start."

"How did they like it?" asked Castillo.

"They loved it! Of course, at first they kept looking behind the screen trying to figure out where the picture was coming from, but eventually they became absorbed by the story. I provided a running commentary."

"Good!"

"They want to see a movie every night now."

"We have plenty in the library."

"Yes, but...*Oh! There they are!*" Lambert pointed excitedly.

The horse and cart came quickly down the path to the water's edge.

"Oh no! Will's hurt, Don. He's bleeding," cried Lambert, her voice tight with emotion.

Then Tanaka and his squad came jogging down the path. They all heard Tanaka's voice in their earpieces, "Go! Go! Riders are coming!" The Kincaids got down along with their escort. They looked briefly at the produce in the back of the cart. "Forget the vegetables!" screamed Tanaka. "Get back to the boat!"

The Kincaids climbed into the inflatable which already had four people in it. A man fired up the small propane outboard and they were away. Tanaka and his men turned to face the oncoming riders and leveled their weapons. As soon as the six horsemen came into view they pulled their horses up, bewildered by what they were seeing. There were six armed men confronting them at the water's edge and a large black object floating about 200 yards out in the loch. *What the hell?* There were people standing on it and a small boat full of people was gliding toward it. The small boat had neither oarsmen nor sails.

The horsemen quickly dismounted and ducked behind trees.

"God!" said Lambert. "I'm a wreck!"

Just then an archer shot from behind a tree. The shaft went through Kevin's upper arm. He cringed, twisted, lost his balance and fell into the water. He began flailing at the surface of the water in fear. Tanaka's squad opened fire on the horsemen.

POP!POP!POP! POP!POP!POP! POP!POP!

Lambert screamed in dismay, then she seemed to go through a transformation. She narrowed her eyes, tucked her lower lip and took on an intense look of determination. She pulled off her headset, her shoes, stripped off her light jacket and began running in her bare feet down the deck. She ran faster and faster until her legs were a blur. She was totally focused on what she had to do. Like an Olympic gymnast making a run at the vault, she was going for gold. She flew down Kansas's sloping deck and launched into the water like a spear. For long seconds she was under the water. Castillo looked for her but saw not a ripple. When finally she broke the surface, she was halfway to Kevin. She began pulling hard with long powerful strokes. She was at his side in four seconds.

"My God!" said Castillo. "She's Superman!"

When the shooting stopped, two of the horsemen lay wounded, and the others came out from behind trees with hands raised…the universal sign of surrender.

Lambert pulled Kevin to Kansas using the lifeguard's side carry. When they bumped the hull, eager hands reached for her and Kincaid, pulling them up onto the deck. Chief Brown snapped off both ends of the arrow piercing Kincaids arm, leaving the center of the shaft still in the arm. This was so they could transport him below deck. When Will Kincaid arrived, Lambert flew to him and examined his throat wound. He appeared dazed and weak.

"I think the wound looks worse than it is," said Lambert. She spoke into her headset, "Maria, tell Doc he has two wounded coming down to him."

"Okay, Susan. I'll alert him," answered Guerrero.

• • •

Doc Aultman cleaned the Kincaid's wounds, dressed them and started them on a course of antibiotics and anti inflammatories. The arrow wound could have been much worse. It missed the brachial artery and the major nerves of Kevin's arm. He expressed the opinion that Kevin would get full use of the arm again if he did some physical therapy.

Kevin didn't know what that was, but he readily agreed to it.

Will pulled a paper from his pocket and unfolded it. "Wae dinna read well, but wae think this is aboot Kanzits, Miss Susan."

Lambert took the paper and scanned it. "I think you're right, Will. I'd better show this to the captain."

The door to Castillo's stateroom was closed. She started to knock but stopped. She heard voices inside. No. It was only one voice. Castillo's. He was discussing something in hushed tones. Her curiosity got the better of her, and she placed an ear to the door and began to eavesdrop.

"I'm sorry, Liz, Robin, Kelly. You'll always be at the center of my universe. It's so hard to go on without you."

He's talking to his family, thought Lambert.

"I know…I know…it's not fair…"

Are they answering him?

"Listen to your mother, girls. And, Kelly, don't get so mad with your sister when she uses your art set. Yours has more colors than hers…and…what's that? No, I'm going to be busy…"

My God! He's carrying on an imaginary conversation with the family he left behind.

"I'll always hold you in my heart, but there are people here who need me. I've got to help them…and… no…I won't be coming home, sweetheart."

What's Castillo's state of mind? Is he fit to command? Is this normal for a man who's just lost his family? Lambert didn't know. She wasn't an expert at these things.

A crewman turned the corner and came down the passageway toward her. Lambert composed herself, cleared her throat and knocked gently on the door. When the door opened, she was staring into Castillo's red-rimmed eyes. "Look at what Will found," she said thrusting the paper into Castillo's hands.

"*The Watch.* What's this?" asked Castillo.

"It's what passes for a newspaper in this century. They sell these things in the market for a half pence. I think it's printed in Glasgow. Read this article here." She pointed.

"Okay." He sniffed and sat heavily into his desk chair.

Fishermen have reported strange sitings in Gare Loch of late. Is there a

> monster in Gare Loch? Ned McPhee
> says yes. It is as big as a cathyedral
> tower and as blacke as a witch's heart,
> says Ned. He and Bill Gentry clymbed
> up on its back and tried to subdue it
> Sundae, but it thrashed the water with
> its powerful tail and cawsed them both
> to fall off. It escaped, according to Ned
> and Bill, but not before it devowred two
> men. We are not of mind whether this
> monster is borne of nature or of Ned
> and Bill's fevered imaginings after a
> nite at the pub, but it makes a grande
> storie.

Castillo shook his head. "We're starting to attract attention. It's time for us to move on."

"I don't think these guys are going to be believed."

"No, but it's a start. And there was that skirmish today with those highwaymen. The curious will come to see what's going on. We've already overstayed our welcome here." He picked up the receiver next to his desk and got Mason Taylor. "Have we recovered all ship's company…who're we missing…okay…as soon as they're aboard, set the maneuvering watch. We're leaving."

"Where're we going?" asked Lambert.

"I'm not sure."

"Have you received any suggestions from the crew?"

"A few." Castillo began to count them on fingers on his right hand. "They want to set up shop in Tahiti, Virginia, Bermuda or Pitcairn Island."

"Pitcairn Island? Isn't that…"

"Yes. Mutiny on the Bounty. When the mutineers wanted to disappear and never be found, they went to Pitcairn Island in the South Pacific. It was uncharted, but it had fresh water and game. They lived there for 150 years before anyone found them."

"Do we want to disappear?" asked Lambert.

"I think we do. Do you know what attracted attention at the market. The Kincaids told Doc it was ice."

"Ice?"

"Everyone wanted to know where they got the ice in the summer to pack the meat in. Little things we do draw attention. If we don't find a remote area, we're going to spur curiosity and get endless questions. And what's worse, if evil men find out the capabilities of this ship, they will stop at nothing to possess it. What do *you* think?"

"I think you're right. Maybe we should seriously consider Pitcairn Island. If we set up there, we would beat the Bounty mutineers by 200 years."

"But what will our descendants do," asked Castillo, "when the Bounty crew shows up?"

"Welcome them!"

"Yeh?"

"Yeh!" nodded Lambert.

"Okay. But we've got a lot to learn. We're children of a modern age and depend too much on technology. We'll have it much harder than the other people of this period. For example, most of us have no idea how to make fire without matches. We're good hunters, but that's because we have guns. Eventually we'll run out of ammo, then what kind of hunters will we be? We've got a lot to overcome."

"We can do it. I'm sure we can, Don." She gave him a measuring glance before continuing. "How are you doing? I mean emotionally."

"Oh…I don't know." Castillo took a deep breath. "Are you my psychiatrist now?"

"No. Just a concerned friend. You're our…head of family now. And we worry because you've suffered a great loss and on top of that captured and tortured. Enough to break many men."

"I am broken, Susan," Castillo said sadly.

"I know it's too early for closure…"

"Closure," snorted Castillo. "What's that? A word made up by psychologists. It means *get over it* and *heal from it*. Well, I'll never heal from it. I will carry a scar deep within me forever. But that's good because to heal means to forget, and I don't want to forget them. They are little pieces of me and if I were to forget them, a little bit of me would die." Castillo snatched a tissue from the dispenser on his desk and dabbed at his wet eyes and when he turned to Lambert he saw that her eyes were wet too. He mopped at his nose and then said, "But we move on. It does no good to dwell on the hurt. We say our good byes and we move on. Right?"

Lambert found she couldn't talk. She could only nod. She took a tissue too and began dabbing at her eyes.

Castillo shifted in his chair, sniffed and cleared his throat, indicating a change of subject. "Now how're we going to keep everyone together. What if a group wants to be let off on the Spanish coast or somewhere?"

"We can't really force them to go where they don't want to."

Castillo eyed her mischievously. "No?"

"What?"

"I think *you* could do it! I've seen you in action. You could just knock a few heads together," he smirked. "What's that SL stand for on your jacket...Super Lady?"

She looked down at the embroidered SL on her jacket, then back at Castillo. "Oh, Ha! Ha!" She punched him playfully.

• • •

When the last crew members were aboard, the maneuvering watch was set and Kansas turned south toward the firth and the Irish Sea. In the bridge well atop the sail were Castillo, the British Captain Simms, Tanaka and Lambert. Taylor had the control room. The rain had almost stopped, but the skies were still very dark. They all wore black rain slickers and hats expecting the rain to start again at any time.

Castillo turned the dial at his station to 1MC, public address system, and began to speak:

Attention all hands! This is Captain Castillo. I would like to welcome all of you aboard our cruise ship as we embark on our world tour.

He glanced at the others and saw a look of surprise.

You will not see many sights from the deck of Kansas, nor will you be able to get much sun on this cruise, but we'll make up for that by stopping at many exotic destinations. You'll all have a chance to explore at each stop.

He turned to Lambert who was wearing an amused smile.

Your social director, Miss Susan Lambert, has planned some wonderful activities for you.

Her smile turned to one of dismay. Castillo and Tanaka chuckled.

But first, I thought you all might want to witness a historic event. The defeat of the great Spanish Armada. We're in time to watch it unfold. I have a personal interest in seeing the Spanish get their asses kicked.

He frowned at his mangled left hand.

"Let's go for it," said Tanaka.

"Hear hear!" said Simms.

He heard agreement in his ear from the control room.

By the time Kansas reached the Irish Sea, the rain had started drumming noisily on Kansas's metal sail surfaces and it was turning dusk. Castillo cleared the bridge, took the boat down to a depth of 100 feet, secured the maneuvering watch, set the underway watch, and they set a course for the English Channel. The following morning they were off Plymouth on the English coast.

Castillo took up station in his command chair in Kansas's control room. "Pilot, take us to periscope depth. Let's take a look."

The control room was packed with people. Castillo almost didn't recognize the Kincaid brothers. They were wearing standard Navy dungaree work uniforms and the official black Kansas crew ball caps. They looked just like crewmen except Kevin had his arm in a sling and Will had a bandage across his throat. "Where did you get the uniforms?" asked Castillo.

"Miss Susan geeve 'em tae us," said Will. "'ese'r the best boots Ay've ever 'ad." He stuck out his right foot to show Castillo.

"Very nice!" said Castillo. They were black standard issue Navy deck boots.

Taylor turned to him and said, "Lambert opened the lockers of all the missing men we left behind in Glasgow. She asked me if she could reassign some of their things, and I said, 'go ahead. Those men won't be needing those clothes anymore.'"

"Okay," said Castillo. Then he noticed that all the civilians in the room also were wearing Navy work uniforms and Kansas ball caps, even Crystal McConnell. It was a sign of solidarity. They were family!

Lambert rushed in and panted, "Don, what do you intend to do about the current crisis?"

Uh oh, thought Castillo. Another crisis? "What's wrong, Susan?"

"What's wrong?" She stared at him incredulously. "We're out of *coffee*!"

"Oh *that*. Yes, Jonesy said we're out, and there isn't any coffee available. But there's lots of tea."

"Tea!" Her eyes were so wide, he thought her eyelids had disappeared. "Tea is not coffee! It's not the same thing at all. I went to Norm Bloomberg and he said that coffee at this time in history is only available in

Africa, Arabia and Turkey. So…when are we going to Turkey?"

Castillo shifted uncomfortably. "Well, Susan, I appreciate the problem and want to address any discomfort you have, but you have to be reasonable. We can't just stop what we're doing and go to Turkey to get you coffee."

"Why not?"

He searched her face for any sign of impishness, but there was none. He saw only stark sincerity in her blue eyes. She truly expected him to stop what he was doing to make a coffee run for her. He couldn't believe what he was about to say. "Okay, Susan. We'll go to Turkey, but first we have some other things to do. Try to make do with tea until then. Okay?"

"Okay." She looked just like a big-eyed little girl who had been denied her request for a Barbie doll.

"We're at periscope depth, sir," said the pilot.

All the viewing screens flickered to life with images. There was a view of the English coast and many views of the empty sea. There was no overcast and the sun struck the waves dramatically causing them to glisten with sparkling diamonds.

"The Armada was engaged here yesterday by the English, July 31st, 1588. I don't see any signs of a battle," said Castillo. "Does anyone else?"

There were murmurings of negativity.

"Maybe we have the date wrong," said Tanaka. "Our history books say July 31st, but we really don't know what date it is. We only have the word of one Spanish sailor."

True," said Castillo, "and he was traumatized." He considered the next course of action. "When is the next Armada battle?"

"According to our history books," said Tanaka, reading from a screen. "The next battle was at the Isle of Portland, August 2nd. The Duke Medina Sidonia, the commander of the Armada, engaged Drake and Howard of the English fleet. The wind was East Northeast."

"Okay, let's go there," said Castillo. "We should be able to see them soon."

"I hope so, sir," said a young sonar watchstander. "These wooden ships don't return much of an echo."

It was obvious to Castillo their sonar was going to be useless in locating these ships. In two hours time they had arrived at the Isle of Portland and all they saw were smaller vessels, fishermen mostly. "Let's go to station keeping," said Castillo, "and see what comes down the channel."

"How long are we going to wait, Don?" asked Taylor.

"I don't know." Castillo sighed. "Not long." In truth he wasn't sure how long to wait, but he wanted to give it a chance.

Lunch was something that tasted exactly like beef stroganoff with scalloped potatoes and fresh garden greens. They were pretty sure it wasn't, but nobody asked questions. It was delicious!

Everyone seemed to be taking Castillo's suggestion seriously to make use of the library and read. Tanaka decided to learn wooden ship building. He was certain this was going to be useful eventually. Anderson was reading and studying metallurgy. Guerrero was studying navigation, but not the modern kind with GPS and nautical gravimetrics, but ancient navigation using sextant and astrolabe. Lambert had begun studying farming and horticulture. Everyone was reading and studying except Castillo. He hadn't decided what to study yet. He wanted it to be something useful. Something for survival. He was in the control room, scanning subjects in the ebook library on his reader when one of the sonar men spoke up.

"I've got something on the wide aperture array, sir."

"What is it?" asked Castillo.

"Don't know."

"Put it on speaker."

"Yessir!" The crewman flipped a switch and on the overhead speakers they heard a muffled staccato.

Bup bup bupbup bup bupbupbup bup bup bupbup bup bup bupbupbupbup bup

"Turn it up," said Castillo.

"I've got it turned all the way up, sir," said the crewman.

"Where's it coming from?"

"Down the channel…" said the crewmen. Two other crewmen walked over and looked over his shoulder, studying the displays. "To the east…maybe 120 miles."

"Okay," said Castillo, "let's go take a look. Navigator, plot us a course for the sound target. Maneuvering, make turns for 25 knots."

"Aye, sir," said Guerrero. "Setting course for sound source."

"Aye, sir," said the maneuvering watch. "Making turns for 25 knots."

As soon as Castillo saw the new course line projected on his plot, he said "Pilot, come to new course 093. Make depth 100 feet."

"Aye, sir," replied the pilot. "Coming to course 093. Going to 100 feet."

Chapter 12

A s they got closer to the sound source, Castillo began to guess what it was. Cannon fire! As the big shipboard guns fired, they recoiled and their carriages thumped the deck hard. The sound was transmitted through the wooden hulls and heard by Kansas's sensitive ears.

When they got within 10 miles, they came to periscope depth and they took a look ahead. They saw a cluster of ships in the far distance. Tall sailing ships.

"I think we found our Armada," said Taylor.

"I think so," replied Castillo.

They continued to close the distance. When they were within 5 miles, they could clearly see ships firing on each other. They could see the flash of cannons in the thick drifting white smoke like camera flashes in mist. Some ships were on fire and disengaging from the fight, listing badly. As they watched, a mast toppled on one of them.

"There must be 100 ships in that cluster," observed Castillo. "It looks like chaos. How can we tell who's winning?"

Tanaka flopped into a chair at one of the workstations, grabbed a joystick and flipped some switches. A red dot appeared on screen. As he talked, he moved the dot about the screen. "See these ships on the left, sir? The tallest mast of each ship is flying the Tudor crest. They are English. The Spanish ships here have a higher stern and larger forecastle or *f'ocsle* as it's properly called, and they're flying red banners with the gold Spanish cross."

"Who's winning?" asked Castillo.

"Uh…don't know, sir," answered Tanaka, studying the scene. "The Spanish are in their famous impenetrable crescent formation and the English are trying to break the formation using a pincer movement."

"Why a crescent formation?" asked Taylor.

"It's like a parabolic dish, sir," said Tanaka, "which focuses light or RF to its center. The crescent formation of ships focuses firepower toward the center of the crescent. It's an ingenious tactic. Notice how the English are trying to avoid that lethal center of the crescent." Tanaka clicked a button and the red dot jumped to the right screen. "Here's another English formation joining the fight from the south. Wind appears to be out of the west, favoring the Spanish."

As they watched, another English warship broke off from the fight. Followed by another and another. Two of them were trailing thick gray smoke and listing badly. Tanaka's dark eyes looked troubled. "This doesn't look right. The English are taking a pounding. They seem to be losing this contest. And the weather was supposed to be stormy."

"The history books could be wrong," said Castillo.

"I suppose," said Tanaka, but he didn't really believe it.

Castillo used his control screen to cycle through all the cameras on the mast. When he got to the rear cameras, he stopped, magnified the image and magnified again. "Another formation of ships behind us."

"Yes, sir. They look Spanish. We must have passed right under them when we came down the channel."

"We were too fixated on the sound we were chasing. How many ships would you say are in that formation?"

"I don't know, sir. The Armada by most reports had 160 ships."

Castillo stared at the oncoming ships. Their white sails were brightly lit by the sun, some of them with red crosses on them. The bows of the heavy ships rose and plunged ponderously with their slow progress down the channel. Castillo pulled the camera view back to get a wider angle. The ships were so numerous it appeared as if a kettle of popcorn had exploded throwing a blanket of kernels across the water.

"Let's get a count," said Castillo. "Everybody grab a pad and get ready to count. Pilot, turn us 180 degrees. Let's head back and find the end of this formation."

"Aye, sir. Turning the ship through 180." The watch-standers picked up notepaper and pens.

Kansas traveled back down the channel staying at periscope depth and never coming closer than 300 yards to a Spanish ship. No one in the Spanish formation saw the small mast protruding above the water's surface. Lookouts and watches on the ships were all watching the horizon. No one looked down. It took a few hours, but when they were done, they had found a total of three crescent formations in the Armada strung out over 25 miles with about 150 ships in each.

"That's 450 ships!" exclaimed Tanaka, his onyx eyes huge. "That's way bigger than the historic reports we have."

"The history books can't be that wrong, can they?" asked Lambert.

"A good question," said Castillo.

When Kansas returned to the main force where the fighting was, it was getting dark. The English had limped back to Portsmouth to regroup and the Spanish had gone to anchor along the northern French coast. Castillo ordered the Kansas to station-keeping off the French coast within sight of the Armada's anchorage.

• • •

That evening after dinner, Castillo and Taylor with great effort helped a wheezing Norm Bloomberg limp to the messdeck where he held court. He setup a laptop and large display screen again and gave a lecture to a full house.

Bloomberg moved a cursor over a map of the English Channel. "The Armada will try to reach Flanders, here, and rendezvous with the Duke of Parma, who has assembled an army of 30,000 men." Bloomberg paused and pushed his glasses back into place with a finger. "They've been ordered to move as a unit up the Thames and capture London and Queen Elizabeth. At least that's what the history books say which are largely based on first person accounts and ship's logs."

"But they were supposed to have been stopped by now," said Lambert.

"Yes, according to the history books, they were slowed by the English fleet and stormy weather, but we've not seen that happen."

"And the Armada was only 160 ships," said Tanaka. "What we're seeing is more like 450!"

There was a long silence.

"Does this mean we're in an alternate reality where the Armada won?" This came from the British captain, Simms. There were deep furrows of concern between his eyebrows.

"Well, not necessarily. Quite often history gets revised in books. This is done for leaders to save face or simply because it makes a better story. Like Columbus proving the world was round. A Greek actually proved the world was round in 240 B.C. But it makes a better story if Columbus did it through bold exploration."

"But why would they alter the Armada story so drastically?" asked Lambert.

"I've no idea. And quite frankly it wouldn't be easy. There were many personal accounts written by the Spanish and English captains and they differ on details but all tell pretty much the same story."

"Do you intend to act, commander?" asked Simms.

All faces swung extectantly to Castillo. "I think we should stay spectators in this thing. Who knows what harm we might…"

"But England can not be allowed to fall to Spain," declared Simms hotly. "That would be unacceptable!"

Castillo understood his concern. He saw similar distressed looks on the faces of others, especially the English. "I think it would be a mistake to get involved in something like this…"

"But this ship has the power to change the outcome," shouted Simms. "When you control something so powerful and don't act for the side of good…why… that's just criminal!"

"Let's calm down," said Castillo. "Let's just wait and see what tomorrow brings. Maybe everything will come out okay. I'm not counting out the English just yet."

Simms crossed his arms and huffed, clearly displeased.

"We should minimize our footprint on the event timeline. Remember? We're not supposed to be here… whether it's our world or not."

"How do you know we're not supposed to be here, Don?" asked Lambert.

Castillo said nothing.

• • •

Castillo turned in early and tried to do some reading. He was still reviewing the ebook index from the ship's library, but he couldn't concentrate, so he tried to sleep, but sleep didn't come either. The events of the day plagued him. He finally gave up, dressed in khakis and went to the control room. There were about 10 men standing watch there.

He flopped into his command chair and looked up at the viewing screen. Someone had switched the cameras to night vision. There was a green glow to the seascape. It looked very peaceful, ships at anchor, rocking gently with tall spindly masts spiderwebbed with rigging and rocking like unsynchronized metronomes. The nightvision brought out the ghostly highlights glistening off wave tops, yardarms and deck rails. There were a few lanterns lit on decks and in cabins. Castillo could imagine they were having briefings and laying out plans for tomorrow.

"What's that?" asked a watchstander, pointing at an object on the left screen.

Castillo brought up his screen controls and magnified the left screen. "It looks like a small cluster of ships." He magnified again. There were about twenty ships under sail, heading toward the anchored Armada. Were they going to attack? Or were they Spanish? Hard to tell. He switched the camera to infra-red. This threw a red cast on the scene, and he could see men on the ships. They were bright white man-shaped blobs. Castillo tried to magnify again, but he was already at maximum. The men were carrying torches, small points of white light. Then there were more points of white light on the decks of the ships. The ships were being set afire!

"It's the fire ships!" someone said.

"Yes, I read about this," said Castillo. "The English sent fire ships into the Armada and caused them to break formation."

This buoyed them. One crewman made a clap. All smiled and leaned forward and watched the attack unfold. They were like kids at the matinee watching the cavalry arrive to rescue the settlers. The fire on each ship grew larger until they were floating bonfires, white hot images on the screen. When the ships were well ablaze and set on course, small boats carried the crews safely away. The first ship approached the Armada, and the watchstanders held their collective breaths, but they exhaled again when a small boat full of oarsmen rowed out from the Armada to meet the fire ship. The men in the boat docked with the first fire ship and did something to it. Castillo killed the infra-red display and brought back the nightvision display trying to see better. The boat rowed away and went to the next ship. There was a bright flash at the first ship, and it began to list.

"They're sinking the fire ships," said a watchstander, disappointment on his face.

It was true. Two more boats rowed out from the Armada and started placing charges on the fire ships, and one by one charges detonated and blew holes in the hulls of the fire ships and sank them. When it was over Castillo said softly, "Well, give them an A for effort."

Castillo impounded the video from the fire ship attack and replayed it for the rest of the crew the following morning.

The Armada slowly got underway. It took almost two hours for them all to weigh anchor and unfurl sail. It was a very labor intense process requiring every crew member of each ship. Castillo could see men scrambling up and down ratlines into the rigging of every ship as they slowly began to make headway.

Kansas shadowed the first crescent formation of the Armada, and once again the control room was crammed with people. The Armada seemed to travel at a speed of 5 knots. This time the skies were gray and overcast and there was a fresh wind out of the southwest again favoring the Spanish fleet. The sea was restless and rolling, but the Armada was unopposed as it moved down the English Channel until it reached Dover. When it reached the channel choke point at the Dover Straits, there was a line of ships blocking their way.

"I think that barricade is the English fleet making their stand," said Castillo.

"I think it is," agreed Taylor.

"Let's go up to the front of the formation to get a better view," said Castillo. "Pilot take us down to 100 feet. Maneuvering, make turns for 25 knots."

"Aye sir, going down to 100."

"Aye sir, making turns for 25 knots."

In a half hour, they were looking back at the Armada's first crescent formation as it approached the English fleet. Soon the English fleet split into two groups of about 50 ships each.

"It's going to be a pincer movement again," said Tanaka.

"I hope they have more ships somewhere," said Lambert. "These just doesn't seem like enough."

Castillo said nothing, but he agreed. This was not going to go well for the English.

The English fleet began to pound on each end of the Spanish crescent, but there were too many ships. They weren't making so much as a dent and several English ships took heavy damage, loosing masts and rigging. One ship's sails began fluttering and, out of control, it drifted into the Spanish formation where it was pounded by cannon until it was nothing but a smoking mastless floating hulk with holes through it.

Castillo took heart when he saw a Spanish ship lose a mast and turn away from the battle, but then he saw what was coming up the channel behind the battle. He magnified the view. Between ships he could see the second Spanish crescent formation coming.

"Shit," he said. "The Spanish are going to execute their own pincer movement. They're going to trap the English between their two 150 ship formations."

"There's no way the English can win this," said Taylor. "They're heavily outnumbered and outgunned."

They watched the brave English make their stand and get outmaneuvered and pounded by the Spanish and the mood in the control room turned heavy. The English ships began to list and smoke and some sank in the angry heaving waves. It was a hard thing to watch. Castillo gulped and looked around at crew members. Lambert was teary-eyed and her hands were balled into fists. Taylor had a moody look, more angry than sad. He heard someone sob and another one sniffle.

He looked around for the British officers and finally saw them sitting next to the nav station. There was blackness in Simms's baleful stare and disappointment in Gastmeyer's. He turned back to watch the battered remnants of the defeated English fleet limping away.

• • •

That night 21 people came as a group to talk to Castillo. There were too many to comfortably fit in his state room, so he decided to take them all to the ward room. It was a tight fit in the small ward room as well. As he looked at all the anguished faces, he recognized many English: Simms, Gastmeyer, McConnell, three of the QVR people whose names he didn't recall, the Kincaid brothers. There was also Lambert, Taylor, Tanaka, Guerrero, Chief Brown and many of the senior staff.

"I think I know your concerns," began Castillo, "but hear me out." He pulled at his lower lip before launching into his argument. "Up until now our involvement with these people has been minimal. We've done only what we've had to to survive and gather intelligence. I've tried to keep our impact to a minimum, although some things just can't be helped." He caught the eye of the Kincaid brothers who looked very serious. "But if we insert ourselves into a battle with the aim of changing its outcome, that is a major impact. I can't think of anything more influential than that. Our being here is purely by accident."

"But…" began Lambert.

Castillo stopped her with an upheld hand. "We did not know, at first, whether we were in our own world or an alternate reality, but I think it's now quite evident that we're in a world where the Armada was intended to win this battle, and who knows what cataclysmic chain of events we might set off by changing it."

"Cataclysmic chain of…" sputtered Simms. "You can't be serious!"

"Don," said Lambert gently. "How do you know the Armada was intended to win this battle?"

"Because they are! Nothing is going according to our history books."

"But maybe we were *intended* to be here," said Crystal McConnell. "Maybe it was God's plan." Her brown eyes were wet and her delicate mouth was trembling with emotion.

"Don't you believe in a God's guiding hand?" asked Lambert.

"Not really. Does God cause famine and disease?" asked Castillo. "Did he cause six million Jews to be exterminated in concentration camps? Where was he then?"

"I don't know," snapped Simms, "but the right people won that contest in the end, didn't they?"

"My point is," said Castillo, "none of us knows what God wants in any situation."

"So, what you're saying is you don't know whether God intends for the Armada to win this contest or not." Simms crossed his arms and glared smugly.

Castillo said nothing. How did this become an argument about God's will?

"There's a lot at stake here, Don," said Lambert. "America is very young right now. If England falls, then a lot of our culture will fall as well. The American ideals of freedom, our rights to free speech and self government. These were all first envisioned in England, Scotland and Ireland. Not Spain."

"As England goes, so goes the world," intoned Simms. "It would also mean the fall of protestantism and the expansion of the Inquisition."

"Did you know," said McConnell, "that your Declaration of Independence is based on the Scottish Oath of Freedom from the time of William Wallace?"

Castillo took a deep breath. They all had good arguments. "Let me think about it."

"Don't think too long," said Simms darkly. "The Spanish are anchored at Flanders now and soon they're going to sail up the Thames with 500 ships and 30,000 troops. We won't be able to stop them once they enter the mouth of the river."

Castillo went back to his stateroom, but once again sleep eluded him. There was too much on his mind. If there really was a God, would he have ripped them all away from their families and friends and caused so much hurt. To what purpose? To fight against the Spanish Armada in a world where the English were not up to the task? It all seemed so improbable. He tossed and turned for two hours trying to find a restful position, finally giving up and getting dressed for the day. He went to the messdeck and made himself a strong cup of tea. It seemed busy for that time of night. Lambert and McConnell were both there.

"What's the matter? Couldn't you sleep either?" asked Lambert.

"No," responded Castillo. "And you're right. Tea is not the same thing as coffee."

She smiled. "You have a lot to think about, I know."

He looked at Lambert, then McConnell. "Yes. I have a feeling if I don't want to act, there will be a mutiny."

"It's your decision, Don," said Lambert. "I'll support you."

Castillo saw trust in her serious blue eyes. He turned to McConnell. "How about you, Crystal?"

"I don't know. Mason says he supports you either way, but there are some who're questioning your leadership."

"You don't have to tell me. I know who it is."

"They say you were affected by your ordeal with that Spaniard and are no longer fit to command."

"I'd better talk to some of my guys," said Castillo. "It's my intention to set up a base of operations somewhere in the world and then have free elections to see who we want to lead our new colony, but right now I'm still the commander and it's my job to protect this ship and this crew. Even those not under my command. I take that responsibility very seriously."

• • •

Castillo and many others watched the viewing screens in the control room all the next day. The Spanish loaded men and supplies onto their ships from the docks at Flanders. They could see men rolling barrels and field cannon and dragging boxes down the dock and leading horses, wagons and goats and loading everything an army needs onto ships and barges. They were obviously making preparations for war. After a ship was loaded, it was moved away from the pier by boats with oarsmen. Then another ship would be brought in for loading. They seemed to be well organized.

Castillo went to his stateroom and brooded. Right now he needed counsel and the best counsel was his wife, Liz. She was smart, and she knew exactly how to distill a problem down into its basic parts and make it seem simple. He wanted badly to talk to her, but that was impossible. He liked to have pretend conversations with her and his girls. It helped him cope with his loss, and for a while, he could pretend they were still here. But that was only *pretend*.

He decided to go see Norm Bloomberg. But Bloomberg did not look well at all. He looked feverish and his face was ashen.

"Are you okay, Norm?"

"Not really. The doc says my sugar is high. Diabetes, you know."

"Oh. Sorry to hear it."

"I've run out of my medication and its starting to affect my kidneys." He smiled weakly. "You don't suppose anybody has a dialysis machine around here, do you?"

Castillo returned his smile. He knew this would happen eventually. Modern medicine is able to keep people leading healthy productive lives even when they have serious illnesses. Without it, we're at the mercy of nature. We've come to a world that is ill equipped to handle kidney failure or coronary artery disease. Damn! He felt so helpless. How many more would fall ill to something like this and force us to stand idly by and watch.

"You're the smartest guy I know, Norm. I just wanted to get your thoughts on what's going on."

Bloomberg seemed to perk up at this. He rolled onto his side and put down his reader. "Talk to me."

"The Spanish are at Flanders and they're loading ships and barges with war supplies…cannon, powder, warhorses, food."

"Sounds like they're getting ready to move against London."

"I'm being pressured to act."

"I see."

Castillo pulled up a chair and sat heavily down. "So…just for argument's sake, let's say we take out the Armada with a Tomahawk strike."

"Yes."

"What would be the down side? What might we set off unintentionally? Just brainstorming here."

"Well, this is extreme speculation, since we just have no way of knowing how the world might react to such a pivotal event. And we're making some pretty big assumptions here. We're assuming the 16th century Spain and England of this world is the same as the ones in ours. "

"We know this England has a Tudor queen, Elizabeth, and Sir·Francis Drake. I learned that much aboard the Spanish ship."

"Yes, and I think it would be safe to say there is an Inquisition going on in Spain. Your captor turned too quickly to torture and coercion when he wanted information. It was as second nature as breathing to him."

"Okay, so let's just say for the sake of argument 16th century Spain and England from where we hail are essentially the same as the ones here." Castillo scratched his face with his right hand. "We would be creating a watershed event in history and possibly establishing a precedent."

"At the least," said Bloomberg. "The first consequence, of course, would be the enormous loss of life."

"Sure. As many as a hundred thousand Spanish." Castillo turned somber. "That's something Spain would take a long time to recover from. It would really set them back to lose that many men and ships."

"And…since we're just spitballing here…it could embolden England. They may begin to believe that God has struck down their enemies. In the absence of any other explanation, it was an act of God. They could feel justified in aggressively expanding their holdings and territories and moving against enemies."

"They already believe God's on their side."

"Yes, everybody has God on their side," said Bloomberg thoughtfully. "That's part of the problem, isn't it?"

"Could it change their national character do you think? Give them a sense of entitlement as God's chosen?"

"I think that ship has sailed," said Bloomberg propping himself on an elbow and peering over the tops of his glasses. "Have you seen some of the art and literature that came out of Elizabethan England? It was rife with angelic messengers and heaven sent visions of victory and conquest."

"I just hate to think that we could be creating a world bully by handing them a victory like this."

Bloomberg rolled onto his back, wheezed loudly, then coughed. "But the impact of doing nothing could be a lot worse for the free world. Like it or not, commander, this is *our* world now. We're stuck in it and you have to think about how you're shaping this new world for our new society and our descendants."

"That's what I was afraid you were going to say." Castillo slouched down in his chair.

When Castillo got back to his stateroom, there was an envelope slid under the door. He opened it and read the note inside:

> Commander,
>
> An explosive device has been improvised on this ship. It will detonate at eighteen hundred hours and only I can

disarm it. You will launch an attack on the Spanish ships. It must be bold and decisive! Make no mistake, commander, if you do not act, I will destroy us all. I regret such extreme measures are required to force you to do the honourable thing. You have six hours.

"Aw, what the hell!" said Castillo.

Chapter 13

"I was half expecting something like this," said Castillo.

Taylor read the note. "You know who it's from, don't you?"

"Sure. Look at the spelling of the word *honourable* and *bold and decisive*. Who do we know talks that way?"

"What are you going to do?"

"About him, I don't know. But I've had the ship checked."

"Do you think he really has a bomb on board?"

"No, Tanaka couldn't find anything. I think it's a bluff." Castillo flexed the remaining fingers on his left hand and inspected them. "I don't think Simms has it in him to kill all of us, but this just shows how desperate he is to save his mother country."

"I think I'd better lay it on the line for Captain Simms. He needs an ass kicking," said Taylor.

"No, Mase. Let me talk to him first. Let's try honey before we use a hammer."

Taylor looked disappointed. "Okay."

"Could you find Mr. Simms and send him to me, please?"

"Sure," replied Taylor.

Soon there was a rap at the door. It was a serious-looking Captain Simms.

"Come in, Miles. Have a seat. Is it okay if I call you Miles?"

Simms nodded and sat. Castillo handed Simms the note and studied him carefully for a reaction.

"What's this?" asked Simms. His bushy eyebrows rose innocently.

"Something I found on the floor about an hour ago."

"Well, this sounds serious. Very serious indeed!"

"Think so? I don't."

"Why not?" Simms blinked.

"I think it's a bluff. I don't think anyone on this boat would do such a thing."

"Oh really?"

"Yes, you need to look at the big picture. A year from now I can envision a community with elected leaders and a bright future. Anyone who threatened that society. Anyone who, let's say, tried to kill people of that society would be an outcast. There are many things we need to fear in this world, but we can't fear each other. We would not want someone in our midst we couldn't turn our back on. Someone we couldn't trust."

Simms said nothing. He only stared ominously.

"And I've already had the places checked where a saboteur would logically place a bomb to destroy us all:

torpedo room, launch tubes, engine room, command and control. They were clean." Castillo sat back and sighed. "I think I'm going to let you keep that note, Miles. Let's just pretend I never saw it. Okay?"

Simms's face looked hateful. "Damn it, Castillo," he bellowed. "I'm a captain and you're only a commander. I outrank you and I know about things like this. I've had more experience than you!"

"Well, with all due respect, *Captain* Simms. The navies that commissioned us no longer exist, so I think ranks don't matter anymore."

"Your navy doesn't exist," snapped Simms. "But mine does. Two weeks ago I served an English monarch named Elizabeth. Remember?"

"A different queen, a different time, Miles!" thundered Castillo. "And I'm still the commander of this ship!" Castillo stopped and took a slow breath to get control of his emotions. "Can we level with each other?"

Simms said nothing. He eyed Castillo suspiciously.

"I've just about made up my mind on this thing. I've looked at all available information, and I've decided we just can't stand idly by, but I'm going to need help. Can I count on you?"

Simms still said nothing. He didn't completely trust Castillo. He only glowered blackly.

"Most of our weapon systems have been compromised by the lightning strike that hit us. To be the most effective, I'm going to need *buy in* by the British admiralty…so we can make maximum use of what we have. Now, I've considered approaching Lord Howard or

Admiral Drake but that just seems like a winless situation to me. 'Hello, Lord Howard, I'm here to help you. I'm from the future.'" Castillo shifted in his chair and scrutinized Simms to see if any of this was having an effect. "They would throw me in an asylum. I'd never see the light of day again."

Simms seemed to change. It was as if a great weight had been lifted from him. He tilted his head and narrowed his eyes, taking Castillo's measure. "Are you serious?"

"Like a heart attack."

"What can *I* do?"

"Bring Drake or Howard to me. I want to put an attack plan together. I need their input."

"How am I going to do that?"

"The English fleet is at anchor at Dover right now, I believe. I would like you to head up a team, Miles. Kansas will get you close. Take an inflatable and anyone else you need."

Simms took a deep breath. "Just to be clear. You want me to kidnap Admiral Drake or Lord Howard?"

"Yes."

He said nothing for long seconds, then, "Okay." He rose from his chair.

Castillo cleared his throat and said, "Oh…and about that note."

Simms tore it carefully into small pieces, smiled and said, "What note?"

• • •

"I've been reading up on Sir Francis Drake," said Tanaka. "I think he's our best bet. He and an Admiral Hawkins were expert seamen, but Lord Howard got his appointment through his political connections, not a seafaring man at all."

Once again there was a crowd in Kansas's control room. They had left the Flemish coast and gone to the English coast to observe the English fleet at anchor off Dover.

"We only have another couple hours of daylight," said Castillo. "Where do you think Drake is?"

"His flagship was the Revenge. A four masted, 46 gun galleon-style warship with decks and sterncastle trimmed in white and red. I have a drawing of it here from a book I found in the ship's library." Tanaka handed out pictures to everyone in the control room.

"These tall ships all look alike to me," said Lambert, frowning.

They were looking at a cluster of 30 ships, some of which were very battered with jagged gaping holes in their sides and missing masts. Castillo slowly swept the cameras over the ships and zoomed occasionally. He moved on to a smaller cluster.

"Drake raided many Spanish outposts and was personally responsible for sinking or capturing over 50 vessels," said Tanaka. "He had a fearsome reputation, and just the rumor that he was coming was enough to turn settlements into ghost towns. The Spanish *hated* him. They called him *El Draque*, which means *the dragon*. Drake liked that nickname so much, he put a dragon on his personal crest."

"How about that one," said Lambert pointing. "It has red and white."

"A three-master," said Tanaka. "We're looking for *four*."

Lambert wrinkled her nose. "How about the one behind it?" She held the drawing at arm's length up to the large viewing screen.

"That looks pretty close," said Castillo.

"Sir," asked Tanaka, "could you zoom on the flag at the top of the third mast on that ship?"

Castillo touched his screen controls and the picture zoomed in on the fluttering flag at the top of the third mast.

"That's it!" exclaimed Tanaka. "That's Drake's crest! The battle ax above the shield with a red dragon! It's the Revenge!"

"Okay," said Castillo, then turning to Simms. "We're going to get you as close as we can after nightfall. Then you and your team will launch in the inflatable. Do you have what you need?"

"I think so. We're going to carry enough tranquilizer darts to knock out half the crew. Hopefully it won't come to that."

"Good luck, Miles! We'll track your progress from here."

• • •

Simms asked for volunteers and got 33. He selected Chief Brown, Lieutenant Anderson, Commander Taylor and at the last minute decided to include Lieutenant Guerrero when she told him she held a black belt in Tae Kwon Do. They took with them grappling hooks, rope, an assault ladder, 2 MP-5 assault rifles, 2 tasers and 3 tranquilizer dart rifles. They all had helmet cams and remote talkers.

The scarlet of the western twilight sky threw crimson rays across the English fleet, highlighting the yard arms and rails of the ships and accenting the ripples around the peaceful hulls of the ships at anchor. Pennants and flags snapped in the breeze. Then the scarlet faded to deep indigo and finally to black. A long dark shape broke the water's surface outside the harbor. A small watercraft separated from it and silently moved toward the anchored ships.

Simms stopped the inflatable when he saw a sailor throw a bucket of something over the side of a nearby ship. He wasn't sure if they'd been spotted. Their propane outboard motor was quiet and there were carpenters hammering. Battle damage was being repaired on several ships. After a time, he decided it was safe to continue. But he stopped again when he saw more men moving along the deck of another ship.

"There seems to be a lot of activity," said Simms.

"Yes," agreed Castillo in Simms's ear.

When they were within 100 yards of Revenge, they saw a small boat alongside, loading. They stopped and watched.

"What's going on?" asked Castillo.

"I think someone's going ashore," said Simms.

"Is it Drake?"

"I don't know." They watched as four men came down a ladder and entered the boat. They all picked up an oar and waited. Another man came into view at the top of the ladder and the oarsmen turned toward him. He was talking to somebody. No, he was giving orders to somebody, thought Simms. "I think that's Drake," said Simms.

"How do you know?" asked Castillo.

"I don't, but he seems to have an air of authority."

The man came down the ladder, got settled into the boat and it cast off. The oarsmen began to pull for shore. Simms had a hunch and he decided to play it. He gunned the motor and closed the distance to the small boat. "Get ready with the tranq rifles, lads," he said. They leveled the tranquilizer rifles and when they were within 20 yards of the small boat, Simms cupped his hands around his mouth and yelled, "Admiral Drake!"

The figure sitting in the center of the boat turned and said, "Yes?"

Pffft! Pffft! Pffft!

Three oarsmen slapped at their necks as if sting by an insect, then they collapsed. The riflemen reloaded.

Pffft! Pffft!

The last oarsman and Admiral Drake collapsed.

• • •

Castillo could not believe he was staring at the great English explorer, privateer and legendary war hero Sir Francis Drake. He expected him to be taller. Although he was laying on a bed in the infirmary, Castillo could estimate his height to be about 5' 7" and he had a substantial pot belly. He was about 49 years old, had a closely cropped reddish brown beard, a round fine-featured face and receding curly coarse brown hair like steel wool. He had a horizontal scar on his right cheek that ran from his right ear half way to his nose. He was wearing a deep blue doublet with gold buttons and fringed gold shoulder caps, under which he wore a white cotton shirt with lace cuffs and a lace collar. His leggings were white cotton and his boots were black, shiny and buckled. His face was absolutely ordinary. It didn't look heroic or movie star handsome. He looked just like a banker or a supermarket manager or something.

"What's that odor?" asked Lambert, sniffing.

Everyone sniffed. Castillo said, "It's kind of a delicate balance between rotting meat, Limburger cheese and…"

"Lilacs?" suggested Lambert.

"Yes, lilacs," said Castillo.

"The English nobility used to use heavy perfumes to make up for their lack of hygiene," said Simms, coughing.

Doc Aultman appeared at the door. "Has he stirred yet?"

"No," responded Castillo.

"It shouldn't be long now. I've put the other four on the tables in the ward room. I made a makeshift infirmary in there. I thought it would be better if they saw each other when they awakened."

"Okay, good!" said Castillo. "Just watch them and make sure no one loses their heads."

Drake began to stir.

"Here we go," said Castillo.

As Drake's eyes fluttered open, Castillo saw the exhaustion. The whites of his olive eyes were laced with red and heavy pouches hung under each. There were spidery lines around his eyes, furrows across his brow and his face was the color of clabbered milk. His breathing seemed to be labored. This was a man who had not slept in some time. He'd obviously been preoccupied.

Drake opened his eyes wide and took in his surroundings. He turned to see four unfamiliar faces staring at him and two more in the passageway. He swung his legs over the edge of the bed, held his head with one hand, looked up and bellowed, "Kill me or ransom me! What's it to be?"

Castillo chuckled. "No, admiral. Neither. We're going to send you back to your ship, but first we have a proposal."

"A…pro…"

Maybe that was a poor choice of words. "We are going to destroy the Spanish fleet," said Castillo. "But we'd like your help."

"Who are you?" asked Drake suspiciously.

"Oh, sorry," said Castillo. "I am Commander Don Castillo, United States Navy."

They each introduced themselves and as they did so, Castillo watched Drake carefully. He was like a predator watching his prey, gaging strengths and weaknesses. He could see him measuring each one of them. He is deciding which one would be the weak link. Who he could take first, second and so forth. Good thing they had taken his weapons.

"If I came to you and said I was going to destroy the Spanish fleet, not only would you not believe me, you would probably have me locked up. So instead, I brought you to my ship."

"Ship?" asked Drake.

"Yes, you're on a ship, admiral," said Simms.

Drake rapped on a wall and scoffed, "This is not a ship. You have sport with me."

"It *is* a ship, sir," said Castillo. "A very advanced ship. Some of what we have here will look like witchcraft to you, but I assure you it's not."

"And believe us when we tell you," said Simms. "We can *destroy* the Spanish."

Drake shook his head as if to clear cobwebs. Then he looked at Castillo suspiciously and said, "Castillo is a Spanish name. Is it not?"

"Yes, but I'm not from Spain."

"Where then? Your manner of speech is not known to me."

"We come from that area you call the Americas. Virginia."

"I've been there," snapped Drake. "'Tis nothing but wilderness and savages. Do I look a fool?"

"Now, yes," said Castillo. "But in a hundred years, there will be many settlements and colonies there. In two hundred years the colonies will break from England and form a new country. In three hundred years there will be one of the most powerful economies in the world and in four hundred years an unrivaled military power and once again allied with England."

Drake said nothing.

"It's true, sir," said Simms. "We want to help."

"God's boots! You're all quite mad!" roared Drake. "And if you've no mind to hold me, free me! I've pressing affairs!" Drake abruptly stood up but swayed slightly, and Castillo reached out to steady him, but Drake shrugged him off.

"I think a tour is in order," said Castillo. They all filed out with Castillo in the lead.

Their first stop was the wardroom. The four groggy oarsmen were sitting up and sipping hot tea. They were quite happy to see Admiral Drake.

"'ey, yer lordship! Is quoyt a place, eh?" said a tall skinny one.

"Don't settle. We're leaving," snapped Drake.

When they got to the control room, Drake stopped dead trying to absorb it all. He scowled at all the screens surrounding them.

"This is our Navigation station," said Castillo pointing. "And this is sonar and communications. Over there is weapons control. In the front is command and control. In the very front on the biggest screen is your ship, the Revenge."

There on the big screen was the Revenge at anchor in the dark, illuminated by the moonlight, a man with a lantern walking on deck. Drake walked to the screen, reached up and touched it. "What sorcery this?"

Castillo was expecting that word. How do you explain something like this to someone who'd never seen anything more complicated than a sextant?

"This is like a window to the outside, admiral. Wally," said Castillo, "can you replay the video from this morning?"

"Yes, sir." Anderson touched controls on his screen and the picture on the large forward screen changed. It showed the scene from that morning with supplies and horses coming down the long pier at Flanders and being loaded onto ships of the Armada.

"What you're seeing here, admiral, is the Spanish loading supplies and men this morning at Flanders. We watched them most of the morning, before we came to Dover to find you."

Drake's jaw dropped. "*God's boots!* It is the eye of *God*!"

"Well, not really. It might seem…"

"It dawns on me, and I embrace it! In our darkest hour, we prayed, and our prayer was heard. You are God sent!" Drake suddenly was very animated. "This is the hand of God!"

"I don't think so, but there are those in my crew who would agree with you."

Drake began to knock on things again with his knuckles. "What is this? Iron?"

"We're made of mostly steel and aluminum."

"Steel and what?"

"A very light strong metal, sir."

"Ah! Where are your sails?"

Castillo chuckled. "No sails. We don't need wind. We use something very powerful. This ship can travel at a speed of 35…let's just say we can travel faster than a galloping horse."

Drake expressed surprise. "You jest with me, verily!"

"Come, admiral. Let's go up above."

Castillo led Drake down the passageway to a ladder trailed by Taylor, Simms and Lambert and finally up through the access trunk in the sail. They emerged in the bridge well at the top of the conning tower. Castillo checked and saw both small boats were tied securely to the Kansas's aft deck and he donned a headset and ordered maneuvering to make turns for 25 knots. As the ship began to move, Drake expressed open-mouthed surprise as the night air began to buffet them and water began to sluice up over the nose of Kansas, split by the sail and sliding off its sides in a loud hiss.

"Your weather deck is spare," asked Drake. "Where be your guns?"

"When we attack, we go under the water so we can not be seen. We have weapons that fly. In jest, we call them *birds*. We also have weapons that travel through the water. We call them *fish*."

"Birds and fish! Ha!"

"How happened you to be here? By what device did God send you?" asked Drake.

Castillo looked from Taylor to Lambert. "Who would like to explain that one?"

They all took a turn at trying to explain the series of events that caused them to time travel, or dimension shift. In the end Drake only shook his head and laughed.

• • •

Castillo reclaimed his wardroom again and sent Drake's recovered oarsmen to the messdeck for food and ale. Around the wardroom table were Castillo, Drake, Taylor, Simms, Tanaka, Anderson, Unger, Guerrero, and Chief Brown. Castillo ordered ale and tea for everyone.

"I'm going to turn the floor over to our weapons officer first," said Castillo. "Lieutenant Walter Anderson."

Anderson had an easy smile and looked every bit the California surfer with his whip thin body, tan face and wind swept blond hair. "The lightning strike took out our horizontal launch tubes and five of our vertical systems. All we have available are seven birds, five Tomahawks and two Harpoons. But the Tomahawks are GPS guided."

There were groans all around the table.

"They can be guided manually, can't they?" asked Tanaka. "From the tactical screens?"

"I don't know. The guy who knows all that stuff…"

"Is not here, I know," said Castillo. "But you can figure it out, right? You have all the manuals."

"Yes, sir. I'm sure I can," answered Anderson, but Castillo detected some doubt in his voice.

"Is there any chance we can get a horizontal tube up and operational?" asked Castillo.

"Well," said Anderson, "we don't have any weapons technicians on board either, sir."

Castillo turned to his left and said, "Unger, you have a lot of comm and sonar technicians. Who's your best?"

Unger had a dark handsome face with pewter framed glasses. "Safir probably. Smitty's pretty good too. But all they know is comm and sonar equipment."

"Get them both working on those tubes. Anderson, give them the manuals and schematics. I need at least *one* horizontal tube! I want to be able to launch Mark 48's."

Drake tried to follow the discussion with raised eyebrow as if he were watching a game of lawn tennis. He concentrated on one speaker, then another, then another.

"Are you aware, sir," said Anderson, "that of our twenty ADCAPs, only twelve are warloads. The rest are dummies."

"Dummies?" asked Tanaka.

"Yes, remember when we were testing torpedo guidance systems? We still have those. They're launchable, but they have dummy heads."

"Even a dummy head traveling at 55 would punch a hole through an old wooden ship," said Tanaka. "A Mark 48 weighs 3000 pounds!"

"True. And a warload carries 650 pounds of high explosive. PBXN-103," replied Anderson.

"My God," said Tanaka. "That would probably turn one of these wooden ships into matchsticks!"

"So would a Tomahawk."

"Okay," interrupted Castillo. "The question is moot anyway if we can't get at least one torpedo tube up and running…and if we can't figure out how to guide our

Tomahawks without GPS. We may not be able to do much of anything."

Drake cleared his throat. "Ha! I give ear to your lively words but little understanding. These *old* wooden ships as you are want to call them are perhaps even more fragile than you believe. The Spanish rushed many of these ships into service using butted plank, which allows for faster assembly. The result is an inferior ship. One that leaks."

"I read about that," said Tanaka. "Many of the old galleons had full time caulking crews. All they did was pump bilges and caulk the whole time they were at sea. Their job was to keep the ship afloat."

"So what you're saying, admiral," began Castillo, "is we don't need to score a direct hit. If we strike a ship, we're likely to take down all ships in the immediate vicinity because we will open up leaks in their hulls."

"I think you take my meaning," replied Drake.

"How would you launch an attack on the Armada using our powerful explosives, admiral?"

"When we strike at their flanks, the Spanish crowd in upon each other. That's when I would direct a powerful explosive. When they're so close, they will entangle each other in their haste to maneuver."

"All that remains then," said Castillo, "is to get our weapon systems up and running."

Drake abruptly stood, holding high his glass of ale and said, "I propose a toast, men!"

All in the room rose, holding out their glasses of ale or mugs of tea.

"To success!" They all clinked glasses and drank. "And thanks be to God for sending you to us by whatever strange device." Drake eyed Castillo, winked and added, "And I don't think we really want to mention this to anyone else. If that glorified clerk, Howard, were to hear of this, he'd want to see for himself, then Hawkins, then Essex, there'd be no end to the parade."

"Agreed!" said Castillo.

"And I think my first act," said Drake, "after battle will be to transfer my flag. This will be my new flagship, and I think I'll rename her *Revenge Almighty*!"

This last statement brought befuddled silence and concerned stares at Castillo.

Chapter 14

"Admiral, we're not joining the English Navy," said Castillo.

"What? Then why come you here?" asked Drake.

"We're here to help you against the Spanish Armada, sir."

"And then what? You're going to take leave?"

"Yes, we're going to establish a colony somewhere."

Drake gaped for long seconds in disbelief. "But that flies in the face of God's plan!"

Would it do any good to explain the *prime directive* to Drake? Probably not, thought Castillo. "I believe God planned for us to create a colony in this world."

There was heavy weather in Drake's stare. Dark storm clouds. "So you ally with us now and who tomorrow?" roared Drake, slapping the table. The gold fringe on his shoulder caps quivered. "The Spanish?"

"No, admiral. After we help you defeat the Spanish, we'll leave. We plan to establish a settlement."

"So taunt us with your God ship and its God-like powers," bellowed Drake, "then dismiss us, leaving us to our never-ending struggle against the tyrants of Spain and France, will you? You'll not leave! I'll not allow it," snarled Drake. He reached for his belt. That's when he realized he did not have his cutlass. "Not only false friends are you, but thieves, as well."

Castillo turned to Anderson. "Could you get the admiral's weapons? I think they're in the infirmary."

"Yes, sir." Anderson exited the wardroom.

"Are you Catholic, Castillo?" asked Drake.

"Yes, but not a practicing one."

"I don't take your meaning."

"I just mean it's been quite a while since I've been to mass."

"So...you are the *worst* of Catholics. A *Godless* one," spat Drake. "You'll be with Spanish whores in a fortnight."

Castillo stood and unbuttoned his shirt to show Drake the two knife scars beneath his collar bone and the two foot long burns that ran across his chest like dark purple ruts in a plowed field. "The Spanish did this to me. And this!" He held up his three-fingered left hand. "I have no love for the Spanish! That's why I'm here. You should understand that, admiral. We're, after all, both men of the sea. We're both..."

"Bah!" blasted Drake. "Men of the sea! Been deafened by cannon fire, have you? Seen smoke so thick across the water it looks a blanket of fleece, have you? Heard the dying screams of your brave men coming to you from across the sea, have you?" He stopped, breathing heavily.

"Okay," said Castillo. "I take your point, admiral. We are from different times. Different worlds. Your battles are a lot more savage. There's a lot more death and suffering. With technology our fighting is a lot more sanitized." Castillo collapsed into a chair, sighed and said, "If you don't want our help, just say so, admiral, and we'll be gone."

Drake had murder in his eye, a vein in his forehead was standing out in bold relief. Then he softened. Castillo could see the wheels turning. The old pirate was scheming. "A colony, say you. Why not here? England has land abundant, and sweet fresh water lakes and good crop land. What better place to consecrate your new endeavor?"

"Well," responded Castillo. He looked about the room and was met with questioning looks. "We'll discuss it. We'll have to take a vote."

"A vote?" Drake said it as if it were a new concept to him.

"Yes, it's an American thing."

"What is to consider? It's for you, no mistake! You'll be given land, all you want. And riches. And titles! You can even have your slaves." Drake gestured to Taylor and Chief Brown, who glared intensely back at him, bristling.

"Slaves?" Castillo couldn't believe it. "You know. I don't think we're going to need a vote after all. I'm going to turn you down on your offer. I can't speak for everyone here, but I am an American and I plan to stay an American even though my country won't exist for another two hundred years. It's a state of mind really. It's belief in families and fairness and a level playing field for everyone. England in this century is not for us."

In a bad bit of timing, Anderson came in and laid before Drake a cutlass and a dagger both with carved ivory handles. Drake reached out, gripped the cutlass tightly, stood and eyed each man in the room, as if issuing a challenge. He was measuring them again, Castillo realized. After long seconds he replaced the cutlass in its sheath on his belt. He did the same with his dagger.

"Before you go, admiral. We want you to take this." Castillo picked up a small cardboard box and opened it to reveal a small black electronic device the size of a broach. "It's a communicator. It goes in your ear like this." Castillo demonstrated on himself. "I will be able to hear your voice and you can hear mine in your ear from a great distance. There is a small button here. See? This turns it on."

Drake made no move to take it. Castillo held his intense stare and felt its heat. "You'd better take it, admiral. You may need to contact us."

Finally he snatched it away from him. "Bah!" he snorted and stormed out. Castillo directed him to the messdeck where his men were waiting and then showed them to the aft deck where their small boat was moored.

Castillo, Taylor and Lambert watched them row away. "Do you think he'll call us?" asked Taylor.

"I don't know," answered Lambert. "He seemed pretty mad."

"He's an explorer," said Castillo. "And a statesman, but first and foremost he's a privateer. He's used to taking what he wants, and this time he saw something he wanted badly but couldn't have, and it rankled him. But I think he'll call."

Hardly a soul slept on Kansas that night. Anderson and Tanaka sat at the tactical Tomahawk control screens, reading manuals and trying to figure out how to manually direct a Tomahawk in flight or at least program a flight path into it without benefit of GPS. There was a lot of head scratching.

Electronic Technicians Jahl Safir and Robert Smith worked on torpedo tube one. They used their analytical skills to troubleshoot the circuitry. They did continuity checks, replaced two bad connectors and poured over schematics. There was more head scratching.

Castillo ordered Kansas back to the Armada staging area off the coast of Flanders. He and the control room crew continued to monitor the Spanish preparing their invasion fleet in the dark. There was a different group of ships being loaded than the ones they saw before. There were lanterns all down the docks and piers where the loading operation was being performed. The flow of supplies and men had slowed. They were approaching readiness. Castillo knew the clock was ticking and wondered how long they really had before this vast fleet of ships sailed against England. There were ten large barge-like ships which appeared to be little more than platforms for hauling troops and horses. This was obviously how they intended to move most of their army up the Thames.

Castillo didn't like the idea of a Tomahawk attack. The detonation of several 1000 pound warheads above these ships would kill many. At least with a torpedo attack, the compression wave would be underwater and the crews would have a chance to abandon ship and possibly be rescued. But he didn't lie to himself. Many would die either way. That's why war is so unthinkable. It's simply homicide on a grand scale.

By morning there were many bleary-eyed crew members but no change of status. Anderson and Tanaka had figured out how to kill the GPS receivers on the Tomahawks but not how to direct them manually. Safir and Smitty had determined that there was power to the function controls on tube one, but no command was reaching the doors. Castillo had determined the Spanish fleet was ready to move.

Lambert found Castillo in his stateroom. She knocked.

"Come in," he called.

She found him sitting at his desk, staring at his family pictures. "How's it going?"

"Okay."

"Has Drake called in?"

"Not yet."

"You look lonely in here." There was worry in her blue eyes.

"One man's loneliness is another man's solitude," said Castillo dismissively.

"What?"

Castillo gave her a smile. "Funny, isn't it? How some people can't stand to be alone and others crave it?"

"Which type are you?"

"A little of both, I guess. Sometimes I want company and other times I want to be alone with my own thoughts."

"Do you want me to go?" She looked slightly hurt.

"No, Susan. I like your company. Maybe a little too much."

"What does that mean?" She asked, puzzled.

"I don't know. I don't know what I'm saying. I'm tired. And I'm concerned about what we're about to do."

"What are your concerns?"

"We're going to *kill* people, Susan. Some of them are evil, but most are not. They're just men following orders…family men…fathers…brothers. I don't like the idea of a Tomahawk strike. I want to use Mark 48's if we can."

Lambert said nothing.

There was a knock on the door frame. It was Lieutenant Guerrero. "It looks like the Armada is getting under way, sir."

"Shit! Okay, thanks, Maria." Castillo and Lambert went up the passageway to the control room. He could see ships unfurling canvas and leaving the piers on the big screen. The sun had been up for only an hour.

"They have the tide and the wind with them," said Tanaka. "And they're taking advantage of it."

Castillo turned to Anderson and asked, "Any progress on the Tomahawks?"

Anderson looked troubled. "No, and we're up against a lot, sir. The vehicle was designed to fly 1000 miles and strike a land target. Eric and I worked on it all night and we came up against the built-in safeguards. The vehicle doesn't arm until it flies a hundred miles. We're too close to our targets, sir. We investigated flying a vehicle 50 miles away and making a U-turn, but if the vehicle tries to boomerang there is another safing mechanism which disarms it. The only way we're going to be able to use these vehicles is if we drive 100 miles away and then launch."

"Shit! At top speed we could be 100 miles away in about three hours. It's a last resort, but it *can* be done."

"The only good news I have for you is our two Harpoons are useable. But they use radar to home on a target at sea and I don't know how strong a return they'll get off a wooden sailing vessel."

"Alright. Thanks, Wally. Right now, I'll take any good news I can get." Castillo turned to Lieutenant Bud Unger and asked, "Any word from Admiral Drake, Bud?"

"No, sir. Nothing so far."

"The comm station is up and running?"

"Yes, sir. Don't worry. As soon as he talks we'll get it here."

"Alright then. Mr. Taylor set the maneuvering watch. We're going to shadow these ships."

"Yes, sir," said Taylor. He picked up a receiver and made an announced throughout the ship:

Set maneuvering watch. Now, set maneuvering watch.

Men filed in and took their stations and soon Kansas was moving very slowly so as not to out pace the slow moving Spanish fleet.

In the center of the first and second crescent formations were the barges holding General Parma's soldiers, horses and cannon. They each had a ship towing them.

It took some time for them to get into formation and then begin moving as a unit.

"With no direction from Drake, I will wait until the English attack the flanks of the first crescent," said Castillo, "before I launch Harpoons. Drake said that the Spanish squeeze together tightly when they're under attack. That will give our Harpoons maximum effect."

Castillo picked up his receiver and dialed the torpedo room.

"Yes, sir," someone answered.

"This is the captain. Do you have a progress report for me?"

"Yes, sir. I think we're close. This is Robert Smith. We've been able to cannibalize from the other controllers, and we got a good health check just now, but I think we've got a problem somewhere else, sir. Jahl is looking at it right now. We really are kind of learning as we go on this thing."

"I understand, Smitty. Thank you and Safir for taking this on. I know it's not your thing. Keep working on it."

He turned to Lambert, "It would be nice to have some teeth. Without weapons we…"

"Sir!…" interrupted Unger. "I think we've got Drake!"

"Put him on speaker." Castillo picked up his receiver.

A voice began speaking from the overhead speakers. "Hello! Hailing Castillo, the American! Can you hear me?"

Castillo spoke into his receiver, "Yes, admiral. I hear you. Can you hear me?"

"God's boots! I can! This is sorcery!"

Castillo heard Lambert giggle. "The Spanish invasion has started, admiral. They are heading for the English coast. We're following them."

"I'm afraid it's over for us. God has sent us an ill wind."

Tanaka turned to Castillo. "The wind is out of the east southeast. I'll bet they're harbor locked."

"You can't leave Dover, admiral?"

"Lest God favors us with a shift of wind." Castillo could hear the fatigue in Drake's voice. "How fares your struggles, commander?"

"We have a few weapons…birds. Still no fish, but I have confidence in my people, admiral. They're very good."

"May God smile upon you, commander. I would wish you fair winds, but you have no need, do you? You and your ship are all that oppose them now. We pray for you."

"Okay, we'll oppose them alone then. If you listen in, we'll keep you updated on what we're doing. Maybe you can offer us advice, sir."

"Yes! Very good! Tell us your actions. We are most fraught with worry here."

"I understand. Have you told your commanders about us?"

"God's boots! No. I've only said, 'our prayers have been answered'. They imagine the Dutch are allying with us or some other nonsense. They'd not believe a God ship lest they see it themselves, no mistake."

"You know best, admiral. Wish us luck."

"Good luck, commander."

Castillo hung up the receiver and realized there were many expectant eyes on him. He sighed and said, "Okay, pilot, take us to 100 feet. Maneuvering, make turns for 35 knots."

"Aye, sir. 100 feet."

"Aye, sir. 35 knots."

Castillo switched the big screen to the navigation display. He watched the green land masses on the navigation screen. He knew where they had to go. He had to race ahead of these ships and put Kansas squarely between the Spanish invasion fleet and the mouth of the Thames. Kansas was the only thing opposing the Spanish now. It was all down to them.

When Kansas finally surfaced. it was 20 miles ahead of the Armada and about 30 miles from the mouth of the Thames. The Spanish fleet was too far away from the Armada to see them visually, but the ship's BPS 16 radar gave them a picture of where the fleet was.

"How's that radar image quality, Wally?" asked Castillo, inspecting the screen. There was a screen full of faint white dots on a field of black with land masses outlined in lime green. "Are those returns good enough for a Harpoon to lock onto?"

"Not sure, sir. Some returns are stronger than others, but we should be able to find a target out of that bunch."

"The problem with this weapon system," said Castillo to Lambert, who was sitting six feet away, "is it was designed to strike heavy surface ships. It depends on a strong radar return and hauls a high explosive 488 pound warhead. I think when it hits, it's going to reduce one of these ships to kindling and kill most of the crew."

Lambert said nothing. She only looked at him dolefully.

"But…it's all we've got. Secure the radar, Mr. Unger. Pilot, let's go down to 100 feet. Mr. Anderson, missile launch stations!"

"Aye, sir. Securing BPS 16."

"Aye, sir. Going to 100 feet."

"Aye, sir. missile launch stations." Anderson began giving orders to the two watchstanders next to him at weapon stations and to unseen crewmen.

Castillo switched the big screen back to the photonics mast and they watched as the restless waves engulfed the cameras and the scene became an aquamarine underwater one. The boat submerged.

Anderson was statusing launch systems when he stopped, turned to Castillo and said, "Sir! Smitty says they have door control on tube one now. They were able to cycle the door open and closed."

"Great!" said Castillo. "They're getting there."

After a time Anderson announced, "Systems are green, sir. Tubes 3 and 4 are ready for Harpoon launch."

"Very well. Begin launch count on tube 3."

"Aye, sir. Beginning count on tube 3 and…mark!" A countdown clock began running in the corner of Anderson's tactical weapon screen.

Castillo watched it tick down past 20 seconds. He looked at Lambert and held up his right hand with crossed fingers. She returned the gesture with her lips set tightly.

Anderson intoned, "5…4…3…2…1…launch."

A tornado of bubbles engulfed the photonics mast cameras, as the missile left its tube and surged upward.

A weapons watchstander responded, "Missile away!"

"Alright!" shouted Anderson, studying his screen. "The missile is flying normally and is getting some radar returns, sir." He could see what the missile was seeing. A smattering of faint white blips ahead of it. "I'm going to try and get a lock on that target in the second row giving us the strongest return."

"Good, Wally. Do it!"

"And…uh…we have a lock!" Anderson pumped his fist.

Castillo suddenly had a remorseful feeling for the unsuspecting men aboard that Spanish ship. They had no idea the hell that was about to come down on them.

Chapter 15
Aboard the Fiorencia
English Channel
20 miles off the Flemish coast

"God smiles on us, Francisco!" exclaimed Gaspar De Sosa. "He gives us a beautiful morning for victory and a good wind."

"Yes, and he keeps Drake and his English dogs locked up in their pen. There is nothing to stop us now, sir."

"It is a magnificent sight, is it not?" De Sosa swept his arm at the view. Ships as far as the eye could see with taut sunlit sails pitching up and down as they plowed through sequined green waves. He breathed in the cool salt air. "We are God's fleet carrying on God's mission, Francisco." He pointed at the great galleon 200 yards to the north. It rolled more slowly because of its great size. "Look at the San Leandro, Francisco. Look at the size of it. The power! How could one doubt it came from God? It must have dropped directly from heaven, for how else could you explain its perfect lines. The perfect way the deck sweeps in such a pure artful manner. It's a force of nature, is it not?" De Sosa laughed a hearty laugh that made his great belly tremble and his black beard quiver.

Francisco laughed too. His thin shoulders shook, and he showed his gap toothed smile, and nervously pulled at his shirt. "I think after we make our landing, we should make every Englishman line up and kiss his Holiness's ring. What say you, De Sosa?"

"A good idea, Francisco, but the Pope is a busy man. He doesn't have time for English scum."

"Maybe they could kiss Admiral Sidonia's ass then. Same thing!"

Both men roared with laughter. De Sosa scanned the horizon ahead and saw nothing but the empty sea and cottony white clouds. There was no sound except the snap of banners in the wind, the rattle of block and tackle and the creak of hull planking as the ship plunged through the waves. Both men gripped the rail tightly to keep their feet as the deck heaved under them.

"Sail!" called the lookout from above. "One point on the bow." He pointed.

Every deck hand turned to where the lookout was pointing.

"That's not a sail," said Francisco.

"What is it?" asked De Sosa.

It was like a tentacle from a Portuguese man of war. One fibrous tentacle extending upward from the sea. It pointed to the sky…up and up. Then it curved down.

"It looks like it's coming toward us," said De Sosa with concern. He extended his spy glass and looked at it.

"I know what it is!" cried Francisco, his brown eyes alive with excitement. "It is a message from God. I have read it many times in the Bible. Heavenly messengers always come from the sky or the sea. It is an angel come to give us a joyful message. God is pleased with us, De Sosa!"

De Sosa's eyes were troubled. He wasn't so sure this was a good thing. It was streaking across the water toward them very fast now. Faster than a racing falcon. He had never seen anything so fast! It was coming straight at them…no…it was coming toward the San Leandro. The men on the San Leandro saw it too. They were at the rails, pointing. There was a sound building like the roar of a lion. It was almost on them. It was…

BOOM!

There was a bright flash and the gunnel beneath De Sosa's arm exploded into fragments and a great invisible hand slapped at him, knocking him end over end. He tumbled from one side of the deck to the other. He grabbed at Francisco and tried to stop him from going over the rail but he failed. He saw the frozen open-mouthed look of horror on Francisco's face as he went over. The Florencia rolled hard over away from the blast. He waited long seconds for the ship to right itself, and when it finally did, he staggered to his feet. There was a sharp pain in his side and when he looked there, he saw a large shard of wood sticking out from between his ribs. Fighting against the pain, he struggled to the rail. The San Leandro was gone! There was nothing but jagged smoking pieces of wood and broken charred planks floating in the water. He also saw bodies floating in the wreckage and heard the cries and entreaties to God of dying men. What could have done such a thing?

De Sosa looked up and saw most of Florencia's sails had been shredded and the mizzen mast had been snapped like a twig. There were only two top gallants still intact. He quickly looked around at the surrounding ships. The Antonio De Palma's sails were fluttering free, having been ripped free of their moorings. Most of the sails of the San Juan De Portugal were shredded like Florencia's. La Trinidad also had shredded sails.

"Capitan!" shouted a crewman. "The larboard hull planking has collapsed, sir! Water is rushing in! We can't stop it!"

"Get boats in the water!" ordered De Sosa. Then he noticed all the nearby ships were listing and putting boats in the water. Others had put up distress flags and were turning around. A distress flag meant the ship had suffered heavy damage and was out of the action.

What could have done this? Is this the hand of God?

"Sir," said a crewman. "You've been injured!"

He looked down at the piece of wood sticking out of his side. "I know." He looked to where the flying demon had come. That's when he saw another one. Another long tentacle reaching toward the sky. It arched, then plunged down and built speed as it came directly at them…no…this time it was going to pass on the other side about 100 yards away. As it roared by, he was able to see it for a split second. It was like a white stove pipe spewing white smoke with triangular attachments on it.

BOOM!

This time the flash was farther away, but it still knocked De Sosa and the crewman next to him off his feet and rolled the Florencia. De Sosa pulled himself up on a rail, crossed himself and said, "We've angered God in some way! He has sent a great demon to smite us!"

• • •

Castillo was talking to Drake by remote communicator. "We've launched two powerful devices, admiral. I'm not sure how much damage we've done. I'm taking the ship closer so we can get a visual assessment."

"Splendid! How goes your attempt to right your weapons?" Asked Drake hopefully.

"We're making progress, but not operational yet."

"Very well, commander. God be with you."

"Thanks, admiral."

Anderson turned to Castillo and said, "Smitty just reported in. They have ATP control on tube one and they were able to cycle the dump valve. They're almost there, sir!"

"Alright!" exclaimed Castillo. "Go Safir and Smitty! Good men!"

When Kansas got to within 3 miles, Castillo brought them up to periscope depth and they took a look.

On the big screen they could see the center of the first crescent formation was in disarray. Some ships were listing heavily and crews were obviously abandoning them in small boats, while others had men aloft cutting away damaged sails and running up new rigging. Two ships were smoking and appeared to be on fire. There was debris in the water that looked like chunks of ship decking, and one large ship was going down by the stern, the bow sticking up high out of the water.

"I'd say they've lost maybe 15 to 20 ships," said Castillo.

"Not enough," remarked Tanaka.

"True. They're probably just going to reform, fill in the hole in their formation and continue." Castillo was frustrated.

"I'm not sure how well a Mark 48 is going to do, sir," said Anderson. "They have active homing heads on them, and I just don't think they're going to get a strong enough sonar return to get a lock on one of those ships."

"I know," replied Castillo. "You're going to have to guide each one in all the way to target from the tactical screen."

"Okay, but it's going to be a lot of guesswork without sonar targets."

"I know," replied Castillo, then thinking aloud. "Any torpedo shot would do more damage, however, if they were closer together."

"But Admiral Drake said they don't tighten their formation unless they're threatened."

Castillo suddenly got an idea. "Maybe *we* can threaten them." He tugged at his chin, then said, "Pilot, take us up."

"Aye, sir. Surfacing."

• • •

Admiral Medina Sidonia was still puzzling over the wreckage. Something had totally destroyed two of his largest galleons. Nothing left but smoking wreckage! And six others are crippled so badly the crews are abandoning them. They're headed for the bottom! And another six so badly damaged, they'll not be afloat much longer. They're running for the French coast!

One of his commanders, Capitan Gaspar De Sosa, was standing before him now. He was wearing a white cotton shirt and leggings, but Sidonia could see under the open shirt a bandage covering his side. It was soaked with blood.

"You got a good look at this flying demon, De Sosa?"

"Not a good look, admiral. Only a fleeting look, sir."

"And what did it look like to you?"

"It looked like a flying smokestack, sir. And it issued white smoke as it passed and made a sound like rolling thunder, sir."

He would normally think a man to be quite mad who told such a story. But something horrible had happened, and he was at a loss to explain it. God? This was not the hand of God! God did not do such things. This was something else. Something English!

"What, Ho!" alerted a lookout, pointing.

Sidonia turned to face that direction and saw nothing but empty sea. Then he *did* see something. There was something low in the water about a mile away. He put his spy glass to his eye. It looked like a great black leviathan with something on its back. A cold trickle of dread ran down his spine. He remembered one of his capitans, Cordova, reporting an encounter with a giant evil leviathan in the Irish Sea a few weeks ago. It sent black clad demon warriors aboard his ship, killed ten of his crew and crippled his ship. He had dismissed it at the time. Cordova was a superstitious fool who made up wild stories to explain his own inadequacies.

"What is it?" gasped De Sosa.

Sidonia said nothing. The unease obvious in his dark eyes. They watched silently as the leviathan swiftly swam to one end of their formation, turned and swam back the other way. It was crossing their path, menacing them, like a great evil shark…waiting for them to come.

"Filipe!" called Sidonia.

"Yes, admiral," answered a small man running down the deck.

"Send a message to Capitan De Recalde and Capitan De Valdez."

The small man pulled out a piece of sharpened lead and a flat board and poised to write.

"Tell them there is a leviathan in our path. It intends to stop us, but we will not be stopped. Use close formation and give Parma and his army maximum protection. That's all."

"Yes, admiral." The little man scurried away.

"This is the greatest and most powerful fleet to ever sail the sea!" exclaimed Sidonia. "The English can not oppose us, so they send a black beast. Well, a beast can not stop us either."

He looked at the beast swimming before them, then at De Sosa's bleeding side wound. This was an English trick of some kind he was sure of it.

• • •

Castillo had been playing his psychological mind game with the Spanish fleet for about a half hour.

"It's working, sir. They're tightening their formation," said Tanaka.

Anderson turned and said, "Smitty and Safir just fired a water slug from tube one, sir."

There was whooping and high fives all over the control room.

"A water slug?" asked Lambert.

"It's the final operational check," said Castillo. "If they can fire a water slug, they can fire a torpedo."

"Ah ha!"

"Okay, Mr. Anderson. Load tube one. I want a warload!"

"Aye, sir. Loading tube one!"

Castillo passed on the good news to Admiral Drake, then began to look at all the available targets in front of them. "I think we should try for the large one in the second row with the red cross on the mainsail."

"How about the one to the left of it?" said Tanaka. "I think that one's a flagship. Look at the banners. And look at the coat of arms on the side of the sterncastle. I think it carries someone important."

"Okay, designate that *Sierra 1*. Bud, can you get a distance and bearing on him with radar?"

"I think so, sir," said Bud Unger. He looked at his radar display, then at the view screen then at his display again. After several back and forths between the two he finally announced, "Distance to *Sierra 1* is 1.42 miles and bearing is 192 relative."

"Good enough," replied Anderson. "It's going to need wire guidance the whole way in. I'll program a course into it and program it to detonate after it runs the distance. We should get pretty close."

"Sounds good."

"Tube one loaded, sir," said Anderson. "And…" He clicked several computer keys. "…uh…programmed!"

"Very good!" Castillo cast a glance at Lambert. "Fire one!"

"Firing one," intoned Anderson.

There was a slight thump. "One away!" said a weapons watchstander.

On the view screen they saw the faint white wake of a Mark 48 torpedo beneath the water's surface as it streaked away from the ship.

• • •

Sidonia kept watching the black beast swimming before them. He was hoping to get close enough to bring his bow guns to bear. They were small rail mounted guns but they could deliver a sting. But the creature seemed to be keeping a steady distance between it and the fleet, just out of gun range. As long as it keeps moving away from us, it won't be a problem, thought Sidonia. If it so much as shows…

WHOOMP!

A monstrous dome of angry white water rose next to his ship. It grew larger and larger until it touched five ships. Sidonia's ship rolled onto its side as if some enormous wind gust had pushed it over. Sidonia reached out and gripped a halyard tightly so as not to be thrown into the water. Several crewmen fell past him and smacked the surface of the water. There was a booming crack, then a series of popings and ripping noises. Sidonia kept waiting for the ship to right itself, but when he looked across the water, he knew it would never happen. He was looking at the stern of his magnificent ship, San Martin. It had no bow attached to it. It righted itself and floated upright with soaked men still hanging to the lines off the sides of it. Where the bow should be was jagged deck boards and bizarre broken hull planks. Some invisible giant had broken San Martin's back and then rent it in two!

When he looked over at the San Pedro, it lie on its side, mortally wounded also. He could only see half of its massive hull protruding from the sea. Many of its hull planks were damaged, stoved in as if a fist had hit it. He heard men's shouts and agonizing calls to God, and he wondered how many other ships were damaged this way.

The last thing Sidonia saw before the bow wreckage rolled over on top of him was the dreaded black beast on the horizon…waiting.

• • •

The Kansas control room crew watched the result of their first torpedo strike on the big screen. "We didn't hit *Sierra 1* directly," said Anderson, "but we got pretty close."

"Yes, *Sierra 1* is done for," said Tanaka. "Some of the surrounding ships as well."

"Let's pick out another target toward the front of the formation," said Castillo. "Reload tube one."

"Aye, sir," replied Anderson. "Reloading tube one."

"How about this one, hauling a barge," said Tanaka. The galleon was pulling a long rectangular raft with structures like long tents that ran the length of it. It was flat with a deck as wide as three galleon decks.

"That barge is full of horses and men," said Castillo. "Let's find another one."

Tanaka found another large galleon. Castillo deemed it suitable. "Designate the target *Sierra 2*."

"Aye, sir," responded Anderson. "*Sierra 2*."

"Distance to *Sierra 2*, 1.96 miles, bearing 265 relative," said Unger.

"Got it," said Anderson. And a few seconds later, "Tube one loaded, sir…a-a-a-and programmed."

"Fire one!"

"Firing one!"

Another slight thump and a weapons watchstander intoned, "One away."

On the view screen they saw another torpedo wake streak away from the ship's bow.

This time they scored a direct hit. Their target ship, *Sierra 2*, was lifted out of the water by a large swell of furious water. When it collapsed, the ship fell into several pieces. The bow held together, but the back of the ship separated from it and then split as if by a giant machette. When the angry swirling stopped, there was only rubble in the water. Castillo zoomed in and saw many bodies floating amid the sections of planking and masts. Two other nearby ships began tilting, then slowly went over on their sides.

"See those flags, sir?" asked Tanaka. "White with a black 'X' on it? I think that means the ship has taken heavy damage and is out of the fight. They're all veering off."

"There are a lot of those," said Castillo.

"I'm guessing thirty, thirty-five," said Tanaka. "They're either damaged or the crews are scared shitless of an unseen enemy. I know *I* would be!"

"I wonder how many men we've killed so far," reflected Castillo. He looked at Lambert through haunted eyes.

"I don't know," said Lambert, "but haven't we saved lives by stopping them?"

"So we're taking lives to save lives. I understand the concept, but it just sounds wrong no matter how you say it."

When he looked into Lambert's eyes, they looked dull not their usual liveliness. "When's the last time you slept, Susan?"

"I don't know. How about you?"

"It's been a while." Castillo squeezed his eyes shut tightly, rubbed them and expelled breath. "Saving the free world is exhausting work." He stared at the screen for a few seconds, then, "I want to communicate with these guys."

"Communicate?" asked Lambert. "With the Spanish? How're you going to do that?"

"I don't know. Do we have a bullhorn or something like that? Does anybody know?"

"I don't think so, sir," said Unger. "I mean, I've never seen one."

"I don't think a bullhorn would reach them anyway, sir," said Tanaka.

"You're probably right." Castillo watched the destruction unfolding on screen. Ships were heeling over. Small lifeboats were bobbing like corks across the water. Some boats were pulling wet bedraggled survivors out of the sea. Abruptly, Castillo turned to Bud Unger and asked, "How many RF buoys do we have on board, Bud?"

"Six, I think, sir."

"Do we have any speakers?"

"I think we have a few spares for the overhead address system, sir"

"Okay, here's what I need." Castillo began to sketch on a screen next to him. "This will at least give me the ability to talk to them. And I need it in an hour!"

Tanaka and Unger turned to each other with surprise. Tanaka silently mouthed, "An hour?"

In a little more than an hour, they had six RF buoys rigged with radios and speakers. They tied bright red strips of cloth on each antenna so it would be easier to see the gray buoys in the water. After some testing, they set them adrift in the path of the Armada spacing them out about 100 yards apart.

The first crescent formation of ships had been decimated. Out of the 150 ships that had started out there were only half that number now. Castillo noticed they had reformed into a smaller crescent and they were slowing down to allow the second crescent formation to come up and reinforce them. If they combined formations, they would have more than 200 ships.

Castillo waited until he judged the leading ships were close enough to hear the speaker buoys. He zoomed in on a buoy, then he zoomed on the ship next to the buoy. He began speaking into his receiver in his best Spanish. He told them to stop and go no further. They must turn back.

He saw men on the deck of the ship stop, go to the gunnels and look down at the buoy. It's obvious they had heard it.

"I'll be damned," said Taylor. "It worked!"

Castillo got inspired. He told them the black beast in the water was not sent by Satan, but by God. It was sent to stop them and it has great power. The eyes of the Spanish sailors turned to Kansas.

"I see fear there," said Castillo. "But there's defiance too. Some of them are hard men. Afraid of very little."

"Maybe they need convincing, sir," said Tanaka.

"Yes, I suppose so. Mr. Anderson, load tube one. I want a dummy."

"A dummy, sir?"

"Yes, this demonstration is going to require some finesse."

"Aye, sir. Loading tube one with a dummy load."

Castillo spoke again to the Spanish. He told them that if they didn't turn back at once, the sea beast would sink the ship in the front row with the red and yellow trim on the bow.

"Do you see the one in the front row, Mr. Anderson? It has red and yellow trim on both sides of the bow. They kind of look like shark's teeth."

"Yes, sir, I've got it."

"Designate that one *Sierra 3* and target it. You're going to have to run shallow or the fish could pass under him. These ships don't have much of a draft."

"Yes, sir. Targeting *Sierra 3*. This is going to take some precision and with no sonar return."

"I'll line up the bow of Kansas with the target. You should be able to steer it visually if the fish is running on the surface."

"Okay, sir. Let's give it a try."

Castillo turned Kansas so its bow was pointing at *Sierra 3*. He picked up his receiver and spoke again to the Spanish fleet. He told them that this was their last warning. They must turn back. God has ordered it. If they do not, God has ordered the sea beast to sink the ship with the red and yellow bow in the front row.

The crewmen on *Sierra 3* were hurrying to load their bow guns. They were ramming charges into the mouths of the cannon and hefting cannon shot. So were crews on several other ships.

"There's your answer," said Taylor. "They're getting ready to fire on us."

G. Ernest Smith

"Tube one is loaded with a dummy fish, sir," announced Anderson.

"Fire one."

"Firing one!"

"One away!" said a weapons watchstander.

They watched the Mark 48 leave the bow tube and begin accelerating to the target. They could easily see it running along the surface. Once it shot between two waves and was briefly out of the water. When it began drifting slightly to the left, Anderson gave it course correction to bring it back on target. It kept building speed until when it finally slammed into the Spanish ship, it was traveling at close to 60 miles per hour.

They knew when the 3000 pound projectile had hit the Spanish ship because they saw the sails and masts shudder slightly. At first nothing happened. Then the ship seemed to settle lower in the water and crewmen became very agitated, running actively across the decks. They lowered boats into the water and the big ship listed away from the strike. Slightly at first, then more and more until it rolled onto its side. Spumes of spray jetted from the ship as inner compartments collapsed and filled with water. They could see half the dark green body of the torpedo protruding from its side.

By now the current had carried the speaker buoys throughout the formation of Spanish ships. Castillo picked up his receiver and told them that they must turn back at once. God demands it. If they do not, God has ordered the black sea beast to kill them all. They can not stop it. No one will be spared.

They waited for something to happen, but nothing did.

"How long should we wait?" asked Lambert.

"I don't know," replied Castillo. He had grown accustomed to having Lambert sitting in the observer seat to his right in the weapons area. She had become a fixture in the control room, and he enjoyed her company.

"Let's load a warshot," sighed Castillo. "They need more convincing."

"Wait, look!" said Lambert, pointing. Some ships began to turn. "They're raising those flags!"

It was true. Most of the ships were raising white flags with the black 'X'. They were taking themselves out of the action and turning toward the French coast.

"Oh no," said Castillo. "Two ships hauling barges have cut them loose."

"They're making a run for it," said Taylor, "and those barges were dead weight. Screw Parma's army!"

"How many hundreds of men are on those barges do you suppose?" asked Castillo.

"And horses," said Lambert.

"The wind and current is going to take them into the rocks on the English coast," said Tanaka.

"Well, Shit!" shouted Castillo in frustration.

Chapter 16

"Admiral Drake, are you there?" asked Castillo.

"Yes, commander," Drake responded from the overhead speakers.

"We've broken up the first two formations of the Armada. Most of the ships are turning toward the French coast."

"Excellent! Good work, commander." Castillo could hear the smile in Drake's voice.

"But we have a problem. Two barges full of soldiers are going to make landfall on the English coast in that area you call Ramsgate."

"I'll alert Colonel Pierce. He'll have his troops there to greet them."

"Good idea, admiral. Good luck."

"Good luck, commander."

"We have to make sure those barges don't hit the rocks, guys," said Castillo. "Kansas is going to become a tug. We have to pull those barges away from the rocks and to a beach where the soldiers and horses can be safely unloaded." Castillo turned to Taylor. "When we get close to those barges, someone may try to take a shot at us. We're going to need cover fire. Can you and Crystal get up in the sail with your guns again?"

"Absolutely," said Taylor. He looked at Crystal Mc-Connell who was sitting across the control room next to Lambert. "What do you say, girl? Are you up for another mission?"

"Sure," she said, beaming at Taylor.

Once again Kansas's crew hauled the big 50 caliber gun to the top of the sail with its ammo cases and Crystal McConnell climbed up the access ladder with the SEAL sniper rifle slung over her shoulder. When Taylor and McConnell were in position and ready, they gave Castillo the go ahead. Kansas slowly approached the first barge as Castillo watched the big screen.

It was apparent the soldiers were aware of their situation. At least two hundred men were standing on deck. Some had hands on hips and some had arms crossed. It was obvious they were drifting toward a rocky shore and had no idea what to do. As Kansas approached, some of them took note and ducked behind splash walls. One soldier picked up a musket, but the man next to him put a hand on the barrel, forcing it down and shook his head.

Kansas launched an inflatable with two volunteers in it. They quickly retrieved the towing line from the barge and tried attaching it to one of Kansas's deck cleats, but the line was too big in diameter, so they had to tie it securely to a narrower braided nylon line, then secure it to Kansas.

Castillo gradually took out the slack in the towing line and then Kansas began to pull. "Watch the heat exchangers, Mr. Tanaka. We don't want anything overheating."

"Yes, sir," responded Tanaka, watching the reactor screens before him.

When they were before a large flat beach, Castillo slackened the tow line and had the crewmen cast it off and allow the barge to drift in to shore and beach itself. When they went to retrieve the second barge, it was almost on the rocks. They began to apply pressure to the tow line and pull with scant feet between the barge and the rocky shoals. Kansas towed the second barge until it was at the same flat beach as the first then they cast it off. The second barge nudged the first barge.

The first barge had lowered its ramps and was starting to unload men and horses. No sooner had the first men stepped onto the beach than hundreds of soldiers on horseback came thundering up the beach. They were flying the Tudor crest high on standards and armed with pikes and long bows. It was Colonel Pierce with the mounted unit of the 3rd battalion of the English Army. The Spanish soldiers quickly threw down their arms and knelt down in surrender.

There were smiles and high fives all around in the control room.

"We have about 2 hours of daylight left," said Castillo. "We need to go see what the third crescent formation of the Armada is doing."

When they got to where the third crescent formation should be, it was not there. Castillo swept the sea in all directions, and finally caught sight of them heading for the French coast.

"They must have figured it out," said Tanaka.

"Or maybe someone got word to them. *Break off the attack*," said Castillo. "I'm not sure how they communicate with each other at sea. They must have a way."

"I'd like to be at *that* debriefing tonight," said Tanaka.

"That would be something!" laughed Castillo. "They're going to compare notes and try to agree on exactly what actually happened today."

"I'd hate to be the one to have to explain it to *King Phillip*," said Lambert.

Castillo chuckled, "Yes!"

Taylor and McConnell stowed their guns away, glad that they weren't needed, Kansas's sail was buttoned up and Kansas submerged. Once again Kansas took up station on the French coast in sight of the Armada remnants. They watched the Spanish fleet secure from their failed invasion, unloading the soldiers, horses and supplies. It went on all night, but Castillo didn't watch it. He was dead on his feet, having not slept for over 48 hours. He was hungry too, but the bed won out. It was calling his name.

Castillo had no trouble sleeping that night.

• • •

Lord Admiral Charles Howard removed his black cloak and flung it across the table on top of his sword, then flung his rangy frame into his padded chair, exhausted. He'd had a long night interrogating Spanish soldiers. He adjusted his leather doublet and stared long and hard at his war council sitting across the large oak table from him.

"Does anyone know what happened?"

This was met with silence and empty faces.

"All I know," bellowed Howard, "is the Spanish invasion fleet was on its way, and we were powerless to stop it. And now it is not!" Howard pulled on his long nose. "And Colonel Pierce has captured over a thousand Spanish soldiers who landed on the beach at Ramsgate. And they are all babbling about being rescued by a sea monster!"

"A sea monster?" scoffed Lord Williams. "The Spanish have always been given to tall tales and imaginative stories."

This earned Howard's intense glare. Williams was a slight man and did not endure Howard's hard glare easily. He suddenly found something of interest on his left hand.

"Drake! What say you?" Howard shifted his concentration to Admiral Drake.

"Why ask me?" responded Drake, locking eyes with Howard.

Howard bored into Drake. "You know something of this, Drake. You disappeared two nights ago. And when reappeared, your manner was different."

Drake said nothing. The silence in the room was deafening. Finally, Drake shifted in his seat and said, "Different?"

"Yes, I'm not the only one to notice." Howard leaned forward. "You acted less concerned about the Spanish, less anxious, and you told Admiral Hawkins here that God was going to intervene in England's behalf. You seemed to take comfort in it."

Drake raised an eyebrow and directed a glance at Admiral Hawkins, who looked away. Hawkins had betrayed a confidence.

Drake had to make a decision. A voice in his head told him to be cautious. Say nothing. His story would never be believed, and he would look ridiculous. He had to think of his career. But… what if he captured this magnificent ship and became its master! What a thing that would be! He would be the most powerful man in the world with such a ship. More powerful than any monarch. It made his head spin. He might be able to do it with Howard's help.

He placed both hands on the smooth surface of the oak table and stood, having made his decision. "Milords, I was taken two nights ago to the most amazing ship. It came from another world. Another time."

He told them all of the ship he had toured. He took a quill and sheets of Howard's writing paper and drew sketches as best he could of what he remembered. When he was done, the looks of disbelief were obvious on every face.

"A ship that travels under the sea at the speed of a galloping horse?" said Howard doubtfully.

"A ship that bombards the enemy with powerful explosives by air and water?" asked a skeptical Admiral

Hawkins. "Drake, someone's poisoned your rum. It has given you a fevered dream."

"Show that drawing to the Spanish soldiers and see if they recognize it," demanded Drake. "And I have a few oarsmen who will verify my story as well." Drake sat back down with a sour expression and crossed his arms. "But you have a doubting nature so discount my story, and explain it to her Majesty as you wish."

"Do you maintain this ship faced and defeated the Armada on its own?" asked Howard.

"Yes. The original plan was for a joint attack, but when our fleet became harbor locked, it had to face the Spanish fleet alone. But it was up to the task. This warship could stand against all of the Spanish empire, no mistake. Maybe even God himself."

Howard thought of the implications. Drake could see the calculation behind his cold brown eyes. "Blasphemy aside, what proof have you of your story, Drake?"

"Only this," said Drake. He laid a small black device the size of a cameo clasp on the table. "It allows me to talk to the ship's commander. A man named *Castillo*."

• • •

They watched the Armada all the following day from the control room, but there was not a lot of activity. The Armada did not look like a fleet that was going anywhere. There was not much happening at all. The only excitement during the day was when Kansas had to relocate because a French fisherman noticed Kansas's photonics mast sticking out of the water and got curious about it.

Castillo had lunch with his senior staff which included Crystal McConnell and Susan Lambert. McConnell was engrossed in something. She had an ebook reader and was reading intently. He was curious. "What are you studying, Crystal?"

"I was trying to figure out how hard it would be to make musical instruments. It looks pretty hard!"

"Musical instruments?" Castillo tried to keep the surprise out of his voice.

"I polled the crew, but all I could find was a guitar and two harmonicas, which is a start, I guess."

"Why are you studying music, Crystal? If I may ask."

"Music is important. Music is therapy, it is emotional expression and much more," replied McConnell. "A society is defined by their music. They use music every time they celebrate, every time they mourn, every time they worship." Her look said, "Need I say more?"

"Really?" responded Castillo.

"Yes," replied McConnell. "In the first few years of our society, we'll have stereo players, but they'll eventually fail and we'll have to make our music the old fashioned way. I'm thinking ahead."

Taylor cleared his throat. "Did you know Crystal is an accomplished pianist?"

"Now, why does that not surprise me?" chuckled Castillo.

"It's true. She's played in a world famous orchestra," crowed Taylor.

"Edinburgh," confirmed McConnell. "But that's in the past, I'm afraid. The piano doesn't exist here yet. I'll never play again and that saddens me."

Castillo had never thought about it before. Music *is* important. People turn to music for solace. Or when work is done to relax. Or sometimes during work, to make the work go easier. He was thankful for talented people like McConnell to think of these things.

When he went to the control room later, he found McConnell standing in the passageway talking to a crewman. "Crystal," said Castillo. "Come to my stateroom. I have something I want you to see."

McConnell nodded, but there were questions in her eyes. When she got to Castillo's stateroom, he closed the door, sat down at his desk and opened his laptop. "You must swear never to reveal what I am about to show you."

"Okay," she said, but her eyebrows were arching in concern. *What could this be?*

Castillo went through some files on his laptop until he found the right one, then clicked on it. It began to play. It was a video:

I'll have a blue Christmas without you
I'll be so blue just thinking about you
Decorations of red on a green Christmas tree
Won't be the same dear, if you're not here with me

Her mouth dropped open. "Oh my God!" she exclaimed. "Is that Mason?"

"Yes," replied Castillo. "That is our very own Commander Taylor performing in a karaoke bar in Norfolk called the Rusty Anchor. When this hit Youtube, it went viral, and he picked up the nickname *Elvis* at command school."

They both listened, saying nothing for a while. McConnell smiled and twisted a finger through her long chestnut locks.

That's when those blue memories start callin'
You'll be doin' all right with your Christmas of white
But I'll have a blue blue blue blue Christmas

The video was not high definition, but was of fairly high quality. Taylor really threw himself into it. He closed his eyes, cradled the microphone and caressed each note with a soulful expression, capturing the emotional baritone of Elvis Presley perfectly.

"He's actually quite good!" said McConnell, surprised.

"I think so too," said Castillo. "Anyway, I just wanted to share that with you since you're interested in music. I thought you might want to know about the XO's talents. I don't think many crewmembers have seen it."

"I'm glad you did! Could I have a copy of that file?"

"Sure, but remember," said Castillo furtively. "It's a secret." Castillo copied the file to a flashdrive for her.

When she left his stateroom, she was as excited as a little girl with a new pony. Castillo felt good about that. He had given her something else she had in common with Taylor. Music. And he had no doubt she would tell people about it. She was bursting to tell someone. He chuckled.

• • •

That evening while Castillo sat in the control room, he checked in with admiral Drake.

"The Armada appears to be dead, admiral," said Castillo. "Very quiet. Minimal crews. We'll watch them awhile, but I don't think they're going to bother you again."

"That's good!" came admiral Drake's voice through the overhead 1MC speakers. "Can I call on you if they threaten us again?"

"Sure, but your communicator is only good for a few more days, then it will die. But we'll keep monitoring the Spanish in our travels. If anything happens, we'll be back." As he said it, he thought it was a pretty tall promise. How would they monitor world events with no electronic media?

"A grateful nation would like to thank you and your crew, commander."

"No thanks necessary, admiral."

"But we disagree. We are having a celebration and an award ceremony tomorrow. You and your crew will be guests of honor. Please come."

"Well…I…"

"Come come! You've nothing better to do. Her Majesty wants to meet you."

"Let me run it by my crew."

"A vote?"

"Yes, a vote."

"Fine! Take your vote," he said disdainfully and disconnected.

Castillo turned to Lambert. "Feel like going to a party?"

Castillo polled the crew and got mixed results. Some were in favor of going to the celebration and meeting the queen, but many, including Taylor and Chief Brown, didn't trust the English and wanted to get on with scouting locations for their new colony. In the end the 'ayes' won, and they made preparations to attend the celebration.

Castillo had one U.S. Navy dress white class 'A' uniform, so he decided to wear that to the ceremony with campaign ribbons. Lambert and McConnell were scrambling. Lambert decided to wear a lemon pant suit she had packed accessorized with a red neck scarf and red pumps. She would have liked to wear something better to meet the queen of England, but it was the best she could do. McConnell opted for a white lacy silk blouse with a black suede jacket and white slacks and black patent leather pumps.

Many crew members opted out, not wishing to attend the ceremony. This made the decision easier for Castillo concerning who to leave behind to man the ship.

Castillo delivered the news to admiral Drake. "We'd be glad to attend your ceremony, admiral. But we would like a discreet place to make anchor so as to protect our ship. You understand. The fewer prying eyes, the better."

"Good news, commander!" responded Drake. "And I give ear to your concerns. We have a safe place for your ship to make harbor. A protected cove south of the Thames where you'll have good cover and few curious eyes."

"Excellent, admiral! Looking forward to seeing you again."

"Yes. Much returned, sir!"

Lieutenant Maria Guerrero found the cove on the English coast Drake described with some help from the radar and Admiral Drake. She plotted a course easy to follow for Castillo. He put the photonics cameras on three screens, and as they pulled into the cove, the control room crew observed their approach. They were surfaced and pulling into a tree-lined estuary.

"It's shallow. We have less than 20 feet under our hull according to the fathometer," said Unger.

There was a 200 foot dock to the right side of the boat with several small skiffs moored there. The crew also noticed a line of carriages and coaches lined up on the access road next to the dock.

"Those must be for us," said Castillo.

"I still don't like this," said Taylor. "I don't trust these people."

"Your concern has been noted."

"But you're going anyway," said Taylor.

"Well, Mase, I think I have to. They're extending us a great honor. We're to meet the queen. I can't just say, 'no thanks'"

Taylor said nothing. He only glowered blackly.

"But I'm going to wear a remote communicator, so we can stay in touch. If you don't hear from me every fifteen minutes, take Kansas out into the Channel and await further orders. If you don't hear from us in 24 hours, take off. Get these people to safety."

"You want me to just take off and leave you and half the crew behind? Not likely."

"Come on, Mase. If it comes to that, then we've been compromised, imprisoned or worse."

"Is that supposed to make me feel better?"

Castillo blew out an exasperated breath. "I think you're worried for no reason. Nothing's going to happen."

"I've heard that before...*sir*."

It was Castillo's turn to say nothing.

Castillo, Lambert and the other crewmen emerged from the aft access hatch blinking in the bright spectacular persimmon sunset. The sun was throwing orange rays across rippled cloud bottoms just visible through the trees on the western shore.

The dock was lined with people having various expressions. Some were beaming. Some were agog with wide eyes and open mouths, obviously amazed by Kansas. The water in the estuary was so glassy, there were two images of everything, dock, skiffs, people...one rightside up and one upside down.

Kansas could not get close enough to the dock to moor because of the lack of depth, so it went to station keeping as close as possible and the skiffs met the boat and ferried crew to the dock in small groups.

Castillo and Lambert were in the first boat. Castillo picked out Admiral Drake in the crowd. "See the tall guy next to Drake with the black cape and plumed black hat?" said Castillo.

"Yes," answered Lambert.

"I think that's Admiral Howard. He's the man in charge."

"He looks like someone important."

When the Kansas crew was all gathered on the dock, Drake approached them. "Is this all?" he asked, disappointment in his voice. There were about 45 people there.

"These are all the people we could spare, I'm afraid," answered Castillo. "Someone has to man the ship."

"I see," said Drake. He introduced them to all the naval high command, Howard, Hawkins, Williams, Sheffield and another Howard. They all shook hands, the English officers noticeably taken aback by the presence of women in the group.

Howard bent at the waist, took Lambert's hand in his and kissed it never taking his eyes from hers. "And what do you do, milady?"

"Test Ops," replied Lambert smiling at him. From his blank expression she could tell she needed to expand on that. "I organize testing on new weapons and counter measures. Everything must be thoroughly tested before it goes out to the fleet."

"Ah! Very good!" responded Howard smiling back at her.

Castillo thought the admiral's heart might have fluttered slightly when he caught sight of Crystal McConnell's flawless face. He had a hard time looking back at Castillo.

When they were all in carriages and the horses began clopping down the path, Castillo checked in, "Are you there, Mase?"

"I'm here."

"So far, so good."

"Noted!"

Castillo removed his earpiece, turned to Lambert and said, "Taylor sounds pissed."

"Why?"

"He thinks we're taking a risk. He doesn't trust Drake and his buddies."

They rolled through the English countryside on a rutted tree lined dirt road going up and down hills and passing grazing cattle bathed in twilight. Occasionally they'd see a barn or house set back off the road with flickering lantern light coming from within.

By the time they arrived at their destination, it was dark. Their destination was apparently a large gray stone Anglican church on a hill. It stood like an ancient impregnable castle keeping watch on the surrounding countryside. It had rows of tall gothic stained glass windows on every side and a tall stone tower topped with a cross. There was a cemetery behind it and two mammoth oak doors in front which were wide open.

Castillo checked in with Taylor. "We've stopped at a large church on a hill set back off the road a ways."

"Okay. Stay on your toes, Don."

"I will."

Castillo adjusted his dress white shirt and removed his hat. Lambert straightened his shoulder boards.

"How do I look?" he asked.

"Quite handsome," replied Lambert. "How about me?"

"Perfect," said Castillo, tucking a stray strand of hair behind her ear. That act seemed so familiar, so natural to him, it made him take pause and hold her gaze for a moment. Lambert looked away, blushing slightly.

"Let's go," he said.

Arm in arm they entered the large church, followed by the rest of the crew. Flickering lanterns along the walls caused their shadows to dance like ghosts and there were long rows of polished wooden pews on each side. The center aisle must have been three hundred feet long, terminating in a raised altar holding a large wooden cross, a baptismal and a polished wooden pulpit elevated about ten feet above the floor. Their footsteps echoed off the stone walls as they walked. It smelled slightly musty with hints of evergreen.

"Wow!" gasped Lambert, her voice echoing slightly. "Look at this place." She and McConnell walked up to the pulpit and began studying the angels carved into the balustrade. "What beautiful work! I can't wait to tell Norm. I wish I had a camera." She stepped back and pretended to snap a picture. "I promised to bring him back a piece of cake too."

"I don't think there's going to be any cake," said McConnell looking around. "I don't see any food."

True, thought Castillo. *What kind of celebration has no food?* Something didn't seem right. That's when he realized Drake was not with them. He decided to go out and see what was keeping him. He went out the doors and to the access road, but there was no one there, and the last of the carriages was pulling away.

When he looked the opposite way up the road, he saw distant lanterns swinging rhythmically. Several horsemen and a coach were approaching. *Maybe this is Drake.* The riders pulled up in front of the church and dismounted. The coach expelled Drake, Howard, Hawkins and Williams.

They walked up to Castillo and Admiral Howard studied the ribbons and insignia on his uniform. "And what navy is this again?" He reached out and touched Castillo's black name badge.

"United States Navy," said Castillo. "You've not heard of it because…"

THUNK! THUNK!

Castillo wheeled around to see that the enormous oak doors on the church had been slammed shut and guards had taken up station in front of each.

"The queen's not coming is she?" said Castillo.

"No, she's not," said Drake without expression. He reached out and plucked the communicator from Castillo's ear.

Chapter 17

"I return this talking device to you, commander," said Drake. "And I instruct you what to say."

Castillo said nothing. He only glared contemptuously at Drake.

"Come, come, commander. Be not angry. You declined land and titles offered you," said Drake, smoothing his reddish brown beard with one hand. "What were we to do? You should have expected this."

Castillo shook his head sadly and said, "I'm not angry. I'm disappointed, admiral." He looked at each face before him and asked, "Is this how a grateful nation shows its gratitude?"

"This is something greater than any of us, commander," said Howard, stepping forward and adjusting his blue doublet. "Give ear to this! Our country is involved in a great struggle and we *need* your ship, and we're prepared to seize it."

"I'm prepared to resist that, admiral. We never agreed to join the English Navy."

Admiral Howard sighed tiredly and said, "Be reasonable, commander. Did you expect us to do naught after seeing what your ship could do?"

"So…if you want something, you take it. It doesn't matter if it doesn't belong to you?"

"Success goes to the strong," said Howard, "and victory to the bold."

"You didn't look that strong or bold against the Armada," stormed Castillo. "If we hadn't been there to oppose them, you'd be fighting the Spanish right now in the heart of London."

They had nothing to say to this.

"What happens to my crew?"

"We'll keep necessary crew at their posts," said Drake. "The others will be settled just as you wished."

"You have some rather handsome women with you, commander," snickered Howard. "I can guess their function."

Castillo knew who Howard was fancying. *The old lech!*

Drake stepped forward and handed Castillo the communicator and said, "Tell your second they're to welcome guests aboard. As I hear from my man that they're safely aboard, I'll let you see your people."

"And if I don't."

"We hold your people, commander," responded Howard. The implied threat was in his voice. "Don't do anything stupid."

"Stupid? You intend to take over my ship and force my people at gunpoint to kill Spanish for you.

That sounds like a very short-sighted and ill con-ceived prospect at best. What happens when we run out of weapons? What happens when the crew has had enough abuse and flatly refuses you? I know my crew and this *will* happen. You're going to need about a hun-dred people to operate that ship. Who's being stupid?" Castillo could tell he had touched on some points not previously considered. There were some uneasy looks shared between the conspirators.

"We know you'll impress upon them, commander," said Howard. "because you'd hate to see something be-fall your people here."

Castillo afixed the communicator to his ear, turned it on and said, "Mase, we have a problem."

"Let me guess," came Taylor's sarcastic voice. "Some bad people are making demands of you."

"Yes," sighed Castillo. "And you're right. I'm too trusting, and it's going to get me killed one day. Maybe today!"

"Brevity, please," said Drake.

"You're going to get some visitors. Once they're on board, they'll tell Drake, and he'll release everyone."

"Okay," said Taylor, "here's what we're going to do…"

Abruptly Drake reached across and yanked the communicator out of Castillo's ear. "Well, done, commander."

• • •

"Hello…Don…," said Taylor. "Are you still there?" Nothing.

"Shit!" Taylor slammed down the receiver. "We're going to have visitors, folks. I want us to be ready to receive them properly."

"Look!" said Lieutenant Unger, pointing at one of the camera screens. Night vision showed large draft horses were coming down the access road being led by soldiers. They were drawing field cannon. The large wheels of the cannon bounced in the ruts and jostled the heavy guns. There were five of them and they were being followed by horses drawing two large wagons.

"Great!" said Taylor. He was in the command chair in the control room. "It sounds like they're holding our shore team hostage." He began looking around to see who was available. Anderson was with the shore team, so was Tanaka, Simms, Gastmeyer, Lambert, McConnell. He looked at the weapons station to his right and saw Chief Greg Brown.

"COB, we can't allow those cannon to threaten us. I don't know how much harm they would do to us. They're larger than the shipboard guns."

"They wouldn't try to destroy the ship if they needed it, would they, sir?" asked Chief Brown.

"I don't know what these psychos might do."

Brown interlaced his fingers and flexed his arms, palms outward. The fabric of his shirt was stressed by the bulge of his mammoth biceps. "Well, sir, I could take a team up there and take out those guns."

"Yes, I'm sure you could, chief, but they'd likely bring in more. We've got to trick them, some how." Taylor watched the parade on screen come to a stop on the road. Soldiers began to back the cannon into position, pointing toward Kansas. "Could you go sneak a look at those cannon, chief. With an eye toward sabotage."

"Sure!"

"Pick a couple people. Take some weapons, just in case."

"On it," said Brown, springing out of his chair.

• • •

When the inflatable was ready, Chief Brown and his small team silently launched into the night. They were not noticed by anyone on shore because they launched toward the opposite shore shielded from watchers by the bulk of Kansas. They beached their small craft, then made their way inside the tree line to the head of the estuary where they could cross a small stream and come up the other side. Brown was a hefty man but he knew how to move with stealth. He and his team moved from tree to tree and stopped when they were within 100 yards.

Brown took out his binoculars and switched them on. The blackness of the night bloomed green in his eyepieces. He could see men moving about the big guns and leading horses away.

"Are you seeing this, sir?"

"Yes, chief," came Taylor's voice in his ear.

• • •

Taylor was looking at a night vision view of the five cannon and soldiers along the road. He could also see Chief Brown's helmet cam on the left screen with a much closer view of the cannon and wagons and soldiers.

"Someone's coming, sir," said Lieutenant Guerrero. "Look!"

On one of the photonics camera screens was a small boat pushing off from the dock. There were nine men in it, four had oars.

"These are probably our baby-sitters," said Taylor. "Bud, why don't you go up and meet them."

"Sure," said Unger, "But what do I tell them?"

"Just escort them down."

"Yes, sir." Unger went up the access hatch on the aft deck to meet the small boat. He could not believe what he was seeing. There were four oarsman and five soldiers in the boat. The soldiers were all wearing armor made of steel or bronze. The armor was quite bulky and covered their torsos. They looked like a family of turtles. They also were wearing helmets with broad brims and a crest that ran down the crown. Two of the soldiers were carrying eight foot pikes, and two were carrying longbows. Unger caught the boat's bow line and secured it to a deck cleat, then watched them struggle to get out of the boat in their heavy armor. They staggered against each other in the moving boat, and one nearly went into the water when he stepped onto Kansas's sloping deck. Eventually they made their way to Unger. The man without weapons had an emblem of some kind on the breastplate of his armor. It looked like a gold and silver coat of arms. His pale face was bony and sported a gray beard.

"Colonel Ashton," he announced. "Here to take command of the ship." He handed Unger a folded sheet of paper. "My commission."

Unger accepted the paper and looked it over. It was some kind of official document with seals and signatures.

"You're going to have to leave your armor and weapons here," said Unger, adjusting his pewter framed glasses. "This is a *submarine*."

The men exchanged looks, then the leader said, "We care not your rules and practices. We keep our weapons…and armor."

"Okay," shrugged Unger. "I'll take you to our commander. Follow me." Unger walked to the hatch and descended the ladder.

The first soldier walked up to the hatch and looked down suspiciously. After a moment of indecision, he decided it looked safe enough. He stepped onto the ladder and descended one step and his turtle shell armor wedged at its widest point in the opening. He climbed free of the hole, turned sideways and tried again. No good. He tried to forcefully slam his body through the hole with a great grunt and a clang.

The soldier squirmed and wiggled but soon found himself wedged solid. He could go neither up nor down. Two other soldiers each took a hand and began to pull but to no avail. A third soldier joined in and began pulling on the first one's head. The first soldier began swearing and bellowing until finally he popped loose. The three soldiers hauled him up onto his feet, and there was momentarily some accusations and finger-pointing, then the colonel stepped in and ordered them all to shed their armor. They piled their helmets and armor on the deck along with most of their weapons. They kept their daggers and the two matchlock pistols they'd brought with them. They were wearing slate muslin shirts with billowy sleeves and loose bloused brown trousers tucked into tall black silver-buckled boots.

When they got to the bottom of the access ladder, Unger was waiting on them, looking slightly bored. He gave the colonel a look that said *I told you so* then turned and led them to the control room.

"This is Lieutenant Commander Taylor," said Unger, then gesturing to the soldiers, "Colonel Ashton and company." Unger noticed that all the viewing screens were dark.

Ashton had to look up at Taylor, who was taller. He frowned and said, "You're in command?"

"Yes. I'm the acting commander."

Ashton cast his brown eyes around the room at the bewildering array of status screens. "But you're a…"

"I'm a what?" asked Taylor. There was a chill in his voice.

Ashton held his gaze for long seconds, then, "I have to send word to Admiral Drake. He said you'd know how to do it. Do you?"

"Yes, I do," responded Taylor slowly. He nodded to Unger.

"And I want all of your weapons."

• • •

"How long do we have to stay here?" asked Lambert.

"For as long as they tell us," said Tanaka.

"Or until Don comes for us," said McConnell sadly.

They were sitting in the front church pews, watching guards search everybody. Four guards had herded everyone to the back of the sanctuary, then searched each person. As they were released, the crewmen were escorted to the front pews near the altar. The guards confiscated anything that looked like a communicator or weapon. They took purses, wallets, knives, watches anything that looked like it could be dangerous. No one on Kansas had thought it necessary to issue sidearms, but now that seemed a woeful oversight.

"I imagine they're making their demands to Castillo right now," said Anderson. "They're using us for leverage."

"Bastards!" scoffed Tanaka. He and all the other U.S. Navy personnel were in dress whites and with the exception of the stubble on their faces looked like navy. "I have a Leatherman."

"A what?" asked Lambert.

"A Leatherman. You know. One of those transformer things that makes into needle-nose pliers and a screwdriver and a saw and a knife. I stuck it in my sock when I saw them searching everyone."

"Good thinking," said Anderson. "It's better than nothing. I should have done that with my Swiss Army knife."

Tanaka looked around the sanctuary, and noticed a door to the left of the altar and what looked like a doorway on the right. "I'm going to go exploring. We need to find another way out of here." He stretched and stood, looking to see if he was being observed.

"That's a good idea," said Anderson. He stood, and scratching at his blond beard, began to slowly saunter toward the right wall of the room.

• • •

Drake stormed up to Castillo. "I just heard from my man, Ashton. He said he is aboard your ship and was presented to a negroid who claimed to be in charge. Explain yourself, commander!"

Castillo said nothing.

"I warn you, Castillo. If you're trying to usurp my authority, you'll be held accountable. You're part of the Royal Navy now, no mistake! And the penalty for mutiny is hanging! We will not hesitate to make an example of you."

"Go ahead and hang me then," said Castillo without emotion.

Drake studied Castillo's face and saw something there. A willingness to sacrifice himself for his country and crew. "No, not you. I think one of your people."

Would he? Castillo felt a sudden chill. "Admiral, there is no way you're going to pull this off. You are out of your depth here. You're dealing with technology you know nothing about. A hundred different things can go wrong. People are going to be killed or badly injured in this reckless gamble."

This didn't seem to hold any sway with Drake. "Do you tell me this *African* is in charge of your ship?"

"Not only is Lieutenant Commander Taylor, *the African*, in charge, he is smarter than anyone you can send against him. He's been ordered to take the ship to safety and that's just what he'll do. He's very resourceful. You *can't* stop him."

"You sacrifice yourself and all your people here to deny us your ship?"

Castillo gave Drake an icy stare. "What do you think?" Drake seemed taken aback by this. "There are some weapons so powerful, so destructive, admiral, they can't be allowed to fall into unconscionable hands. Our lives are insignificant compared to the destruction you could so casually inflict with such a weapon."

It was Drake's turn to say nothing.

"I used to respect you, admiral. Your name is in our history books. You're a great man, they said. *Sir Francis Drake!* An explorer, a statesman, a war hero, a man of integrity. I'm very disappointed, admiral." Castillo paused, looking at the massive locked front doors of the Anglican church. "I expected something like this from the short-sighted power-hungry men surrounding you. They're more concerned with career advancement and power than the welfare and rights of people. But I expected more from you."

Drake scowled and looked at the church.

• • •

"These are our weapons," said Taylor, sliding open the doors to Kansas's weapons locker. There was a row of vertical assault rifles and sidearms.

Ashton reached out and tentatively touched one, a look of awe on his face. Then he took one from the rack and turned it over in his hands. "How does it work?"

Taylor pulled out a tray in the locker and picked up a clip. "The bullets go in here. It fits into the gun here." He took the rifle and slammed the clip into the bottom of the gun. "But these are specially made rifles. They will not fire inside this ship. Too dangerous. See?" He pulled the trigger, but nothing happened because a round was not chambered and the safety was set. He didn't see any reason why he should arm these men beyond what they already had.

Taylor put the rifle back in the locker, slid the doors closed and locked them. Ashton held out his open palm and Taylor put the key in it.

They went back to the control room where they sat staring at each other. Colonel Ashton and his soldiers had searched the control room and crew for weapons. The English soldiers were rough-looking bearded men. Many of the Kansas crew were bearded too, but they had only been working on it for about three weeks. The best Taylor could do was a face full of scraggly black stubble, his bald head was not as bald, however. It had a thin carpet of black hair peppered with gray. He'd stopped shaving that too. Unger's beard had grown in thick and heavily peppered with gray to his surprise. It was a contrast to his thick wavy black hair and made him look much older than his twenty five years.

When Chief Brown showed up, the English soldiers jumped. "Where has this one been?" demanded Ashton.

"Who me?" asked Brown, quickly grasping the situation. "I was up in the sail, doing inventory."

"Yes," said Taylor. "I forgot to mention him." Taylor could tell the English soldiers were surprised by the appearance of Brown. The fact that he had the build of a bodybuilder did not help.

"Search him," said Ashton.

"Now, just wait a minute," snapped Brown. "What's going on here?" He took a step back.

At this two of the men took out small metal boxes and began doing something with cord. Taylor could smell smoke over the stench of the men. When the men squared themselves and leveled their pistols, Taylor could see that the matches had been lit in the matchlocks and the guns were ready to fire.

Taylor stood up and said, "Okay, I've tolerated this for about as long as I can."

Without moving any other part of his body, Unger reached his right hand under his control station just above his knees and gripped a small device that looked like a soldering gun.

"Sit down," ordered Ashton. "I'm in command here."

"I think it's time to *neutralize* the situation."

Zap! Zap! Zap! Zap!

At the word *neutralize* Unger and three other crewmen drew and fired tasers at the soldiers. The soldiers all did a spastic dance, their eyes wide.

POW!

One of the matchlocks fired when the soldier twitched his trigger finger. Then the men collapsed to the floor in full seizure.

"What have you done?" demanded the colonel. "This is an outrage!"

"It certainly is," said Taylor. "But it stops now." Then to Unger he said, "Let's tie these guys up and…" But Unger didn't hear him. The lieutenant's gray eyes were open, but they weren't seeing anything. There was a hole in his right temple and a trickle of blood oozing from it. "Fuck!" cried Taylor.

Lieutenant Guerrero dropped her taser and ran to Unger. "Oh no," she sobbed. "Bud!"

The other crewmen set about angrily zip-tying and gagging the disabled men and removing their weapons.

Colonel Ashton huffed and shouted, "My superiors will hear about this!"

Before Taylor could respond, Chief Brown had the colonel's throat in his big hands, lifting him off his feet. "Listen, you asshole!" he snarled. "You just killed one of my friends. He was worth a hundred of you! Give me a good reason I shouldn't put an end to you right now!"

The colonel's face was filled with open-mouthed terror. He was trying to pry Brown's hands off him and turning the color of a plum. His eyes bulged and his lips were moving, but nothing coming out but gagging noises.

Taylor decided to put an end to it. "Let him go, chief. Zip him up and put him with the others." Chief Brown seemed not to hear him, so he repeated himself more forcefully, "Let him go, chief!" He tapped Brown on the shoulder.

Finally, Brown let go and the colonel collapsed in a heap on the deck, massaging his throat. Brown delivered a vicious kick to his ribs, spat on him and walked away.

"You should see him when he gets *mad*," said Taylor.

Crewmen drug the trussed men to the back of the control room and then carried Bud Unger's body to the dispensary. When they returned from their somber task, they settled into the control room with a new man in Unger's position. The mood was heavy. It was as if the crew had been dealt a mortal blow.

Taylor stood in the center of the room and coughed. "I'm not as good with words as the skipper is, so I'll keep this brief. Bud was a guy we all loved. He played a mean harmonica, he knew some pretty good jokes, he was a good poker player and we're going to miss him. But we'll carry him in our hearts always. I think we owe it to Bud to avenge his death." Taylor paused and looked at the trussed up men in the back of the room. The colonel suddenly began to squirm. "And the best way to do that is to deny these sons of bitches what they want…this ship. Let's make ready to get underway."

"But, sir," sniffled Guerrero, "we're not going to leave the skipper and half our crewmates behind, are we?"

"Only temporarily. Castillo and I are a team. We can practically read each other's thoughts. Right now, he is depending on me to get this ship out of here, and I'm depending on him to watch over the rest of our crew and keep them safe until we can mount a rescue." Taylor picked up the receiver, dialed and said:

Set the maneuvering watch! Now, set the maneuvering watch!

"With what, sir?" asked Guerrero. "I don't think we have enough people to cover the maneuvering watch."

"Some are going to have to perform double duty," said Taylor. "Pilot, is there enough room in this waterway to swing us 180?"

"I think so, sir," replied the pilot. "Executing a stationery 180."

Taylor began flipping switches and all the viewing screens came to life. It was still dark out, but the sky was starting to lighten in the east. As soon as Kansas began its 180 degree pirouette, the men on the shore became excited. Taylor could see them shouting, pointing and scrambling. Some of them carried and stacked cannon balls next to the cannon. Crews rammed bagged charges down the barrels of the cannon, followed by cannon balls.

"Uh, chief?" said Taylor. "About those cannon."

"Oh, you don't have to worry about them, sir."

"I don't?"

"No. We took them out of commission."

Taylor watched nervously as the crews inserted fuses in the breech of each cannon and fired up torches. "You're sure?"

"Yes, sir."

The gun crews were sighting the guns now, elevating the butt of each gun, drawing a bead on Kansas.

• • •

"Something's amiss," said Howard, looking through his spy glass. "They've a distress flag at Jessup's Cove. There's a problem."

Howard approached Castillo. "I hope your people are cooperating, commander. If they try to escape, the gunnery crews are under orders to destroy your ship. We brought in the biggest guns we could find."

"I don't think you'd do that, admiral. You want my ship."

"It's not your ship any longer, commander. And we will destroy it, no mistake. We can't let it escape and fall into the wrong hands. The possibility we might oppose it some day on the high seas can not be allowed."

"So, if you can't have it, no one can!" snapped Castillo.

"You take my meaning," said Howard, oozing confidence.

Castillo stormed off, and when he was out of ear-shot, Howard turned to his aide and said, "Send someone to see what matters at the cove." The man turned to go, but Howard stopped him and added, "And take the tall wench to my quarters. You know the one, long tresses and fair of face. I want to give her my personal attention."

Chapter 18

"Maneuvering, make turns for 4 knots," ordered Taylor.

"Aye, sir. Making turns for 4 knots."

Taylor watched the gun crews with angst. They were standing at the ready beside their guns, obviously awaiting orders to fire. As the submarine began to move, the guns were retrained to track its progress. Chief Brown had said that the guns had been taken out, but they looked fully functional to Taylor. Just before they got to the mouth of the estuary, the crews were ordered to fire. The torch men stepped forward and touched off the fuses. The fuses sparked to life. Taylor's face tensed. The fuses burned down to the breech and…nothing. The gun crews looked to each other in askance. There was some shrugging and some head scratching. *What the hell?* They touched the torches to the flash holes. Nothing. They hurriedly cleared the flash holes in the breech and reinserted fuses, thinking the first fuses were bad. But they got the same result the second time.

"I told you," said Chief Brown. "I got your back, sir."

Taylor smiled and said, "What did you do?"

"Well, we were watching them, see, and…"

"Oh no!" said Guerrero. "What's that?"

Taylor looked at the screen and saw…a net? "When did they string a net across?"

"I don't know," said Guerrero.

"I wonder how strong it is," wondered Taylor. "See if you can break through it, pilot."

"Aye, sir."

They couldn't. Kansas contacted the net at the narrow mouth of the estuary and stretched it, but couldn't break it.

"Must be some kind of anti-shipping thing," said Chief Brown. "It looks pretty strong."

"Probably hemp," said Guerrero.

Taylor studied the screen, ran a hand over the thin carpet of hair on his scalp and said, "Well, we're too close to use a fish. Let's try MP-5's from the sail. You and me, chief."

"Sounds good, sir. I'm on it."

"Oh…and the colonel has the key to the weapons locker."

Chief Brown approached the colonel on the floor and grinned evilly.

Kansas had a conning tower that sat far forward, like all Virginia class submarines. It was so far forward, it was less than sixty feet from the bow.

When Brown returned with two assault rifles, Taylor made a sketch on an edit screen at one of the work stations. "I think we should concentrate our fire here and here. If we can break through that top hawser, I think the net will collapse. It looks to be about 4 inches in diameter and is providing the strength and most of the support for the thing." He indicated the two anchoring points of the net at each end. "Try to get all your shots into the same spot. The distance is going to be about 90 feet. We want to do this fast to eliminate exposure. Their rifles aren't very good, but they could get lucky."

"Piece of cake, sir," said Brown, displaying white teeth.

They climbed up the access ladder with the rifles into the sail and emerged into the bridge well. Kansas was still straining against the heavy net. Taylor crouched down and briefly popped up to scout the banks on both sides of the narrow mouth. On their right about 100 feet away was a line of trees, but on their left on an elevation even with the top of the sail were about ten soldiers. Taylor counted five rifles. They were about 150 feet away.

"Okay, chief. Pick your spot."

Brown popped his head up, took a look and said, "Got it."

"On three." Taylor tucked his lower lip, then said, "One…two…three…"

POP!POP!POP! POP!POP!POP! POP!POP!POP! POP!POP!POP! POP!POP!POP! POP!

POP!POP!POP! POP!POP!POP! POP!POP!POP! POP!POP!POP! POP!POP!POP! POP!

They hammered at both ends of the net until their clips were empty. Then they ducked back down, ejected their empties and inserted fresh clips. They repeated the procedure.

POP!POP!POP! POP!POP!POP! POP!POP!POP! POP!POP!POP! POP!POP!POP! POP!

POP!POP!POP! POP!POP!POP! POP!POP!POP! POP!POP!POP! POP!POP!POP! POP!

Taylor could see his end of the net fraying. Loose strands were hanging out of it. One more time should do it. They ducked down and replaced clips again. "Doing any good, chief?"

"Yeh, let's hit it one more time."

They popped up again

POP!POP!POP! POP!POP!POP!

POW!

A bullet careened off the edge of the bridge well. Someone had taken a shot at them.

POP!POP!POP! POP!POP!POP! POP!POP!POP! POP!POP!POP!

POW! POW!

Taylor heard Brown grunt and he knew he had been hit. "Chief!"

"Keep going, sir," said Brown. The bullet had struck him in the upper left arm.

POP!POP!POP! POP!POP!POP!

The net on Taylor's side parted. The net on Brown's side looked ragged but was still holding together. Taylor slung both rifles and supported the grimacing chief down the ladder. He got him to the infirmary and Doc Aultman.

Taylor returned to the control room, sat in the command chair and said, "Maneuvering, give me turns for 35 knots!"

"Aye, sir. Making turns for 35 knots."

Taylor watched all the camera screens both in front and behind. The water behind Kansas began to froth and foam violently. Four foot waves fanned out across the estuary and lapped up onto the shore. At first the boiling water was white, then it became the color of mud. The net was under tremendous strain, stretching taut. The left side of the net had collapsed, but there were enough lines still holding across the opening to stop Kansas from moving. The place where the chief had shot the hawser was frayed but still holding together.

"Pilot, give it a little left rudder."

"Aye, sir. Left rudder."

Kansas's tail slowly shifted to the right.

"Give it a little right rudder."

"Aye, sir. Right rudder."

Kansas's tail shifted to the left. More frayed strands unraveled from the hawser.

"Left rudder."

"Aye, sir. Left rudder."

Kansas's tail shifted to the right again.

They repeated this slow fish-tailing procedure two more times putting pressure on the net until abruptly it collapsed, and Kansas shot through the narrow mouth of the estuary and into the open channel. The control room crew cheered, pumped fists and gave high fives.

Taylor turned the control room over to Guerrero and went to check on Chief Brown.

• • •

Crystal McConnell was fast asleep on a pew. She used her folded hands as a pillow. Many others of the Kansas crew were also sleeping. They'd had a long night. She was awakened by two men wearing brown leather waistcoats. They looked like soldiers or guards. They had daggers, swords and flat black hats with badges on them.

"Could you come with us, milady," said the one with the short cropped sandy hair and beard.

"Wh-What? Why?" she asked sleepily.

"Admiral Howard would like to see you."

"But why?" she repeated. Her thin eyebrows formed a peak.

"What's going on?" asked Tanaka, sitting nearby. He saw the guards looming over McConnell, and he leaped to his feet and walked up to them.

"Official business," said the darker one. He put a hand on the handle of his sword.

"What official business does the admiral have with *her*?" Tanaka crossed his arms in challenge.

"Don't know. We just 'ave to fetch 'er. Do ye mean ta stop us?"

Tanaka took a step forward with his lower jaw jutting out. "I just might."

"No," said McConnell. "I'll go."

"What's happening here?" inquired Lambert, approaching the group. Sleep was still in her eyes. She massaged them gently with her fingertips.

"These guys are taking Crystal to meet the admiral," said Tanaka. "It doesn't sound right to me. Something's fishy."

"I'll go," said McConnell. "I don't want any trouble."

"I'll go with you," said Lambert.

"Me too!" Tanaka gave the closest guard a steely-eyed squint.

"No," said the darker guard. "Just the lady comes. Orders!"

"Crystal, are you sure about this?" asked Lambert.

"Yes. If you try to fight these guys, someone's going to get hurt." She turned to the two guards. "Come on. Let's go see the admiral."

They watched McConnell and the two guards depart. "I don't like this," said Lambert.

"Something's not right," said Tanaka.

• • •

Castillo was sitting behind the church under a large elm tree, staring at the morning sun coming up over the cemetery. The sun threw a fan of peach colored rays through the spotty cloud cover over the rolling green hills. It was quite a striking landscape, but Castillo's mood was black. He wanted to talk to Taylor. And he wanted to check on his people. He'd been cut off from everyone. His head was full of questions. *How do they intend to force us to do their bidding? It was madness. Has*

Taylor taken the ship and crew to safety? He was jolted out of his thoughts by someone approaching. It was Admirals Howard and Drake.

"Commander Castillo!" Howard thundered. "You'd better get your ship back here or it will go very badly for you and your people."

Castillo searched their faces. They were furious. He smiled and said, "I told you he was good. He got away, didn't he?"

"The penalty for mutiny is hanging, commander," snapped Howard. "And I'm going to start hanging your people one at a time until that ship returns."

Drake handed Castillo the communicator. "Talk to your man Taylor. Tell him to return with the ship or your lives will be forfeited."

Castillo made no move to take the communicator. He only glowered at both men.

"I'm warning you, commander," said Howard. "I'm not to be trifled with."

Castillo finally sighed deeply and said, "There's a big problem here, admiral."

Howard tilted his head, questioning.

"You said we were going to meet the queen. That was a *lie,* wasn't it? Then you said if I told Taylor to admit your people to my ship, you'd let me see my people. That was a *lie* too, wasn't it?" There was accusation in his voice. He waited for a response, but getting none, he went on. "Now, you tell me if my ship returns, you won't execute my people. Can you see the problem yet, admiral?"

"Commander…" said Drake.

"The problem is," roared Castillo, "you're word is worthless, admiral! It doesn't matter what I do! You're going to do what you want. Go ahead, admiral. Execute us all! It won't change a damn thing!"

Castillo snatched the communicator out of Drake's hand, turned it on and put it in his ear. "Kansas, this is Castillo…Kansas, this is Castillo…how do you read?" He looked at Drake. "Kansas may be out of range. I don't know how far…" Then he heard a voice in his ear.

"Sir! Is that you?" It was Maria Guerrero.

"Yes, Maria. Is Mason there?"

"Yes, sir. He's coming. We had a problem here with some men who boarded us, sir. Bud Unger is dead!"

The words hit him like a blow to the stomach. *Bud Unger is dead!* "How?"

"He was shot. Chief Brown was shot too, but the doc thinks he's going to be okay."

He repeated the news for the benefit of the two eavesdropping admirals. "So Lieutenant Unger has been killed and Chief Brown is wounded."

Admiral Drake looked at his shoes.

"Yes…oh…Here's Commander Taylor."

Howard leaned forward and said, "Just tell him to return the ship. If he does not, I will kill your people one at a time, no mistake."

"Don, is that you?" It was Taylor.

"Yes, Mase. Maria said Unger's dead."

"Yes." There was sadness in Taylor's voice. "We had to disable our boarders and…well…it was an accident.

Unger got in the way of a bullet." He cleared his throat. "Is Howard standing there?"

"Yes."

"How about Drake. Is he there?"

"Yes."

"Commander," insisted Howard hotly. "Tell your man to return the ship!"

"We've done some research on Drake and Howard. I want you to say the following loudly."

"Okay." Taylor had a plan. *He was up to something.*

"Say, 'targets' and then say 'Effingham in Surrey'."

What was he up to? "Targets!" said Castillo loudly, then "Effingham in Surrey!"

At this Howard snapped around and locked eyes with Castillo.

"Did you get a reaction?"

"Yes."

"Good. I'm running a bluff here. That's where Admiral Howard's primary residence is and his family. Now say, 'Buckland Abbey in Devon'. That's Drake's family residence."

"Buckland Abbey in Devon. Okay." At this Drake looked up and glared at Castillo.

"Tell them the countdown clock is running. They have until nightfall to release you."

"Okay. And whatever you do. Do *not* bring the ship back here." Castillo removed the communicator from his ear, switched it off and handed it back to Drake.

"He's getting ready to hit two targets, gentlemen. You heard me name them. He's set the machinery into motion. The only way to stop it is to release us. You have until nightfall."

"I don't believe you have such a weapon!" said Howard.

"Oh but we do! Tomahawks! Admiral Drake here has heard us talk of them. With a Tomahawk we can reach out and completely destroy a small village hundreds of miles away. But don't take my word for it. Ask any of my crew."

Howard's mouth opened, then closed again. He was at a loss for words.

"Even if you do have such a weapon," said Drake, "I doubt that you would have the resolve to use it so savagely."

"Your right. I wouldn't, but Taylor would. He's one of those emotional *Africans*, you know. And he's mad! You killed one of his crew!" He paused and watched his words sink in.

The admirals exchanged a look and Castillo could see *fear* there.

"You gentlemen are very powerful, but not untouchable." Castillo looked toward the church and said, "I think I'll go see my people now." He began walking away.

"But," said Howard. "I thought you wanted to help England."

"England. Yes," called Castillo, "but not unprincipled hooligans, who feel justified in using any amount of coercion or force to further their own ambitions!"

When he arrived at the front doors to the church, the guards stood blocking his path. He stood there face to face with one of them, saying nothing. He heard Drake's voice call out, "Pass" and the guard stood aside. Castillo hauled open one of the mammoth doors and entered.

Lambert was the first to greet him. She ran to him and said, "Oh, Don. I was worried about you."

"I'm okay. How are you guys?"

Tanaka came up. "We're okay, sir. Hungry and tired, but otherwise…"

"And they took Crystal," said Lambert.

"Who took her?"

"Two guards," said Tanaka. "They said Howard wanted to see her."

"That bastard!" spat Castillo.

"Are we going to go get her?" asked Tanaka.

"Definitely! Taylor took the Kansas and the rest of the crew to safety. We're trying something that's going to get us all out of here…maybe." He debated telling them about Bud Unger.

"In case it doesn't work, I think I've found another way out, sir," said Tanaka.

Castillo felt energized being back with his crew. These talented people renewed him.

• • •

Crystal McConnell took in her surroundings. There was a fancy wingback armchair covered in some kind of fancy print fabric and a sofa made out of red velvet or something, and there was a large polished table of maple stacked with papers and books and a fireplace with a deer head above the mantle.

They had taken her by coach to this clapboard farm house with weather worn unpainted boards. An older lady in a white apron met her at the door and showed her to this room. It had the most beautiful old antique brass lantern, it looked like a swan, except it wasn't really an antique to these people. There was a silver candlestick holder and there were beautiful oil paintings too. One of a magnificent castle on a rocky mountain top and one of an old sailing ship, except it really wasn't an old ship, was it? The lady who met them at the door had explained that the admiral was using this house as his temporary quarters.

The aproned lady brought in some tea and scones. The scones were delicious and Crystal devoured them all. She was quite hungry.

• • •

"We saw these guys in the wagon measuring black powder," said Chief Brown. "They put it onto these pieces of cloth, then they tied it up with twine. When they were done, they had a bag of black powder about the size of a bowling ball, see?"

"Yes," replied Taylor.

"We discussed it and decided these must be the charges they use in the big guns when they load 'em." Chief Brown winced when Doc Aultman pressed the tape on his dressing into place on his arm. "Anyway, when they were finished, they went to dinner and didn't post a guard. So we took the bagged charges of powder down to the shoreline and emptied each one and then refilled them with sand and ve-e-e-ery carefully retied them exactly like they were. Then we restacked them by the wagon exactly where we found them. It took us about 45 minutes."

Taylor let loose a belly laugh and Brown joined in. "So you swapped their gunpowder with sand and they didn't detect it?"

"No, sir! And when one of those big muzzle loaders gets jammed up, it's not an easy thing to unload!"

"You're right! I watched them scramblin'." Taylor and Brown both laughed long and hard. Tears came to Taylor's eyes. "That was a damn good trick, chief!"

"Yeh. I'm pretty proud of that too. It was Douglas's idea though."

"Good job. You saved our skin. But we're not out of this thing yet."

"Just tell me what you need me to do, sir."

"You should rest, chief. You're hurt."

"Aw hell! This is barely a scratch!"

"Well, more than a scratch," said Aultman, packing up his tape and dressings. "It could have been much worse. You're lucky, chief. The ball passed clean through and didn't involve much muscle tissue. Subcutaneous mostly."

"Like he said. A scratch, sir. I can still hold a gun." Brown flexed his left hand and made a fist.

"Well, if you're up for it. I've got one more mission for you, chief."

Chapter 19

"On the other side of this wall," said Tanaka, "is the firewood box."

"What is that awful smell?" asked Castillo. They were in a small dark room at the back of the church behind the altar. It had only one narrow window that was very high up at the ceiling.

"That's the chamber pot in the corner. This serves as the bathroom here too."

"You're kidding!"

"No I'm not, sir. And the ladies don't like it much either," said Tanaka wrinkling his nose. He knelt down and pointed to a wooden panel. "See this?" He slid the panel open. "This is a pass through. I'm guessing they use this to get firewood when its cold out." The firewood box appeared to be only a third full. There was nothing blocking the opening.

"Let me try it," said Castillo, removing his hat. He knelt down and twisted his body through the opening. It was about 4 feet wide and about 18 inches high.

Immediately when he flexed his torso, his chest wounds began to throb and the pain made his eyes water. He was not yet healed from his ordeal with the Spaniard. He could not stand up in the firewood box. It was too small. He was able to lift the cover, however, and peer out. He could see Admirals Drake and Howard with several other people. The two admirals appeared to be arguing. He hoped it was about Taylor's ultimatum. He wanted to increase discord between the two.

When Castillo came back through the opening, he stood, smiled and said, "Look what I found!" He was holding an ax. It was coated with dirt and had a rusted head, and when Castillo pulled on it, the head came off easily. He wiped away the dirt from the ax handle and took an experimental swing. It was as solid as a Louisville slugger.

"Now we have a weapon," said Tanaka.

"And a way out," said Castillo.

"Shouldn't we wait to see if they're going to release us, sir?"

"I think we better escape if we can. I don't think Mason's going to wait either. His bluff against the admirals was just a ploy to buy us time. And maybe cause dissension. We just have to deal with the two guards at the back of the sanctuary. I don't trust myself to swing this thing with any accuracy though. I have too many injuries."

"Want me to try, sir?"

"Sure. But don't we have a crewman who played baseball? Italian guy?"

"Deangelo! He was scouted by the Atlanta Braves!"

"Is he with us?"

"I think he is!"

"Could you go get him?"

"Yes, sir. Be right back."

When Tanaka returned, he was trailed by a petty officer, second class, in dress white uniform. He was a young man with dark hair, serious eyes and a good set of shoulders. He immediately saluted Castillo.

Castillo returned the salute and said, "That's another navy reg we're going to do away with. No more saluting."

"Yes, sir," said Deangelo.

Castillo scratched his whiskered chin then said, "If we distract a guard, could you knock him out with this?" He put the ax handle in Deangelo's hand.

Deangelo got into a batter's stance and made a test swung. "Yes, sir. It shouldn't be a problem."

"That will handle one guard," said Castillo, "but there are two."

Deangelo walked over to a small table with a candle set in a round pewter candle holder. He picked up the candle holder and removed the candle. It was a small carved head about the size of an orange, the likeness of a saint probably. He tossed it up gently, getting the heft of it. "I have an idea, sir," said Deangelo.

The three discussed a strategy and finally agreed on a plan they thought would work and came back out to the sanctuary. Tiny motes of dust wafted in the rose colored beams of sunlight streaming through the stained glass windows on the south side of the building.

The tall Gothic windows brightly illustrated the virgin Mary and various saints in heroic poses, in battle and slaying dragons.

"Why were you gone so long?" asked Lambert. "And what happened to your uniform?"

"We were coming up with a plan," said Castillo, dusting dirt off his trousers.

"Why is Tony walking like he has a stick up his ass?" asked Lambert.

Castillo studied Deangelo. He *was* walking very awkwardly, with stiff legs. Castillo removed his hat, finger combed his dark brown hair, sighed and said, "It's not a stick. It's an ax handle. *God!* I hope no one else notices." He turned to Lambert. "Susan, we're about to make a move. Go around and wake up anyone who's asleep. Tell them to be ready."

"Sure," said Lambert. She began to move through the crowd, gently shaking them and whispering.

Both guards were standing alert with their backs to the wall beside the heavy doors. Castillo nodded to Tanaka and Deangelo who were standing together at the far right wall. At his nod, they separated. Tanaka began walking out into the center of the room, humming. Deangelo began to make his way along the wall toward the guards.

Tanaka took out his Leatherman multi-tool as he slowly ambled toward the center of the room. The guards both followed him with their eyes.

When he was sure the guards were both watching Tanaka, Deangelo slowly undid his belt and unfastened his trousers enough that he could reach inside and withdraw the ax handle. He leaned against the wall, trapping the ax handle between the wall and his back. He refastened his pants, then began slowly stepping in the direction of the nearest guard with the ax handle in one hand behind his back.

Tanaka made a great show of turning the tool into a pair of pliers. He opened and closed the jaws of the pliers, then he folded the tool and unfolded a knife blade. He swished the air with the blade as if sword fighting.

One guard frowned and called, "'ey, wo's 'at?" Tanaka continued to make passes at the air, slicing and cutting. "'ey!" said the guard louder. Tanaka paid him no mind. Finally the guard pushed off the wall and began approaching Tanaka with his hand extended. "You better give 'at ta me."

Deangelo was almost to the other guard when he pushed off the wall too and began to follow the first guard. Deangelo decided to follow the second guard, but almost bumped into him when he abruptly stopped. Deangelo thought he might turn around, but he seemed to be focused on what was going on with the other guard and Tanaka in the center of the room.

"No," thundered Tanaka. "It's mine. You can't have it, you big ape!" Both guards put hands on their swords and began to draw them.

Thunk!

Deangelo hit a home run on the head of the guard in front of him. The other guard turned in time to see the stricken guard hit the ground…and…

Thok!

…catch a pewter candle holder in the forehead. Deangelo had withdrawn the orb from his waistband and had whipped it as hard as he could, like he was throwing out a runner at first.

Deangelo dropped like a bag of cement on the guard in front of him. Tanaka fell on the other one. Castillo walked up and nodded with approval. "Well done, guys!" Both guards appeared to be stunned.

"We need something to tie them up with," said Tanaka.

"Here," said Lambert. "Take my belt." She undid her long white thin leather belt and handed it to Tanaka.

Another crewmember volunteered a white navy uniform belt for Deangelo to use. They tied the guards up, hands to feet with arched backs, and gagged them with strips of a red scarf volunteered by Lambert. They took swords and daggers off the guards and handed them to crewmembers.

Castillo herded them as a group to the small room behind the altar, then he wiggled through the firewood opening first to scout ahead. When he lifted the wooden lid of the firewood box, he didn't see the admirals anymore, but there were two other men there. Aides probably. They were approximately 250 feet away, at the edge of the cemetery.

Castillo called back inside the room and said, "Deangelo, I need an instant replay."

• • •

"It is time to admit defeat, Howard," said Drake, collapsing into a padded chair. They had taken over a banquet room at a nearby tavern to eat, drink and have a planning session. They were accompanied by five guards and two aides.

"When victory is at hand? I think not!" said Admiral Howard, spearing a piece of beef with his knife and putting in his mouth.

"This was destined to fail. We take away no shame. These are extraordinary people."

"I believe not that doubtful fiction of flying weapons destroying Effingham and Devon. Do you?"

Drake blinked. "You don't?"

Admiral Howard stared hard at Drake, chewing.

"I've been inside the God ship. Howard. It travels as fast as a hawk in flight with sails unseen. It has a great God's eye that can look *anywhere* and see *anything*. I saw the Spanish loading their ships and making ready to invade us. They were parading wagons and horses down the piers at Flanders. *I saw it! I fear they watch us right now!* If Castillo claims weapons that dance on the head of a pin, I believe him!"

"I think you're hysterical, Drake! These are only mortal men with fancy magic. I wager they dance a macabre dance when their necks are stretched by the hangman. Same as anyone. And it's time to stop bargaining with them and demonstrate our willful intent."

"What is your intent?"

"I'm going to hang one of them with Castillo as witness. We'll see if that gives him cause to swear oath."

Drake put down his knife. "I want no part of it."

"Then that's just what you'll have…no part of it!" snapped Howard. He finished his ale, banged the tankard on the wooden table then stood.

"Are we going back already?"

"No. There is an urgent matter I must attend to at my quarters." He donned his long cloak and his black hat of office and exited.

• • •

Castillo and Deangelo lifted the lid of the firebox and exited as quietly as a summer breeze. Castillo motioned for Deangelo to stay behind. He approached the two men and said, "Say, could you help me? I'm trying to figure out what's happened to one of my people?"

The two turned to face him. One had a round boyish face with not much beard and a ruddy complexion, the other was taller and pale and sniffed nervously. Castillo nodded to Deangelo who began his stealthy approach from behind.

"Which one, commander?" asked the shorter boyish one.

"The tall woman who was with us," replied Castillo. "I need to find her."

"Did she possibly wander?"

"No, she was with us under guard when two guards came and took her away," said Castillo, raising his voice. "I want to know where she is!"

He advanced on them both. They seemed to shrink under his onslaught. "We did not take her, sir."

"Well, someone did!" shouted Castillo. "And I think you know who!"

"no, sir," said the shorter one. "I assure you I…"

Thunk!

The short aide collapsed in a heap with Deangelo standing over him. When Deangelo turned to the second aide, weapon raised, he dropped to the ground, cowering with his arms over his head. "No," he wailed. "Don't hit me! I didn't take your lady, sir."

Castillo waved off Deangelo, and he lowered his weapon. "Where did Howard take her?" he demanded.

"I don't know, sir, verily," cried the aide. "I make no deception!"

"Maybe this guy knows," said Deangelo, prodding the unconscious aide on the ground.

Castillo shook his head in frustration. "Go get the rest of the crew, Tony. Tell them it's safe."

One at a time Deangelo helped them out of the firebox until there were 44 people clustered in a group, unsure where to go next.

"What's up, sir?" asked Tanaka.

"We have to find Crystal," said Castillo. "I think Howard took her."

"Why?" asked Tanaka.

"He's a lecherous old man."

Understanding dawned in Tanaka's eyes.

Castillo looked down at the cowering aide. He reached down and pulled him to his feet. "Where does Howard go to sleep at night?"

"He's taken a house down the road," blurted the aide. His fearful eyes were on Deangelo who was still carrying the ax handle. "It's his temporary field quarters."

"How far is it?"

"Four furlongs, maybe five."

"How far is a furlong?" asked Castillo.

"Not far, sir," said the aide. "A ten minute ride. It's just past the Kilborn Tavern, down Slocum Road."

"I think that's our best bet," said Castillo. "Eric, I think we need to go to that house and try to find her. I don't want to take everybody. I need to move fast. Just you, me and Deangelo."

"I'm with ya, skipper!"

"Me too," said Lambert, approaching.

Castillo took her by the shoulders and said, "Susan, this is likely to get dangerous."

Lambert just stared at him, mouth set.

Castillo recognized that look. The one she had when her mind was set and no argument was going to dissuade her. "I can't talk you out of this, can I?"

"Crystal is my *friend*," said Lambert, stubbornly, as if that's all the argument she needed.

• • •

Crystal McConnell was feeling sleepy after consuming scones and tea and getting comfortable in the large stuffed chair. She yawned and looked out the window at the tree lined lake. There were black ducks floating on it beneath a clear blue sky. It was a peaceful scene, but she was jolted out of her reverie by the slam of a door.

"There you are," said Howard as he entered the room. He removed his hat and long black cloak, closed the door, smiled broadly and said, "Would you fancy some claret, my sweet?"

McConnell stood to face him. She guessed him to be about fifty something because of the crow's feet and the gray in his hair and beard. She didn't like the way he was looking at her. It was the look of the wolf. Predatory. She'd seen it before in men. Men who thought they could have their way with her just because they had bought her dinner or favored her with a compliment and a hungry look. "No, thank you, admiral. What did you want to see me about?" She was beginning to guess.

"Why do you wear britches, dear? You're dressed in a *man's* clothes!" He walked over and took hold of the black gabardine fabric and pulled at it. "But you're definitely *not* a man!"

McConnell pulled away from him. He uncorked a bottle of wine and began pouring into two ceramic cups. He held out one to her, but she didn't take it. "Come! Come! It's quite good."

"No thanks." She stared at him without expression.

He brought his face up quite close to her. Close enough she could smell his foul breath and see how yellow his teeth were when he smiled at her. He was a little taller than she was. Maybe an inch. She began to calculate the distance to the door. It was either that or the window. She needed an escape route.

"I think you should disown that ridiculous garb and don something more suitable."

"I think I should be getting back to my friends," said McConnell, taking a cautious step toward the door. "They're going to miss me."

"But you just got here," said Howard.

"No, I have to go."

She tried to push past him, but he grabbed her roughly by her upper arms, spun her and slammed her against the closed door. "You'll go when I counsel you to go!"

McConnell gasped and blinked, stunned. Then she recovered and pushed against him, escaping the admiral's grip, backing against the table. "You can't keep me here!" she shouted.

"But I can," said Howard. "Who's going to mount rescue? Your captain? Now shed those ridiculous clothes, so I can behold the glory beneath."

"I will not submit to you, Admiral Howard!" said McConnell hotly. She began to circle the table. "Maybe you're used to getting your way, but not this time."

He made a quick move toward her, and she picked up the brass swan lantern and drew back, ready to throw it.

"Well, my dear," sighed Howard, resignedly. "You leave me no choice."

He left the room and McConnell breathed a sigh of relief and put down the lantern. But he returned seconds later with two men. She recognized them immediately. They were the guards who had come for her in the church.

"Hold her!" snapped Howard. The two men stepped forward and each seized one of her arms tightly. Howard withdrew a dagger from his waistband and beamed at her saying, "Now, let's unwrap this tender morsel. Shall we?"

• • •

Lieutenant Commander Mason Taylor was a highly trained well disciplined Naval officer, but if he had been a ship, he would say his hull had been holed because an important piece of him was missing. Castillo had entrusted him with the safekeeping of Kansas and her crew, but his heart was somewhere else. Someone he cared for deeply was in danger. He could sense it. When he got the assault teams ready to go, he knew he was going to go with them. At some point, he didn't know exactly when, he'd made the decision to go. His soul was being pulled by a powerful force.

The SEAL special equipment locker had enough to equip a twelve man team, so Taylor decided to send twelve. This meant Kansas's inflatables would be full. There wouldn't be any room to transport Kansas's crew. They would have to "borrow" boats to make the evacuation. Each member of the assault team carried an assault rifle, five grenades, communicator, combat knife, 9mm pistol and extra ammo clips and wore black kevlar body armor and helmets. Five people were designated to carry tranquilizer rifles and five others had stun guns and four had helmet cams. They had just about emptied the SEAL special equipment locker.

Taylor knew that they would be on foot and moving fast so he only wanted the fittest crewmen. He hand picked the team and then picked a likely landing spot away from the estuary. It was to the north about half mile. A spot where the trees came down to the water's edge. It provided good cover and there wasn't likely to be anyone there. He didn't like the idea of a strike in broad daylight, but he felt they couldn't wait.

Taylor's hopes of being unobserved were quickly dashed, however. As they pulled their inflatables in to shore, he saw a man and two boys wading in the shallows. They had been catching something in a net. They immediately stopped what they were doing and watched curiously as the black clad invaders came in. They made no move to flee, but Taylor decided to leave a man behind to watch the boats and their observers.

• • •

Drake decided to go see Castillo. He had to talk to him and try to head off what was about to happen. When he got to the church, he exited his coach, and the guards at the front door stepped aside. Drake went in, then bellowed, "Gods boots!"

The guards entered behind Drake and stared dumbfounded at the room. It was empty except for the two bound guards laying in the aisle.

These people were difficult to contain, thought Drake. They were extremely resourceful. "Well, where are they?" he demanded.

"They didn't get past us," assured a front door guard.

"I may as well have posted blind monkeys!" bellowed Drake. "Howard will explode! Better find them!"

They freed the two bound guards and soon found two admiralty aides laying behind the church, bound also.

"I think they went to the admiral's quarters, sir," said one aide.

Drake turned to the guards standing behind him. "Get to Howard's quarters immediately!"

• • •

Crystal McConnell was weeping uncontrollably. She was being held tightly by two rough-looking men and almost all her clothes had been cut away. All she was wearing was her white cotton panties and her brassiere. Howard was running his finger around the inside of her panties. He had never seen an undergarment like this. He was more accustomed to the heavy knickers worn by his wife and the chamber maids. And he was astounded at the brassiere. He plucked at it experimentally.

"What is this?" he asked. But he got no answer, only sobbing. "I asked you a question!" he roared. When he got only sobbing again, he backhanded her, snapping her head around from the force of the blow.

Then he ran his hand down her flat white stomach. Her warm smooth unblemished skin was like satin to touch. The fires of lust ignited in him. He tried to put his mouth on hers, but she turned away. He grabbed two handfuls of her hair and held her head still as he pressed his lips to hers then began probing her mouth with his tongue. She shuddered and squirmed trying desperately to pull away.

"Ow!" screamed Howard. "She bit me!" He reached up and touched his sore tongue. Then he gave her another vicious backhand, staggering her.

Howard turned her face toward him. She looked at him with her tear-streaked face then, smiled and said, "Oh thank you, God! Thank you! Thank you!"

Howard frowned at this. Then he realized she was looking beyond him at something in the doorway. He turned to see Castillo and three others in the doorway. Castillo and the oriental looking one next to him were carrying swords.

"What are you going to do, commander? Match swords with us? These are two of the best swordsmen in the land."

"No," said Castillo. "I'm not." He stepped aside, pointed and another man threw a pewter ball very forcefully hitting the left guard in the forehead. He collapsed. "Release her now, admiral, or you'll be next."

Admiral Howard's shocked eyes went to his stricken guard, then slowly back at Castillo. Howard nodded to the guard. The guard let go of her and McConnell ran sobbing to Lambert who shrugged out of her yellow pantsuit jacket and draped it around her, then wrapped her in her arms.

"What should we do with Admiral Howard, Crystal?" asked Castillo. "Should we maybe use him as a punching bag?"

Howard huffed disdainfully and McConnell looked at him with hateful wet eyes.

"I must say," said Castillo. "You're not a very good host, admiral. You've lied to us, imprisoned us and then…" Castillo gestured to McConnell.

Howard glanced out the window and said, "Where are the rest of you?"

"I sent them away. Out of your clutches."

"I want to go," sniffed McConnell.

"As you wish," said Castillo. "Let's go!" They started to turn around.

"Stop!" commanded Howard.

Castillo heard a click behind him. It was the sound a hammer makes when it's cocked on a firearm. Down through the centuries firearms have gone through many developmental modifications, but that sound has stayed unchanged and is universally recognized. The chilling sound of a firearm being cocked and readied to fire. When he turned to look, he saw three guards with pistols leveled. He could see the faint trails of smoke coming from the lit matches. They were primed to fire.

Howard sneered at Castillo. "Don't leave, commander. I insist." He pointed a finger at the man who had thrown the ball and said, "Kill him!" The guard standing behind him fired.

POP!

The man's mouth and eyes opened wide in surprise, he clutched at his chest and fell face forward down on the floor. There was a stain of blood spreading in the middle of his back.

Chapter 20

"They were here," said Chief Brown. "Look what I found." He held up a burlap bag.

The Kansas assault team was standing in the sanctuary of the large Anglican church, but it was empty.

Taylor took the bag, looked inside and saw a collection of purses, wallets and pocket knives. "They were here alright." He looked out the front door where the rest of the team was assembled. "I wonder where they went."

"Dunno, sir. Let's see if we can pick up the scent."

"Okay. Take the bag along. Some people might want their stuff back."

"Yes, sir."

• • •

Castillo felt Deangelo's neck for a pulse. Nothing. He stood and faced Howard with stormy eyes. "You son of a bitch! You're going to pay for that, admiral!"

Howard appeared to be unconcerned. "Now that your…*throwing man* has been subtracted, I would that you return your ship."

"That's not going to happen."

"Oh, I think t'will," said Howard coldly. "Hold him." Guards stepped up and took Castillo by both arms. Howard cut away Castillo's white uniform shirt exposing his scarred chest. "Behold! What's this?" he asked, looking at the fresh wounds and ugly purple burns.

"Go ahead, admiral. Do your worst! I've been through this before."

"I can see. Who visited this upon you?"

Castillo said nothing.

Howard looked around and spying a corkscrew, picked it up. Smiling viciously, he pressed it into the left side of Castillo's chest until it pierced him, then he began to slowly turn it, screwing it in. Castillo tightened the cords in his neck against the pain and hardened his arms and fists. Howard continued to turn it.

"Stop this!" shouted Lambert. She looked as if she were the one being tortured.

"Only *he* can make it stop," said Howard. He screwed the device half way into Castillo's chest and Castillo had clamped his mouth and eyes shut tightly against the sharp stabbing pain but had not uttered a sound. He struggled to breathe and fought against nausea, but at the same time, he was struck with a sudden epiphany. He saw with absolute clarity that he could hold out against any amount of pain this man could offer because he had a reason. The best of reasons. He had to protect his ship and his crew, and there was no amount of pain he could not withstand for his people. His crew would do anything for him and he could endure anything for them and do it proudly. He clenched his teeth, opened his eyes and gave Howard the full force of his defiant hateful stare.

Howard got the message and stopped. He took Castillo's measure and determined that this was not going to work. He needed something better. He caught the look in Lambert's eyes and grabbed her wrist, pulling her to him.

"I think I'll kill this one," said Howard, pulling his dagger. He held her in front of him with the dagger to her throat. "Do you have anything to say about that, commander?"

Castillo stared into Lambert's glistening blue eyes and felt more helpless than he'd ever felt before. He did not feel as defiant now. The game had changed. "This is not going to work, admiral. You've tried to bend us to your will and failed."

"'Tis not a failure yet." He stuck the tip of the knife into Lambert's neck until it penetrated about an inch, and blood began to run down her neck. Lambert gave out a whimpering sob, tears made trails down her face.

Howard had discovered Castillo's weakness. He couldn't bear to see Susan hurt. "Okay!" yelled Castillo. "You win! I'll get my ship back here."

"No, Don," cried Lambert. "You can't."

"Good," said Howard. "I knew you'd see it my way."

"I need my communicator. Do you have it?"

"No," said Howard. "It's at the church."

"Better go get it, admiral," said Tanaka.

"We'll all go," said Howard, and then to one of his men. "Get the coaches…and get more men. Find the rest of these people."

• • •

Wally Anderson was leading 41 people back to the ship. There was just one problem. He had no idea how they were going to get back. He thought it best to stay off the road so they wouldn't run into any soldiers. They followed a drainage ditch, skirting oak trees and small bushes and made their way back to the cove. It became obvious some of them knew nothing about stealth as they crashed through the underbrush, tripping on roots and cursing. Those wearing Navy whites were now besmirched with dirt and grass stain.

Anderson conferred with several others and decided the best thing to do would be to steal a couple boats and start ferrying the group out into the channel. Kansas would be sure to see them. Castillo had said to be on the lookout. The XO would probably send an extraction team. But he hadn't seen anyone so far.

They went as far as they could, right down to the water's edge. "Now we need boats," said Anderson.

"There are boats just on the other side of that rise, sir," said Petty Officer Grogan pointing to the right.

"I know," said Anderson. "And armed men." He looked up to where the elevated road started. He could see horses, men and what looked like cannon pointing toward the cove. "I wish we had some weapons."

"We better move everyone back into the trees before we're seen, sir."

"Yes. Good idea."

They all began to move toward the tree line but someone tripped and swore. A soldier on the road turned and saw them, then there were two soldiers watching them, then five.

"Oh no," said Anderson. "We've been noticed."

There were ten soldiers running on the road now and seven of them had rifles.

"Get these people moving north, Grogan," said Anderson. "Away from the cove. *Fast!*"

"Come on, people," screamed Grogan. "Move!" He started pointing north.

• • •

Mason Taylor had left a man to guard the inflatables and keep an eye on the nearby observers. He was Lieutenant JG Trent Kenaston, and he was watching them intently. They appeared to be a father and two adolescent sons catching something in a cast net. After each cast they would haul in their net and pluck small things out of it and deposit them into a large basket strapped to the father. What were they netting? Shellfish?

They at first had stopped and watched as the strange intruders came ashore, but now seemed to be back at their task of netting and collecting. They wore long white shirts and had bare legs and had expressions of concentration on their faces.

Kenaston itched at his chin. After days of growing facial hair he had only blond peach fuzz to show for it. What's worse, his face was kind of round…like a peach. He just knew someone was going to hang the name *peaches* on him sooner or later.

He heard the sharp report of shots! At least three of them! It was to the south of him. The other three heard it too. They all were looking south. Kenaston got up on a root ball of a tree. It was the highest platform he could find. He needed elevation. When he looked to the south, he could see men running. They were wearing Navy whites! It was Kansas crewmen! He jumped off his perch and began running through the tall dune grass toward them.

Then he heard three more shots and realized they were being pursued.

• • •

"Coaches are coming!" shouted Chief Brown.

"Everyone out of sight!" barked Taylor.

One massive oak door to the church entrance was open and one closed. Taylor ducked behind the closed one along with two other men. The rest hid behind the church and in the cemetery.

Taylor watched as the occupants of the two coaches emerged. There were several guards, and someone wearing a cape and a fancy black hat with a gold emblem on it. He saw Castillo! His shirt was in tatters and he was bleeding from a chest wound. Tanaka! Lambert was bleeding too from the neck. And…he had mixed emotions as he gazed on Crystal. He was so glad to see her, but she was almost naked and her beautiful face was swollen and red on the right side. Who had done this to her?

Suddenly his communicator came alive.

"XO, this is Kenaston back on the beach. I've found the crew, they're heading this way…"

"That's good, Trent. Tell them to stay there until we get back…"

"…but, sir…they're being chased! It looks like a whole rifle company's after them!"

"Shit! Okay, hang on! I'm sending help right away." He looked around for Chief Brown. Not seeing him, he said into his headset. "Take five men, chief, and get back to the beach, pronto. Kenaston needs help."

"Yes, sir. I heard." Taylor could hear Brown calling out names over the comm net and ordering them to follow.

Taylor turned to the two petty officers next to him and noticed they were both carrying tranquilizer rifles. "Get those things loaded guys. I want you to dart some people."

They nodded silently and unslung the tranquilizer guns.

• • •

It was easy to pick out the civilians in the group, thought Kenaston. They were the only ones not wearing white. There appeared to be five of them. Three were wearing royal blue windbreakers with QVR over the left breast pocket. The others were wearing tan and black jackets respectively.

As they ran, he noticed some of them were limping. Shot probably. He ran toward them as fast as his short legs could carry him. He recognized Wally Anderson and beckoned to him. Anderson saw him and waved.

"Get to the boats," Kenaston shouted, pointing. "I'll hold them off."

He unslung his rifle and leveled it at the advancing riflemen. The crewmen rushed past him in groups of three and four. The lead rifleman was about 150 yards away. Kenaston tried to draw a bead on him, but people kept getting in his line of fire. Finally he got a clear view and fired a burst of three.

POP!POP!POP!

He missed, but this caused the rifle company to stop their pursuit. They shifted their focus to him.

POW! POW!

He heard one rifle ball zipped past his ear, and the second one struck him in the chest. He went down from the impact and dropped his rifle. He looked where it had struck him. He was going to have a bruise there. He picked up his rifle, shouldered it, popped up out of the tall dune grass and laid down deadly fire.

POP!POP!POP! POP!POP!POP! POP!POP!POP! POP!POP!POP! POP!POP!POP! POP!POP!POP!

The riflemen were shocked to see him jump up unharmed and begin firing. Kenaston saw two of them spin around, hit by his spray of bullets and he saw two others clutch at their chests and drop onto their backs. The rest ducked down and tried to disappear in the grass. Kenaston decided that was a good idea, so he did too. Score one for the good guys, he thought. There were about twelve of them and he had hit four, maybe more. So he only had to deal with eight of them. They were in tall grass a little more than 100 yards away. He decided to pop his head up and take a look, and when he did he saw another twenty men coming down the embankment from the road. Christ! They were about 200 yards away, maybe more. He probably couldn't hit them, but he opened fire anyway.

POP!POP!POP! POP!POP!POP! POP!POP!POP! POP!POP!POP! POP!POP!POP! POP!POP!POP!

The men immediately flattened to the ground. Good! That would keep them occupied. He stuck his head up to take another look and…

POW!

It was as if someone had clubbed him with a hammer. Hard! The helmet took the brunt of that one. He was going to have to be more careful. These guys had zeroed in on him. They knew about where he was.

• • •

Taylor peered through a crack in the door. He could see them at the edge of the access road about 50 yards away. "Take out the guys with the guns," said Taylor.

"But there are three guys with guns," said one of the shooters.

"Take out the guys on each end. I'll take the one in the middle." There were a total of five guards in the party. Castillo and Tanaka were in front, with the gunmen right behind them. "Okay? Ready?" Both men nodded and put their rifles to their shoulders. Taylor let the party get closer. They were only twenty yards away now. "Now!" They swung around the door. When Castillo and Tanaka saw them, they dropped to the ground.

Pffft! Pffft! POP!

They had all hit their man, but one dart had bounced off the left guard's leather doublet. The middle guard caught the bullet in the chest and went down immediately. The darted guard turned and fired his pistol at Taylor…

POW!

…and missed. The untouched guard fired at the man to Taylor's left…

POW!

…and hit him. He went down. Taylor then fired a three round burst into the man…

POP!POP!POP!

…and he went down, followed by the man who had been darted. The startled admiral looked at his three guards on the ground. Lambert pulled free of him and ran to Castillo.

"Mason!" cried McConnell and ran to his side, sobbing. They kissed, and the Howard's face twisted in distaste.

Taylor knelt to check on his man. "You okay, Jimmy?"

"Yes, sir. My fiber stopped it." He pointed to a frayed spot on his body armor.

"Good!"

The two remaining guards drew swords. Taylor drew his 9mm Sig and tossed his assault rifle to Castillo. "It's over, men. Drop your weapons!" ordered Taylor. They only scowled at him.

"Do it now!" bellowed Castillo and gestured with the rifle. They threw down their swords.

Two aides came through the doors walking haltingly. They were being prodded from behind by two of the Kansas assault team.

"Where's Will?" asked Taylor.

"Watching the road," replied one of them.

Taylor nodded, then took McConnell's chin and tilted her teary face up toward him. "Who did this to you, babe?"

Her eyes slid toward Howard. Taylor cocked the 9mm Sig walked up to the admiral and put the barrel in his mouth. "This guy?" he demanded. The admiral's eyes were full of fear and darting nervously right and left pleadingly at Castillo and McConnell. His teeth were chattering against the cold steel of the gun and sweat began beading on his forehead.

"Wait!" said McConnell. "Hold him!" Taylor withdrew the pistol, gestured to two crewmen who came forward and each grabbed an arm. The admiral struggled, but they held fast. "I want to see what he looks like naked! Cut off his clothes," commanded McConnell.

With too much glee Taylor handed his pistol to McConnell, pulled his combat knife, and cut the admiral's cloak from him, pulled off his hat and threw it in on the floor.

"Stop this!" roared Howard. "I'll see every one of you swing from a yard arm for this, damn you! I'll make every one of you…"

Taylor slammed Howard in the mouth with a vicious right fist, snapping his head back. "Don't talk until I tell you to," barked Taylor.

Howard blinked, shook his head, sniffed and said, "Castillo, you'd better get your African under control or…"

Taylor hit Howard again even harder. This time he felt Howard's large nose break. Taylor grabbed a hand full of Howard's hair, pulled his head slowly forward and blood began to run from his mouth and nose. "I said, 'no talking'!" bellowed Taylor.

He returned to cutting away Howard's clothes.

"Jesus!" said Castillo. "Go easy on him, Mase. He's an old man."

"He's an old *asshole*!" raged Taylor. "What he did would have earned him jail time where we come from."

"True," sighed Castillo.

• • •

They knew just about where he was.

POW! POW! POW!

Shots were snapping through the tall grass all around him. Between the grass blades he saw one brave soldier on foot approaching him. He was about 50 yards away, so Kenaston lined him up in his sights and squeezed off a three round burst.

POP!POP!POP!

The man fell and five others leaped to their feet and began running towards him.

POW! POW! POW! POW!POW! POW!

It began to rain bullets. His body armor stopped one, but one ball struck him in the right shoulder and one in the right arm. There was a burst of searing pain in his arm, but his trigger finger still worked. He aimed and squeezed.

POP!POP!POP! POP!POP!POP! POP!POP!POP! POP!POP!POP! POP!POP!POP! POP!POP!POP!

The five running soldiers dropped to the ground, either hit or taking cover. He wasn't sure which. Then he saw ten men leap to their feet and began running toward him. Shit! They were about fifty yards away and closing the distance fast.

POW! POW! POW!POW!

A ball struck him in between the left shoulder and his neck, under his armor. It felt like a freight train had hit him, and it burned like a white hot poker. His assault rifle felt like it weighed a ton! With difficulty he aimed and pulled the trigger.

POP!

That was it. He was out of ammo. He had another clip on his belt, but in his painful state he would never reach it and insert it in time. They were almost on him. He could see the angry face of the man coming at him. His teeth were clenched and his lips were peeled back. There was blood in his eye. I probably shot his buddy, thought Kenaston. He braced and waited for the end. The rifleman in the lead was less than 20 feet away now. Kenaston could see the pores in his sallow skin. The man aimed his rifle and…

POW! POW!

POP!POP!POP!POP!   POP!POP!POP!
POP!POP!POP!   POP!POP!POP!   POP!POP!POP!
POP!POP!POP!POP!POP!POP!   POP!POP!POP!
POP!POP!POP!   POP!POP!POP!   POP!POP!POP!
POP!POP!POP!

Automatic weapons fire! The man over him went down clutching his side. Kenaston heard a voice in his ear.

"Trent, where are you? We can't see you anywhere." It was Chief Brown!

"I'm gon' try ta stand up," replied Kenaston. He tried to push himself up, but he couldn't. He couldn't get leverage against the ground with his arms. Damn! It hurt! He was getting dizzy. He was only able to roll over. He stuck his left hand up in the air.

"Okay, I see you. Stay right there. We'll be there as soon as we mop up."

"Okay," said Kenaston.

POP!POP!POP!POP!   POP!POP!POP!
POP!POP!POP!   POP!POP!POP!   POP!POP!POP!
POP!POP!POP!POP!POP!POP!   POP!POP!POP!
POP!POP!POP!   POP!POP!POP!   POP!POP!POP!
POP!POP!POP!

When he craned his neck and tried to see, he saw the riflemen jumping up and trying to run back up the embankment, but as soon as they did they fell under a hail of gunfire. Many of them were holding up their arms in surrender.

• • •

Admiral Howard's naked body was *not* a beautiful thing to behold. It featured loose pale skin and saggy pouches everywhere. There were two saggy bags of skin on his chest. Breasts! And there was a larger saggy deformed bulge hanging at his midsection like some kind of satchel. His belly! And there was his flaccid penis which looked like a chubby grubworm hanging its head in shame.

McConnell giggled. "You were going to assault me with that?" she said, pointing.

Howard only made a noise that was between a whine and a whimper. The fire had gone out of him.

"Who's in charge of Kansas?" asked Castillo.

"Maria," answered Taylor.

Castillo said nothing.

"What? She's command qualified."

"I know," answered Castillo. "But she's young. What did she do when you told her to disappear with the ship if none of us made it back?"

"Nothing."

Castillo said nothing again.

Okay, she freaked…a little." Taylor could hear female laughter in his earpiece. "I think she's listening."

"Tell her we'll be back soon," said Castillo.

"We'll be back soon, Maria."

"Good! Stay safe!"

Then Taylor heard another voice in his ear. "XO, we've got everybody on the beach. Kenaston and a couple others have been shot up." It was Chief Brown.

"Okay, chief. I'm here with the skipper and the others. We'll be right there."

They heard something that sounded like running water splashing on the ground. It was the Admiral Howard urinating.

"Let him go," said Taylor. The two crewmen made faces of disgust and released him, stepping back out of the slick of urine. The admiral collapsed into a heap on the cobblestone floor in the puddle of his own urine, groaning.

Castillo began to examine the men on the ground. "This guy isn't hurt too bad. He took a bullet just below his right clavicle. But this other one is done for. Three bullets through the gut. That's pretty much a death sentence in this age."

"I didn't really want to kill him," said Taylor.

"I know," said Castillo. "This is the one who killed Deangelo."

"Deangelo?" said Taylor, thoughtfully. "Wasn't he..."

"Yes, a Navy nuclear technician with major league baseball potential."

Taylor just shook his head sadly.

"He was instrumental in our escape from that church. Eric," said Castillo, turning to Tanaka, "take two men and a coach and retrieve Deangelo. I don't want to leave anybody behind. He was family. Meet us at the cove." Castillo handed Tanaka the assault rifle.

"Yes, sir." Tanaka motioned to the two of the crewmen in body armor and they all exited.

Chapter 21

Admiral Howard felt nauseous. His head was throbbing, his vision was blurred and his mouth hurt.
He wanted to escape, but he didn't think he could stand,
much less run. His useless guards had all been tied up
on the floor. He began to crawl toward the doorway,
dragging his naked body over the cobblestones of the
floor, slick with blood and urine.

He crawled around the guard that was near death…
or maybe he was dead. It served him right. He was a
terrible guard. He had been charged with protecting
him and had failed miserably. He stared down at something, at first not recognizing it. He shook his head
trying to focus. Gradually he recognized it as a pistol.
One of his guards had dropped it. It was…still cocked
and the match was…still lit. He could see the wispy
smoke rising from it. He reached out and touched it.
Yes, it was real!

He cautiously looked at the small group huddled
to his left, but they were discussing something and no

one was watching him. The large African had his back turned to him. He could shoot him and get his revenge. The fires of rage grew in him. He wanted only to kill the monster before him. The one who had denied him his prize…the God ship…and the woman. He deserved death. And Howard deserved glory and power and now he would never have them because of this man. And the…whore had kissed him! Unthinkable!

He slowly picked up the gun. He would kill the devil, but he would have to take careful aim. The black clothing gave these men protection from firearms. He would have to shoot him in the head to kill him.

• • •

"I don't know how we'll be able to evacuate everyone," said Castillo. "We're going to need boats. About five or six at least."

"I only saw two at the cove," said Taylor.

"I know. I think the only…

POW!

Blood sprayed Castillo and McConnell who were standing in front of Taylor. Taylor looked at McConnell in wide-eyed astonishment. His mind rejected what had just happened. Blood began pumping out of a ragged messy hole in his neck. He clasped a hand over it.

McConnell put it together quickly. She saw Howard holding a smoking gun, and she was still holding Taylor's 9mm Sig Sauer. She clicked off the safety and fired.

POW! POW! POW! POW! POW! POW!

The admiral twitched with every bullet. He fell onto his back and his life drained away, eyes staring lifelessly at the ceiling. McConnell looked down at him with lips quivering, then she dropped the gun and ran back to Taylor. He was on the ground still holding his neck.

"Quick," barked Castillo, "get him to the coach outside! We've got to get him to the doc right now! I think his carotid's been hit!"

"No, no no!" sobbed McConnell, cradling his head. Taylor smiled up at her. Then carefully Castillo, Lambert, McConnell and two other crewmen carried Taylor out to the black coach with the silver trim on the access road. They ordered the driver to take them to the cove at once and they were soon speeding down the road behind two galloping white horses. During the rough ride, Taylor lost consciousness and let go of his neck, and his neck wound began to gush again.

"Crystal, keep pressure on his neck," yelled Castillo. "Don't let him lose too much blood."

"Okay," she replied, sniffling. She straddled Taylor and put her right hand tightly over his neck wound. "Hang on, Mason!"

Castillo took the communicator from Taylor's ear and clipped it to his own. "Chief Brown. This is Castillo. Are you there?"

A reply came at once. "Here, skipper!"

"We're coming in with Taylor. He's been hit and about to go critical. We're in a coach coming down the access road. We need to get him to the boat immediately."

"Okay, sir. I understand! I'm going to have the inflatables waiting for you at the bottom of the embankment. Trent Kenaston and Lauren Gastmeyer are both in bad shape too."

"We'll take them all with us." The coach hit a pot hole and Castillo hit his head on the ceiling. "Ouch!"

"Commander, is that you?" It was Maria Guerrero.

"Yes, Maria. Tell the doc that he's got wounded incoming."

"He's already set up," said Guerrero. "Listen, Admiral Drake just came up on his channel. He wants to talk to you. I'm patching him in."

"Okay."

"Commander?" It was Drake.

"Yes, admiral."

"You've got to get your people out straight away. A regiment has made ready and is mobilizing for Jessup's Cove. Someone has told them another Spanish barge has landed."

"Oh my God!" said Castillo. "There's going to be a blood bath!" The coach hit another pothole and jostled everybody. McConnell lost her grip on Taylor, but quickly regained it. The floor of the coach was soaked with blood. "I can't get my people out without boats, admiral."

"I've found a boat and sent it your way. It should be there shortly."

"Is it big enough to carry everybody?"

"Yes, it should suffice nicely."

"Thanks, admiral."

"Offer me no thanks, commander." There was strife in Drake's voice. "This fault lays at *my* feet. You did England a service in her hour of need and then suffered terribly at the hands of her admiralty. For that I am sorry."

"I don't blame England, admiral. I blame power hungry men and human nature." Castillo had offered no distinction which power hungry men he referred to, but Drake knew. Castillo could hear the heavy silence at the other end.

"God be with you, commander." Drake signed off.

"Drake said he's sending us a boat."

"What kind of boat?" asked Lambert.

"I don't know. I hope it gets here in time."

The clopping of the horses began to slow. From a gallop to a trot, then to a walk. Castillo looked out the windows of the coach. On the right of the elevated road was the cove with the dock and about twenty hostile looking men. Their weapons were all on the ground. Six black clad Kansas crewmen had them surrounded. Castillo shifted over and looked out the left window. There was an embankment down to the water's edge littered with the bodies of English soldiers. Their brown leather doublets were stitched with bullet holes oozing blood. He could see the two inflatables about fifty yards off shore heading in toward the beach.

"Okay, guys, let's get Mason down to the water's edge and into an inflatable."

They carefully inched the unconscious Taylor out of the coach and down the hillside to the water's edge. Castillo was dismayed at the sight of the inflatables with so many wounded laying in them. Lauren Gastmeyer looked unconscious and ghostly white and Trent Kenaston had his head tilted back and his mouth agape, looking lifeless. There were two other men looking pale and sickly their Navy whites with blossoms of red on them. They gingerly lay Taylor in the floor of one of the boats and McConnell got in with him, keeping her hold on his neck.

"Okay," said Castillo. "Go! Go!" He stepped clear of the water. His feet and lower pant legs were soaked. "Maria, get ready. They're coming to you!"

"Yes, sir!"

He heard her in the background barking orders. "Pilot, take us up! Come to course two four four! Make turns for four knots!"

Castillo shaded his eyes with his right hand and watched the distant western horizon, waiting. Finally, he saw it. About five miles out Kansas broke the surface with her sail and turned toward them. What a welcome sight! He got a lump in his throat and was suddenly overcome with emotion. Then was surrounded by his crew! Where had they all come from? He hadn't seen them approach. They were all looking at him pensively.

"Is that our boat?" asked Lambert.

"Yes," answered Castillo. "That's Kansas. Isn't she beautiful?"

"No, not that. That!" She pointed.

There was a single masted ship approaching. A sloop. It was about sixty feet in length. It was pulling into the cove. "Yes," said Castillo. "I believe that's the transportation Admiral Drake arranged for us."

They all scrambled up the embankment and down the other side to the dock and watched the sloop pull in, throw lines and dock. The tiller man yelled, "Commander Castillo!"

"Right here!" called Castillo, raising a hand.

"Admiral Drake said to ride you and your people to your ship."

"Yes, we've been expecting you."

One at a time crewmen boarded the boat. There wasn't enough room for everyone to sit, so many had to stand.

"What about Eric?" asked Lambert. "We can't leave without him…and his men."

Castillo looked down the access road for any sign of a coach. The air was thick with tension. Eight members of the Kansas assault team kept their assault rifles trained on the angry looking men on the shore and the road.

"Eric, where are you?" asked Castillo into his communicator. Nothing. "Eric?" He waited. Nothing. Then to Lambert. "I hope he hasn't run into trouble. I don't know how long we can wait."

"We can't leave him!" said Lambert emotionally.

"I know. I don't want…"

Suddenly Tanaka's voice was in his ear. "We're on our way, but there are a lot of soldiers coming in wagons. They're right behind us!"

"Okay. We're ready to cast off as soon as you're aboard. Hurry!"

Castillo and Lambert climbed the hill and looked down the road for any sign of a coach approaching. Finally they saw it. It came around the bend with horses at full gallop. It got closer and closer and then slowed and finally came to a stop. Tanaka and his men piled out, then they reached inside and two of them slid the body of Deangelo out. They carried him down the hill and tenderly placed him on the deck of the boat.

"Everybody!" screamed Castillo and beckoned to the assault team. They all turned and ran for the boat just as they cast off. They all made the leap across the gap from dock to boat. One of the English soldiers on the ground leaped to his feet with a rifle. Tanaka leveled the assault rifle he was holding and…

POP!POP!POP!

…the soldier fell. Wagons pulled up behind the two coaches and men piled out. They took aim at the boat.

"Everyone get down on the deck!" ordered Castillo. They all did.

POW! POW! POW!POW!

Bullets began to impact the gunnels of the boat. Then an arrow shafted the tillerman steering the boat. It entered through his back and exited his stomach. He grimaced and fell, holding his stomach. Tanaka stepped up, handed his assault rifle to Castillo and grabbed the tiller, steadying the boat and steering a course for the channel. Another arrow flew by narrowly missing Castillo's head as he laid down deadly fire.

POP!POP!POP! POP!POP!POP! POP!POP!POP! POP!POP!POP! POP!POP!POP! POP!POP!POP!

Another three crewmen joined in. Adding to the barrage.

POP!POP!POP! POP!POP!POP! POP!POP!POP! POP!POP!POP! POP!POP!POP! POP!POP!POP!

POP!POP!POP! POP!POP!POP! POP!POP!POP! POP!POP!POP! POP!POP!POP! POP!POP!POP!

When they finally stopped about twenty English soldiers and two horses lay wounded or dead and the remainder of the soldiers had taken cover behind the wagons.

They cleared the cove and began to steer for Kansas. Tanaka gave orders to the boatmen, but they didn't seem to understand, but eventually through much screaming and pointing, they understood and resheeted sails and tightened the downhauls as they made their turn across the wind. Castillo saw something come alive in Tanaka's face as he steered the sloop and inspected the set of the sails.

• • •

Doc Aultman was nothing short of a miracle worker. He set up surgeries in the infirmary and in the ward room. He knew the blood types of everyone except Lauren Gastmeyer and one of the injured civilians, but he had enlisted blood donors from the crew and was ready to transfuse as soon as the injured came aboard. Taylor was near death when Aultman got to him. He carefully closed the hole in his neck artery, dressed his wound and began transfusion, then he went to the next injured.

A bullet had struck Kenaston and traveled through his thoracic cavity and come to rest...where? Aultman did not have an X-ray machine so he didn't know. Tanaka got a brilliant idea! He had an instrument that was used for inspecting compressor blades in the engine turbine. It was a snake-like borescope with a light at the tip of it. They sterilized it as best they could and Aultman was able to insert the device, find and extract the bullet and inspect damage with minimal invasion. Aultman was very pleased with the device.

Lauren Gastmeyer was another difficult case. She had taken a bullet to the back. It had passed between two ribs right next to the tenth thoracic vertebra, and from her heart palpitations, Aultman was afraid it had done heart damage. With the borescope, he could see the bullet. It had nicked the left ventricle but had not penetrated. He extracted the bullet through a small incision beneath her rib cage.

Aultman tried to save the life of the tillerman who had caught an arrow, but was unable to. There had been too much damage to his liver and kidney.

Everything else was an assortment of leg and arm wounds. There were seven injured in all. Aultman reported to Castillo that everyone would survive, but all medical supplies were almost exhausted. They were out of pain killers, antibiotics and anti-inflammatories.

The first thing they did was have a burial service at sea for Bud Unger and Tony Deangelo. Everyone attended except for Taylor, Kenaston, Gastmeyer and Bloomberg, who were all too weak to move. Castillo took these deaths hard. These two fine young men had died because of him. He had not taken the advice of his XO and had stubbornly insisted on the ill-fated venture that led to their deaths.

Castillo dropped in on Taylor, who looked lethargic. His skin was clammy, and his eyes were rheumy, not their usual clarity, and a white bandage stood out in stark contrast against the skin of his brown neck. Crystal McConnell was sitting with him, holding his hand. When Taylor saw Castillo, he smiled weakly. "H'lo, skipper."

"How you feel, big guy?"

"Been better."

"He has to get better," said McConnell. "So he can serenade me. I want to hear *Are you Lonesome Tonight*."

"Did you show her that…video?" he said groggily.

"What video?" asked Castillo innocently. McConnell giggled. Castillo perched on the side of Taylor's bed. "I haven't heard your input on where we should go to establish our new society."

"You want…my opinion?" Taylor tried to act surprised.

"Yes. You have some kind of uncanny ability to see the future. You've been right twice now. Do you have a crystal ball?"

"No," replied Taylor. "Jus' a Crystal." McConnell beamed. "I wanna go somewhere far from Englan' and Spain an' Europe. Somewhere nice. With good weather an' good fishin'. An' somewhere a black boy can walk down the street with a white girl…an' not get shot!"

Castillo laughed. "Deal!"

"Don' we hafta go ta Turkey so Susan can have coffee?"

"No, she withdrew her request. She said she's gotten used to tea now."

"So, where we going first?" asked McConnell.

"Bermuda! I'm going to take them in order from east to west. Bermuda was requested, so we'll check that out first."

"What else have you got?" asked McConnell.

"Tahiti, Virginia, and Pitcairn Island"

• • •

The scarred and battered crew of Kansas bid good-bye to the English Channel and Kansas entered the Atlantic. Castillo relaxed the rules on alcohol and many got drunk that night, and there was music on the messdeck with performances on guitar and harmonica. They all felt a close personal connection to each other. It was the kind of thing survivors feel after they've come through something horrific. The bond people have when they've come face to face with their own mortality.

Kansas at top speed could reach Bermuda in three days, but Castillo did not want to push his ship at top speed. The reactor had a long life ahead of it, but there were components which wore out and should be replaced and serviced at regular intervals. Things like bearings and seals and lubricants. Castillo had to make Kansas last without benefit of a shipyard, so they went slowly and reached Bermuda in a week.

Bermuda was a tropical paradise with bone white beaches and iridescent aquamarine waters and tropical vegetation that beckoned. Every direction looked like an exotic travel poster. They took turns going ashore, but one of the inflatables hit a hidden reef and sprung a leak. There seemed to be reefs everywhere. They found game on the island. Large sea birds mostly. They harvested about fifty of them. Enough to fill Kansas's meat locker. That night they applied a patch to the damaged inflatable and dined on chicken marinara. Everyone knew it wasn't really chicken, but it was damn good!

On the third day two Spanish ships sailed into view. Castillo read that both the Spanish and English liked to use Bermuda as a stopping point when coming from the New World to replenish their water and food supplies. At least Kansas did not have to take on fresh water. She had two desalination plants to make her own.

The crew took a vote and decided Bermuda was too close to Europe for comfort and not for them. They moved on. In a little less than two days they were off the coast of Virginia at the mouth of the Chesapeake. It didn't look anything like the place they had left a few months ago. It was all wilderness. They went ashore and Chief Brown gave lessons to the Kincaid brothers on firearm safety and then equipped each with a rifle. They were thrilled and set about hunting deer, rabbit and turkey. They were very successful. Castillo one day found himself standing on a beach watching some small wading shore birds. He was crying. He couldn't help himself. It was the same beach where two beautiful laughing little girls had frolicked.

Lambert found him, a forlorn solitary figure standing on the beach. "You're the one who requested Virginia, weren't you."

"Yes," replied Castillo, wiping his eyes. "I had to see it one more time. I can almost feel them here."

They held each other for a long time saying nothing. When Lambert turned her face to Castillo, he could see she was weeping too. Then something unexpected happened. He kissed her. He didn't know why. And she returned the kiss passionately. They parted and he searched her face. He was very conflicted about this. It felt like an act of betrayal, but it also felt so right. He had never been very good at expressing his emotions, but he knew he was violating his wedding vows and his promise to Liz, but at the same time acknowledging his love for the amazing woman at his side. The silence was now embarrassing.

"I…uh…," began Castillo.

"Shhh!" said Lambert, taking his hand. "No apologies, please."

It's as if she could read his mind. "How did you get so smart?" asked Castillo.

"I dunno. Just…born that way, I guess." She laughed. They walked hand in hand down the beach toward the small group of crewmen there. "Do you think this would be a good place to set up our colony?"

"No," replied Castillo. "We're going to have a problem with the English here. I don't think they would actively hunt us, but you never know. We killed a few

of them during our visit, including their lord admiral."
He looked up at a gull screaming overhead. "And then
there's the slavery thing going on too. Some of our crew
will be very uncomfortable here. We should move on."

"Where to next?"

"Tahiti."

"Let's go!"

It took three weeks to reach Tahiti because there
was no Panama Canal. They had to go the long way;
around Cape Horn. When they took their first look
at Tahiti, it was another one of those picture postcard
places with coral reefs and palm trees and water that
varied from light azure to aquamarine and shimmered
in the sunlight. When finally they sent a shore party
out led by Chief Brown, they were attacked by fierce
tattooed warriors. They flooded out of the jungle without warning in great numbers and hurled spears at
them. The crew quickly scrambled back into the inflatables and launched. Two people were injured by the
spears and the inflatables were pierced. They tried to
make it back to Kansas, but the inflatables were losing air too quickly. Chief Brown knew they were not
going to make it. They were going to have to swim
for it through shark infested waters with people who
were bleeding! The tattooed warriors came after them
in outrigger dugout canoes.

Brown's inflatable was almost awash. Water was
pouring in. When the first canoe got close enough,
Brown shot the lead warrior in the chest, then the next
one, then the next until they were all laying wounded
in the bottom of the boat, then he handed his rifle to

another man and directed him to shoot everybody in the second canoe. Brown leaped into the water, swam to the first canoe, climbed in and emptied it of people, then he began paddling. He reached the inflatable just as it was disappearing under the waves. He fished Kansas crewmen out of the water and into the canoe. Someone did the same with the second canoe until everyone in the water had been rescued.

They returned to Kansas where Doc Aultman went to work on the injured. He pronounce that the injuries were not too serious. They had lost their inflatables but had gained two dugout canoes. The only problem was there was no place to store them, so they tethered the canoes to Kansas with long lines. Kansas could tow them. Kansas could still dive, but not very deeply if they wanted to keep the canoes. Castillo did not consider it a great loss. The inflatables were temporary short term vessels anyway and the propane cannisters were almost spent. They had gotten a lot of use out of them. Castillo later read that the Spanish explorer Jaun Fernandez had visited Tahiti in 1577 and there had been a disagreement about something and bloodshed. The natives probably thought the Europeans had returned with their bearded faces and their strange boats.

They decided to go next door and take a look at Pitcairn Island. It looked very forbidding. Not like a tropical paradise at all. There were steep cliffs that rose straight up out of the water. No place to land a small boat. Castillo could immediately see why the Bounty mutineers liked it. It was isolated and built like a mighty fortress. They could see what was coming from a long way off and hold off an assault easily from here. But it didn't appeal to anyone. They decided to continue their search for a new home to the west.

On their eighth day after Pitcairn they found an island identified on modern charts as Sarno Island, a part of French Polynesia. In the world they had come from Sarno Island had a major city, Simone, with a population of 200,000, but now it was almost bare of any people. It was about 54 square miles and had a small village of Polynesians on the north shore where there was a protected cove. It was every bit as lush and beautiful as Tahiti. They loaded up their dugout canoes and went ashore. Cautiously this time. There was fresh water streams and coconut trees and a tree that bore fruit which looked like small bananas. For the next two days all took turns coming ashore, walking on the beach and smelling the fragrant orchids that adorned the trees. When they took a vote it was unanimous. This was the place.

"But it's not a done deal yet," said Castillo. "I need to go have a meeting with the chief of the village on the other side of the island."

Castillo decided to wear his Navy dress white uniform. Most of the dirt had come out of it when it was washed. He wanted to impress this Polynesian chief as best he could. Castillo walked into the village one night with Tanaka, Anderson, Brown, Taylor, Lambert and McConnell in tow. The village consisted of an assortment of huts with walls made of…bamboo? And palm frond roofs arranged in a fan like shape to come to a point. There was a larger structure in the center of the village which Castillo assumed was a general meeting place. Castillo knew that these people had been watching them. He recognized a couple faces he had seen shyly looking at them from behind palm trees.

"I think we're in luck," said Castillo. "I don't think they've ever seen Europeans before."

"That's good," said Lambert hopefully.

Most of the villagers stopped what they were doing, cooking, weaving, cutting and came over to the Kansas group. One of them said something to Taylor. Taylor just smiled and waved. These people were caramel colored, had broad faces and were all small of stature. At 6' 3" Mason Taylor was a giant among them. They were all bare chested, even the women. They only wore loincloths made of some kind of hide. Some of them wore a mocassin like foot covering.

"They're like children," said McConnell as one of them plucked at her blouse and made a curious face.

Eventually a squat thick-waisted little man approached them. Castillo guessed him to be in his fifties, but he could be wrong. He wore a band around his head adorned with red feathers and another one around his waist and had two black swirls tattooed on his chest. This had to be the chief, thought Castillo.

He led them into the structure at the center of the village. They went in and it was very dark. Hardly any sunlight penetrated the large room, and it took a while for their eyes to adjust to it. There was a large woman with great ponderous bare breasts sitting on a reed mat. She also had red feathers on her head and a garland of flowers around her neck. She seemed to be tattooed over every inch of her body. She looked to be about sixty, Castillo guessed. There were four men sitting on her right and two men and two women sitting on her left.

"I think this is the tribal council," said Castillo.

She said something to them and gestured at the mats in front of her. Castillo took this to mean sit. So they all sat down cross legged. Castillo opened the first box they had brought with them. He took out black Kansas ball caps. He passed them out to the Kansas crew. They all put them on their heads, then he counted out ten more and passed them to the queen and her council. They all accepted them, sniffed them, then donned them the same as the Kansas crew had done.

"Why are we doing this?" whispered Lambert.

"This is our bonding ceremony," said Castillo quietly.

"Since when?"

"Since I made it up. About an hour ago."

Lambert giggled.

The queen, if that's what she was, barked orders and servers came in and with something in cups. Each person got a cup of…tea? Castillo tasted it experimentally. No, it tasted more like broth.

"What is this?" asked Lambert.

"Don't ask. Just smile and drink up." Castillo smiled broadly.

The queen held up her left hand and pointed to Castillo. Castillo waved at her and pointed back.

"I think she wants to see your hand," said Lambert.

"Oh!" Castillo got up and went to her and let her look at his mangled left hand. She held it gently and turned it over looking at it from both sides and said something to the man next to her. He said something back. Castillo could imagine the conversation. *Musta hurt! Yeh, like a bitch!*

Castillo opened up the second box and pulled out a jug of English ale. He walked around and filled all the cups. "I don't know if they're going to like this. It's kind of an acquired taste."

The village council took sips of it and smacked their lips curiously. The queen set hers aside. Castillo opened the last box and withdrew a sheathed combat knife. He withdrew the knife from the sheath and allowed them to see the polished blade. They were taken aback by its stainless steel beauty, murmuring to each other. Then Castillo sheathed the knife and made a great show of bowing to the queen and presenting the knife to her.

She took it and unsheathed it with a look of awe. Then she began to chatter excitedly and barking commands. Soon men came in with a young girl. She was pushed forward. She looked to be in her early teens and very frightened.

"*Oh…my…God!*" said Lambert slowly.

"What?" asked a clueless Castillo.

"You gave her a knife, and she gave you a *girl!*" said Lambert.

"A girl?" asked Castillo.

Lambert elevated her eyebrows. "Yes. A girl!"

"Oh!" It slowly dawned on Castillo. "Wait! No no! We really don't need a girl right now, but it's kind of you to offer." He shook his head and made negative gestures.

The queen raised her voice and yelled something at him.

"I don't think you can refuse, Don," said Taylor. "This is part of their code. To refuse is to dishonor them."

"Well, shit! What are we going to do with a little girl?" Castillo looked helplessly to Lambert.

"Feed her?" said Lambert.

Chapter 22

Castillo reported to the crew that it was a done deal. They had communicated with the village chieftan, or whatever she was, and conducted a bonding ceremony, and they now had a new home. They also introduced their newest member. The young girl's name was Mapua and she had large brown sad eyes. Lambert took her aboard Kansas and made her a bed in her stateroom using blankets and a pillow, but she was horrified by her strange surroundings and began to cry. Lambert sat on the floor with her, cradled her in her arms, sang softly to her and rocked her until she fell asleep.

The following morning they began to unload tools. They didn't have many. Kansas's damage control team had four axes, a cordless reciprocating saw, a cordless drill, a cordless Jaws of Life and various sledge hammers and pry bars. All these things were designed to free trapped crewmen from collapsed bulkheads and machinery, but they would never be used for that. The crew would make use of them now to build their new community. There was a good spot on the southeast side of the island which had a natural harbor. It would be perfect to shelter boats.

The whole crew pitched in and began to clear trees until by week's end they had a modest clearing. Their newest crew member turned out to be invaluable. Mapua showed them edible fruits and berries. She also taught them how to dig a root that tasted like sweet potato and how to make a good fishing net. With her help they ate well. Jonesy lamented that he had no more tomatoes or tomato sauce and the closest ones at this time in history were in Central America. But he was very inventive with what he had and was able to create dishes that tantalized.

In the coming weeks they began to build domiciles out of bamboo similar to the natives, but a lot more solid because they used cable and wire from the comm systems on the ship to secure the corner joints. They also built two good sized rafts of bamboo. They used the rafts to transport building materials from all over the island to where they needed it. Some people were assigned the task of building bamboo furniture; simple tables and chairs. Others cut bamboo to uniform lengths for walls, using axes and the one power saw. When the first home was complete Castillo did a walk through. It was a solid little house with three rooms, two doors and three windows. It was very primitive, but they were living in primitive times. There was no running water, no electricity, a dirt floor and no glass in the windows. But it would be good protection for someone. He suggested they anchor it to the ground, so they made anchors out of piping they cannibalized from the Kansas living spaces and anchored it firmly to the ground.

They had to stop their furious building activity to bury Norm Bloomberg. His kidneys failed, he slipped into a coma and a week later he was gone. It was a sad day for everyone. A piece of them was gone. That night they sat around a fire, drank the last of the ale and whiskey and told Norm Bloomberg stories.

"At least we were able to lay him to rest in our new home," sniffed Lambert.

"Yes, too bad he couldn't enjoy any of it though," replied Castillo. "I think he was the true renaissance man. He seemed to know about just about everything."

"Yes. He knew about everything." She sighed. "Except maybe the dangers of obesity."

Castillo shamed her with a look.

"Well, it's true! His health problems were caused by his size. He loved food and drink a little too much. Oh that reminds me. We're hosting the villagers next week. Where's Mapua?" Lambert began to look around.

"She's over there next to Crystal." Castillo pointed.

"Oh." Lambert said, "Mapua," and beckoned to her.

She ran over to Lambert, smiling and said "Yes, Zoozan?"

"We're having a dinner. Big dinner! Seven nights." She held up seven fingers. "You bring everybody! Okay?"

"Everybody! Okay! Me bring in zeven nights!" She smiled held up seven fingers and raced off.

Castillo's mouth fell open. "How much English does she understand?"

"A lot I think."

"She learned that much in two *weeks*?"

"Yes!"

"You taught her?"

"As much as I can tell, no one taught her. She learned it all from hanging around and watching us… and listening!"

"*Oh, my God!* Are they *all* that smart?"

"Could be." The flickering firelight danced in her eyes.

Castillo reflected on it. These people *could* be very intelligent.

"What are you thinking about?"

"Oh, nothing. We're taking Kansas out tomorrow to a neighboring island. We're trying to locate a good source of bamboo. We've used up most of the construction grade bamboo here. It shouldn't take more than a couple days. You want to come?"

"No. Think I'll stay. I'm working on my garden plot. I'm going to try and grow some of those turnips and beets we got from Scotland and Jonesy says he has some tomato seeds for me."

"Okay. Give some thought to a name."

"Name?" asked Lambert blankly.

"For..our place." Castillo was still seeing blankness in Lambert's eyes. "Our little settlement here."

"Oh!" Lambert reflected briefly, then said, "Why not Bloomberg? It sort of sounds like a city, doesn't it?"

"Bloomberg! Sure! I'll run it past the crew and see what they say."

• • •

The following day the crew secured their dugout canoes and bamboo rafts to the deck cleats on Kansas's aft deck and they left the island behind. The weather was good so the submarine ran on the surface. If they detected a ship on radar, then they either diverted or submerged and ran just beneath the surface. No one would be able to see Kansas. They would only see her trailing canoes and rafts being pulled along the surface apparently be a mysterious sea creature.

They saw not a single ship before they reached their first stop. It was a small island called Gatuama about 150 miles away. There were natives there, but they did not seem aggressive. The crew found a great deal of high quality construction grade bamboo, so they warily harvested as much as they could. In two days they loaded both rafts and then constructed two more rafts and loaded them too. With their heavy load of bamboo they began their trek back to their home island, but they hadn't traveled far when something got their attention.

"Two ships, sir," said the radar watch stander. "…74 miles."

"Which way are they heading?" asked Castillo, frowning at the radar plot.

"Uh…the lead ship is steering 166 and the other ship is steering an intercept course of 112."

"They're going to cross our path, aren't they?"

"Yes, sir. It looks like we're all heading for the same spot of ocean."

Castillo carefully watched the two ships. When they got to within 24 miles, he ordered Kansas to periscope depth. He watched the camera screens from the photonics mast and saw one ship closing on another.

"That first ship looks like a Spanish Galleon," said Tanaka. "Not enough guns to be a man of war. I'll bet its a silver ship coming from Central America. This is a major route for them. They haul silver and sometimes sugar and tobacco."

"What about the other ship?" asked Castillo.

"That looks like an attack vector. I'd say he's probably a French privateer. Can you get a close up on his flag, sir?"

Castillo zoomed in on the flag flying from the second mast. It appeared to be a red heart on a black background with a single drop of blood coming from it.

"Yep," said Tanaka. "A pirate!"

"I thought they flew the jolly roger," said Taylor.

"That didn't come along 'til later, sir."

They watched as the two ships closed on each other. The Galleon was a good sized four master with an elaborately carved and painted figurehead and high stern castle and fo'csle trimmed in red and black. The other ship was three masted, but was all black, had a much lower silhouette, almost no stern castle at all, but two gun decks and two flying jibs. It had lots of firepower and looked fast! They were still a few miles apart.

"He's going to disable the Spanish ship, steal the cargo and then kill the crew."

"Why would they kill the crew?" asked Taylor.

"No witnesses," said Tanaka.

Castillo was staring hard at the screen. Taylor could see wheels turning.

"You're not thinking of intervening, are you?"

Castillo said nothing. He pursed his lips.

"Don," said Taylor in exasperation, "every time we get involved with these people, it has disastrous consequences. Need I remind you…" Taylor stopped because Castillo had held up his hand.

"Eric," said Castillo, "do you think you could command that pirate ship?"

Tanaka's black eyes popped wide. "By myself?"

"No, of course not. I was just thinking it would be very nice to have a ship we could use to sail into a trade port and get supplies. It's just too difficult with Kansas. But it all hinges on one question. Can you command that ship if we took it over?"

"Um…yes!" replied Tanaka, nodding positively. "Yes, I can, sir!"

"Good! Then we'll have to disable it some way and overwhelm the crew with force."

"I can't believe I'm saying this," said Taylor. "But why don't we just pop up next to them on the side away from their target. We can catch them looking the other way."

"Yes, sir," said Tanaka. "That's a very good idea! They usually have enough men to man one battery of guns. They'll have their starboard battery fully manned, the side toward the Spaniard. The port side batteries won't be manned at all. And it won't be easy to move everyone to the other side and prime the port guns."

"Okay, we're going to cut lose our load of bamboo," said Castillo. "It's going to slow us down."

"But we need it, sir," said Anderson.

"We'll come back and get it," said Castillo. "How much scuba gear have we got on board?"

"Scuba gear?" Taylor and Tanaka exchanged puzzled glances.

• • •

Kansas slowed to a stop while Chief Brown, Tanaka, and Anderson exited the lockout trunk on Kansas in scuba gear and made their way to the ship's sail with their support equipment. When they were in position and lashed down, Kansas resumed speed and closed on the French privateer. When Kansas's sail broke the water, it was twenty feet from the hull on the port side of the privateer and just as Taylor had predicted, the entire crew was looking the other way. They were all sizing up the fat Spanish plum in the water a few hundred yards away. All gun crews were at the ready on the starboard side.

Brown, Anderson and Tanaka each threw a line with a grappling hook and climbing stirrups over the port side rails of the ship. Then they swung down and began climbing. Kansas surfaced completely and

Castillo, Taylor and two other men came out of the hatch wearing body armor and carrying assault rifles. They were 25 feet above sea level and able to look down on the weather deck of the privateer. It had tan decks and was about 180 feet long.

Soon a man walked by, looked up and screamed in horror at the ominous men dressed in black looking at him from a black tower coming out of the sea. Men turned around and began shouting orders and running. A man raised a rifle and was shot…

POP!

…and fell. Another man raised a rifle and another…

POP!POP!POP! POP!POP!POP!

…and they both fell. One more man tried it…

POP!

… and met the same end. The pirates were horror-stricken by the masked invaders in black climbing over the rails. Five men rushed them with cutlasses…

POP!POP!POP! POP!POP!POP! POP!POP!POP! POP!POP!POP! POP!POP!POP! POP!POP!POP!

…and all five fell. Now the French crew was petrified with terror. Nobody moved. They only stared in naked fear. Tanaka pulled off his scuba mask, pointed his rifle and began barking orders.

"Unsheet the mains and heave to!" He immediately ran into a problem. Most of them only spoke French.

But one man clearly understood him. He began running around on the deck and casting off sheet lines. The sails began to spill air and the ship slowed.

Twenty more Kansas crewmen scrambled aboard, and then they began sorting through the French crew. Tanaka had to figure out who to keep and who to get rid of. He discerned who the captain was. All he had to do is bellow, "I'm going to cut off the balls of your captain!" There were enough English speakers there who understood him. Their eyes went to one large bearded evil looking man with a scar on his cheek.

Tanaka pointed out to Castillo about twenty men he didn't want and Castillo put them into the dugout canoes and on a raft and towed them to within sight of land and cast them off.

Taylor expressed surprise at how hard-hearted Castillo had become, and Castillo expressed surprise at how tepid Taylor had become.

There was a great deal of surprise when they finally returned to the settlement of Bloomberg. Tanaka pulled the French ship into the little bay and dropped anchor. The sun glistened on its black lacquered rails and yards and it swung easily on its anchor as they put boats in the sparkling light azure colored water. Kansas went to its normal parking spot off shore and disembarked all personnel except those on watch. Then the ship was submerged.

"What a beautiful ship!" exclaimed Lambert, standing on the beach. "Where did you get it?"

"Found it!" said Castillo. "That's Eric Tanaka's first command."

Lambert laughed. "Really?"

"Yes. Now we can sail into any port and pick up supplies."

"Great!"

"But wait! It gets better! Do you know what we found in the hold?"

"What?" giggled Lambert.

"Silver, tobacco and rum! We can now afford to *buy* anything too!"

"Wow!"

"It's called the *Feu Infernal* which means hellfire I've been told. We'll have to rename it. And alter its appearance."

"Let's celebrate!"

"Why not? We have plenty of rum to celebrate with."

The sunlight accented the faint laugh lines around her smiling mouth and the long lashes over her laughing blue eyes, and Castillo suddenly was hungry for another kiss. And he could read the unvoiced invitation in her face. So he took her in his arms. And this time they threw themselves into it, passionately embracing and lovingly touching and probing each other's bodies and mouths.

Chapter 23
Old Bloombers
September 23, 1912

Eliza Davenport turned her blue eyes toward the stormy skies. It did not look promising. Professor Goolong was supposed to be on this flight, but the weather looked bad. Not even the seabirds were flying. She felt the first drops of rain and decided to go into the terminal and wait with the others. She looked up at the tracking screen and saw the flight still inbound, about 50 miles out.

She reflected on Kami Goolong. She hadn't seen her for over five years. She wondered if she still looked the same, jet black hair, caramel skin, long exquisite neck, a picture of tall elegance. She would be almost fifty now. Davenport envied her because of her grace and beauty, but the tables would be turned this time because of her find. Eliza would be famous for this find. She couldn't wait to tell her.

Finally a loud voice blared from the speakers:

Arriving Flight 212 from New Kansas! Behind blast protection get everyone grace until the warn is terminated. Arriving Flight 212 from New Kansas! Behind blast protection get everyone grace until the warn is terminated.

People who had been outside quickly hurried into the terminal building and turned to look out the large glass windows. Davenport stared at the large sign in the distance surrounded by the agitated palm trees.

Welcome to Old Bloomberg – Where Lives History!

She watched as the white stubby winged craft approached. It was only a bright speck in the dark sky, but growing. As it got closer, she could see the silver arrow graphics and logo of Hough Transport. It looked like an egg with wings. It slowed, stopped and hovered over the landing sight while stilt like legs extended. Then it settled on them, blasting dust and debris for a hundreds of yards in all directions. This was one of the older Sebring sky skimmers. This route never got the shiny newer ones. Old Bloomberg just didn't get a lot of high profile traffic. There were only two flights a day now and it was mostly tourists wanting to see the memorial or the historic reenactment.

She watched the ramp extend from the body of the skimmer and travelers disembark. She walked out onto the wet cement surface and into the light rain. The wind tugged at her coat. There she was! Goolong smiled and waved at her. She was just as beautiful as ever. Damn!

"Honor to you!" Davenport smiled and kissed her.

"Honor to you!" returned Goolong. "Look good you! Compliments you well this quiet life."

"Tired are you?" asked Davenport, hoping she would say no.

"No," replied Goolong. "Want I to see what drug you out me to this place for."

"Hoped I did you would say that," bubbled Davenport. "Come! Must see you this!"

They entered Davenport's small red ground runner and traveled down the cement ribbon of road that trailed through the jungle. Goolong jumped every time a large pinnate leaf slapped at the windshield.

"Beautiful here it is!" exclaimed Goolong. "Spend I too much time in the city."

Davenport frowned and cleared her throat thinking how to start. "Wondered have you who our forefathers were?"

"Knows every school child. Donald and Susan Castillo."

"No. Mean I…Come from where did they?"

"Donald from Spain. Susan from England."

"Speculation is that!"

Goolong studied her for a few seconds before speaking. "*Found* something you did."

"I did! Something big!" Davenport's freckles seemed to dance on her light brown skin in the filtered sunlight coming through the palms.

"Found you a reference to *Toto*!"

"Toto? Oh, from the inscription? No!" The inscription on Castillo's headstone originally was, *I don't think we're in Kansas any more, Toto*. No one knows what it refers to. Some say it was Castillo's last words. Kansas was his first ship, but no one knew who Toto was. She stopped the red runner at the edge of a clearing and pointed. "Opening we are the new monument next week." There was a large white cement domed building standing all alone in the clearing. It had double glass doors in the front and a long walkway leading up to it. On its very peak was a bronze statue of Don Castillo dressed like a 16th century European with long cloak, doublet and large floppy hat. There were flowerbeds on both sides of the walkway and a carpet of bright red and yellow blooms spread from both sides of the building. There were many workers still planting small trees and shrubs.

"Beautiful! But must work they even in the rain?" asked Goolong.

"Have they much work still to do," replied Davenport. They drove on.

Soon they arrived at Davenport's office in a small two story complex resembling a cluster of stacked bird houses. Once inside it seemed to be a hive of activity with people and robots scurrying down hallways and flickering screens everywhere.

When finally they arrived, Davenport motioned to a chair for Goolong to take. Goolong dumped her purse and her carry bag and collapsed into a chair. She saw the picture of the smiling couple on Davenport's desk and asked, "Is Chad well he?"

"Yes! Is at Magellan Base he."

"The moon?"

"Yes. Leaves he for Drake Base in two days."

"Mars? Is a space traveler he!"

"Yes. Received I a call two hours ago. Good he is. Misses me he does. And miss I him too." Davenport's blue eyes grew wet and she sniffed.

"So!" said Goolong crossing her long legs. "I am here why?"

"Wondered have you why this place…the South Pacific is prosperous? Is Castillo the most powerful nation on earth! Is New Kansas the most prosperous city on earth! Wondered have you why? Was here nothing, three hundred years ago. No technology! No resources! Came Castillos, Taylors, Bloomberg and all the others. Come from where did they?"

"Have found you *what*?" demanded Goolong eyebrows arched.

"Moved we the bodies of Donald and Susan from the mausoleum, so could work we on rebuilding it. For the new center."

"Yes?" said Goolong transfixed. "And?"

"And found we a cement chamber under the floor. And found we in that chamber a sealed metal box. A big box. Very old." She gestured with her hands about three feet apart. "And found we in that box the personal account of Donald Castillo."

Goolong gasped.

"In the hand of Donald Castillo!"

Goolong gasped again. "Must see I!"

"Have sent I the artifacts to the university."

Goolong blinked. "Which university?"

"East Castillo National. Have they the best lab."

"But, Eliza. Am I a professor of history," she said sadly.

"Yes," said Davenport. "At Aultman. But are you my friend, so must call I you. Must see you this."

"See…" Goolong's communicator began to buzz in her ear. She took it out and threw it angrily against the wall. "See I what?" she shouted.

"This!" said Davenport. She reached behind her chair and pulled up a large three foot square piece of cardboard against the wall and laid it flat on the desk. She slid clips from its edges and the cardboard sheet turned into two. She carefully lifted the top piece off to reveal something wrapped in tissue.

Goolong got up and walked around to look over her shoulder. "Is this the only piece did send I not to them. The preface it is. Has taken everyone an oath of secrecy and so must you." Goolong reached out to touch it and Davenport grabbed her wrist. "Touch you must not. Very fragile it is. Very old."

"Can read I?" She whispered reverently.

"Yes. But hard it is. Is made the paper of rice. Dim it is and although English, structed differently the sentences are. Not like speak we at all."

Goolong began to read:

I've decided to detail our adventures here just in case someone wants to know what we went through. It's been quite a ride, so far. Whoever reads this will understand

why we're here and some of the sacrifices
we've made so far to get here.
Don Castillo, October 8, 1588
Dear Liz, Kelly and Robin,

I'm writing this journal in the form
of letters to you although I know you'll
never read them. But each time I write,
I'm reminded that you are alive somewhere and happy, I hope. It's enough
to know you're all safe somewhere. Also,
you've always been good listeners. You
know. Easy to talk to. I can picture in my
mind's eye all of you gathered around
the fireplace with cups of cocoa listening
to me spin my tales. Thinking about it
makes me smile. I'm going to finish this
later, something's in my eyes.

"Liz, Kelly and Robin are who?" asked Goolong.

"Explains he that later."

Goolong rushed around and collected her purse and
her carry bag and picked up her communicator laying
on the floor. "Go I must!"

"Where?" asked Davenport.

"To the ECN lab, Eliza! Must read I the rest of this!
Ground-breaking this is!"

"But have I the text here. Scanned the ECN lab it
and sent me it by wire three days ago."

"You…sent they…" Goolong stopped mid stride and fixed Davenport with a stare.

"Thought you called I you to see a scrap of paper?" Davenport held out a flat reader to Goolong.

"On here it is?" asked Goolong.

"It is," replied Davenport. "'Bloomberg41' the unlock is."

"Authenticated ECN the documents?"

"Not completely. Passed it the dating authentication. Three hundred years!"

Goolong dropped her purse and bag and settled into a chair holding the reader gingerly as if she were cradling the Holy Grail.

"Read I the account three times and afraid am I that believe it not will some. Fantastic it is! Like witchcraft will say some. The year 1912 this is! Believes no one that stuff in this day and age."

She looked at Goolong, but Goolong was no longer listening to her, she was concentrating on the text:

Dear Liz, Kelly and Robin,

We have a new island home. On modern charts it's called Sarno Island. It's an island about 400 miles north of New Zealand in the South Pacific. It has coconuts and a small banana-like fruit that's quite tasty and there's an animal that looks like a large hedgehog which tastes like pork when it's prepared by an expert chef like Jonesy.

We've built a small community here. We have about 100 small homes and a larger meeting lodge built of bamboo.

Our population is about 157 now. We've grown beyond the original crew because we invited crew members from another ship to join us.

We also have a ship. A sailing ship, I mean. It's a French galleon. Eric Tanaka is in charge of that. It's original name was Feu Infernal and it belonged to pirates, but we renamed it New Adventure. Susan's idea. I like it. It has an optimistic sound to it. It kind of conveys our positive attitude toward our challenges.

What I have to say to you guys now is difficult, but I don't know any other way to say it than to just come right out with it. I've fallen in love with a woman named Susan Lambert. She's an amazing woman. She was assigned to Kansas as the chief test conductor. She holds a PHD in computer science from Duke University and she's a two time winner of the Virginia Old Dominion Triathlon. But that's not why I love her. She has pretty blue eyes, sandy hair and a delicate little face like an angel, and she rescued me when I was abducted and tortured by a crazed Spaniard. But that's not why I love her. I love her because she's so sunny and never gives up. She finds the good in just about everything although she left loved ones behind too. She had a brother, sister, nieces and nephews. And she was close to her mother. I love her because her fluttery laugh comes so easily. I love her because she sings

Niel Diamond when she works in her garden and dances when she thinks no one is watching. I love her because she gets a certain twinkle in her eye and wrinkles her nose when she's about to tell the punch line to a joke. I love her mostly because she loves me despite my many flaws.

The Kinkaid boys, Kevin and Will, consider Susan their mom although they're almost grown. They lost their real mom when they were young so Susan is the only mom they've ever known probably. They came with us from Scotland. A little island girl, Mapua, also considers Susan mom, I think. Susan is a good mom to the three of them. She makes sure they have clothes and get enough to eat, and she takes a personal interest in everything they do. She's teaching Mapua to read English.

That's all for now. I'll write again next week.
Don Castillo, October 9, 1588

Goolong said, "Understand I not much of this."

Davenport replied, "Understand you will much more during the second reading. Must read you it all."

Goolong frowned and went to the next entry.

Dear Liz, Kelly and Robin,
We just held our first free election to elect a president and the settlement of Bloomberg has elected me, no surprise, as their first president. I've agreed to serve, but I'm going to step down after

four years and give someone else a chance.

Everyone has tried to learn a skill or specialty to help us survive and grow as a community, and I just didn't know what to do. It looks like, however, by default (that means no one else wants to do it) I am the camp administrator. That means I have to record all important transactions and contracts: marriages, deaths, births, bills of sale, etc. I came up with a fancy little certificate of marriage and another one for births and deaths and I printed a bunch on the ship's printer. But we ran out of paper fast. Kansas did not carry much paper.

But on a trip to Kanta we found a merchant selling rice paper from the Phillipines. We bought all he had and told him we'd be back for more. We also found a merchant in Corchado who was selling squid ink, so we bought all he had of that too. Everyone is trying to copy important books and writing notes and papers on every subject of interest. We all feel we're racing the clock. Our technology will fail some day and that will be the end of our knowledge base. Maria Guerrero wants to copy all the nautical charts we have. That's like 1000 charts! Susan and I watched her do it. She displays a chart on her navigation plot screen, lays a sheet of paper over it, anchors it with clips, then carefully traces it, marking channels and depths and contours. It took her about 30 minutes to do one!

It's going to take a long time to copy them all. But she said she doesn't really need them all, just the approaches to ports we're likely to visit. The more I think about it, the more I like it. We have the most advanced precision navigational charts in the world. It would be shame to lose them. I assigned two people to help her.

I'm trying to learn the Machuan language. That's the language of our Island here before we got here anyway. The natives call themselves Machua and the island is called Apanuchu. The language is like all Polynesian languages. The verb is first. Different than the English language. If I'm in a boat, I might say, "I sail the boat," but they would say, "Sail I the boat." Strange, huh? Like that little character in the Star Wars movies. I forget his name. They talk that way all over the South Pacific.

That's all for now,
Don Castillo, October 16, 1588

Dear Liz, Kelly and Robin,

They want me to perform marriages because I'm the official administrator. But we have a young man named Olson who would like to start a church. At first I had mixed feelings about that because religion has created so many problems in the world. We've seen it at its worst! Why can't this be a religion free zone? But there is no denying that it has done a lot of good too. It has provided a moral compass and hope in dark times and maybe we need that. Some deity to believe in and offer thanks to. We need to trust that a higher power will show us the way when we've lost the path.

I invited Olson, now known as the Reverend Matthew Olson to perform the ceremony. It was a double ceremony. Mason and Crystal stood on the specially built platform in the meeting hall next to Susan and me. It was a beautiful ceremony. The crew built an archway out of vines laced with big showy red and purple jungle orchids and Susan and Crystal were in white lace dresses and had white hibiscus blossoms in their hair. They were breathtaking. Mason and I wore our Navy dress white uniforms. (I was able to get most of the stains out of mine.) A young man named Douglas played his guitar and sang a Neil Diamond song *Hello Again Hello.* (That was requested by Susan.)

Susan and I decided to do some home improvements. We doubled the size of our little house so we could have the Kinkaids and Mapua under our roof. It only took about two weeks to do that.

The villagers, the Machua, have taken a real interest in the houses we've built. Our homes stand up better to the severe weather than theirs. So we've started building homes for them too. We've started cannibalizing some of the Tomahawk missiles just to get the wiring and the sheet metal.

That's all for now,
Don Castillo, October 30, 1588

Dear Liz, Kelly and Robin,

I know it's been awhile since I've written, but there's been a lot going on.

Eric Tanaka is a damn genius! He looked at our captured cannons and rifles and said these can be greatly improved. He devised a way to rifle the barrel of a large cannon we acquired. He epoxied diamonds, we bought them in Papua, to a steel shaft from Kansas and created a cutting head he could use to force down the cannon's muzzle over and over by hammering it with an ax to create rifling. He lost the cutting head once when it got jammed, but he got it back. He also created a resin-coated fabric that seals the space between the cannon ball and gun barrel better than anything currently available. Anyway, we have a gun now that will fire a 9 pound ball twice the distance of anything in Europe. Eric says he's going to mount it on the bow of New Adventure. He's designing a swivel mount that will attach to the deck and absorb the recoil of the big gun.

He's also decided to rifle the shipboard guns. He's created more cutting heads using the rest of the diamonds we purchased, and enlisted the help of about ten people. He has plans to rifle the barrels of the muskets and other black powder guns we have too. In the world we came from, flintlocks reigned supreme for about 200 years. Then the percussion cap was invented. Here, we will never see a flintlock rifle or musket because we have made the leap to cap and ball technology. Eric was able make a working percussion cap from things he bought from an apothecary in Galle. Potassium chlorate, Sulfur and powdered flint. He made a paste out of this stuff using resin from a tree in our jungle here. The outside of the cap was actually formed of paper treated with resin so it would not be affected by moisture. He modified the flash pan and hammer of the gun to accept and detonate the cap. It works quite well and will fire even in the rain. It also shortens the loading time of a black powder weapon.

Oh, and also in Galle, we found a vendor selling coffee. We bought all he had, eleven bags of coffee beans. Susan is thrilled to have coffee again. I'm not sure how long eleven 35 pound bags will last her. Her garden is beginning to produce tomatoes. They're delicious and Jonesy has big plans for them. She's enlarged her garden now and is trying to grow things we've found in the markets: onions, radishes, cabbages and something called cobe. There are a lot of gardens being grown on the island now.

That's all for now,
Don Castillo, December 20, 1588

Dear Liz, Kelly and Robin,

We had a very nice Christmas. The Reverend Matthew Olson held a special Christmas service and Crystal and Douglas played and provided a musical program on guitar and harpsichord. Did I forget to mention that Crystal has a harpsichord? Mason found it in a market somewhere and bought it for her. She plays very well. She also organized a choir and they sound very good! They've really worked very hard and have a superb sound. They performed 'O Come All Ye Faithful' and a variety of Christmas songs and one original written by Mr. Douglas and sung by none other than Mason Taylor. He has an exceptional voice!

That's all for now,
Don Castillo, December 28, 1588

Dear Liz, Kelly and Robin,

Big news! Crystal and Susan are both pregnant! Doc Aultman has examined them in his little clinic and pronounced them healthy. It seems like the fates have joined the four of us somehow. We are destined to travel through life on parallel paths.

We've made some money transporting things, like a freight company. Many vendors want things hauled, spices mostly, so we've taken on some cargoes and were paid quite well. As administrator and self-appointed negotiator, I've drawn up legal contracts and bills of sale for everything should we ever be legally challenged.

We may have found our niche in this world as a maritime freight company. Maria Guerrero has excellent charts and has great skill as a navigator. She's very good with a sextant and has taught five other people how to use one. We're the most reliable shipping company available.

Wally Anderson has expressed the desire to build a foundry! He says we need to be able to produce high quality steel and other alloys. That way, we will always have the best tools and weapons. I said fine, but just how are we going to do that? To have a foundry you need a furnace that will generate about 2000+ degrees of heat which means blowers and forced air. I don't see how it would be possible. He said he could do it if we could harness a river. (?) We don't have any rivers here. Just some streams. He's going to work on it.

That's all for now,
Don Castillo, February 11, 1589

Dear Liz, Kelly and Robin,
I knew this was going to happen!

We've attracted the attention of the French. This is, after all, French Polynesia. Some French official, a Monsieur Arnaud Somebody, paid us a visit, looked at our work here, you know, with weapons and the writing of technical papers we're doing and said we should be under French "protection" at once. He drew up a treaty for me to sign. I'm not a lawyer but I took one look at it and refused. It benefited France greatly, but not us. In exchange for French protection, we would have to turn over everything we produce here to them.

When I refused, the Frenchman said, "But these waters are dangerous! Spanish and English privateers are everywhere. Without France's protection, you will not last." I told him we'd take our chances.

About a week later, our ship, New Adventure, was on a run to the Dutch East Indies and a ship approached them at sea. I was not aboard, but according to Tanaka, it flew no colors and began to close on them, demonstrating hostile intent. By this time Tanaka had perfected his big swiveling bow gun. When the ship had closed to within a mile and a half, Tanaka opened fire. He had the distance, but missed. The second shot was fired when they were just over a mile away and it was a direct hit to their foc'sle, shattering their bowsprit. I think it shocked them. They left the area. Tanaka has plans now to build a second swiveling heavy gun mount on the stern.

Our population is about 260 now. Many of our young men are finding wives in some of the ports we visit, and I've run out of my marriage certificates. But I discovered that Lauren Gastmeyer is a very fine artist. She's done some beautiful drawings of the local birds and flowers, and she's agreed to pen some very professional looking certificates for me. I can't get over all the talent around me!

Susan and Crystal are both due the same week in September. It should be interesting.

That's all for now,
Don Castillo, March 30, 1589

Dear Liz, Kelly and Robin,

I could see this coming!

The French have tried to take us over by force! They showed up with two warships off our eastern coast. Two warships was a little too much for us to handle, so I called up Mason. He had the watch on Kansas. I told him to put a fish into the smaller of the two ships. And use a dummy head. He said, "Right away! What do you want to do about the other one?"

I told him that we could handle that one. The French warships put boats in the water and started sending soldiers ashore. When the first two boats were almost ashore, the smaller of the two ships was struck. It made a mighty boom! We could hear it from across the water. The boats stopped, the soldiers stood up and watched as it rolled onto its side and slipped beneath the surface. Anyway, after they made their landing, we surprised them with an ambush. They quickly surrendered. They realized they were no match for our firepower. A few of them were wounded. We used the same trick to capture all the soldiers in the third and fourth boats too. Then a bunch of us put on their uniforms (they smelled awful) and returned to the first ship and pulled another ambush as soon as we were aboard. We were successful, but we lost a young man. His name was Sinclair and he was shot in the back by one of the French sailors. The bullet struck him in the head just beneath his helmet. I really regret that. It's a brutal world here, and many have fallen needlessly.

We had a funeral for Sinclair and the many Frenchmen who died too on the ship we sank. I'm sure most of them were honorable men simply carrying out orders.

Well, we have two ships now and many French prisoners. I was not sure what to do with them. We already have some French speaking men in our little community, so they helped me communicate with them. Some of them had no desire to return to the French Navy. They had been pressed into service and wanted to join us, so I let them stay. The others we took to a port in Australia and put ashore. I'm sure I'm going to hear about this from the French. I've assigned a dive team to go look at the sunken French ship and salvage whatever they can off her.

That's all for now,
Don Castillo, June 7, 1589

Dear Liz, Kelly and Robin,
I'm a father! Again! Susan gave birth to a little girl, 6 pounds, 8 ounces on

September 14th. Susan wants to name her Anna Lee after her mother. Mason and Crystal had a little boy, 7 pounds, 3 ounces, they're going with Anthony William. We're talking about building a school. We're going to need one. There are many pregnancies here.

On a more serious note, an island girl here was raped by one of the Frenchmen who joined us. We've not had much in the way of a government up until now, but I can see we need something. I've appointed Chief Brown as head of our police force and Mason Taylor as head of our judiciary. So, their first job is to try the Frenchman and decide on his guilt and his punishment.

I received a diplomatic pouch from France. Tanaka was given it when we were at one of our regular stops with New Adventure. Our other ship we have named New Hope. The pouch had a letter in it from the French Defense Minister. It was in French so I had to have it translated. It said that by sinking his majesty's ship and stealing another one, the township of Bloomberg has declared war on France. We must surrender to French authority at once or there would be dire consequences.

I wrote a letter back in English stating that France committed an act of war on the sovereign peace-loving people of Bloomberg when it violated our international waters and sent soldiers to our shores. Our two countries are currently in a state of war! If you wish to sue for peace, we are willing to discuss the terms of your surrender. I told Tanaka to carry this pouch back out the next time he goes out.

Meanwhile, Tanaka is busy outfitting our new ship, New Hope, with a heavy bow gun and stern gun.

We recovered some valuable things from the salvaged French warship. For some reason, it was carrying gold bullion and some ship building tools, saws, hammers, nails, etc. We could use all that stuff.

Wally Anderson says he would like to locate a foundry on New Zealand where there is a good strong river he can harness.

That's all for now,
Don Castillo, September 26, 1589

"Respond to Castillo did the French?" asked Goolong, looking up to Davenport.

"Yes, the following year. Show I you, you want?"

"Yes, grace!"

Davenport picked up the reader and pressed a few onscreen buttons. "Oh! Read this one first. Odd it is!"

Dear Liz, Kelly and Robin,

CATS ARE MARSUPIALS! CATS ARE MARSUPIALS! CATS ARE MARSUPIALS! When I found this out I screamed it as loud as I could. I checked this out with different hunters and trappers. House cats, tigers, lions, leopards are all marsupials. Like kangaroos. They give birth to these little hairless things the size of your thumbnail. They stay inside the mother's pouch and attach themselves to the mother's nipples, then when they grow big enough, they come out of the pouch.

This is proof to me that we are in a different parallel world to our own. Kansas's presence could not have caused this! This condition existed before we got here! This is an enormous load off my mind. Just to know that we're not affecting anyone's future. I mean any one I know and love. We're affecting the futures of people in this world of course. But we're always affecting the future wherever we are and whatever we do.

I'm just so happy to have proof of our dimension jump. Everyone I told about this greeted it the same way, with complete and utter joy. Except the Frenchmen, of course. They think we're all a bit mad.

This kind of releases any restraints on us, although, to be honest, we haven't demonstrated a lot of restraint so far.

That's all for now,
Don Castillo, March 13, 1590

Chapter 24

"Most odd!" remarked Goolong.

"Yes," agreed Davenport.

"Is what kind of ship Kansas?" asked Goolong.

"A military underwater antiship," replied Davenport.

"Eliza! An underwater antiship in 1588!?" Goolong looked doubtful.

"Yes. Call they it a submarine." Davenport took the reader, began to look through the entries, then handed the reader to Goolong. "Respond the French here."

> Dear Liz, Kelly and Robin,
> We're at war with the French!
> We found ourselves surrounded one morning. Wally Anderson was on duty in Kansas. He called up and told me there were French warships on the horizon, eight of them. I told him to wait and see what they wanted. Looking back, that was a stupid decision. We're at war! With the French! And they take war very seriously. One ship came up

and opened fire while I was looking at her through my binoculars. The first salvo mostly missed us, but two shots landed in our settlement and took out a house on the edge of the village. I told Anderson quick put a fish into that ship, use a dummy head. I've discovered that if we use dummy heads, there's minimum damage to the ship and its worth more for salvage.

The ship was struck before she could reload her gun batteries. A second ship fired a salvo at us, but never landed a shot in Bloomberg. I ordered that ship torpedoed too. Finally I just said torpedo all of them. To which Anderson replied, "But we only have five more dummy loads left."

Okay, I told him, then sink five more ships and we'll try to take the other two. One by one the French warships were struck and began listing heavily. You could see men running and screaming on the decks, trying to get boats in the water. The two untouched French ships fled. A good decision on their part!

The house that was hit was not occupied. The owners had gotten up early to go get a bath in the stream.

There were about 800 survivors from the wrecked French ships. We rounded them up and loaded them onto our third ship, New Fortune, and took them all to a port in New Caledonia.

Wally Anderson has started building his foundry in New Zealand next to a raging river. We've hauled several loads of brick and stone for the furnaces.

Oh, and we've started building a school. We have twelve children here now and many more to come. The Machuans have kind of taken over that project.

That's all for now,
Don Castillo, June 1, 1590

Dear Liz, Kelly and Robin

Our population is at 1251 and climbing rapidly.

Word has spread about our stand off with the French and everyone wants to join us. People are showing up in boats almost everyday. They want our protection. I guess the French, well, all Europeans actually, have made a lot of enemies. They are Polynesians mostly, but many others too.

I fear we're going to outgrow our little island. We may have to start another colony and probably the best place would be where Wally is building his foundry in New Zealand. It's beautiful there. There are tall majestic gray and purple snow capped mountains and beautiful beaches.

Oh! We have a guy who wants to jump off one of those mountains. His name is Sebring. He's not Navy. He was a QVR guy, and he was a private pilot. He used to really enjoy flying. He misses it so much he decided to build his own glider out of bamboo and sail cloth. According to all his calculations, it should fly, but he can't find a good launching point. He wants go to New Zealand and jump off one of those 10,000+ foot peaks.

That's all for now,
Don Castillo, September 2, 1590

Dear Liz, Kelly and Robin

I know I haven't written in a while but I've been very busy.

Our population is up to 2000+ now and we're getting ready to move to New Zealand and set up there.

We've been getting lots of work. Shipping! We only send out our three ships in convoy now, shadowed by Kansas. It's safer that way. We've only had to sink one ship though. Three French warships came at us in the Spice Islands. The wind was against us, making maneuvering hard. New Adventure opened up on the first ship with its bow gun. The other French ships were attempting to bracket us by spreading out. I was aboard Kansas at the time. I really didn't want to use a warload ADCAP on a single ship so instead, we "broke polar ice". We retracted all masts and antennas, buttoned up tight, matched speed with one of the ships and slowly came up under him until we heard the polar ice crack. Pop! We cracked the hull of that wooden ship like it was an egg and it went down.

Maria Guerrero is pregnant. Did I tell you that she and Wally Anderson got married? I really didn't see that one coming.

Something else I didn't see coming. Tanaka asked to talk to me in private one day about an important matter. An important matter? When we got alone, he asked for Mapua's hand in marriage. I was stunned! Tanaka and Mapua! I said, "Of course not, Eric. You're twice her age!" He said okay, thanked me and left. I thought originally Mapua was about 12 years old, but she was closer to fifteen, sixteen now, almost seventeen. Her people are small in stature, so although she's only 4 foot 11 inches tall, she may be fully grown. I asked Tanaka how old he was and he said thirty, he had a birthday last week. That's the kind of guy he is. He has a birthday and doesn't tell a soul.

I told Susan about this and she said, "Well, I saw that coming, didn't you?" I said no and she said I was impossible!

I'm really conflicted about this whole thing. I regard Mapua as my daughter and Tanaka is like my son. But the air changed between Tanaka and me. He was a lot more terse and a little too re-spectful. I didn't like it. It made me very uncomfortable. I began watching them together and that's when I noticed the furtive looks he gave her and the ado-ration in her eyes when she was with him. Yes, I'd seen that look before. I was up against something huge here. They were in love!

I'm aware that in some cultures girls are married off when they're twelve, but not where I come from. It's just hard for me to come to grips with. But in the end I consented. Mapua is a young woman and of legal age in most states in the U.S. When I told Tanaka, he hugged me. Hard! I thought he was going to break my ribs!

> That's all for now,
> Don Castillo, November 23, 1590

Goolong stood up yawned and said, "Tired am I!"

Davenport took the reader and began jumping ahead. "Read this one. Very sad it is."

Dear Liz, Kelly and Robin

Today we said good bye to Kansas. She was a good ship and served us well. She was home to us and protected us and stood silent guard over us. We celebrated on her, mourned, bonded and became a family while on her. We all felt better knowing she was near by, but now we must say good bye. We'd been putting this off, but it must be done.

She is but a hulk, an empty shell, stripped bare of anything useful. Even her weapons were dismantled. Her generators failed years ago. Her reactor is still good, but her propulsor will not turn anymore. Her seals are shot, as are her thrust bearings. Once the pride of the U.S. Navy, she can't move under her own power anymore.

Kansas has been sitting on its barnacle encrusted bottom for many years in the shallows next to Bloomberg. The Machua and several crewmen camouflaged it with netting covered with palm fronds. From the water it looks just like part of the island.

We had a hard time floating it free, but once we had a good high tide and towed it out of its lagoon with our ships, we towed it to deep water and sent it to the bottom. We had a small ceremony first though. Reverend Olson said a prayer of thanks and we laid wreaths in the water and silently said thanks to her for protecting us through our incredible odyssey. I cried like a baby, and when I looked around, I was not alone. Susan's eyes were awash. So was Crystal's and Mason's.

By unanimous decision of the council, we voted to rename our new city New Kansas. There is talk of naming our island nation Castillo, but I stopped that. I appreciate the honor, but it would be a lot to live up to. I'm not a god.

We are very prosperous here. We have a fleet of 42 ships now. France, Spain and England all leave us alone. In the past thirty years we've sent nine ships to the bottom during hostilities and let everyone know that we will not attack any other nation, but will respond with deadly force if fired upon. They still approach us with treaties but according to my son, Bud, they have different tenor than they used to. There is no more talk of protecting us. There is more give and take. Bud is two years into his term as president and is doing a fine job I think. Susan and I are very proud of him. And all our others too. We have five not counting the Kincaids and Mapua.

I turn 69 next week and I hope they don't throw me any surprise parties. I'm old, and I can't take a lot of shock. We're all getting old and handing over the reins to the next generation.

Wally Anderson and his sons Toby and Charlie are producing the best carbon steel and aluminum alloys in the world. There are several manufacturing companies making tools and implements using these fine metals. The Tanaka kids are trying to build a steam engine. They have constructed a good boiler, but they still have some work to do.

Remember that guy who was trying to fly, Sebring? He has a series of gliders he's made, using aluminum frames, and some of them have small chemical engines which will keep them in the air for up to thirty minutes!

Our school system is really expanding. The Machua people are very smart and excellent educators. They have taken over our education system and are doing a terrific job. They teach science, nature, social studies, math and of course English.

That's all for now,
Don Castillo, April 14, 1620

Davenport took the reader and began jumping ahead. "Read you this one too. Another sad one. And really, The beginning it is."

Goolong gave her a questioning look. She took the reader and began reading.

Dear Liz, Kelly and Robin,

A piece of me died last week. I am alone now and lost, and I don't think I can go on. I put my Susan in the ground. She was 84.

My world has gone dark and cold! Because my life has been sucked away. The most tender loving generous woman I have ever known is gone. I'm not good for anything now. And I was never as good a person as Susan. She was an angel.

I am 89 and in pain every day! My joints are stiff and hurt, and it is all I can do to get out of bed in the mornings. I am useless now. If there is a God, why did he let me live so long? Why did he take my angel?

At least she did not leave this world alone. When she passed, she was surrounded by family. Our five children, who are not really children now, and their spouses and children and our five great grandchildren. All the Kincaids and all the Tanakas were at her side too.

At the funeral there were about 1000+ people in attendance, although we tried to keep it private. It was mostly the old Kansas crew and all their offspring. I hadn't seen some of them in years and I was surprised by how old they all had gotten. They all offered condolences and tried to comfort me, but I could take no comfort in it. I am in a desolate place.

A few hours ago Anna, Bud and Thomas came over to see how I'm doing. Not well, I guess. They were concerned. I've been sleeping twenty hours a day. During my waking hours I sit and stare out the window at Susan's beautiful flower garden. She loved that garden so much. I still expect to see her there, happily digging and planting seedlings.

Anna asked when was the last time I ate. I didn't know so she made me some shepherd's stew, but I couldn't eat it. It made me feel a little better just to see Anna. She has Susan's bright blue eyes and sandy hair. The same petite nose. She's taller than Susan and her cheeks are chubbier. That's my fault, I guess.

I told her my life was over too. There was nothing left for me to do. It would rather be with Susan. This troubled the three of them greatly.

Anna asked to see what I was writing so I showed her. She took all my pages away and read them and when she returned, she said, "Father, you're not finished with your story. What about the beginning? You never explained how you and mom got here. You still have much more to do here."

She's absolutely right! It seems kind of backwards to me, but I must now tell the beginning.

> I was born Donald William Castillo
> to Hector Miguel and Delores Lucinda
> Castillo on April 20, 1977 in Smithtown,
> Long Island...

• • •

Davenport curled up and went to sleep on her desk using her carry bag as a pillow. She didn't know how long she had slept when Goolong shook her.

"Finished I the account," said Goolong yawning. "And right you are. Believe this no one will. Sounds this like witchcraft."

"Played my son Norm Bloomberg in the Founder's Day pageant," said Davenport. "Would like he not the truth. Thinks he Bloomberg a great warrior who fell in battle."

"If truth this is," cautioned Goolong.

"Think you it is not?" asked Davenport.

"Think I…" began Goolong, searching for words, "Would be better it if stayed this truth only with us. Have we 300 million people all over the South Pacific must think we about. The entire nation of Castillo. Would throw this into turmoil many."

"But explains this the defeat of the Spanish Armada. Did believe you a sea monster it was? And about the artifacts found we here? Ancient advanced alloys and weapons out-of-place?"

Goolong blew out a long breath through pursed lips. "Descended from the Taylors am I," said Goolong quietly. "Think you my ancestors came from another world? Another dimension? Will say they belong we not here. Belonged we here never." She studied Davenport intently.

"Know I not," she said softly. She could see fame slipping away. If Goolong chose not to endorse this find, it would be a blow to her.

Goolong picked up her purse and carry bag and asked, "Could keep I this?" She held up the reader.

"Yes."

"Grace! Have to go I. Late it is but still can I catch a Sebring back to New Kansas. And grace for showing you this to me. Will call I you." Davenport watched her walk out and down the sidewalk into the cool night air. She bent her tall frame into the doorway of the little vehicle and folded her long legs into the runner and then looked toward Davenport in the doorway.

Davenport blinked tears from her blue eyes. "But descended from Castillos am I," she said to nobody. "And the truth want I the world to know." She shrugged on her brown jacket, picked up the keys to the old runner and trudged down the stairs and into the cool night.

Notes From the Author

I must admit I've been out of submarines for a long time and do not know a lot about the Virginia class boats, but I read everything I could find on them and when I couldn't get answers, I made some leaps in logic. I'm sure I've drawn some incorrect conclusions and someone will be sure to tell me where.

Sarno Island does not really exist. It's based loosely on Tahiti. The Machua people are based on several different Polynesian cultures.

Lord Admiral Howard was a wonderful man by all accounts. He organized the English Navy, led them against the Spanish Armada and later he created a charity for impoverished and homeless seamen. But I needed a villain for my story, so I chose him because he was convenient. To anyone who takes issue with this, I say this is an *alternate* dimension. Things are different here! *This* Lord Howard is different!

The 2008 Helium accident at the Hadron Collider actually happened. But hyperdensification did not occur and is still pretty much the stuff of speculation. Some scientists think it can be done, but controlling it is another matter.

Other Books by G. Ernest Smith

Assassin Awaken

Look Down

Bone Maze

About the Author

G. Ernest Smith is a retired Space Shuttle launch team member who lives near Cape Canaveral, Florida with his wife, Mary Beth. He has a son, Brandon, and a daughter, Mona, a brother, Jeff, and a sister, Gwen, who all live in California.

He enjoys sailing, Harley Davidsons, fishing, flying, writing, Miatas and eating (not necessarily in that order).

He is a graduate of Rollins College and the Florida Institute of Technology and holds a Masters degree in Computer Science.

https://www.gernestsmith.com

58995905R00238

Made in the USA
Charleston, SC
24 July 2016